The Collected Stories of
Robert Silverberg

VOLUME THREE

Something Wild is Loose
1969-72

The Collected Stories of
Robert Silverberg

VOLUME THREE

Something Wild is Loose
1969-72

ROBERT SILVERBERG

SUBTERRANEAN PRESS 2012

Trade Paperback

978-1-59606-509-3

Subterranean Press
PO Box 190106
Burton, MI 48519

www.subterraneanpress.com

ACKNOWLEDGMENTS

"Something Wild is Loose" first appeared in *The Many Worlds of Science Fiction.*

"In Entropy's Jaws, "Caliban," and "What We Learned from This Morning's Newspaper" first appeared in *Infinity.*

"The Reality Trip" first appeared in *If.*

"Going" first appeared in *Four Futures.*

"Good News from the Vatican," "When We Went to See the End of the World," and "Many Mansions" first appeared in *Universe.*

"Thomas the Proclaimer" first appeared in *The Day the Sun Stood Still.*

"Push No More" first appeared in *Strange Bedfellows.*

"The Wind and the Rain" first appeared in *Saving Worlds.*

"Some Notes on the Pre-Dynastic Epoch" first appeared in *Bad Moon Rising.*

"The Feast of St. Dionysus" first appeared in *An Exaltation of Stars.*

"The Mutant Season" first appeared in *Androids, Time Machines, and Blue Giraffes.*

"Caught in the Organ Draft" first appeared in *And Walk Now Gently Through the Fire....*

TABLE OF CONTENTS

For Ben Bova
Bob Hoskins
Ejler Jakobsson
Terry Carr
Roger Elwood
Tom Disch

INTRODUCTION

The title that I've chosen for this third volume of my Collected Stories is not just the title of one of the stories in the book; it is indicative of the state of the world, and of the author of these stories, during the years (1969-72) when they were written.

Science fiction is supposed to be about the future, but in fact it has always been deeply rooted in the present, and its nature changes as our perception of the present-day world changes. For example, the science fiction of the dark, gloomy, hopeless 1930s tended to be bright, optimistic stuff, looking forward to a happy world in which technology would lead us out of the economic morass of the Great Depression. The science fiction of the 1940s, when the world was riven by war, was generally built around simple melodramatic conflicts between good and evil, which was the way we were encouraged to perceive that war. In the 1950s, when a period of relative tranquility held sway most of the time and we managed even to keep the fear of atomic doom well under control, a kind of slick, suburban s-f evolved, smoothly written and published in shiny-looking magazines. It dealt with such matters as what it was like to be the hostess at a cocktail party for aliens, and how to program your household robot to serve low-calorie meals.

Then came the 1960s, when that serene suburban world fell apart, and the 1970s, when we were left with the task of putting the lopsided pieces back together. During that crazy time—which began, I think, with the bullet that took John F. Kennedy's life in Dallas in 1963 and needed twenty years to play through to its end—science fiction and fantasy reached unparalleled prosperity in the United States and most other Western industrial nations. That should not be very surprising. When the world turns incomprehensible, it makes sense to look for answers from some other world. In former times it was sufficient to look no farther than the Church: God was there, emanating love and security, offering the hope of passing onward from this vale of tears to the true life beyond. One of the difficulties of modern life is that most of us have lost the option of using religious faith as a consolation. It may be that science fiction has evolved into a sort of substitute: a body of texts offering an examination of absolute values and the hypothetical construction of alternative modes of living.

But, as I have already observed, the science fiction of the moment is always rooted in the moment. As the traditional values of American society and much of Western Europe crumbled in the late 1960s, the science fiction written at that time reflected the dislocations and fragmentations that our society was experiencing. New writers, armed with dazzling new techniques, took up the materials of s-f and did strange new things with it. Older writers, formerly content to produce the safe and simple stuff of previous decades, were reborn with sudden experimental zeal. It was a wild and adventurous time, when we were all improvising our way of life from day to day or even from hour to hour, and the science fiction of that period certainly shows it.

The stories in this volume were written in those troubled times when there was no longer any safe zone in the world—the years from 1969 to 1972. People wore strange clothes and strange hair, doped themselves with strange drugs, read and wrote strange things. These manifestations of the times—beginning now to seem quaint to us oldsters, and almost unreal to those young adults of today who hadn't yet been born when we were living through that bizarre era—were symptoms, naturally, of deeper malaise and confusion. I have pegged the onset of that time of troubles to the moment of the Kennedy assassination not because Kennedy himself was a peerless leader—he had his personal flaws, as we now know all too well, and at the time of his death he was finding it almost impossible to win support in Washington for his political agenda—but because he was a perfect symbol of energy and youth and the promise of the future. When he was stuck down, it seemed to me and a great many others that this shining promise had been forfeited and that the commonwealth itself had been ripped apart. And so it was. I think we would probably have had the troubles that followed even if Kennedy had lived, just as we would have had World War One eventually even if the Archduke Franz Ferdinand had not been assassinated at Sarajevo; but in each case the murder proved to be an historical catalyst.

After Kennedy came new and more foolish leaders who mired us in a dismal and hopeless war against which the nation's young rebelled, and everything fell into chaos. Two consecutive presidents were overthrown and driven from office, the result of popular outcry against their philosophies and methods. On all levels of society, desperate new styles of behavior reflected the desperation within. We slid into a widespread and catastrophic societal breakdown and it was years before the necessary repairs were made. The upheaval that we call, in historical shorthand, "the Sixties" brought us into blunt confrontation with the future, and what we saw—energy crises, uncontrollable inflation, free-floating terrorism, the threat of atomic destruction from, perhaps, some randomly self-appointed enemy—frightened us into becoming a nation of science-fiction fans, seeking for answers in the literature of tomorrow.

Things are a little quieter now, though no less perilous. Instead of the Soviet Union to worry about, we have radical Islam. Inflation seems to have subsided, but global temperatures are rising and the long-term environmental prognosis looks strikingly ungood. The fear of a worldwide population explosion that obsessed us back then has been replaced by something more complex, the fear of a Third World population explosion while First World countries shrink from generation to generation. The plague of AIDS has entered the world. Interesting computer viruses propagate among us daily, sowing chaos. Et cetera, et cetera. Curiously, we no longer turn to science fiction for answers to these problems. The disturbing, fragmented s-f of the Sixties is all but forgotten, supplanted by the bland, comforting, predictable fantasy novels of recent times, in which benevolent wizards hold out the hope that the Staff of Power will ultimately return to the hands of the High King and all will be made right in the world.

The stories in this book are, by and large, not like that. The world that they sprang from was the troubled, bewildering, dangerous, and very exciting world of those weird years when the barriers were down and the future was rushing into the present with the force of a river unleashed. But of course I think these stories speak to our times, too, and that most of them will remain valid as we go staggering onward through the brave new world of the twenty-first century. I am not one of those who believes that all is lost and the end is nigh. Like William Faulkner, I do think we will somehow endure and prevail against increasingly stiff odds.

A great many strange and dizzying things happen to the characters in these sixteen stories, and in the fourteen stories of the 1972-73 volume that will follow. The reader who makes the journey from beginning to end of all thirty stories will be taken on many a curious trip, that I promise—as was their author during the years when they were being written.

Robert Silverberg

SOMETHING WILD IS LOOSE

By the late months of 1969 I had shaken off most of the fatigue that the various stresses of the fire that wrecked my house in New York City in February, 1968 had caused, and was hitting my full stride as a writer—pouring forth novel after novel, Downward to the Earth *and* Tower of Glass *and* Son of Man *all in 1969,* The World Inside *and* A Time of Changes *and* The Second Trip *in 1970 (along with a huge non-fiction work exploring the origins of the Prester John myth.) My production of short stories diminished drastically as I concentrated on these demanding books.*

But I could be cajoled to do one occasionally. My friend Ben Bova had joined the swiftly growing roster of original-anthology editors with a book that was to be called The Many Worlds of Science Fiction, *and he insisted that my presence on the contents page was obligatory. Well, so be it: in the final weeks of 1969, just after coming up out of the psychedelic frenzies of* Son of Man, *I wrote the relatively conservative (for that era) "Something Wild is Loose" for Ben's anthology. I've been waiting ever since for someone to make a movie out of it.*

The Vsiir got aboard the Earthbound ship by accident. It had absolutely no plans for taking a holiday on a wet, grimy planet like Earth. But it was in its metamorphic phase, undergoing the period of undisciplined change that began as winter came on, and it had shifted so far up-spectrum that Earthborn eyes couldn't see it. Oh, a really skilled observer might notice a slippery little purple flicker once in a while, a kind of snore, as the Vsiir momentarily dropped down out of the ultraviolet; but he'd have to know where to look, and when. The crewman who was responsible for putting the Vsiir on the ship never even considered the possibility that there might be something invisible sleeping atop one of the crates of cargo being hoisted into the ship's hold. He simply went down the row, slapping a floater-node on each crate and sending it gliding up the gravity wall toward the open hatch. The fifth crate to go inside was the one on which the Vsiir had decided to take its nap. The spaceman didn't know that he had inadvertently given an alien organism a free ride to Earth. The Vsiir didn't know it, either, until the hatch was sealed and an oxygen-nitrogen atmosphere began to hiss from the vents. The Vsiir did not happen to breathe those gases, but, because it was in its time of metamorphosis, it was able to adapt itself quickly and nicely to the sour, prickly vapors seeping into its metabolic cells. The next step was to fashion a set of full-spectrum scanners and learn something about its surroundings. Within a few minutes, the Vsiir was aware—

—that it was in a large, dark place that held a great many boxes containing various mineral and vegetable products of its world, mainly branches of the greenfire tree but also some other things of no comprehensible value to a Vsiir—

—that a double wall of curved metal enclosed this place—

—that just beyond this wall was a null-atmosphere zone, such as is found between one planet and another—

—that this entire closed system was undergoing acceleration—

—that this therefore was a spaceship, heading rapidly away from the world of Vsiirs and in fact already some ten planetary diameters distant, with the gap growing alarmingly moment by moment—

—that it would be impossible, even for a Vsiir in metamorphosis, to escape from the spaceship at this point—

—and that, unless it could persuade the crew of the ship to halt and go back, it would be compelled to undertake a long and dreary voyage to a strange and probably loathsome world, where life would at best be highly inconvenient, and might present great dangers. It would find itself cut off painfully from the rhythm of its own civilization. It would miss the Festival of Changing. It would miss the Holy Eclipse. It would not be able to take part in next spring's Rising of the Sea. It would suffer in a thousand ways.

There were six human beings aboard the ship. Extending its perceptors, the Vsiir tried to reach their minds. Though humans had been coming to its planet for many years, it had never bothered making contact with them before; but it had never been in this much trouble before, either. It sent a foggy tendril of thought, roving the corridors, looking for traces of human intelligence. Here? A glow of electrical activity within a sphere of bone: a mind, a mind! A busy mind. But surrounded by a wall, apparently; the Vsiir rammed up against it and was thrust back. That was startling and disturbing. What kind of beings were these, whose minds were closed to ordinary contact? The Vsiir went on, hunting through the ship. Another mind: again closed. Another. Another. The Vsiir felt panic rising. Its mantle fluttered; its energy radiations dropped far down into the visible spectrum, then shot nervously toward much shorter waves. Even its physical form experienced a series of quick involuntary metamorphoses, to the Vsiir's intense embarrassment. It did not get control of its body until it had passed from spherical to cubical to chaotic, and had become a gridwork of fibrous threads held together only by a pulsing strand of ego. Fiercely it forced itself back to the spherical form and resumed its search of the ship, dismally realizing that by this time its native world was half a stellar unit away. It was without hope now, but it continued to probe the minds of the crew, if only for the sake of thoroughness. Even if it made contact, though, how could it communicate the nature of its plight, and even if it communicated, why would the humans be disposed to help it? Yet it went on through the ship. And—

Here: an open mind. No wall at all. A miracle! The Vsiir rushed into close contact, overcome with joy and surprise, pouring out its predicament. *Please listen. Unfortunate nonhuman organism accidentally transported into this vessel during loading of cargo. Metabolically and psychologically unsuited for prolonged life on Earth. Begs pardon for inconvenience, wishes prompt return to home planet recently left, regrets disturbance in shipping schedule but hopes that this large favor will not prove impossible to grant. Do you comprehend my sending? Unfortunate nonhuman organism accidentally transported—*

Lieutenant Falkirk had drawn the first sleep-shift after floatoff. It was only fair; Falkirk had knocked himself out processing the cargo during the loading stage, slapping the floater-nodes on every crate and feeding the transit manifests to the computer. Now that the ship was spaceborne he could grab some rest while the other crewmen were handling the floatoff chores. So he settled down for six hours in the cradle as soon as they were on their way. Below him, the ship's six gravity-drinkers spun on their axes, gobbling inertia and pushing up the acceleration, and the ship floated Earthward at a velocity that would reach the galactic level before Falkirk woke. He drifted into drowsiness. A good trip: enough greenfire bark in the hold to see Earth through a dozen fits of the molecule plague, and plenty of other potential medicinals besides, along with a load of interesting mineral samples, and—Falkirk slept. For half an hour he enjoyed sweet slumber, his mind disengaged, his body loose.

Until a dark dream bubbled through his skull.

Deep purple sunlight, hot and somber. Something slippery tickling the edges of his brain. He lies on a broad white slab in a scorched desert. Unable to move. Getting harder to breathe. The gravity—a terrible pull, bending and breaking him, ripping his bones apart. Hooded figures moving around him, pointing, laughing, exchanging blurred comments in an unknown language. His skin melting and taking on a new texture: porcupine quills sprouting inside his flesh and forcing their way upward, poking out through every pore. Points of fire all over him. A thin scarlet hand, withered fingers like crab claws, hovering in front of his face. Scratching. Scratching. Scratching. His blood running among the quills, thick and sluggish. He shivers, struggling to sit up—lifts a hand, leaving pieces of quivering flesh stuck to the slab—sits up—

Wakes, trembling, screaming.

Falkirk's shout still sounded in his own ears as his eyes adjusted to the light. Lieutenant Commander Rodriguez was holding his shoulders and shaking him.

"You all right?"

Falkirk tried to reply. Words wouldn't come. Hallucinatory shock, he realized, as part of his mind attempted to convince the other part that the dream was over. He was trained to handle crises; he ran through a quick disciplinary countdown and calmed himself, though he was still badly shaken. "Nightmare," he said hoarsely. "A beauty. Never had a dream with that kind of intensity before."

Rodriguez relaxed. Obviously he couldn't get very upset over a mere nightmare. "You want a pill?"

Falkirk shook his head. "I'll manage, thanks."

But the impact of the dream lingered. It was more than an hour before he got back to sleep, and then he fell into a light, restless doze, as if his mind were on guard against a return of those chilling fantasies. Fifty minutes before his programmed wake-up time, he was awakened by a ghastly shriek from the far side of the cabin.

Lieutenant Commander Rodriguez was having a nightmare.

When the ship made floatdown on Earth a month later it was, of course, put through the usual decontamination procedures before anyone or anything aboard it was allowed out of the starport. The outer hull got squirted with sealants designed to trap and smother any microorganism that might have hitchhiked from another world; the crewmen emerged through the safety pouch and went straight into a quarantine chamber without being exposed to the air; the ship's atmosphere was cycled into withdrawal chambers, where it underwent a thorough purification, and the entire interior of the vessel received a six-phase sterilization, beginning with fifteen minutes of hard vacuum and ending with an hour of neutron bombardment.

These procedures caused a certain degree of inconvenience for the Vsiir. It was already at the low end of its energy phase, due mainly to the repeated discouragements it had suffered in its attempts to communicate with the six humans. Now it was forced to adapt to a variety of unpleasant environments with no chance to rest between changes. Even the most adaptable of organisms can get tired. By the time the starport's decontamination team was ready to certify that the ship was wholly free of alien life-forms, the Vsiir was very, very tired indeed.

The oxygen-nitrogen atmosphere entered the hold once more. The Vsiir found it quite welcome, at least in contrast to all that had just been thrown at it. The hatch was open; stevedores were muscling the cargo crates into position to be floated across the field to the handling dome. The Vsiir took advantage of this moment to extrude some legs and scramble out of the ship. It found itself on a broad concrete apron, rimmed by massive buildings. A yellow sun was shining in a blue sky; infrared was bouncing all over the place, but the Vsiir speedily made arrangements to deflect the excess. It also compensated immediately for the tinge of ugly hydrocarbons in the atmosphere, for the frightening noise level, and for the leaden feeling of homesickness that suddenly threatened its organic stability at the first sight of this unfamiliar, disheartening world. How to get home again? How to make contact, even? The Vsiir sensed nothing but closed minds—sealed like seeds in their shells. True, from time to time the minds of these humans opened, but even then they seemed unwilling to let the Vsiir's message get through.

Perhaps it would be different here. Perhaps those six were poor communicators, for some reason, and there would be more receptive minds available in this place. Perhaps. Perhaps. Close to despair, the Vsiir hurried across the field and slipped into the first building in which it sensed open minds. There were hundreds of humans in it, occupying many levels, and the open minds were widely scattered. The Vsiir located the nearest one and, worriedly, earnestly, hopefully, touched the tip of its mind to the human's. *Please listen, I mean no harm. Am nonhuman organism arrived on your planet through unhappy circumstances, wishing only quick going back to own world.*

The cardiac wing of Long Island Starport Hospital was on the ground floor, in the rear, where the patients could be given floater therapy without upsetting the gravitational ratios of the rest of the building. As always, the hospital was full—people were always coming in sick off starliners, and most of them were hospitalized right at the starport for their own safety—and the cardiac wing had more than its share. At the moment it held a dozen infarcts awaiting implant, nine postimplant recupes, five coronaries in emergency stasis, three ventricle-regrowth projects, an aortal patch job, and nine or ten assorted other cases. Most of the patients were floating, to keep down the gravitational strain on their damaged tissues—all but the regrowth people, who were under full Earthnorm gravity so that their new hearts would come in with the proper resilience and toughness. The hospital had a fine reputation and one of the lowest mortality rates in the hemisphere.

Losing two patients the same morning was a shock to the entire staff.

At 0917 the monitor flashed the red light for Mrs. Maldonado, 87, postimplant and thus far doing fine. She had developed acute endocarditis coming back from a tour of the Jupiter system; at her age there wasn't enough vitality to sustain her through the slow business of growing a new heart with a genetic prod, but they'd given her a synthetic implant and for two weeks it had worked quite well. Suddenly, though, the hospital's control center was getting a load of grim telemetry from Mrs. Maldonado's bed: valve action zero, blood pressure zero, respiration zero, pulse zero, everything zero, zero, zero. The EEG tape showed a violent lurch—as though she had received some abrupt and intense shock—followed by a minute or two of irregular action, followed by termination of brain activity. Long before any hospital personnel had reached her bedside, automatic revival equipment, both chemical and electrical, had gone to work on the patient, but she was beyond reach: a massive cerebral hemorrhage, coming totally without warning, had done irreversible damage.

At 0928 came the second loss: Mr. Guinness, 51, three days past surgery for a coronary embolism. The same series of events. A severe jolt to the nervous system, an immediate and fatal physiological response. Resuscitation procedures negative. No one on the staff had any plausible explanation for Mr. Guinness' death. Like Mrs. Maldonado, he had been sleeping peacefully, all vital signs good, until the moment of the fatal seizure.

"As though someone had come up and yelled *boo* in their ears," one doctor muttered, puzzling over the charts. He pointed to the wild EEG track. "Or as if they'd had unbearably vivid nightmares and couldn't take the sensory overload. But no one was making noise in the ward. And nightmares aren't contagious."

Dr. Peter Mookherji, resident in neuropathology, was beginning his morning rounds on the hospital's sixth level when the soft voice of his annunciator, taped behind his left ear, asked him to report to the quarantine building immediately. Dr. Mookherji scowled. "Can't it wait? This is my busiest time of day, and—"

"You are asked to come at once."

"Look, I've got a girl in a coma here, due for her teletherapy session in fifteen minutes, and she's counting on seeing me. I'm her only link to the world. If I'm not there when—"

"You are asked to come at once, Dr. Mookherji."

"Why do the quarantine people need a neuropathologist in such a hurry? Let me take care of the girl, at least, and in forty-five minutes they can have me."

"Dr. Mookherji—"

It didn't pay to argue with a machine. Mookherji forced his temper down. Short tempers ran in his family, along with a fondness for torrid curries and a talent for telepathy. Glowering, he grabbed a data terminal, identified himself, and told the hospital's control center to reprogram his entire morning schedule. "Build in a half-hour postponement somehow," he snapped. "I can't help it—see for yourself. I've been requisitioned by the quarantine staff." The computer was thoughtful enough to have a rollerbuggy waiting for him when he emerged from the hospital. It whisked him across the starport to the quarantine building in three minutes, but he was still angry when he got there. The scanner at the door ticked off his badge and one of the control center's innumerable voice-outputs told him solemnly, "You are expected in Room 403, Dr. Mookherji."

Room 403 turned out to be a two-sector interrogation office. The rear sector of the room was part of the building's central quarantine core, and the front sector belonged to the public-access part of the building, with a thick glass wall in between. Six haggard-looking spacemen were slouched on sofas behind the wall, and three members of the starport's quarantine staff paced about in the front. Mookherji's irritation ebbed when he saw that one of the quarantine men was an old medical-school friend, Lee Nakadai. The slender Japanese was a year older than Mookherji—29 to 28; they met for lunch occasionally at the starport commissary, and they had double-dated a pair of Filipina twins earlier in the year, but the pressure of work had kept them apart for months. Nakadai got down to business quickly now: "Pete, have you ever heard of an epidemic of nightmares?"

"Eh?"

Indicating the men behind the quarantine wall, Nakadai said, "These fellows came in a couple of hours ago from Norton's Star. Brought back a cargo of greenfire bark. Physically they check out to five decimal places, and I'd release them except for one funny thing. They're all in a bad state of nervous exhaustion, which they say is the result of having had practically no sleep during their whole month-long return trip. And the reason for that is that they were having nightmares—every one of them—real mind-wrecking dreams, whenever they tried to sleep. It sounded so peculiar that I thought we'd better run a neuropath checkup, in case they've picked up some kind of cerebral infection."

Mookherji frowned. "For this you get me out of my ward on emergency requisition, Lee?"

"Talk to them," Nakadai said. "Maybe it'll scare you a little."

Mookherji glanced at the spacemen. "All right," he said. "What about these nightmares?"

A tall, bony-looking officer who introduced himself as Lieutenant Falkirk said, "I was the first victim—right after floatoff. I almost flipped. It was like, well, something touching my mind, filling it with weird thoughts. And everything absolutely real while it was going on—I thought I was choking, I thought my body was changing into something alien, I felt my blood running out my pores—" Falkirk shrugged. "Like any sort of bad dream, I guess, only ten times as vivid. Fifty times. A few hours later Lieutenant Commander Rodriguez had the same kind of dream. Different images, same effect. And then, one by one, as the others took their sleep-shifts, they started to wake up screaming. Two of us ended up spending three weeks on happy-pills. We're pretty stable men, doctor—we're trained to take almost anything. But I think a civilian would have cracked up for good with dreams like those. Not so much the images as the intensity, the realness of them."

"And these dreams recurred, throughout the voyage?" Mookherji asked.

"Every shift. It got so we were afraid to doze off, because we knew the devils would start crawling through our heads when we did. Or we'd put ourselves real down on sleeper-tabs. And even so we'd have the dreams, with our minds doped to a level where you wouldn't imagine dreams would happen. A plague of nightmares, doctor. An epidemic."

"When was the last episode?"

'The final sleep-shift before floatdown."

"You haven't gone to sleep, any of you, since leaving ship?"

'No," Falkirk said.

One of the other spacemen said, "Maybe he didn't make it clear to you, doctor. These were killer dreams. They were mind-crackers. We were lucky to get home sane. If we did."

Mookherji drummed his fingertips together, rummaging through his experience for some parallel case. He couldn't find any. He knew of mass hallucinations, plenty of them, episodes in which whole mobs had persuaded themselves they had seen gods, demons, miracles, the dead walking, fiery symbols in the sky. But a series of hallucinations coming in sequence, shift after shift, to an entire crew of tough, pragmatic spacemen? It didn't make sense.

Nakadai said, "Pete, the men had a guess about what might have done it to them. Just a wild idea, but maybe—"

"What is it?"

Falkirk laughed uneasily. "Actually, it's pretty fantastic, doctor."

"Go ahead."

"Well, that something from the planet came aboard the ship with us. Something, well, telepathic. Which fiddled around with our minds whenever we went to sleep. What we felt as nightmares was maybe this thing inside our heads."

"Possibly it rode all the way back to Earth with us," another spaceman said. "It could still be aboard the ship. Or loose in the city by now."

"The Invisible Nightmare Menace?" Mookherji said, with a faint smile. "I doubt that I can buy that."

"There *are* telepathic creatures," Falkirk pointed out.

"I know," Mookherji said sharply. "I happen to be one myself."

"I'm sorry, doctor, if—"

"But that doesn't lead me to look for telepaths under every bush. I'm not ruling out your alien menace, mind you. But I think it's a lot more likely that you picked up some kind of inflammation of the brain out there. A virus disease, a type of encephalitis that shows itself in the form of chronic hallucinations." The spacemen looked troubled. Obviously they would rather be victims of an unknown monster preying on them from outside than of an unknown virus lodged in their brains. Mookherji went on, "I'm not saying that's what it is, either. I'm just tossing around hypotheses. We'll know more after we've run some tests." Checking his watch, he said to Nakadai, "Lee, there's not much more I can find out right now, and I've got to get back to my patients. I want these fellows plugged in for the full series of neuropsychological checkouts. Have the outputs relayed to my office as they come in. Run the tests in staggered series and start letting the men go to sleep, two at a time, after each series—I'll send over a technician to help you rig the telemetry. I want to be notified immediately if there's any nightmare experience."

"Right."

"And get them to sign telepathy releases. I'll give them a preliminary mind-probe this evening after I've had a chance to study the clinical findings. Maintain absolute quarantine, of course. This thing might just be infectious. Play it very safe."

Nakadai nodded. Mookherji flashed a professional smile at the six somber spacemen and went out, brooding. A nightmare virus? Or a mind-meddling alien organism that no one can see? He wasn't sure which notion he liked less. Probably, though, there was some prosaic and unstartling explanation for that month of bad dreams—contaminated food supplies, or something funny in the atmosphere recycler. A simple, mundane explanation.

Probably.

⁂

The first time it happened, the Vsiir was not sure what had actually taken place. It had touched a human mind; there had been an immediate vehement reaction; the Vsiir had pulled back, alarmed by the surging fury of the response, and then, a moment later, had been unable to locate the mind at all. Possibly it was some defense mechanism, the Vsiir thought, by which the humans guarded their minds against intruders. But that seemed unlikely since the humans' minds were quite effectively guarded most of the time anyway. Aboard the ship, whenever the Vsiir had managed to slip past the walls that shielded the minds of the crewmen, it had always encountered a great deal of turbulence—plainly these humans did not enjoy mental contact with a Vsiir—but never this complete shutdown, this total cutoff of signal. Puzzled, the Vsiir tried again, reaching toward an open mind situated not far from where the one that had vanished had been. *Kindly attention, a moment of consideration for confused other-worldly individual, victim of unhappy circumstances, who—*

Again the violent response: a sudden tremendous flare of mental energy, a churning blaze of fear and pain and shock. And again, moments later, complete silence, as though the human had retreated behind an impermeable barrier. *Where are you? Where did you go?* The Vsiir, troubled, took the risk of creating an optical receptor that worked in the visible spectrum—and that therefore would itself be visible to humans—and surveyed the scene. It saw a human on a bed, completely surrounded by intricate machinery. Colored lights were flashing. Other humans, looking agitated, were rushing toward the bed. The human on the bed lay quite still, not even moving when a metal arm descended and jabbed a long bright needle into his chest.

Suddenly the Vsiir understood.

The two humans must have experienced termination of existence!

Hastily the Vsiir dissolved its visible-spectrum receptor and retreated to a sheltered corner to consider what had happened. *Datum:* two humans had died. *Datum:* each had undergone termination immediately after receiving a mental transmission from the Vsiir. *Problem:* had the mental transmission brought about the terminations?

The possibility that the Vsiir might have destroyed two lives was shocking and appalling, and such a chill went through its body that it shrank into a tight, hard ball, with all thought-processes snarled. It needed several minutes to return to a fully functional state. If its attempts at communicating with these humans produced such terrible effects, the Vsiir realized, then its prospects of finding help on this planet were slim. How could it dare risk trying to contact other humans, if—

A comforting thought surfaced. The Vsiir realized that it was jumping to a hasty conclusion on the basis of sketchy evidence, while overlooking some powerful arguments against that conclusion. All during the voyage to this world the Vsiir had been making contact with humans, the six crewmen, and none of them had terminated. That was ample evidence that humans could withstand contact with a Vsiir mind. Therefore contact alone could not have caused these two deaths.

Possibly it was only coincidental that the Vsiir had approached two humans in succession that were on the verge of termination. Was this the place where humans were brought when their time of termination was near? Would the terminations have happened even if the Vsiir had not tried to make contact? Was the attempt at contact just enough of a drain on dwindling energies to push the two over the edge into termination? The Vsiir did not know. It was uncomfortably conscious of how many important facts it lacked. Only one thing was certain: its time was running short. If it did not find help soon, metabolic decay was going to set in, followed by metamorphic rigidity, followed by a fatal loss in adaptability, followed by...termination.

The Vsiir had no choice. Continuing its quest for contact with a human was its only hope of survival. Cautiously, timidly, the Vsiir again began to send out its probes, looking for a properly receptive mind. This one was walled. So was this. And all these: no entrance, no entrance! The Vsiir wondered if the barriers these humans possessed were designed merely to keep out intruding nonhuman consciousnesses, or actually shielded each human against mental contact of all kinds, including contact with other humans. If any human-to-human contact existed, the Vsiir had not detected it, either in this building or aboard the spaceship. What a strange race!

Perhaps it would be best to try a different level of this building. The Vsiir flowed easily under a closed door and up a service staircase to a higher floor. Once more it sent forth its probes. A closed mind here. And here. And here. And then a receptive one. The Vsiir prepared to send its message. For safety's sake it stepped down the power of its transmission, letting a mere wisp of thought curl forth. *Do you hear? Stranded extraterrestrial being is calling. Seeks aid. Wishes—*

From the human came a sharp, stinging displeasure-response, wordless but unmistakably hostile. The Vsiir at once withdrew. It waited, terrified, fearing that it had caused another termination. No: the human mind continued to function, although it was no longer open, but now surrounded by the sort of barrier humans normally wore. Drooping, dejected, the Vsiir crept away. Failure, again. Not even a moment of meaningful mind-to-mind contact. Was there no way to reach these people? Dismally, the Vsiir resumed its search for a receptive mind. What else could it do?

The visit to the quarantine building had taken forty minutes out of Dr. Mookherji's morning schedule. That bothered him. He couldn't blame the quarantine people for getting upset over the six spacemen's tale of chronic hallucinations, but he didn't think the situation, mysterious as it was, was grave enough to warrant calling him in on an emergency basis. Whatever was troubling the spacemen would eventually come to light; meanwhile they were safely isolated from the rest of the starport. Nakadai should have run more tests before asking him. And he resented having to steal time from his patients.

But as he began his belated morning rounds, Mookherji calmed himself with a deliberate effort: it wouldn't do him or his patients any good if he visited them while still loaded with tensions and irritations. He was supposed to be a healer, not a spreader of anxieties. He spent a moment going through a de-escalation routine, and by the time he entered the first patient's room—that of Satina Ransom—he was convincingly relaxed and amiable.

Satina lay on her left side, eyes closed, a slender girl of sixteen with a fragile-looking face and long, soft straw-colored hair. A spidery network of monitoring systems surrounded her. She had been unconscious for fourteen months, twelve of them here in the starport's neuropathology ward and the last six under Mookherji's care, As a holiday treat, her parents had taken her to one of the resorts on Titan during the best season for viewing Saturn's rings; with great difficulty they succeeded in booking reservations at Galileo Dome, and were there on the grim day when a violent Titanquake ruptured the dome and exposed a thousand tourists to the icy moon's poisonous methane atmosphere. Satina was one of the lucky ones: she got no more than a couple of whiffs of the stuff before a dome guide with whom she'd been talking managed to slap a breathing mask over her face. She survived. Her mother, father, and young brother didn't. But she had never regained consciousness after collapsing at the moment of the disaster. Months of examination on Earth had shown that her brief methane inhalation hadn't caused any major brain damage; organically there seemed to be nothing wrong with her, but she refused to wake up. A shock reaction, Mookherji believed: she would rather go on dreaming forever than return to the living nightmare that consciousness had become. He had been able to reach her mind telepathically, but so far he had been unable to cleanse her of the trauma of that catastrophe and bring her back to the waking world.

Now he prepared to make contact. There was nothing easy or automatic about his telepathy; "reading" minds was strenuous work for him, as difficult and as taxing as running a cross-country race or memorizing a lengthy part in Hamlet. Despite the fears of laymen, he had no way of scanning anyone's intimate thoughts with a casual glance. To enter another mind, he had to go through an elaborate procedure of warming up and reaching out, and even so it was a slow business to tune in on somebody's "wavelength", with little coherent information coming across until the ninth or tenth attempt. The gift had been in the Mookherji family for at least a dozen generations, helped along by shrewdly planned marriages designed to conserve the precious gene; he was more adept than any of his ancestors, yet it might take another century or two of Mookherjis to produce a really potent telepath. At least he was able to make good use of such talent for mind-contact as he had. He knew that many members of his family in earlier times had been forced to hide their gift from those about them, back in India, lest they be classed with vampires and werewolves and cast out of society.

Gently he placed his dark hand on Satina's pale wrist. Physical contact was necessary to attain the mental linkage. He concentrated on reaching her. After months of teletherapy, her mind was sensitized to his; he was able to skip the intermediate steps, and, once he was warmed up, could plunge straight into her troubled soul. His eyes were closed. He saw a swirl of pearly-gray fog before him: Satina's mind. He thrust himself into it, entering easily. Up from the depths of her spirit swam a question mark.

—*Who is it? Doctor?*

—*Me, yes. How are you today, Satina?*

—*Fine. Just fine.*

—*Been sleeping well?*

—*It's so peaceful here, doctor.*

—*Yes. Yes, I imagine it is. But you ought to see how it is here. A wonderful summer day. The sun in the blue sky. Everything in bloom. A perfect day for swimming, eh? Wouldn't you like a swim?* He puts all the force of his concentration into images of swimming: a cold mountain stream, a deep pool at the base of a creamy waterfall, the sudden delightful shock of diving in, the crystal flow tingling against her warm skin, the laughter of her friends, the splashing, the swift powerful strokes carrying her to the far shore—

—*I'd rather stay where I am,* she tells him.

—*Maybe you'd like to go floating instead?* He summons the sensations of free flight: a floater-node fastened to her belt, lifting her serenely to an altitude of a hundred feet, and off she goes, drifting over fields and valleys, her friends beside her, her body totally relaxed, weightless, soaring on the updrafts, rising until the ground is a checkerboard of brown and green, looking down on the tiny houses and the comical cars, now crossing a shimmering silvery lake, now hovering over a dark, somber forest of thick-packed spruce, now simply lying on her back, legs crossed, hands clasped behind her head, the sunlight on her cheeks, three hundred feet of nothingness underneath her—

But Satina doesn't take his bait. She prefers to stay where she is. The temptations of floating are not strong enough.

Mookherji does not have enough energy left to try a third attempt at luring her out of her coma. Instead he shifts to a purely medical function and tries to probe for the source of the trauma that has cut her off from the world. The fright, no doubt; and the terrible crack in the dome, spelling the end to all security; and the sight of her parents and brother dying before her eyes; and the swampy reek of Titan's atmosphere hitting her nostrils—all of those things, no doubt. But people have rebounded from worse calamities. Why does she insist on withdrawing from life? Why not come to terms with the dreadful past, and accept existence again?

She fights him. Her defenses are fierce; she does not want him meddling with her mind. All of their sessions have ended this way: Satina clinging to her retreat, Satina blocking any shot at knocking her free of her self-imposed prison. He has gone on hoping that one day she will lower her guard. But this is not to be the day. Wearily, he pulls back from the core of her mind and talks to her on a shallower level.

—*You ought to be getting back to school, Satina.*

—*Not yet. It's been such a short vacation!*

—*Do you know how long?*

—*About three weeks, isn't it?*

—*Fourteen months so far,* he tells her.

—*That's impossible. We just went away to Titan a little while ago—the week before Christmas, wasn't it, and—*

—*Satina, how old are you?*

—*I'll be fifteen in April.*

—*Wrong,* he tells her. *That April's been here and so has the next one. You were sixteen two months ago. Sixteen, Satina.*

—*That can't be true, doctor. A girl's sixteenth birthday is something special, don't you know that? My parents are going to give me a big party. All my friends invited. And a nine piece robot orchestra with synthesizers. And I know that that hasn't happened yet, so how can I be sixteen?*

His reservoir of strength is almost drained. His mental signal is weak. He cannot find the energy to tell her that she is blocking reality again, that her parents are dead, that time is passing while she lies here, that it is too late for a Sweet Sixteen party.

—*We'll talk about it…another time, Satina. I'll…see…you…again… tomorrow…Tomorrow…morning…*

—*Don't go so soon, doctor!* But he can no longer hold the contact, and lets it break.

Releasing her, Mookherji stood up, shaking his head. A shame, he thought. A damned shame. He went out of the room on trembling legs and paused a moment in the hall, propping himself against a closed door and mopping his sweaty forehead. He was getting nowhere with Satina. After the initial encouraging period of contact, he had failed entirely to lessen the intensity of her coma. She had settled quite comfortably into her delusive world of withdrawal, and, telepathy or no, he could find no way to blast her loose.

He took a deep breath. Fighting back a growing mood of bleak discouragement, he went toward the next patient's room.

The operation was going smoothly. The dozen third-year medical students occupied the observation deck of the surgical gallery on the starport hospital's third floor, studying Dr. Hammond's expert technique by direct viewing and by simultaneous microamplified relay to their individual desk-screens. The patient, a brain-tumor victim in his late sixties, was visible only as a head and shoulders protruding from a life-support chamber. His scalp had been shaved; blue lines and dark red dots were painted on it to indicate the inner contours of the skull, as previously determined by short-range sonar bounces; the surgeon had finished the job of positioning the lasers that would excise the tumor. The hard part was over. Nothing remained except to bring the lasers to full power and send their fierce, precise bolts of light slicing into the patient's brain. Cranial surgery of this kind was entirely bloodless; there was no need to cut through skin and bone to expose the tumor, for the beams of the lasers, calibrated to a millionth of a millimeter, would penetrate through minute openings and, playing on the tumor from different sides, destroy the malignant growth without harming a bit of the surrounding healthy brain tissue. Planning was everything in an operation like this. Once the exact outlines of the tumor were determined, and the surgical lasers were mounted at the correct angles, any intern could finish the job.

For Dr. Hammond it was a routine procedure. He had performed a hundred operations of this kind in the past year alone. He gave the signal; the warning light glowed on the laser rack; the students in the gallery leaned forth expectantly—

And, just as the lasers' glittering fire leaped toward the operating table, the face of the anesthetized patient contorted weirdly, as though some terrifying dream had come drifting up out of the caverns of the man's drugged mind. His nostrils flared; his lips drew back; his eyes opened wide; he seemed to be trying to scream; he moved convulsively, twisting his head to one side. The lasers bit deep the patient's left temple, far from the indicated zone of the tumor. The right side of his face began to sag, all muscles paralyzed. The medical students looked at each other in bewilderment. Dr. Hammond, stunned, retained enough presence of mind to kill the lasers with a quick swipe of his hand. Then, gripping the operating table with both hands in his agitation, he peered at the dials and meters that told him the details of the botched operation. The tumor remained intact; a vast sector of the patient's brain had been devastated. "Impossible," Hammond muttered. What could goad a patient under anesthesia into jumping around like that? "Impossible. Impossible." He strode to the end of the table and checked the readings on the life-support chamber. The question now was not whether the brain tumor would be successfully removed; the immediate question was whether the patient was going to survive.

By four that afternoon Mookherji had finished most of his chores. He had seen every patient; he had brought his progress charts up to date; he had fed a prognosis digest to the master computer that was the starport hospital's control center; he had found time for a gulped lunch. Ordinarily, now, he could take the next four hours off, going back to his spartan room in the residents' building at the edge of the starport complex for a nap, or dropping in at the recreation center to have a couple rounds of floater-tennis, or looking in at the latest cube-show, or whatever. His next round of patient-visiting didn't begin until eight in the evening. But he couldn't relax: there was that business of the quarantined spacemen to worry about. Nakadai had been sending test outputs over since two o'clock, and now they were stacked deep in Mookherji's data terminal. Nothing had carried an *urgent* flag, so Mookherji had simply let the reports pile up; but now he felt he ought to have a look. He tapped the keys of the terminal, requesting printouts, and Nakadai's outputs began to slide from the slot.

Mookherji ruffled through the yellow sheets. Reflexes, synapse charge, degree of neural ionization, endocrine balances, visual response, respiratory and circulatory, cerebral molecular exchange, sensory percepts, EEG both enhanced and minimated...No, nothing unusual here. It was plain from the tests that the six men who had been to Norton's Star were badly in need of a vacation—frayed nerves, blurred reflexes—but there was no indication of anything more serious than chronic loss of sleep. He couldn't detect signs of brain lesions, infection, nerve damage, or other organic disabilities.

Why the nightmares, then?

He tapped out the phone number of Nakadai's office. "Quarantine," a crisp voice said almost at once, and moments later Nakadai's lean, tawny face appeared on the screen. "Hello, Pete. I was just going to call you."

Mookherji said, "I didn't finish up until a little while ago. But I've been through the outputs you sent over. Lee, there's nothing here."

"As I thought."

"What about the men? You were supposed to call me if any of them went into nightmares."

"None of them have," Nakadai said. "Falkirk and Rodriguez have been sleeping since eleven. Like lambs. Schmidt and Carroll were allowed to conk out at half past one. Webster and Schiavone hit the cots at three. All six are still snoring away, sleeping like they haven't slept in years. I've got them loaded with equipment and everything's reading perfectly normal. You want me to shunt the data to you?"

"Why bother? If they aren't hallucinating, what'll I learn?"

"Does that mean you plan to skip the mind-probes tonight?"

"I don't know," Mookherji said, shrugging. "I suspect there's no point in it, but let's leave that part open. I'll be finishing my evening rounds about eleven, and if there's some reason to get into the heads of those spacemen then, I will." He frowned. "But look—didn't they say that each one of them went into the nightmares on *every single sleep-shift?*"

"Right."

"And here they are, sleeping outside the ship to for the first time since the nightmares started, and none of them having any trouble at all. And no sign of possible hallucinogenic brain lesions. You know something, Lee? I'm starting to come around to a very silly hypothesis that those men proposed this morning."

"That the hallucinations were caused by some unseen alien being?" Nakadai asked.

"Something like that. Lee, what's the status of the ship they came in on?"

"It's been through all the routine purification checks, and now it's sitting in an isolation vector until we have some idea of what's on."

"Would I be able to get aboard it?" Mookherji asked.

"I suppose so, yes, but—why—?"

"On the wild shot that something external caused those nightmares and that that something may still be aboard the ship. And perhaps a lowlevel telepath like myself will be able to detect its presence. Can you set up clearance fast?"

"Within ten minutes," Nakadai said. "I'll pick you up."

Nakadai came by shortly in a rollerbuggy. As they headed toward the landing field, he handed Mookherji a crumpled spacesuit and told him to put it on.

"What for?"

"You may want to breathe inside the ship. Right now it's full of vacuum—we decided it wasn't safe to leave it under atmosphere. Also it's still loaded with radiation from the decontamination process. Okay?"

Mookherji struggled into the suit.

They reached the ship: a standard interstellar null-gravity-drive job, looking small and lonely in its corner of the field. A robot cordon kept it under isolation, but, tipped off by the control center, the robots let the two doctors pass. Nakadai remained outside; Mookherji crawled into the safety pouch and, after the hatch had gone through its admission cycle, entered the ship. He moved cautiously from cabin to cabin, like a man walking in a forest that was said to have a jaguar in every tree. While looking about, he brought himself as quickly as possible up to full telepathic receptivity, and, wide open, awaited telepathic contact with anything that might be lurking in the ship.

—Go on. Do your worst.

Complete silence on all mental wavelengths. Mookherji prowled everywhere: the cargo hold, the crew cabins, the drive compartments. Everything empty, everything still. Surely he would have been able to detect the presence of a telepathic creature in here, no matter how alien; if it was capable of reaching the mind of a sleeping spaceman, it should be able to reach the mind of a waking telepath as well. After fifteen minutes he left the ship, satisfied.

"Nothing there," he told Nakadai. "We're still nowhere."

The Vsiir was growing desperate. It had been roaming this building all day; judging by the quality of the solar radiation coming through the windows, night was beginning to fall now. And, though there were open minds on every level of the structure, the Vsiir had had no luck in making contact. At least there had been no more terminations. But it was the same story here as on the ship: whenever the Vsiir touched a human mind, the reaction was so negative as to make communication impossible. And yet the Vsiir went on and on and on, to mind after mind, unable to believe that this whole planet did not hold a single human to whom it could tell its story. It hoped it was not doing severe damage to these minds it was approaching; but it had its own fate to consider.

Perhaps this mind would be the one. The Vsiir started once more to tell its tale—

Half past nine at night. Dr. Peter Mookherji, bloodshot, tense, hauled himself through his neuropathological responsibilities. The ward was full: a schizoid collapse, a catatonic freeze, Satina in her coma, half a dozen routine hysterias, a couple of paralysis cases, an aphasic, and plenty more, enough to keep him going for sixteen hours a day and strain his telepathic powers, not to mention his conventional medical skills, to their limits. Some day the ordeal of residency would be over; some day he'd be quit of this hospital, and would set up private practice on some sweet tropical isle, and commute to Bombay on weekends to see his family, and spend his holidays on planets of distant stars, like any prosperous medical specialist...Some day. He tried to banish such lavish fantasies from his mind. If you're going to look forward to anything, he told himself, look forward to midnight. To sleep. Beautiful, beautiful sleep. And in the morning it all begins again, Satina and the coma, the schizoid, the catatonic, the aphasic...

As he stepped into the hall, going from patient to patient, his annunciator said, "Dr. Mookherji, please report at once to Dr. Bailey's office."

Bailey? The head of the neuropathology department, still hitting the desk this late. What now? But of course there was no ignoring such a summons. Mookherji notified the control center that he had been called off his rounds, and made his way quickly down the corridor to the frosted-glass door marked SAMUEL F. BAILEY, M.D.

He found at least half the neuropath staff there already: four of the other senior residents, most of the interns, even a few of the high-level doctors. Bailey, a puffy-faced, sandy-haired, fiftyish man of formidable professional standing, was thumbing a sheaf of outputs and scowling. He gave Mookherji a faint nod by way of greeting. They were not on the best of terms; Bailey, somewhat old-school in his attitudes, had not made a good adjustment to the advent of telepathy as a tool in the treatment of mental disturbance. "As I was just saying," Bailey began, "these reports have been accumulating all day, and they've all been dumped on me, God knows why. Listen: two cardiac patients under sedation undergo sudden violent shocks, described by one doctor as sensory overloads. One reacts with cardiac arrest, the other with cerebral hemorrhage. Both die. A patient being treated for endocrine restabilization develops a runaway adrenaline flow while asleep, and gets a six-month setback. A patient undergoing brain surgery starts lurching around on the operating table, despite adequate anesthesia, and gets badly carved up by the lasers. Et cetera. Serious problems like this all over the hospital today. Computer check of general EEG patterns shows that fourteen patients, other than those mentioned, have experienced exceptionally severe episodes of nightmare in the last eleven hours, nearly all of them of such impact that the patient has sustained some degree of psychic damage and often actual physiological harm. Control center reports no case histories of previous epidemics of bad dreams. No reason to suspect a widespread dietary imbalance or similar cause for the outbreak. Nevertheless, sleeping patients are continuing to suffer, and those whose condition is particularly critical may be exposed to grave risks. Effective immediately, sedation of critical patients has been interrupted where feasible, and sleep schedules of other patients have been rearranged, but this is obviously not an expedient that is going to do much good if this outbreak continues into tomorrow."

Bailey paused, glanced around the room, let his gaze rest on Mookherji. "Control center has offered one hypothesis: that a psychopathic individual with strong telepathic powers is at large in the hospital, preying on sleeping patients and transmitting images to them that take the form of horrifying nightmares. Mookherji, what do you make of that idea?"

Mookherji said, "It's perfectly feasible, I suppose, although I can't imagine why any telepath would want to go around distributing nightmares. But has control center correlated any of this with the business over at the quarantine building?"

Bailey stared at his output slips. "What business is that?"

"Six spacemen who came in early this morning, reporting that they'd all suffered chronic nightmares on their voyage homeward. Dr. Lee Nakadai's been testing them; he called me in as a consultant, but I couldn't discover anything useful. I imagine there are some late reports from Nakadai in my office, but—"

Bailey said, "Control center seems only to be concerned about events in the hospital, not in the starport complex as a whole. And if your six spacemen had their nightmares during their voyage, there's no chance that their symptoms are going to find their way onto—"

"That's just it!" Mookherji cut in. "They had their nightmares in space. But they've been asleep since morning, and Nakadai says they're resting peacefully. Meanwhile an outbreak of hallucinations has started over here. Which means that whatever was bothering them during their voyage has somehow got loose in the hospital today—some sort of entity capable of stirring up such ghastly dreams that they bring veteran spacemen to the edge of nervous breakdowns and can seriously injure or even kill someone in poor health." He realized that Bailey was looking at him strangely, and that Bailey was not the only one. In a more restrained tone, Mookherji said, "I'm sorry if this sounds fantastic to you. I've been checking it out all day, so I've had some time to get used to the concept. And things began to fit together for me just now. I'm not saying that my idea is necessarily correct. I'm simply saying that it's a reasonable notion, that it links up with the spacemen's own idea of what was bothering them, that it corresponds to the shape of the situation—and that it deserves a decent investigation, if we're going to stop this before we lose some more patients."

"All right, doctor," Bailey said. "How do you propose to conduct the investigation?"

Mookherji was shaken by that. He had been on the go all day; he was ready to fold. Here was Bailey abruptly putting him in charge of this snark-hunt, without even asking! But he saw there was no way to refuse. He was the only telepath on the staff. And, if the supposed creature really was at large in the hospital, how could be tracked except by a telepath?

Fighting back his fatigue, Mookherji said rigidly, "Well, I'd want a chart of all the nightmare cases, to begin with, a chart showing the location of each victim and the approximate time of onset hallucination—"

They would be preparing for the Festival of Changing, now, the grand climax of the winter. Thousands of Vsiirs in the metamorphic phase would be on their way toward the Valley of Sand, toward that great natural amphitheater where the holiest rituals were performed. By now the firstcomers would already have taken up their positions, facing the west, waiting for the sunrise. Gradually the rows would fill as Vsiirs came in from every part of the planet, until the golden valley was thick with them, Vsiirs that constantly shifted their energy levels, dimensional extensions, and inner resonances, shuttling gloriously through the final joyous moments of the season of metamorphosis, competing with one another in a gentle way to display the great variety of form, the most dynamic cycle of physical changes—and, when the first red rays of the sun crept past the Needle, the celebrants would grow even more frenzied, dancing and leaping and transforming themselves with total abandon, purging themselves of the winter's flamboyance as the season of stability swept across the world. And finally, in the full blaze of sunlight, they would turn to one another in renewed kinship, embracing, and—

The Vsiir tried not to think about it. But it was hard to repress that sense of loss, that pang of nostalgia. The pain grew more intense with every moment. No imaginable miracle would get the Vsiir home in time for the Festival of Changing, it knew, and yet it could not really believe that such a calamity had befallen it.

Trying to touch minds with humans was useless. Perhaps if it assumed a form visible to them, and let itself be noticed, and then tried to open verbal communication—

But the Vsiir was so small, and these humans were so large. The dangers were great. The Vsiir, clinging to a wall and carefully keeping its wavelength well beyond the ultraviolet, weighed one risk against another, and, for the moment, did nothing.

"All right," Mookherji said foggily, a little before midnight. "I think we've got the trail clear now." He sat before a wall-sized screen on which the control center had thrown a three-dimensional schematic plan of the hospital. Bright red dots marked the place of each nightmare incident, yellow dashes the probable path of the unseen alien creature. "It came in the side way, probably, straight off the ship, and went into the cardiac wing first. Mrs. Maldonado's bed here, Mr. Guinness' over here, eh? Then it went up to the second level, coming around to the front wing and impinging on the minds of patients here and here and here between ten and eleven in the morning. There were no reported episodes of hallucination in the next hour and ten minutes, but then came that nasty business in the third-level surgical gallery, and after that—" Mookherji's aching eyes closed a moment; it seemed to him that he could still see the red dots and yellow dashes. He forced himself to go on, tracing the rest of the intruder's route for his audience of doctors and hospital security personnel. At last he said, "That's it. I figure that the thing must be somewhere between the fifth and eighth levels by now. It's moving much more slowly than it did this morning, possibly running out of energy. What we have to do is keep the hospital's wings tightly sealed to prevent its free movement, if that can be done, and attempt to narrow down the number of places whom it might be found."

One of the security men said, a little belligerently, "Doctor, just how are we supposed to find an invisible entity?"

Mookherji struggled to keep impatience out of his voice. "The visible spectrum isn't the only sort of electromagnetic energy in the universe. If this thing is alive, it's got to be radiating *somewhere* along the line. You've got a master computer with a million sensory pickups mounted all over the hospital. Can't you have the sensors scan for a point-source of infrared or ultraviolet moving through a room? Or even X-rays, for God's sake: we don't know where the radiation's likely to be. Maybe it's a gamma emitter, even. Look, something wild is loose in this building, and we can't see it, but the computer can. Make it search."

Dr. Bailey said, "Perhaps the energy we ought to be trying to trace it by is, ah, telepathic energy, doctor."

Mookherji shrugged. "As far as anybody knows, telepathic impulses propagate somewhere outside the electromagnetic spectrum. But of course you're right that I might be able to pick up some kind of output, and I intend to make a floor-by-floor search as soon as this briefing session is over." He turned toward Nakadai. "Lee, what's the word from your quarantined spacemen?"

"All six went through eight-hour sleep periods today without any sign of a nightmare episode: there was some dreaming, but all of it normal. In the past couple of hours I've had them on the phone talking with some of the patients who had the nightmares, and everybody agrees that the kind of dreams people have been having here today are the same in tone, texture, and general level of horror as the ones the men had aboard the ship. Images of bodily destruction and alien landscapes, accompanied by an overwhelming, almost intolerable, feeling of isolation, loneliness, separation from one's own kind."

"Which would fit the hypothesis of an alien being as the cause," said Martinson of the psychology staff. "If it's wandering around trying to communicate with us, trying to tell us it doesn't want to be here, say, and its communications reach human minds only in the form of frightful nightmares—"

"Why does it communicate only with sleeping people?" an intern asked.

"Perhaps those are the only ones it can reach. Maybe a mind that's awake isn't receptive," Martinson suggested.

"Seems to me," a security man said, "that we're making a whole lot of guesses based on no evidence at all. You're all sitting around talking about an invisible telepathic thing that breathes nightmares in people's ears, and it might just as easily be a virus that attacks the brain, or something in yesterday's food, or—"

Mookherji said, "The ideas you're offering now have already been examined and discarded. We're working on this line of inquiry now because it seems to hold together, fantastic though it sounds, and because it's all we have. If you'll excuse me, I'd like to start checking the building for telepathic output, now." He went out, pressing his hands to his throbbing temples.

Satina Ransom stirred, stretched, subsided. She looked up and saw the dazzling blaze of Saturn's rings overhead, glowing through the hotel's domed roof. She had never seen anything more beautiful in her life. This close to them, only about 750,000 miles out, she could clearly make out the different zones of the rings, each revolving about Saturn at its own speed, with the blackness of space visible through the open places. And Saturn itself, gleaming in the heavens, so bright, so huge—

What was that rumbling sound? Thunder? Not here, not on Titan. Again: louder. And the ground swaying. A crack in the dome! Oh, no, no, no, feel the air rushing out, look at that cold greenish mist pouring in—people falling down all over the place—what's happening, what's happening, what's happening? Saturn seems to be falling toward us. That taste in my mouth—oh—oh—oh—

Satina screamed. And screamed. And went on screaming as she slipped down into darkness, and pulled the soft blanket of unconsciousness over her, and shivered, and gave thanks for finding a safe place to hide.

Mookherji had plodded through the whole building accompanied by three security men and a couple of interns. He had seen whole sectors of the hospital that he didn't know existed. He had toured basements and sub-basements and sub-sub-basements; he had been through laboratories and computer rooms and wards and exercise chambers. He had kept himself in a state of complete telepathic receptivity throughout the trek, but he had detected nothing, not even a fit of mental current anywhere. Somehow that came as no surprise to him. Now, with dawn near, he wanted nothing more than sixteen hours or so of sleep. Even with nightmares. He was tired beyond all comprehension of the meaning of tiredness.

Yet something wild was loose, still, and the nightmares still were going on. Three incidents, ninety minutes apart, had occurred during the night: two patients on the fifth level and one on the sixth awakened in states of terror. It had been possible to calm them quickly, and apparently no lasting harm had been done, but now the stranger was close to Mookherji's neuropathology ward, and he didn't like the thought of exposing a bunch of mentally unstable patients to that kind of stimulus. By this time, the control center had reprogrammed all patient-monitoring systems to watch for the early stages of nightmare—hormone changes, EEG tremors, respiration rate rise, and so forth—in the hope of awakening a victim before the full impact could be felt. Even so, Mookherji wanted to see that thing caught and out of the hospital before it got to any of his own people.

But how?

As he trudged back to his sixth-level office, he considered some of the ideas people had tossed around in that midnight briefing session. *Wandering around trying to communicate with us,* Martinson had said. *Its communications reach human minds only in the form of frightful nightmares. Maybe a mind that's awake isn't receptive.* Even the mind of a human telepath, it seemed, wasn't receptive while awake. Mookherji wondered if he should go to sleep and hope the alien would reach him, and then try to deal with it, lead it into a trap of some kind—but no. He wasn't that different from other people. If he slept, and the alien did open contact, he'd simply have a hell of a nightmare and wake up, and nothing gained. That wasn't the answer. Suppose, though, he managed to make contact with the alien through the mind of a nightmare victim—someone he could use as a kind of telepathic loudspeaker—someone who wasn't likely to wake up while the dream was going on—

Satina.

Perhaps. Perhaps. Of course, he'd have to make sure the girl was shielded from possible harm. She had enough horrors running free in her head as it was. But if he lent her his strength, drained off the poison of the nightmare, took the impact himself via their telepathic link, and was able to stand the strain and still speak to the alien mind—that might just work. Might.

He went to her room. He clasped her hand between his.

—*Satina?*

—*Morning so soon, doctor?*

—*It's still early, Satina. But things are a little unusual here today. We need your help. You don't have to if you don't want to, but I think you can be of great value to us, and maybe even to yourself. Listen to me very carefully, and think it over before you say yes or no—*

God help me if I'm wrong, Mookherji thought, far below the level of telepathic transmission.

Chilled, alone, growing groggy with dismay and hopelessness, the Vsiir had made no attempts at contact for several hours now. What was the use? The results were always the same when it touched a human mind; it was exhausting itself and apparently bothering the humans, to no purpose. Now the sun had risen. The Vsiir contemplated slipping out of the building and exposing itself to the yellow solar radiation while dropping all defenses; it would be a quick death, an end to all this misery and longing. It was folly to dream of seeing the home planet again. And—

What was that?

A call. Clear, intelligible, unmistakable. *Come to me.* An open mind somewhere on this level, speaking neither the human language nor the Vsiir language, but using the wordless, universally comprehensible communion that occurs when mind speaks directly to mind. *Come to me. Tell me everything. How can I help you?*

In its excitement the Vsiir slid up and down the spectrum, emitting a blast of infrared, a jagged blurt of ultraviolet, a lively blaze of visible light, before getting control. Quickly it took a fix on the direction of the call. Not far away: down this corridor, under this door, through this passage. *Come to me.* Yes. Yes. Extending its mind-probes ahead of it, groping for contact with the beckoning mind, the Vsiir hastened forward.

⁂

Mookherji, his mind locked to Satina's, felt the sudden crashing shock of the nightmare moving in, and even at second remove the effect was stunning in its power. He perceived a clicking sensation of mind touching mind. And then, into Satina's receptive spirit, there poured—

A wall higher than Everest. Satina trying to climb it, scrambling up a smooth white face, digging fingertips into minute crevices. Slipping back one yard for every two gained. Below, a roiling pit, flames shooting up, foul gases rising, monsters with needle-sharp fangs waiting for her to fall. The wall grows taller. The air is so thin she can barely breathe, her eyes are dimming, a greasy hand is squeezing her heart, she can feel her veins pulling free of her flesh like wires coming out of a broken plaster ceiling, and the gravitational pull is growing constantly—pain, her lungs crumbling, her face sagging hideously—a river of terror surging through her skull—

—None of it is real, Satina. They're just illusions. None of it is really happening.

—*Yes,* she says, *yes, I know,* but still she resonates with fright, her muscles jerking at random, her face flushed and sweating, her eyes fluttering beneath the lids. The dream continues. How much more can she stand?

—*Give it to me,* he tells her. *Give me the dream!*

She does not understand. No matter. Mookherji knows how to do it. He is so tired that fatigue is unimportant; somewhere in the realm beyond collapse he finds unexpected strength, and reaches into her numbed soul, and pulls the hallucinations forth as though they were cobwebs. They engulf him. No longer does he experience them indirectly; now all the phantoms are loose in his skull, and, even as he feels Satina relax, he braces himself against the onslaught of unreality that he has summoned into himself. And he copes. He drains the excess of irrationality out of her and winds it about his consciousness, and adapts, learning to live with the appalling flood of images. He and Satina share what is coming forth. Together they can bear the burden; he carries more of it than she does, but she does her part, and now neither of them is overwhelmed by the parade of bogeys. They can laugh at the dream monsters; they can even admire them for being so richly fantastic. That beast with a hundred heads, that bundle of living copper wires, that pit of dragons, that coiling mass of spiky teeth—who can fear what does not exist?

Over the clatter of bizarre images Mookherji sends a coherent thought, pushing it through Satina's mind to the alien.

—*Can you turn off the nightmares?*

—*No,* something replies. *They are in you, not in me. I only provide the liberating stimulus. You generate the images.*

—*All right. Who are you, and what do you want here?*

—*I am a Vsiir.*

—*A what?*

—*Native life form of the planet where you collect the greenfire branches. Through my own carelessness I was transported to your planet.* Accompanying the message is an overriding impulse of sadness, a mixture of pathos, self-pity, discomfort, exhaustion. Above this the nightmares still flow, but they are insignificant now. The Vsiir says, *I wish only to be sent home. I did not want to come here.*

And this is our alien monster? Mookherji thinks. This is our fearsome nightmare-spreading beast from the stars?

—*Why do you spread hallucinations?*

—*This was not my intention. I was merely trying to make mental contact. Some defect in the human receptive system, perhaps—I do not know. I do not know. I am so tired, though. Can you help me?*

—*We'll send you home, yes,* Mookherji promises. *Where are you? Can you show yourself to me? Let me know how to find you, and I'll notify the starport authorities, and they'll arrange for your passage home on the first ship out.*

Hesitation. Silence. Contact wavers and perhaps breaks.

Well? Mookherji says, after a moment. *What's happening? Where are you?*

From the Vsiir an uneasy response:

—*How can I trust you? Perhaps you merely wish to destroy me. If I reveal myself—*

Mookherji bites his lip in sudden fury. His reserve of strength is almost gone; he can barely sustain the contact at all. And if he now has to find some way of persuading a suspicious alien to surrender itself, he may run out of steam before he can settle things. The situation calls for desperate measures.

—*Listen, Vsiir. I'm not strong enough to talk much longer, and neither is this girl I'm using. I invite you into my head. I'll drop all defenses if you can look at who I am, look hard, and decide for yourself whether you can trust me. After that it's up to you. I can help you get home, but only if you produce yourself right away.*

He opens his mind wide. He stands mentally naked.

The Vsiir rushes into Mookherji's brain.

A hand touched Mookherji's shoulder. He snapped awake instantly, blinking, trying to get his bearings. Lee Nakadai stood above him. They were in—where?—Satina Ransom's room. The pale light of early morning was coming through the window; he must have dozed only a minute or so. His head was splitting.

"We've been looking all over for you, Pete," Nakadai said.

"It's all right now," Mookherji murmured. "It's all right." He shook his head to clear it. He remembered things. Yes. On the floor, next to Satina's bed, squatted something about the size of a frog, but very different in shape, color, and texture from any frog Mookherji had ever seen. He showed it to Nakadai. "That's the Vsiir," Mookherji said. "The alien terror. Satina and I made friends with it. We talked it into showing itself. Listen, it isn't happy here, so will you get hold of a starport official fast, and explain that we've got an organism here that has to be shipped back to Norton's Star at once, and—"

Satina said, "Are you Dr. Mookherji?"

"That's right. I suppose I should have introduced myself when—*you're awake?"*

"It's morning, isn't it?" The girl sat up, grinning. "You're younger than I thought you were. And so serious-looking. And I *love* that color of skin. I—"

"You're awake?"

"I had a bad dream," she said. "Or maybe a bad dream within a bad dream—I don't know. Whatever it was, it was pretty awful but I felt so much better when it went away—I just felt that if I slept any longer I was going to miss a lot of good things, that I had to get up and see what was happening in the world—do you understand any of this, doctor?"

Mookherji realized his knees were shaking. "Shock therapy," he muttered. "We blasted her loose from the coma—without even knowing what we were doing." He moved toward the bed. "Listen, Satina.

I've been up for about a million years, and I'm ready to burn out from overload. And I've got a thousand things to talk about with you, only not now. Is that okay? Not now. I'll send Dr. Bailey in—he's my boss—and after I've had some sleep I'll come back and we'll go over everything together, okay? Say, five, six this evening. All right?"

"Well, of course, all right," Satina said, with a twinkling smile. "If you feel you really have to run off, just when I've—sure. Go. Go. You look awfully tired, doctor."

Mookherji blew her a kiss. Then, taking Nakadai by the elbow, he headed for the door. When he was outside he said, "Get the Vsiir over to your quarantine place pronto and try to put it in an atmosphere it finds comfortable. And arrange for its trip home. And I guess you can let your six spacemen out. I'll go talk to Bailey—and then I'm going to drop."

Nakadai nodded. "You get some rest, Pete. I'll handle things."

Mookherji shuffled slowly down the hall toward Dr. Bailey's office, thinking of the smile on Satina's face, thinking of the sad little Vsiir, thinking of nightmares—

"Pleasant dreams, Pete," Nakadai called.

IN ENTROPY'S JAWS

This is a story that I began in January, 1970 and finished, after taking a little break for a winter holiday in a warmer place than the one in which I lived, early in March of that year. It was written at a time when I was still reasonably comfortable with the conventions of science fiction and had not yet entered into the period of literary and personal chaos that would complicate my life from 1973 or so through the early 1980s. And so I blithely tackled this long, complex, challenging story, which moves among changing levels of ureality and shifting zones of time, with the sort of confidence that I would later lose and be a long time regaining.

I don't recall much about the genesis of "In Entropy's Jaws," only that I wrote it for the second issue of Bob Hoskins' paperback anthology, Infinity. *Hoskins, a long-time science-fiction figure whom I had known glancingly for many years, paid me well and gave me a free hand artistically, a combination that—not too surprisingly—I found irresistible, and so I did a story for each of the five issues of his anthology that appeared between 1970 and 1973. Some of my best work, too. (The first of them was included in the previous volume of this series; three of them are in here, and the fifth, done in that troubled time when I was beginning to lose all faith in the value of science fiction, will be in the next one.)*

Static crackles from the hazy golden cloud of airborne loudspeakers drifting just below the ceiling of the spaceliner cabin. A hiss: communications filters are opening. An impending announcement from the bridge, no doubt. Then the captain's bland, mechanical voice: "We are approaching the Panama Canal. All passengers into their bottles until the all-clear after insertion. When we come out the far side, we'll be travelling at eighty lights toward the Perseus relay booster. Thank you." In John Skein's cabin the warning globe begins to flash, dousing him with red, yellow, green light, going up and down the visible spectrum, giving him some infra– and ultra– too. Not everybody who books passage on this liner necessarily has human sensory equipment. The signal will not go out until Skein is safely in his bottle. Go on, it tells him. Get in. Get in. Panama Canal coming up.

Obediently he rises and moves across the narrow cabin toward the tapering dull-skinned steel container, two and a half meters high, that will protect him against the dimensional stresses of canal insertion. He is a tall, angular man with thin lips, a strong chin, glossy black hair that clings close to his high-vaulted skull. His skin is deeply tanned but his eyes are those of one who has been in winter for some time. This is the fiftieth year of his second go-round. He is travelling alone toward a world of the Abbondanza system, perhaps the last leg on a journey that has occupied him for several years.

The passenger bottle swings open on its gaudy rhodium-jacketed hinge when its sensors, picking up Skein's mass and thermal output, tell it that its protectee is within entry range. He gets in. It closes and seals, wrapping him in a seamless magnetic field. "Please be seated," the bottle tells him softly. "Place your arms through the stasis loops and your feet in the security platens. When you have done this the pressor fields will automatically be activated and you will be fully insulated against injury during the coming period of turbulence." Skein, who has had plenty of experience with faster-than-light travel, has anticipated the instructions and is already in stasis. The bottle closes. "Do you wish music?" it asks him. "A book? A vision spool? Conversation?"

"Nothing, thanks," Skein says, and waits.

He understands waiting very well by this time. Once he was an impatient man, but this is a thin season in his life, and it has been teaching him the arts of stoic acceptance. He will sit here with the Buddha's own complacency until the ship is through the canal. Silent, alone, self-sufficient. If only there will be no fugues this time. Or, at least—he is negotiating the terms of his torment with his demons—at least let them not be flashforwards. If he must break loose again from the matrix of time, he prefers to be cast only into his yesterdays, never into his tomorrows.

"We are almost into the canal now," the bottle tells him pleasantly.

"It's all right. You don't need to look after me. Just let me know when it's safe to come out."

He closes his eyes. Trying to envision the ship: a fragile glimmering purple needle squirting through clinging blackness, plunging toward the celestial vortex just ahead, the maelstrom of clashing forces, the soup of contravariant tensors. The Panama Canal, so-called. Through which the liner will shortly rush, acquiring during its passage such a garland of borrowed power that it will rip itself free of the standard fourspace; it will emerge on the far side of the canal into a strange, tranquil pocket of the universe where the speed of light is the downside limiting velocity, and no one knows where the upper limit lies.

Alarms sound in the corridor, heavy, resonant: clang, clang, clang. The dislocation is beginning. Skein is braced. What does it look like out there? Folds of glowing black velvet, furry swatches of the disrupted continuum, wrapping themselves around the ship? Titanic lightnings hammering on the hull? Laughing centaurs flashing across the twisted heavens? Despondent masks, fixed in tragic grimaces, dangling between the blurred stars? Streaks of orange, green, crimson: sick rainbows, limp, askew? In we go. Clang, clang, clang. The next phase of the voyage now begins. He thinks of his destination, holding an image of it rigidly in mind. The picture is vivid, though this is a world he has visited only in spells of temporal fugue. Too often; he has been there again and again in these moments of disorientation in time. The colors are wrong on that world. Purple sand. Blue-leaved trees. Too much manganese? Too little copper? He will forgive it its colors if it will grant him his answers. And then. Skein feels the familiar ugly throbbing at the base of his neck, as if the tip of his spine is swelling like a balloon. He curses. He tries to resist. As he feared, not even the bottle can wholly protect him against these stresses. Outside the ship the universe is being wrenched apart; some of that slips in here and throws him into a private epilepsy of the timeline. Spacetime is breaking up for him. He will go into fugue. He clings, fighting, knowing it is futile. The currents of time buffet him, knocking him a short distance into the future, then a reciprocal distance into the past, as if he is a bubble of insect spittle glued loosely to a dry reed. He cannot hold on much longer. Let it not be flashforward, he prays, wondering who it is to whom he prays. Let it not be flashforward. And he loses his grip. And shatters. And is swept in shards across time.

Of course, if x is before y then it remains eternally before y, and nothing in the passage of time can change this. But the peculiar position of the "now" can be easily expressed simply because our language has tenses. The future will be, *the present* is, *and the past* was; *the light will be red, it is now yellow, and it was green. But do we, in these terms, really describe the "processional" character of time? We sometimes say that an event* is *future, then it* is *present, and finally it* is *past; and by this means we seem to dispense with tenses, yet we portray the passage of time. But this is really not the case; for all that we have done is to translate our tenses into the words "then" and "finally", and into the order in which we state our clauses. If we were to omit these words or their equivalents, and mix up the clauses, our sentences would no longer be meaningful. To say that the future, the present, and the past* are *in some sense is to dodge the problem of time by resorting to the tenseless language of logic and mathematics. In such an* atemporal *language it would be meaningful to say that Socrates is mortal because all men are mortal and Socrates is a man, even though Socrates has been dead many centuries. But if we cannot describe time either by a language containing tenses or by a tenseless language, how shall we symbolize it?*

He feels the curious doubleness of self, the sense of having been here before, and knows it is flashback. Some comfort in that. He is a passenger in his own skull, looking out through the eyes of John Skein on an event that he has already experienced, and which he now is powerless to alter.

His office. All its gilded magnificence. A crystal dome at the summit of Kenyatta Tower. With the amplifiers on he can see as far as Serengeti in one direction, Mombasa in another. Count the fleas on an elephant in Tsavo Park. A wall of light on the east-southeast face of the dome, housing his data-access units. No one can stare at that wall more than thirty seconds without suffering intensely from a surfeit of information. Except Skein; he drains nourishment from it, hour after hour.

As he slides into the soul of that earlier Skein he takes a brief joy in the sight of his office, like Aeneas relishing a vision of unfallen Troy, like Adam looking back into Eden. How good it was. That broad sweet desk with its subtle components dedicated to his service. The gentle psychosensitive carpet, so useful and so beautiful. The undulating ribbon-sculpture gliding in and out of the dome's skin, undergoing molecular displacement each time and forever exhibiting the newest of its infinity of possible patterns. A rich man's office; he was unabashed in his pursuit of elegance. He had earned the right to luxury through the intelligent use of his innate skills. Returning now to that lost dome of wonders, he quickly seizes his moment of satisfaction, aware that shortly some souring scene of subtraction will be replayed for him, one of the stages of the darkening and withering of his life. But which one?

"Send in Coustakis," he hears himself say, and his words give him the answer. That one. He will again watch his own destruction. Surely there is no further need to subject him to this particular reenactment. He has been through it at least seven times; he is losing count. An endless spiralling track of torment.

Coustakis is bald, blue-eyed, sharp-nosed, with the desperate look of a man who is near the end of his first go-round and is not yet sure that he will be granted a second. Skein guesses that he is about seventy. The man is unlikable: he dresses coarsely, moves in aggressive blurting little strides, and shows in every gesture and glance that he seethes with envy of the opulence with which Skein surrounds himself. Skein feels no need to like his clients, though. Only to respect. And Coustakis is brilliant; he commands respect.

Skein says, "My staff and I have studied your proposal in great detail. It's a cunning scheme."

"You'll help me?"

"There are risks for me," Skein points out. "Nissenson has a powerful ego. So do you. I could get hurt. The whole concept of synergy involves risk for the Communicator. My fees are calculated accordingly."

"Nobody expects a Communicator to be cheap," Coustakis mutters.

"I'm not. But I think you'll be able to afford me. The question is whether I can afford you."

"You're very cryptic, Mr. Skein. Like all oracles."

Skein smiles. "I'm not an oracle, I'm afraid. Merely a conduit through whom connections are made. I can't foresee the future."

"You can evaluate probabilities."

"Only concerning my own welfare. And I'm capable of arriving at an incorrect evaluation."

Coustakis fidgets. "Will you help me or won't you?"

"The fee," Skein says, "is half a million down, plus an equity position of fifteen percent in the corporation you'll establish with the contacts I provide."

Coustakis gnaws at his lower lip. "So much?"

"Bear in mind that I've got to split my fee with Nissenson. Consultants like him aren't cheap."

"Even so. Ten percent."

"Excuse me, Mr. Coustakis. I really thought we were past the point of negotiation in this transaction. It's going to be a busy day for me, and so—" Skein passes his hand over a black rectangle on his desk and a section of the floor silently opens, uncovering the dropshaft access. He nods toward it. The carpet reveals the colors of Coustakis's mental processes: black for anger, green for greed, red for anxiety, yellow for fear, blue for temptation, all mixed together in the hashed pattern betraying the calculations now going on in his mind. Coustakis will yield. Nevertheless Skein proceeds with the charade of standing, gesturing toward the exit, trying to usher his visitor out. "All right," Coustakis says explosively, "fifteen percent!"

Skein instructs his desk to extrude a contract cube. He says, "Place your hand here, please," and as Coustakis touches the cube he presses his own palm against its opposite face. At once the cube's sleek crystalline surface darkens and roughens as the double sensory output bombards it. Skein says, "Repeat after me. I, Nicholas Coustakis, whose handprint and vibration pattern are being imprinted in this contract as I speak—"

"I, Nicholas Coustakis, whose handprint and vibration pattern are being imprinted in this contract as I speak—"

"—do knowingly and willingly assign to John Skein Enterprises, as payment for professional services to be rendered, an equity interest in Coustakis Transport Ltd or any successor corporation amounting to—"

"—do knowingly and willingly assign—"

They drone on in turns through a description of Coustakis's corporation and the irrevocable nature of Skein's part ownership in it. Then

Skein files the contract cube and says, "If you'll phone your bank and put your thumb on the cash part of the transaction, I'll make contact with Nissenson and you can get started."

"Half a million?"

"Half a million."

"You know I don't have that kind of money."

"Let's not waste time, Mr. Coustakis. You have assets. Pledge them as collateral. Credit is easily obtained."

Scowling, Coustakis applies for the loan, gets it, transfers the funds to Skein's account. The process takes eight minutes; Skein uses the time to review Coustakis's ego profile. It displeases Skein to have to exert such sordid economic pressure; but the service he offers does, after all, expose him to dangers, and he must cushion the risk by high guarantees, in case some mishap should put him out of business.

"Now we can proceed," Skein says, when the transaction is done.

Coustakis has almost invented a system for the economical instantaneous transportation of matter. It will not, unfortunately, ever be useful for living things, since the process involves the destruction of the material being shipped and its virtually simultaneous reconstitution elsewhere. The fragile entity that is the soul cannot withstand the withering blast of Coustakis's transmitter's electron beam. But there is tremendous potential in the freight business; the Coustakis transmitter will be able to send cabbages to Mars, computers to Pluto, and, given the proper linkage facilities, it should be able to reach the inhabited extrasolar planets.

However, Coustakis has not yet perfected his system. For five years he has been stymied by one impassable problem: keeping the beam tight enough between transmitter and receiver. Beamspread has led to chaos in his experiments; marginal straying results in the loss of transmitted information, so that that which is being sent invariably arrives incomplete. Coustakis has depleted his resources in the unsuccessful search for a solution, and thus has been forced to the desperate and costly step of calling in a Communicator.

For a price, Skein will place him in contact with someone who can solve his problem. Skein has a network of consultants on several worlds, experts in technology and finance and philology and nearly everything else. Using his own mind as the focal nexus, Skein will open telepathic communion between Coustakis and a consultant.

"Get Nissenson into a receptive state," he orders his desk.

Coustakis, blinking rapidly, obviously uneasy, says, "First let me get it clear. This man will see everything that's in my mind? He'll get access to my secrets?"

"No. No. I filter the communion with great care. Nothing will pass from your mind to his except the nature of the problem you want him to tackle. Nothing will come back from his mind to yours except the answer."

"And if he doesn't have the answer?"

"He will."

Skein gives no refunds in the event of failure, but he has never had a failure. He does not accept jobs that he feels will be inherently impossible to handle. Either Nissenson will see the solution Coustakis has been overlooking, or else he will make some suggestion that will nudge Coustakis toward finding the solution himself. The telepathic communion is the vital element. Mere talking would never get anywhere. Coustakis and Nissenson could stare at blueprints together for months, pound computers side by side for years, debate the difficulty with each other for decades, and still they might not hit on the answer. But the communion creates a synergy of minds that is more than a doubling of the available brainpower. A union of perceptions, a heightening, that always produces that mystic flash of insight, that leap of the intellect.

"And if he goes into the transmission business for himself afterward?" Coustakis asks.

"He's bonded," Skein says curtly. "No chance of it. Let's go, now. Up and together."

The desk reports that Nissenson, half the world away in São Paulo, is ready. Skein's power does not vary with distance. Quickly he throws Coustakis into the receptive condition, and swings around to face the brilliant lights of his data-access units. Those sparkling, shifting little blazes kindle his gift, jabbing at the electrical rhythms of his brain until he is lifted into the energy level that permits the opening of a communion. As he starts to go up, the other Skein who is watching, the time-displaced prisoner behind his forehead, tries frenziedly to prevent him from entering the fatal linkage. *Don't. Don't. You'll overload. They're too strong for you.* Easier to halt a planet in its orbit, though. The course of the past is frozen; all this has already happened; the Skein who cries out in silent anguish is merely an observer, necessarily passive, here to view the maiming of his earlier self.

Skein reaches forth one tendril of his mind and engages Nissenson. With another tendril he snares Coustakis. Steadily, now, he draws the two tendrils together.

There is no way to predict the intensity of the forces that will shortly course through his brain. He has done what he could, checking the ego profiles of his client and the consultant, but that really tells him little. What Coustakis and Nissenson may be as individuals hardly matters; it is what they may become in communion that he must fear. Synergistic intensities are unpredictable. He has lived for a lifetime and a half with the possibility of a burnout.

The tendrils meet.

Skein the observer winces and tries to armor himself against the shock. But there is no way to deflect it. Out of Coustakis's mind flows a description of the matter transmitter and a clear statement of the beam-spread problem; Skein shoves it along to Nissenson, who begins to work on a solution. But when their minds join it is immediately evident that their combined strength will be more than Skein can control. This time the synergy will destroy him. But he cannot disengage; he has no mental circuitbreaker. He is caught, trapped, impaled. The entity that is Coustakis/Nissenson will not let go of him, for that would mean its own destruction. A wave of mental energy goes rippling and dancing along the vector of communion from Coustakis to Nissenson and goes bouncing back, pulsating and gaining strength, from Nissenson to Coustakis. A fiery oscillation is set up. Skein sees what is happening; he has become the amplifier of his own doom. The torrent of energy continues to gather power each time it reverberates from Coustakis to Nissenson, from Nissenson to Coustakis. Powerless, Skein watches the energy-pumping effect building up a mighty charge. The discharge is bound to come soon, and he will be the one who must receive it. How long? How long? The juggernaut fills the corridors of his mind. He ceases to know which end of the circuit is Nissenson, which is Coustakis; he perceives only two shining walls of mental power, between which he is stretched ever thinner, a twanging wire of ego, heating up, heating up, glowing now, emitting a searing blast of heat, particles of identity streaming away from him like so many liberated ions—

Then he lies numb and dazed on the floor of his office, grinding his face into the psychosensitive carpet, while Coustakis barks over and over, "Skein? Skein? Skein? Skein?"

Like any other chronometric device, our inner clocks are subject to their own peculiar disorders and, in spite of the substantial concordance between private and public time, discrepancies may occur as the result of sheer inattention. Mach noted that if a doctor focuses his attention on the patient's blood, it may seem to him to squirt out before the lancet enters the skin and, for similar reasons, the feebler of two stimuli presented simultaneously is usually perceived later...Normal life requires the capacity to recall experiences in a sequence corresponding, roughly at least, to the order in which they actually occurred. It requires in addition that our potential recollections should be reasonably accessible to consciousness. These potential recollections mean not only a perpetuation within us of representations of the past, but also a ceaseless interplay between such representations and the uninterrupted input of present information from the external world. Just as our past may be at the service of our present, so the present may be remotely controlled by our past: in the words of Shelley, "Swift as a Thought by the snake Memory stung."

"Skein? Skein? Skein? Skein?"

His bottle is open and they are helping him out. His cabin is full of intruders. Skein recognizes the captain's robot, the medic, and a couple of passengers, the little swarthy man from Pingalore and the woman from Globe Fifteen. The cabin door is open and more people are coming in. The medic makes a cuff-shooting gesture and a blinding haze of metallic white particles wraps itself about Skein's head. The little tingling prickling sensations spur him to wakefulness. "You didn't respond when the bottle told you it was all right," the medic explains. "We're through the canal."

"Was it a good passage? Fine. Fine. I must have dozed."

"If you'd like to come to the infirmary—routine check, only—put you through the diagnostat—"

"No. No. Will you all please go? I assure you, I'm quite all right."

Reluctantly, clucking over him, they finally leave. Skein gulps cold water until his head is clear. He plants himself flatfooted in mid-cabin, trying to pick up some sensation of forward motion. The ship now is travelling at something like fifteen million miles a second. How long is fifteen million miles? How long is a second? From Rome to Naples it was a morning's drive on the autostrada. From Tel Aviv to Jerusalem was the time between twilight and darkness. San Francisco to San Diego spanned lunch to dinner by superpod. As I slide my right foot two inches forward we traverse fifteen million miles. From where to where? And why? He has not seen Earth in twenty-six months. At the end of this voyage his remaining funds will be exhausted. Perhaps he will have to make his home in the Abbondanza system; he has no return ticket. But of course he can travel to his heart's discontent within his own skull, whipping from point to point along the timeline in the grip of the fugues.

He goes quickly from his cabin to the recreation lounge.

The ship is a second-class vessel, neither lavish nor seedy. It carries about twenty passengers, most of them, like him, bound outward on one-way journeys. He has not talked directly to any of them, but he has done considerable eavesdropping in the lounge, and by now can tag each one of them with the proper dull biography. The wife bravely joining her pioneer husband, whom she has not seen for half a decade. The remittance man under orders to place ten thousand light-years, at the very least, between himself and his parents. The glittery-eyed entrepreneur, a Phoenician merchant sixty centuries after his proper era, off to carve an empire as a middleman's middleman. The tourists. The bureaucrat. The colonel. Among this collection Skein stands out in sharp relief; he is the only one who has not made an effort to know and be known, and the mystery of his reserve tantalizes them.

He carries the fact of his crackup with him like some wrinkled dangling yellowed wen. When his eyes meet those of any of the others he says silently, You see my deformity? I am my own survivor. I have been destroyed and lived to look back on it. Once I was a man of wealth and power, and look at me now. But I ask for no pity. Is that understood?

Hunching at the bar, Skein pushes the node for filtered rum. His drink arrives, and with it comes the remittance man, handsome, young, insinuating. Giving Skein a confidential wink, as if to say, *I* know. You're on the run, too.

"From Earth, are you?" he says to Skein.

"Formerly."

"I'm Pid Rocklin."

"John Skein."

"What were you doing there?"

"On Earth?" Skein shrugs. "A Communicator. I retired four years ago."

"Oh." Rocklin summons a drink. "That's good work, if you have the gift."

"I had the gift," Skein says. The unstressed past tense is as far into self-pity as he will go. He drinks and pushes for another one. A great gleaming screen over the bar shows the look of space: empty, here beyond the Panama Canal, although yesterday a million suns blazed on that ebony rectangle. Skein imagines he can hear the whoosh of hydrogen molecules scraping past the hull at eighty lights. He sees them as blobs of brightness millions of miles long, going *zip!* and *zip!* and *zip!* as the ship spurts along. Abruptly a purple nimbus envelopes him and he drops into a flashforward fugue so quickly there is not even time for the usual futile resistance. "Hey, what's the matter?" Pid Rocklin says, reaching for him. "Are you all—" and Skein loses the universe.

He is on the world that he takes to be Abbondanza VI, and his familiar companion, the skull-faced man, stands beside him at the edge of an oily orange sea. They appear to be having the debate about time once again. The skull-faced man must be at least a hundred and twenty years old; his skin lies against his bones with, seemingly, no flesh at all under it, and his face is all nostrils and burning eyes. Bony sockets, sharp shelves for cheekbones, a bald dome of a skull. The neck no more than wrist-thick, rising out of shrivelled shoulders. Saying, "Won't you ever come to see that causality is merely an illusion, Skein? The notion that there's a consecutive series of events is nothing but a fraud. We impose form on our lives, we talk of time's arrow, we say that there's a flow from A through G and Q to Z, we make believe everything is nicely linear. But it isn't, Skein. It isn't."

"So you keep telling me."

"I feel an obligation to awaken your mind to the truth. G can come before A, and Z before both of them. Most of us don't like to perceive it that way, so we arrange things in what seems like a more logical pattern, just as a novelist will put the motive before the murder and the murder before the arrest. But the universe isn't a novel. We can't make nature imitate art. It's all random, Skein, random, random! Look there. You see what's drifting on the sea?"

On the orange waves tosses the bloated corpse of a shaggy blue beast. Upturned saucery eyes, drooping snout, thick limbs. Why is it not waterlogged by now? What keeps it afloat?

The skull-faced man says, "Time is an ocean, and events come drifting to us as randomly as dead animals on the waves. We filter them. We screen out what doesn't make sense and admit them to our consciousness in what seems to be the right sequence." He laughs. "The grand delusion! The past is nothing but a series of films slipping unpredictably into the future. And vice versa."

"I won't accept that," Skein says stubbornly. "It's a demonic, chaotic, nihilistic theory. It's idiocy. Are we greybeards before we're children? Do we die before we're born? Do trees devolve into seeds? Deny linearity all you like. I won't go along."

"You can say that after all you've experienced?"

Skein shakes his head. "I'll go on saying it. What I've been going through is a mental illness. Maybe I'm deranged, but the universe isn't."

"Contrary. You've only recently become sane and started to see things as they really are," the skull-faced man insists. "The trouble is that you don't want to admit the evidence you've begun to perceive. Your filters are down, Skein! You've shaken free of the illusion of linearity! Now's your chance to show your resilience. Learn to live with the real reality. Stop this silly business of imposing an artificial order on the flow of time. Why should effect follow cause? Why shouldn't the seed follow the tree? Why must you persist in holding tight to a useless, outworn, contemptible system of false evaluations of experience when you've managed to break free of the—"

"Stop it! Stop it! Stop it! Stop it!"

"—right, Skein?"

"What happened?"

"You started to fall off your stool," Pid Rocklin says. "You turned absolutely white. I thought you were having some kind of a stroke."

"How long was I unconscious?"

"Oh, three, four seconds, I suppose. I grabbed you and propped you up, and your eyes opened. Can I help you to your cabin? Or maybe you ought to go to the infirmary."

"Excuse me," Skein says hoarsely, and leaves the lounge.

When the hallucinations began, not long after the Coustakis overload, he assumed at first that they were memory disturbances produced by the fearful jolt he had absorbed. Quite clearly most of them involved scenes of his past, which he would relive, during the moments of fugue, with an intensity so brilliant that he felt he had actually been thrust back into time. He did not merely recollect, but rather he experienced the past anew, following a script from which he could not deviate as he spoke and felt and reacted. Such strange excursions into memory could be easily enough explained: his brain had been damaged, and it was heaving old segments of experience into view in some kind of attempt to clear itself of debris and heal the wounds. But while the flashbacks were comprehensible, the flashforwards were not, and he did not recognize them at all for what they actually were. Those scenes of himself wandering alien worlds, those phantom conversations with people he had never met, those views of spaceliner cabins and transit booths and unfamiliar hotels and passenger terminals, seemed merely to be fantasies, random fictions of his injured brain. Even when he started to notice that there was a consistent pattern to these feverish glimpses of the unknown, he still did not catch on. It appeared as though he was seeing himself performing a sort of quest, or perhaps a pilgrimage; the slices of unexperienced experience that he was permitted to see began to fit into a coherent structure of travel and seeking. And certain scenes and conversations recurred, yes, sometimes several times the same day, the script always the same, so that he began to learn a few of the scenes word for word. Despite the solid texture of these episodes, he persisted in thinking of them as mere brief flickering segments of nightmare. He could not imagine why the injury to his brain was causing him to have these waking dreams of long space voyages and unknown planets, so vivid and so momentarily real, but they seemed no more frightening to him than the equally vivid flashbacks.

Only after a while, when many months had passed since the Coustakis incident, did the truth strike him. One day he found himself living through an episode that he considered to be one of his fantasies. It was a minor thing, one that he had experienced, in whole or in part, seven or eight times. What he had seen, in fitful bursts of uninvited delusion, was himself in a public garden on some hot spring morning, standing before an immense baroque building while a grotesque group of nonhuman tourists filed past him in a weird creaking, clanking procession of inhalator suits and breather-wheels and ion-disperser masks. That was all. Then it happened that a harrowing legal snarl brought him to a city in North Carolina about fourteen months after the overload, and, after having put in his appearance at the courthouse, he set out on a long walk through the grimy, decayed metropolis, and came, as if by an enchantment, to a huge metal gate behind which he could see a dark sweep of lavish forest, oaks and rhododendrons and magnolias, laid out in an elegant formal manner. It was, according to a sign posted by the gate, the estate of a nineteenth-century millionaire, now open to all and preserved in its ancient state despite the encroachments of the city on its borders.

Skein bought a ticket and went in, on foot, hiking for what seemed like miles through cool leafy glades, until abruptly the path curved and he emerged into the bright sunlight and saw before him the great grey bulk of a colossal mansion, hundreds of rooms topped by parapets and spires, with a massive portico from which vast columns of stairs descended. In wonder he moved toward it, for this was the building of his frequent fantasy, and as he approached he beheld the red and green and purple figures crossing the portico, those coiled and gnarled and looping shapes he had seen before, the eerie horde of alien travellers here to take in the wonders of Earth. Heads without eyes, eyes without heads, multiplicities of limbs and absences of limbs, bodies like tumors and tumors like bodies, all the universe's imagination on display in these agglomerated life forms, so strange and yet not at all strange to him. But this time it was no fantasy. It fit smoothly into the sequence of the events of the day, rather than dropping, dreamlike, intrusive, into that sequence. Nor did it fade after a few moments; the scene remained sharp, never leaving him to plunge back into "real" life. This was reality itself, and he had experienced it before.

Twice more in the next few weeks things like that happened to him, until at last he was ready to admit the truth to himself about his fugues, that he was experiencing flashforwards as well as flashbacks, that he was being subjected to glimpses of his own future.

T'ang, the high king of the Shang, asked Hsia Chi saying, "In the beginning, were there already individual things?" Hsia Chi replied, "If there were no things then, how could there be any now? If later generations should pretend that there had been no things in our time, would they be right?" Tang said, "Have things then no before and no after?" To which Hsia Chi replied, "The ends and the origins of things have no limit from which they began. The origin of one thing may be considered the end of another; the end of one may be considered the origin of the next. Who can distinguish accurately between these cycles? What lies beyond all things, and before all events, we cannot know."

They reach and enter the Perseus relay booster, which is a whirling celestial anomaly structurally similar to the Panama Canal but not nearly so potent, and it kicks the ship's velocity to just above a hundred lights. That is the voyage's final acceleration; the ship will maintain this rate for two and a half days, until it clocks in at Scylla, the main deceleration station for this part of the galaxy, where it will be seized by a spongy web of forces twenty light-minutes in diameter and slowed to sublight velocities for the entry into the Abbondanza system.

Skein spends nearly all of this period in his cabin, rarely eating and sleeping very little. He reads, almost constantly, obsessively dredging from the ship's extensive library a wide and capricious assortment of books. Rilke. Kafka. Eddington, *The Nature of the Physical World.* Lowry, *Hear Us O Lord From Heaven Thy Dwelling Place.* Elias. Razhuminin. Dickey. Pound. Fraisse, *The Psychology of Time.* Greene, *Dream and Delusion.* Poe. Shakespeare. Marlowe. Tourneur. *The Waste Land. Ulysses. Heart of Darkness.* Bury, *The Idea of Progress.* Jung. Buechner. Pirandello. *The Magic Mountain.* Ellis, *The Rack.* Cervantes. Blenheim. Fierst. Keats. Nietzsche. His mind swims with images and bits of verse, with floating sequences of dialogue, with unscaffolded dialectics. He dips into each work briefly, magpielike, seeking bright scraps. The words form a scaly impasto on the inner surface of his skull. He finds that this heavy verbal overdose helps, to some slight extent, to fight off the fugues; his mind is weighted, perhaps, bound by this leaden clutter of borrowed genius to the moving line of the present, and during his debauch of reading he finds himself shifting off that line less frequently than in the recent past.

His mind whirls. *Man is a rope stretched between the animal and the Superman—A rope over an abyss.* My patience are exhausted. *See, see where Christ's blood streams in the firmament! One drop would save my soul.* I had not thought death had undone so many. These fragments I have shored against my ruins. *Hoogspanning. Levensgevaar. Peligro de Muerte. Electricidad. Danger.* Give me my spear. *Old father, old artificer, stand me now and ever in good stead.* You like this garden? Why is it yours? We evict those who destroy! *And then went down to the ship, set keel to breakers, forth on the godly sea.* There is no "official" theory of time, defined in creeds or universally agreed upon among Christians. Christianity is not concerned with the purely scientific aspects of the subject nor, within wide limits, with its philosophical analysis, except insofar as it is committed to a fundamentally realist view and could not admit, as some Eastern philosophies have done, that temporal existence is mere illusion. *A shudder in the loins engenders there the broken wall, the burning roof and tower and Agamemnon dead.* Stately, plump Buck Mulligan came from the stairhead, bearing a bowl of lather on which a mirror and a razor lay crossed. *In what distant deeps or skies burnt the fire of thine eyes? On what wings dare he aspire? What the hand dare seize the fire?* These fragments I have shored against my ruins. Hieronymo's mad again. *Then felt I like some watcher of the skies when a new planet swims into his ken.* It has also lately been postulated that the physical concept of information is identical with a phenomenon of reversal of entropy. The psychologist must add a few remarks here: It does not seem convincing to me that information is *eo ipso* identical with a *pouvoir d'organisation* which undoes entropy. *Datta. Dayadhvam. Damyata. Shantih shantih shantih.*

Nevertheless, once the ship is past Scylla and slowing toward the Abbondanza planets, the periods of fugue become frequent once again, so that he lives entrapped, shuttling between the flashing shadows of yesterday and tomorrow.

After the Coustakis overload he tried to go on in the old way, as best he could. He gave Coustakis a refund without even being asked, for he had been of no service, nor could he ever be. Instantaneous transportation of matter would have to wait. But Skein took other clients. He could still make the communion, after a fashion, and when the nature of the task was sufficiently low-level he could even deliver a decent synergetic response.

Often his work was unsatisfactory, however. Contacts would break at awkward moments, or, conversely, his filter mechanism would weaken and he would allow the entire contents of his client's mind to flow into that of his consultant. The results of such disasters were chaotic, involving him in heavy medical expenses and sometimes in damage suits. He was forced to place his fees on a contingency basis: no synergy, no pay. About half the time he earned nothing for his output of energy. Meanwhile his overhead remained the same as always: the domed office, the network of consultants, the research staff, and the rest. His effort to remain in business was eating rapidly into the bank accounts he had set aside against just such a time of storm.

They could find no organic injury to his brain. Of course, so little was known about a Communicator's gift that it was impossible to determine much by medical analysis. If they could not locate the centre center from which a Communicator powered his communions, how could they detect the place where he had been hurt? The medical archives were of no value; there had been eleven previous cases of overload, but each instance was physiologically unique. They told him he would eventually heal, and sent him away. Sometimes the doctors gave him silly therapies: counting exercises, rhythmic blinkings, hopping on his left leg and then his right, as if he had a stroke. But he had not had a stroke.

For a time he was able to maintain his business on the momentum of his reputation. Then, as word got around that he had been hurt and was no longer any good, clients stopped coming. Even the contingency basis for fees failed to attract them. Within six months he found that he was lucky to find a client a week. He reduced his rates, and that seemed only to make things worse, so he raised them to something not far below what they had been at the time of the overload. For a while the pace of business increased, as if people were getting the impression that Skein had recovered. He gave such spotty service, though. Blurred and wavering communions, unanticipated positive feedbacks, filtering problems, information deficiencies, redundancy surpluses—"You take your mind in your hands when you go to Skein," they were saying now.

The fugues added to his professional difficulties.

He never knew when he would snap into hallucination. It might happen during a communion, and often did. Once he dropped back to the moment of the Coustakis-Nissenson hookup and treated a terrified client to a replay of his overload. Once, although he did not understand at the time what was happening, he underwent a flashforward and carried the client with him to a scarlet jungle on a formaldehyde world, and when Skein slipped back to reality the client remained in the scarlet jungle. There was a damage suit over that one, too.

Temporal dislocation plagued him into making poor guesses. He took on clients whom he could not possibly serve and wasted his time on them. He turned away people whom he might have been able to help to his own profit. Since he was no longer anchored firmly to his timeline, but drifted in random oscillations of twenty years or more in either direction, he forfeited the keen sense of perspective on which he had previously founded his professional judgments. He grew haggard and lean, also. He passed through a tempest of spiritual doubts that amounted to total submission and then total rejection of faith within the course of four months. He changed lawyers almost weekly. He liquidated assets with invariably catastrophic timing to pay his cascading bills.

A year and a half after the overload, he formally renounced his registration and closed his office. It took six months more to settle the remaining damage suits. Then, with what was left of his money, he bought a spaceliner ticket and set out to search for a world with purple sand and blue-leaved trees, where, unless his fugues had played him false, he might be able to arrange for the repair of his broken mind.

Now the ship has returned to the conventional fourspace and dawdles planetward at something rather less than half the speed of light. Across the screens there spreads a necklace of stars; space is crowded here. The captain will point out Abbondanza to anyone who asks: a lemon-colored sun, bigger than that of Earth, surrounded by a dozen bright planetary pips. The passengers are excited. They buzz, twitter, speculate, anticipate. No one is silent except Skein. He is aware of many love affairs; he has had to reject several offers just in the past three days. He has given up reading and is trying to purge his mind of all he has stuffed into it. The fugues have grown worse. He has to write notes to himself, saying things like *You are a passenger aboard a ship heading for Abbondanza VI, and will be landing in a few days,* so that he does not forget which of his three entangled timelines is the true one.

Suddenly he is with Nilla on the island in the Gulf of Mexico, getting aboard the little excursion boat. Time stands still here; it could almost be the twentieth century. The frayed, sagging cords of the rigging. The lumpy engine inefficiently converted from internal combustion to turbines. The mustachioed Mexican bandits who will be their guides today. Nilla, nervously coiling her long blonde hair, saying, "Will I get seasick, John? The boat rides right in the water, doesn't it? It won't even hover a little bit?"

"Terribly archaic," Skein says. "That's why we're here."

The captain gestures them aboard. Juan, Francisco, Sebastián. Brothers. *Los hermanos.* Yards of white teeth glistening below the drooping moustaches. With a terrible roar the boat moves away from the dock. Soon the little town of crumbling pastel buildings is out of sight and they are heading jaggedly eastward along the coast, green shoreward water on their left, the blue depths on the right. The morning sun coming up hard. "Could I sunbathe?" Nilla asks. Unsure of herself; he has never seen her this way, so hesitant, so abashed. Mexico has robbed her of her New York assurance. "Go ahead," Skein says. "Why not?" She drops her robe. Underneath she wears only a waist-strap; her heavy breasts look white and vulnerable in the tropic glare, and the small nipples are a faded pink. Skein sprays her with protective sealant and she sprawls out on the deck. *Los hermanos* stare hungrily and talk to each other in low rumbling tones. Not Spanish. Mayan, perhaps? The natives have never learned to adopt the tourists' casual nudity here. Nilla, obviously still uneasy, rolls over and lies face down. Her broad smooth back glistens.

Juan and Francisco yell. Skein follows their pointing fingers. Porpoises! A dozen of them, frisking around the bow, keeping just ahead of the boat, leaping high and slicing down into the blue water. Nilla gives a little cry of joy and rushes to the side to get a closer look. Throwing her arm self-consciously across her bare breasts. "You don't need to do that," Skein murmurs. She keeps herself covered. "How lovely they are," she says softly. Sebastián comes up beside them. "*Amigos,*" he says. "They are. My friends." The cavorting porpoises eventually disappear. The boat bucks bouncily onward, keeping close to the island's beautiful empty palmy shore. Later they anchor, and he and Nilla swim masked, spying on the coral gardens. When they haul themselves on deck again it is almost noon. The sun is terrible. "Lunch?" Francisco asks. "We make you good lunch now?" Nilla laughs. She is no longer hiding her body. "I'm starved!" she cries.

"We make you good lunch," Francisco says, grinning, and he and Juan go over the side. In the shallow water they are clearly visible near the white sand of the bottom. They have spear guns; they hold their breaths and prowl. Too late Skein realizes what they are doing. Francisco hauls a fluttering spiny lobster out from behind a rock. Juan impales a huge pale crab. He grabs three conchs also, surfaces, dumps his prey on the deck. Francisco arrives with the lobster. Juan, below again, spears a second lobster. The animals are not dead; they crawl sadly in circles on the deck as they dry. Appalled, Skein turns to Sebastián and says, "Tell them to stop. We're not that hungry." Sebastián, preparing some kind of salad, smiles and shrugs. Francisco has brought up another crab, bigger than the first. "Enough," Skein says. *"Basta! Basta!"* Juan, dripping, tosses down three more conchs. "You pay us good," he says. "We give you good lunch." Skein shakes his head. The deck is becoming a slaughterhouse for ocean life. Sebastián now energetically slits conch shells, extracts the meat, drops it into a vast bowl to marinate in a yellow-green fluid. *"Basta!"* Skein yells: Is that the right word in Spanish? He knows it's right in Italian. *Los hermanos* look amused. The sea is full of life, they seem to be telling him. We give you good lunch. Suddenly Francisco erupts from the water, bearing something immense. A turtle! Forty, fifty pounds! The joke has gone too far. "No," Skein says. "Listen, I have to forbid this. Those turtles are almost extinct. Do you understand that? *Muerto. Perdido. Desaparecido.* I won't eat a turtle. Throw it back. Throw it back." Francisco smiles. He shakes his head. Deftly he binds the turtle's flippers with rope. Juan says, "Not for lunch, señor. For us. For to sell. *Mucho dinero."* Skein can do nothing. Francisco and Sebastián have begun to hack up the crabs and lobsters. Juan slices peppers into the bowl where the conchs are marinating. Pieces of dead animals litter the deck. "Oh, I'm *starving,"* Nilla says. Her waist-strap is off too, now. The turtle watches the whole scene, beady-eyed. Skein shudders. Auschwitz, he thinks. Buchenwald. For the animals it's Buchenwald every day.

Purple sand, blue-leaved trees. An orange sea gleaming not far to the west under a lemon sun. "It isn't much farther," the skull-faced man says. "You can make it. Step by step by step is how."

"I'm winded," Skein says. "Those hills—"

"I'm twice your age, and I'm doing fine."

"You're in better shape. I've been cooped up on spaceships for months and months."

"Just a short way on," says the skull-faced man. "About a hundred meters from the shore."

Skein struggles on. The heat is frightful. He has trouble getting a footing in the shifting sand. Twice he trips over black vines whose fleshy runners form a mat a few centimeters under the surface; loops of the vines stick up here and there. He even suffers a brief fugue, a seven-second flashback to a day in Jerusalem. Somewhere at the core of his mind he is amused by that: a flashback within a flashforward. Encapsulated concentric hallucinations. When he comes out of it, he finds himself getting to his feet and brushing sand from his clothing. Ten steps onward the skull-faced man halts him and says, "There it is. Look there, in the pit."

Skein sees a funnel-shaped crater right in front of him, perhaps five meters in diameter at ground level and dwindling to about half that width at its bottom, some six or seven meters down. The pit strikes him as a series of perfect circles making up a truncated cone. Its sides are smooth and firm, almost glazed, and the sand has a brown tinge. In the pit, resting peacefully on the flat floor, is something that looks like a golden amoeba the size of a large cat. A row of round blue-black eyes crosses the hump of its back. From the perimeter of its body comes a soft green radiance.

"Go down to it," the skull-faced man says. "The force of its power falls off with the cube of the distance; from up here you can't feel it. Go down. Let it take you over. Fuse with it. Make communion, Skein, make communion!"

"And will it heal me? So that I'll function as I did before the trouble started?"

"If you let it heal you, it will. That's what it wants to do. It's a completely benign organism. It thrives on repairing broken souls. Let it into your head, let it find the damaged place. You can trust it. Go down."

Skein trembles on the edge of the pit. The creature below flows and eddies, becoming first long and narrow, then high and squat, then resuming its basically circular form. Its color deepens almost to scarlet, and its radiance shifts toward yellow. As if preening and stretching itself. It seems to be waiting for him. It seems eager. This is what he has sought so long, going from planet to wearying planet. The skull-faced man, the purple sand, the pit, the creature. Skein slips his sandals off. *What have I to lose?* He sits for a moment on the pit's rim; then he shimmies down, sliding part of the way, and lands softly, close beside the being that awaits him. And immediately feels its power.

He enters the huge desolate cavern that is the cathedral of Haghia Sophia. A few Turkish guides lounge hopefully against the vast marble pillars. Tourists shuffle about, reading to each other from cheap plastic guidebooks. A shaft of light enters from some improbable aperture and splinters against the Moslem pulpit. It seems to Skein that he hears the tolling of bells and feels incense prickling at his nostrils. But how can that be? No Christian rites have been performed here in a thousand years. A Turk looms before him. "Show you the mosyics?" he says. *Mosyics.* "Help you understand this marvelous building? A dollar. No? Maybe change money? A good rate. Dollars, marks, Eurocredits, what? You speak English? Show you the mosyics?" The Turk fades. The bells grow louder. A row of bowed priests in white silk robes files past the altar, chanting in—what? Greek? The ceiling is encrusted with gems. Gold plate gleams everywhere. Skein senses the terrible complexity of the cathedral, teeming now with life, a whole universe engulfed in this gloom, a thousand chapels packed with worshippers, long lines waiting to urinate in the crypts, a marketplace in the balcony, jeweled necklaces changing hands with low murmurs of negotiation, babies being born behind the alabaster sarcophagi, the bells tolling, dukes nodding to one another, clouds of incense swirling toward the dome, the figures in the mosaics alive, making the sign of the Cross, smiling, blowing kisses, the pillars moving now, becoming fat-middled as they bend from side to side, the entire colossal structure shifting and flowing and melting. And a ballet of Turks. "Show you the mosyics?" "Change money?" "Postcards? Souvenir of Istanbul?" A plump, pink American face: "You're John Skein, aren't you? The Communicator? We worked together on the big fusion-chamber merger in '53." Skein shakes his head. "It must be that you are mistaken," he says, speaking in Italian. "I am not he. Pardon. Pardon." And joins the line of chanting priests.

Purple sand, blue-leaved trees. An orange sea under a lemon sun. Looking out from the top deck of the terminal, an hour after landing,

Skein sees a row of towering hotels rising along the nearby beach. At once he feels the wrongness: there should be no hotels. The right planet has no such towers; therefore this is another of the wrong ones.

He suffers from complete disorientation as he attempts to place himself in sequence. *Where am I?* Aboard a liner heading toward Abbondanza VI. *What do I see?* A world I have previously visited. Which one? The one with the hotels. The third out of seven, isn't it?

He has seen this planet before, in flashforwards. Long before he left Earth to begin his quest he glimpsed those hotels, that beach. Now he views it in flashback. That perplexes him. He must try to see himself as a moving point travelling through time, viewing the scenery now from this perspective, now from that.

He watches his earlier self at the terminal. Once it was his future self. How confusing, how needlessly muddling! "I'm looking for an old Earthman," he says. "He must be a hundred, hundred-twenty years old. A face like a skull—no flesh at all, really. A brittle man. No? Well, can you tell me, does this planet have a life-form about this big, a kind of blob of golden jelly, that lives in pits down by the seashore, and—no? No? Ask someone else, you say? Of course. And perhaps a hotel room? As long as I've come all this way."

He is getting tired of finding the wrong planets. What folly this is, squandering his last savings on a quest for a world seen in a dream! He would have expected planets with purple sand and blue-leaved trees to be uncommon, but no, in an infinite universe one can find a dozen of everything, and now he has wasted almost half his money and close to a year, visiting two planets and this one and not finding what he seeks.

He goes to the hotel they arrange for him.

The beach is packed with sunbathers, most of them from Earth. Skein walks among them. "Look," he wants to say, "I have this trouble with my brain, an old injury, and it gives me these visions of myself in the past and future, and one of the visions I see is a place where there's a skull-faced man who takes me to a kind of amoeba in a pit that can heal me, do you follow? And it's a planet with purple sand and blue-leaved trees, just like this one, and I figure if I keep going long enough I'm bound to find it and the skull-face and the amoeba, do you follow me? And maybe this is the planet after all, only I'm in the wrong part of it. What should I do? What hope do you think I really have?" This is the third world. He knows that he must visit a number of wrong ones before he finds the right one. But how many? How many? And when will he know that he has the right one?

Standing silent on the beach, he feels confusion come over him, and drops into fugue, and is hurled to another world. Purple sand, blue-leaved trees. A fat, friendly Pingalorian consul. "A skull-faced man? No, I can't say I know of any." Which world is this, Skein wonders? One that I have already visited, or one that I have not yet come to? The manifold layers of illusion dazzle him. Past and future and present lie like a knot around his throat. Shifting planes of reality; intersecting films of event. Purple sand, blue-leaved trees. Which planet is this? Which one? Which one? He is back on the crowded beach. A lemon sun. An orange sea. He is back in his cabin on the spaceliner. He sees a note in his own handwriting: *You are a passenger aboard a ship heading for Abbondanza VI, and will be landing in a few days.* So everything was a vision. Flashback? Flashforward? He is no longer able to tell. He is baffled by these identical worlds. Purple sand. Blue-leaved trees. He wishes he knew how to cry.

Instead of a client and a consultant for today's communion, Skein has a client and a client. A man and a woman, Michaels and Miss Schumpeter. The communion is of an unusually intimate kind. Michaels has been married six times, and several of the marriages apparently have been dissolved under bitter circumstances. Miss Schumpeter, a woman of some wealth, loves Michaels but doesn't entirely trust him; she wants a peep into his mind before she'll put her thumb to the marital cube. Skein will oblige. The fee has already been credited to his account. Let me not to the marriage of true minds admit impediments. If she does not like what she finds in her beloved's soul, there may not be any marriage, but Skein will have been paid.

A tendril of his mind goes to Michaels, now. A tendril to Miss Schumpeter. Skein opens his filters. "Now you'll meet for the first time," he tells them. Michaels flows to her. Miss Schumpeter flows to him. Skein is merely the conduit. Through him pass the ambitions, betrayals, failures, vanities, deteriorations, disputes, treacheries, lusts, generosities, shames, and follies of these two human beings. If he wishes, he can examine the most private sins of Miss Schumpeter and the darkest yearnings of her future husband. But he does not care. He sees such things every day. He takes no pleasure in spying on the psyches of these two. Would a surgeon grow excited over the sight of Miss Schumpeter's Fallopian tubes or

Michaels's pancreas? Skein is merely doing his job. He is no voyeur, simply a Communicator. He looks upon himself as a public utility.

When he severs the contact, Miss Schumpeter and Michaels both are weeping.

"I love you!" she wails.

"Get away from me!" he mutters.

*

Purple sand. Blue-leaved trees. Oily orange sea.

The skull-faced man says, "Won't you ever come to see that causality is merely an illusion, Skein? The notion that there's a consecutive series of events is nothing but a fraud. We impose form on our lives, we talk of time's arrow, we say that there's a flow from A through G and Q to Z, we make believe everything is nicely linear. But it isn't, Skein. It isn't."

"So you keep telling me."

"I feel an obligation to awaken your mind to the truth. G can come before A, and Z before both of them. Most of us don't like to perceive it that way, so we arrange things in what seems like a more logical pattern, just as a novelist will put the motive before the murder and the murder before the arrest. But the universe isn't a novel. We can't make nature imitate art. It's all random, Skein, random, random!"

*

"Half a million?"

"Half a million."

"You know I don't have that kind of money."

"Let's not waste time, Mr. Coustakis. You have assets. Pledge them as collateral. Credit is easily obtained." Skein waits for the inventor to clear his loan. "Now we can proceed," he says, and tells his desk, "Get Nissenson into a receptive state."

Coustakis says, "First let me get it clear. This man will see everything that's in my mind? He'll get access to my secrets?"

"No. No. I filter the communion with great care. Nothing will pass from your mind to his except the nature of the problem you want him to tackle. Nothing will came come back from his mind to yours except the answer."

"And if he doesn't have the answer?"

"He will."

"And if he goes into the transmission business for himself afterward?"

"He's bonded," Skein says curtly. "No chance of it. Let's go, now. Up and together."

"Skein? Skein? Skein? Skein?"

The wind is rising. The sand, blown aloft, stains the sky grey. Skein clambers from the pit and lies by its rim, breathing hard. The skull-faced man helps him get up.

Skein has seen this series of images hundreds of times. "How do you feel?" the skull-faced man asks.

"Strange. Good. My head seems so clear!"

"You had communion down there?"

"Oh, yes. Yes."

"And?"

"I think I'm healed," Skein says in wonder. "My strength is back. Before, you know, I felt cut down to the bone, a minimum version of myself. And now. And now." He lets a tendril of consciousness slip forth. It meets the mind of the skull-faced man. Skein is aware of a glassy interface; he can touch the other mind, but he cannot enter it. "Are you a Communicator too?" Skein asks, awed.

"In a sense. I feel you touching me. You're better, aren't you?"

"Much. Much. Much."

"As I told you. Now you have your second chance, Skein. Your gift has been restored. Courtesy of our friend in the pit. They love being helpful."

"Skein? Skein? Skein? Skein?"

We conceive of time either as flowing or as enduring. The problem is how to reconcile these concepts. From a purely formalistic point of view there exists no difficulty, as these properties can be reconciled by means of the concept of a duratio successiva. *Every unit of time measure has this characteristic of a flowing permanence: an hour streams by while it lasts and so long as it lasts. Its flowing is thus identical with its duration. Time, from this point of view, is transitory; but its passing away lasts.*

In the early months of his affliction he experienced a great many scenes of flashforward while in fugue. He saw himself outside the nineteenth-century mansion, he saw himself in a dozen lawyers' offices, he saw himself in hotels, terminals, spaceliners, he saw himself discussing the nature of time with the skull-faced man, he saw himself trembling on the edge of the pit, he saw himself emerging healed, he saw himself wandering from world to world, looking for the right one with purple sand and blue-leaved trees. As time unfolded most of these flashforwards duly entered the flow of the present; he did come to the mansion, he did go to those hotels and terminals, he did wander those useless worlds. Now, as he approaches Abbondanza VI, he goes through a great many flashbacks and a relatively few flashforwards, and the flashforwards seem to be limited to a fairly narrow span of time, covering his landing on Abbondanza VI, his first meeting with the skull-faced man, his journey to the pit, and his emergence, healed, from the amoeba's lair. Never anything beyond that final scene. He wonders if time is going to run out for him on Abbondanza VI.

The ship lands on Abbondanza VI half a day ahead of schedule. There are the usual decontamination procedures to endure, and while they are going on Skein rests in his cabin, counting minutes to liberty. He is curiously confident that this will be the world on which he finds the skull-faced man and the benign amoeba. Of course, he has felt that way before, looking out from other spaceliners at other planets of the proper coloration, and he has been wrong. But the intensity of his confidence is something new. He is sure that the end of his quest lies here.

"Debarkation beginning now," the loudspeakers say.

He joins the line of outgoing passengers. The others smile, embrace, whisper; they have found friends or even mates on this voyage. He remains apart. No one says goodbye to him. He emerges into a brightly lit terminal, a great cube of glass that looks like all the other terminals scattered across the thousands of worlds that man has reached. He could be in Chicago or Johannesburg or Beirut: the scene is one of porters, reservations clerks, customs officials, hotel agents, taxi drivers, guides. A blight of sameness spreading across the universe. Stumbling through the customs gate, Skein finds himself set upon.

Does he want a taxi, a hotel room, a woman, a man, a guide, a homestead plot, a servant, a ticket to Abbondanza VII, a private car, an interpreter, a bank, a telephone? The hubbub jolts Skein into three consecutive ten-second fugues, all flashbacks; he sees a rainy day in Tierra del Fuego, he conducts a communion to help a maker of sky-spectacles perfect the plot of his latest extravaganza, and he puts his palm to a cube in order to dictate contract terms to Nicholas Coustakis. Then Coustakis fades, the terminal reappears, and Skein realizes that someone has seized him by the left arm just above the elbow. Bony fingers dig painfully into his flesh. It is the skull-faced man. "Come with me," he says. "I'll take you where you want to go."

"This isn't just another flashforward, is it?" Skein asks, as he has watched himself ask so many times in the past. "I mean you're really here to get me."

The skull-faced man says, as Skein has heard him say so many times in the past, "No, this time it's no flashforward. I'm really here to get you."

"Thank God. Thank God. Thank God."

"Follow along this way. You have your passport handy?"

The familiar words. Skein is prepared to discover he is merely in fugue, and expects to drop back into frustrating reality at any moment. But no. The scene does not waver. It holds firm. It holds. At last he has caught up with this particular scene, overtaking it and enclosing it, pearl-like, in the folds of the present. He is on the way out of the terminal. The skull-faced man helps him through the formalities. How withered he is! How fiery the eyes, how gaunt the face! Those frightening orbits of bone jutting through the skin of the forehead. That parched cheek. Skein listens for a dry rattle of ribs. One sturdy punch and there would be nothing left but a cloud of white dust, slowly settling.

"I know your difficulty," the skull-faced man says. "You've been caught in entropy's jaws. You're being devoured. The injury to your mind—it's tipped you into a situation you aren't able to handle. You *could* handle it, if you'd only learn to adapt to the nature of the perceptions you're getting now. But you won't do that, will you? And you want to be healed. Well, you can be healed here, all right. More or less healed. I'll take you to the place."

"What do you mean, I could handle it, if I'd only learn to adapt?"

"Your injury has liberated you. It's shown you the truth about time. But you refuse to see it."

"What truth?" Skein asks flatly.

"You still try to think that time flows neatly from alpha to omega, from yesterday through today to tomorrow," the skull-faced man says, as they walk slowly through the terminal. "But it doesn't. The idea of the forward flow of time is a deception we impose on ourselves in childhood. An abstraction, agreed upon by common convention, to make it easier for us to cope with phenomena. The truth is that events are random, that chronological flow is only our joint hallucination, that if time can be said to flow at all, it flows in all 'directions' at once. Therefore—"

"Wait," Skein says. "How do you explain the laws of thermodynamics? Entropy increases, available energy constantly diminishes, the universe heads toward ultimate stasis."

"Does it?"

"The second law of thermodynamics—"

"Is an abstraction," the skull-faced man says, "which unfortunately fails to correspond with the situation in the true universe. It isn't a divine law. It's a mathematical hypothesis developed by men who weren't able to perceive the real situation. They did their best to account for the data within a framework they could understand. Their laws are formulations of probability, based on conditions that hold within closed systems, and given the right closed system the second law is useful and illuminating. But in the universe as a whole it simply isn't true. There is no arrow of time. Entropy does not necessarily increase. Natural processes can be reversible. Causes do not invariably precede effects. In fact, the concepts of cause and effect are empty. There are neither causes nor effects, but only events, spontaneously generated, which we arrange in our minds in comprehensible patterns of sequence."

"No," Skein mutters. "This is insanity!"

"There are no patterns. Everything is random."

"No."

"Why not admit it? Your brain has been injured. What was destroyed was the centre center of temporal perception, the node that humans use to impose this unreal order on events. Your time filter has burned out. The past and the future are as accessible to you as the present, Skein: you can go where you like, you can watch events drifting past as they really do. Only you haven't been able to break up your old habits of thought. You still try to impose the conventional entropic order on things, even though you lack the mechanism to do it, now, and the conflict between what you perceive and what you think you perceive is driving you crazy. Eh?"

"How do you know so much about me?"

The skull-faced man chuckles. "I was injured in the same way as you. I was cut free from the timeline long ago, through the kind of overload you suffered. And I've had years to come to terms with the new reality. I was as terrified as you were, at first. But now I understand. I move about freely. I know things, Skein." A rasping laugh. "You need rest, though. A room, a bed. Time to think things over. Come. There's no rush now. You're on the right planet; you'll be all right soon."

Further, the association of entropy increase with time's arrow is in no sense circular; rather, it both tells us something about what will happen to natural systems in time, and about what the time order must be for a series of states of a system. Thus, we may often establish a time order among a set of events by use of the time-entropy association, free from any reference to clocks and magnitudes of time intervals from the present. In actual judgments of before-after we frequently do this on the basis of our experience (even though without any explicit knowledge of the law of entropy increase): we know, for example, that for iron in air the state of pure metal must have been before that of a rusted surface, or that the clothes will be dry after, not before, they have hung in the hot sun.

A tense, humid night of thunder and temporal storms. Lying alone in his oversize hotel room, five kilometers from the purple shore, Skein suffers fiercely from fugue.

"Listen, I have to forbid this. Those turtles are almost extinct. Do you understand that? *Muerto. Perdido. Desaparecido.* I won't eat a turtle. Throw it back. Throw it back."

"I'm happy to say your second go-round has been approved, Mr. Skein. Not that there was ever any doubt. A long and happy new life to you, sir."

"Go down to it. The force of its power falls off with the cube of the distance; from up here you can't feel it. Go down. Let it take you over. Fuse with it. Make communion, Skein, make communion!"

"Show you the mosyics? Help you understand this marvelous building? A dollar. No? Maybe change money? A good rate."

"First let me get it clear. This man will see everything that's in my mind? He'll get access to my secrets?"

"I love you."

"Get away from me!"

"Won't you ever come to see that causality is merely an illusion, Skein? The notion that there's a consecutive series of events is nothing but a fraud. We impose form on our lives, we talk of time's arrow, we say that there's a flow from A through G and Q to Z, we make believe everything is nicely linear. But it isn't, Skein. It isn't."

Breakfast on a leafy veranda. Morning light out of the west, making the trees glow with an ultramarine glitter. The skull-faced man joins him. Skein secretly searches the parched face. Is everything an illusion? Perhaps he is an illusion.

They walk toward the sea. Well before noon they reach the shore. The skull-faced man points to the south, and they follow the coast; it is often a difficult hike, for in places the sand is washed out and they must detour inland, scrambling over quartzy cliffs. The monstrous old man is indefatigable. When they pause to rest, squatting on a timeless purple strand made smooth by the recent tide, the debate about time resumes, and Skein hears words that have been echoing in his skull for four years and more. It is as though everything up till now has been a rehearsal for a play, and now at last he has taken the stage.

"Won't you ever come to see that causality is merely an illusion, Skein?"

"I feel an obligation to awaken your mind to the truth."

"Time is an ocean, and events come drifting to us as randomly as dead animals on the waves."

Skein offers all the proper cues.

"I won't accept that! It's demonic, chaotic, nihilistic theory."

"You can say that after all you've experienced?"

"I'll go on saying it. What I've been going through is a mental illness. Maybe I'm deranged, but the universe isn't."

"Contrary. You've only recently become sane and started to see things as they really are. The trouble is that you don't want to admit the evidence you've begun to perceive. Your filters are down, Skein! You've shaken free of the illusion of linearity! Now's your chance to show your resilience. Learn to live with the real reality. Stop this silly business of imposing an artificial order on the flow of time. Why should effect follow cause? Why shouldn't the seed follow the tree? Why must you persist in holding tight to a useless, outworn, contemptible system of false evaluations of experience when you've managed to break free of the—"

"Stop it! Stop it! Stop it! Stop it!"

By early afternoon they are many kilometers from the hotel, still keeping as close to the shore as they can. The terrain is uneven and divided, with rugged fingers of rock running almost to the water's edge, and Skein finds the journey even more exhausting than it had seemed in his visions of it. Several times he stops, panting, and has to be urged to go on.

"It isn't much farther," the skull-faced man says. "You can make it. Step by step is how."

"I'm winded. Those hills—"

"I'm twice your age, and I'm doing fine."

"You're in better shape. I've been cooped up on spaceships for months and months."

"Just a short way on," says the skull-faced man. "About a hundred meters from the shore."

Skein struggles on. The heat is frightful. He trips in the sand; he is blinded by sweat; he has a momentary flashback fugue. "There it is," the skull-faced man says finally. "Look there, in the pit."

Skein beholds the conical crater. He sees the golden amoeba

"Go down to it," the skull-faced man says. "The force of its power falls off with the cube of the distance; from up here you can't feel it. Go down. Let it take you over. Fuse with it. Make communion, Skein, make communion!"

"And will it heal me? So that I'll function as I did before the trouble started?"

"If you let it heal you, it will. That's what it wants to do. It's a completely benign organism. It thrives on repairing broken souls. Let it into your head; let it find the damaged place. You can trust it. Go down."

Skein trembles on the edge of the pit. The creature below flows and eddies, becoming first long and narrow, then high and squat, then resuming its basically circular form. Its color deepens almost to scarlet, and its radiance shifts toward yellow. As if preening and stretching itself. It seems to be waiting for him. It seems eager. This is what he has sought so long, going from planet to wearying planet. The skull-faced man, the purple sand, the pit, the creature. Skein slips his sandals off. *What have I to lose?* He sits for a moment on the pit's rim; then he shimmies down, sliding part of the way, and lands softly, close beside the being that awaits him. And immediately feels its power. Something brushes against his brain. The sensation reminds him of the training sessions of his first go-round, when the instructors were showing him how to develop his gift. The fingers probing his consciousness. Go on, enter, he tells them. I'm open. And he finds himself in contact with the being of the pit. Wordless. A two-way flow of unintelligible images is the only communion; shapes drift from and into his mind. The universe blurs. He is no longer sure where the center of his ego lies. He has thought of his brain as a sphere with himself at its center, but now it seems extended, elliptical, and an ellipse has no center, only a pair of focuses, here and here, one focus in his own skull and one—where?—within that fleshy amoeba.

And suddenly he is looking at himself through the amoeba's eyes. The large biped with the bony body. How strange, how grotesque! Yet it suffers. Yet it must be helped. It is injured. It is broken. We go to it with all our love. We will heal. And Skein feels something flowing over the bare folds and fissures of his brain. But he can no longer remember whether he is the human or the alien, the bony one or the boneless. Their identities have mingled. He goes through fugues by the scores, seeing yesterdays and tomorrows, and everything is formless and without content; he is unable to recognize himself or to understand the words being spoken. It does not matter. All is random. All is illusion. Release the knot of pain you clutch within you. Accept. Accept. Accept. Accept.

He accepts.

He releases.

He merges.

He casts away the shreds of ego, the constricting exoskeleton of self, and placidly permits the necessary adjustments to be made.

The possibility, however, of genuine thermodynamic entropy decrease for an isolated system—no matter how rare—does raise an objection to the definition of time's direction in terms of entropy. If a large, isolated system did by chance go through an entropy decrease as one state evolved from another, we would have to say that time "went backward" if our definition of time's arrow were basically in terms of entropy increase. But with an ultimate definition of the forward direction of time in terms of the actual occurrence of states, and measured time intervals from the present, we can readily accommodate the entropy decrease; it would become merely a rare anomaly in the physical processes of the natural world.

The wind is rising. The sand, blown aloft, stains the sky grey. Skein clambers from the pit and lies by its rim, breathing hard. The skull-faced man helps him get up.

Skein has seen this series of images hundreds of times. "How do you feel?" the skull-faced man asks.

"Strange. Good. My head seems clear!"

"You had communion down there?"

"Oh, yes. Yes."

"And?"

"I think I'm healed," Skein says in wonder. "My strength is back. Before, you know, I felt cut down to the bone, a minimum version of myself. And now. And now." He lets a tendril of consciousness slip forth. It meets the mind of the skull-faced man. Skein is aware of a glassy interface; he can touch the other mind, but he cannot enter it. "Are you a Communicator too?" Skein asks, awed.

"In a sense. I feel you touching me. You're better, aren't you?"

"Much. Much. Much."

"As I told you. Now you have your second chance, Skein. Your gift has been restored. Courtesy of our friend in the pit. They love being helpful."

"What shall I do now? Where shall I go?"

"Anything. Anywhere. Anywhen. You're free to move along the timeline as you please. In a state of controlled, directed fugue, so to speak. After all, if time is random, if there is no rigid sequence of events—"

"Yes."

"Then why not choose the sequence that appeals to you? Why stick to the set of abstractions your former self has handed you? You're a free man, Skein. Go. Enjoy. Undo your past. Edit it. Improve on it. It isn't your past, any more than this is your present. It's all one, Skein, all *one*. Pick the segment you prefer."

He tests the truth of the skull-faced man's words. Cautiously Skein steps three minutes into the past and sees himself struggling up out of the pit. He slides four minutes into the future and sees the skull-faced man, alone, trudging northward along the shore. Everything flows. All is fluidity. He is free. He is free.

"You see, Skein?"

"Now I do," Skein says. He is out of entropy's jaws. He is time's master, which is to say he is his own master. He can move at will. He can defy the imaginary forces of determinism. Suddenly he realizes what he must do now. He will assert his free will; he will challenge entropy on its home ground. Skein smiles. He cuts free of the timeline and floats easily into what others would call the past.

"Get Nissenson into a receptive state," he orders his desk.

Coustakis, blinking rapidly, obviously uneasy, says, "First let me get it clear. This man will see everything that's in my mind? He'll get access to my secrets?"

"No. No. I filter the communion with great care. Nothing will pass from your mind to his except the nature of the problem you want him to tackle. Nothing will come back from his mind to yours except the answer."

"And if he doesn't have the answer?"

"He will."

"And if he goes into the transmission business for himself afterward?" Coustakis asks.

"He's bonded," Skein says curtly. "No chance of it. Let's go, now. Up and together."

The desk reports that Nissenson, half the world away in São Paulo, is ready. Quickly Skein throws Coustakis into the receptive condition, and swings around to face the brilliant lights of his data-access units. Here is the moment when he can halt the transaction. Turn again, Skein. Face Coustakis, smile sadly, inform him that the communion will be impossible. Give him back his money, send him off to break some other Communicator's mind. And live on, whole and happy, ever after. It was at this point, visiting this scene endlessly in his fugues, that Skein silently and hopelessly cried out to himself to stop. Now it is within his power, for this is no fugue, no illusion of time-shift. He has shifted. He is here, carrying with him the knowledge of all that is to come, and he is the only Skein on the scene, the operative Skein. Get up, now. Refuse the contract.

He does not. Thus he defies entropy. Thus he breaks the chain.

He peers into the sparkling, shifting little blazes until they kindle his gift, jabbing at the electrical rhythms of his brain until he is lifted into the energy level that permits the opening of a communion. He starts to go up. He reaches forth one tendril of his mind and engages Nissenson. With another tendril he snares Coustakis. Steadily, now, he draws the two tendrils together. He is aware of the risks, but believes he can surmount them.

The tendrils meet.

Out of Coustakis's mind flows a description of the matter transmitter and a clear statement of the beam-spread problem; Skein shoves it along to Nissenson, who begins to work on a solution. The combined strength of the two minds is great, but Skein deftly lets the excess charge bleed away and maintains the communion with no particular effort, holding Coustakis and Nissenson together while they deal with their technical matters. Skein pays little attention as their excited minds rush toward answers. *If you. Yes, and then. But if. I see, yes. I could. And. However, maybe I should. I like that. It leads to. Of course. The inevitable result. Is it feasible, though? I think so. You might have to. I could. Yes. I could. I could.*

"I thank you a million times," Coustakis says to Skein. "It was all so simple, once we saw how we ought to look at it. I don't begrudge your fee at all. Not at all."

Coustakis leaves, glowing with delight. Skein, relieved, tells his desk, "I'm going to allow myself a three-day holiday. Fix the schedule to move everybody up accordingly."

He smiles. He strides across his office, turning up the amplifiers, treating himself to the magnificent view. The nightmare undone. The past revised. The burnout avoided. All it took was confidence. Enlightenment. A proper understanding of the processes involved.

He feels the sudden swooping sensations of incipient temporal fugue. Before he can intervene to regain control, he swings off into darkness and arrives instantaneously on a planet of purple sand and blue-leaved trees. Orange waves lap at the shore. He stands a few meters from a deep conical pit. Peering into it, he sees an amoebalike creature lying beside a human figure; strands of the alien's jellylike substance are wound around the man's body. He recognizes the man to be John Skein. The communion in the pit ends; the man begins to clamber from the pit. The wind is rising. The sand, blown aloft, stains the sky grey. Patiently he watches his younger self struggling up from the pit. Now he understands. The circuit is closed; the knot is tied; the identity loop is complete. He is destined to spend many years on Abbondanza VI, growing ancient and withered. He is the skull-faced man.

Skein reaches the rim of the pit and lies there, breathing hard. He helps Skein get up.

"How do you feel?" he asks.

THE REALITY TRIP

This one also dates from January, 1970. I was thirty-five years old and had spent just about half my life thus far intensely involved with the craft of writing; I had moved from an early apprenticeship as a tireless producer of prefabricated literary merchandise into a maturity of some literary distinction, and the rewards were arriving steadily now, not just financial ones but awards (the Nebula in 1969 for "Passengers," a Hugo later that year for the novella version of "Nightwings," and more to come) and accolades (I was named to the presidency of the Science Fiction Writers of America in 1967-68, and I was asked to be the Guest of Honor at the World Science Fiction Convention in Heidelberg in 1970). I was about as well established as a writer could be; virtually everything I wrote was on commission now, and my writing time was committed well into the future while my agent fended off additional requests for contributions.

I should have been happy with what I had accomplished, and I suppose that much of the time I was. But there was trouble ahead as I edged into the dreaded mid-life years. Already my extraordinary output of words was slackening from the legendary millions and millions of my youth: I managed only a trifling (for me) 668,000 words in 1969 and there was a further drop in production to 571,000 the next year. This was in part due to the increasing care I was devoting to my work, but also I was encountering mysterious resistances to writing at all—as is shown by the steep drop from 1970's already reduced output to 1971's even more sharply reduced 269,000 words, not much more than I would have been able to turn out in a single month in a wild year like 1963. In another few years I would find myself unable to write at all. There was the move to California in my future, too, and a marital breakup, and a host of other complexities were looming on the horizon for me as well. In 1970 I had only an inkling of what lay ahead, but it was enough to make me apprehensive and to intensify the already apparent darkening of the tone of my fiction, a development that would culminate in 1971's The Book of Skulls *and* Dying Inside *and the dramatic changes in my life that would follow later that year.*

Some of that, perhaps, is already evident in "The Reality Trip," which I wrote in January, 1970 for Ejler Jakobsson, the new editor of Galaxy *and* If. *Ejler published it, with amazing swiftness, in the May, 1970 issue of* If. *It's a lighthearted story with some very dark corners; and certainly it demonstrates that I had come a long way indeed from the simplicities of "Gorgon Planet" and "The Silent Colony," and even from the somber "Road to Nightfall" that stands as a strange beacon almost at the very beginning of my writing career. I see in it a foreshadowing of the volatility to come in my life. A time of changes lay ahead for me; and when it was done I would be a very different person living in a very different place.*

I am a reclamation project for her. She lives on my floor of the hotel, a dozen rooms down the hall: a lady poet, private income. No, that makes her sound too old, a middle-aged eccentric. Actually she is no more than thirty. Taller than I am, with long kinky brown hair and a sharp, bony nose that has a bump on the bridge. Eyes are very glossy. A studied raggedness about her dress; carefully chosen shabby clothes. I am in no position really to judge the sexual attractiveness of Earthfolk but I gather from remarks made by men living here that she is not considered good-looking. I pass her often on my way to my room. She smiles fiercely at me. Saying to herself, no doubt, You poor lonely man. Let me help you bear the burden of your unhappy life. Let me show you the meaning of love, for I too know what it is like to be alone.

Or words to that effect. She's never actually said any such thing. But her intentions are transparent. When she sees me, a kind of hunger comes into her eyes, part maternal, part (I guess) sexual, and her face takes on a wild crazy intensity. Burning with emotion. Her name is Elizabeth Cooke. "Are you fond of poetry, Mr. Knecht?" she asked me this morning, as we creaked upward together in the ancient elevator.

And an hour later she knocked at my door. "Something for you to read," she said. "I wrote them." A sheaf of large yellow sheets, stapled at the top; poems printed in smeary blue mimeography. *The Reality Trip,* the collection was headed. *Limited Edition: 125 Copies.* "You can keep it if you like," she explained. "I've got lots more." She was wearing bright corduroy slacks and a flimsy pink shawl , through which her breasts plainly showed. Small tapering breasts, not very functional-looking. When she saw me studying them her nostrils flared momentarily and she blinked her eyes three times swiftly. Tokens of lust?

I read the poems. Is it fair for me to offer judgment on them? Even though I've lived on this planet eleven of its years, even though my command of colloquial English is quite good, do I really comprehend the inner life of poetry? I thought they were all quite bad. Earnest, plodding poems, capturing what they call slices of life. The world around her, the cruel, brutal, unloving city. Lamenting failure of people to open to one another. The title poem began this way:

> He was on the reality trip. Big black man,
> bloodshot eyes, bad teeth. Eisenhower jacket,
> frayed. Smell of cheap wine. I guess a knife
> in his pocket. Looked at me mean. Criminal
> record. Rape, child-beating, possession of drugs.
> In his head saying, slavemistress bitch, and me in
> my head saying, black brother, let's freak in together,
> let's trip on love—

And so forth. Warm, direct emotion; but is the urge to love all wounded things a sufficient center for poetry? I don't know. I did put her poems through the scanner and transmit them to Homeworld, although I doubt they'll learn much from them about Earth. It would flatter Elizabeth to know that while she has few readers here, she has acquired some ninety light-years away. But of course I can't tell her that.

She came back a short while ago. "Did you like them?" she asked.

"Very much. You have such sympathy for those who suffer."

I think she expected me to invite her in. I was careful not to look at her breasts this time.

The hotel is on West 23rd Street. It must be over a hundred years old; the façade is practically baroque and the interior shows a kind of genteel decay. The place has a bohemian tradition. Most of its guests are permanent residents and many of them are artists, novelists, playwrights, and such. I have lived here nine years. I know a number of the residents by name, and they me, but I have discouraged any real intimacy, naturally, and everyone has respected that choice. I do not invite others into my room. Sometimes I let myself be invited to visit theirs, since one of my responsibilities on this world is to get to know something of the way Earthfolk live and think. Elizabeth is the first to attempt to cross the invisible barrier of privacy I surround myself with. I'm not sure how I'll handle that. She moved in about three years ago; her attentions became noticeable perhaps ten months back, and for the last five or six weeks she's been a great nuisance. Some kind of confrontation is inevitable: either I must tell her to leave me alone, or I will find myself drawn into a situation impossible to tolerate. Perhaps she'll find someone else to feel even sorrier for, before it comes to that.

My daily routine rarely varies. I rise at seven. First Feeding. Then I clean my skin (my outer one, the Earth-skin, I mean) and dress. From eight to ten I transmit data to Homeworld. Then I go out for the morning field trip: talking to people, buying newspapers, often some library research. At one I return to my room. Second Feeding. I transmit data from two to five. Out again, perhaps to the theater, to a motion picture, to a political meeting. I must soak up the flavor of this planet. Often to saloons; I am equipped for ingesting alcohol, though of course I must get rid of it before it has been in my body very long, and I drink and listen and sometimes argue. At midnight back to my room. Third Feeding. Transmit data from one to four in the morning. Then three hours of sleep, and at seven the cycle begins anew. It is a comforting schedule. I don't know how many agents Homeworld has on Earth, but I like to think that I'm one of the most diligent and useful. I miss very little. I've done good service, and, as they say here, hard work is its own reward. I won't deny that I hate the physical discomfort of it and frequently give way to real despair over my isolation from my own kind. Sometimes I even think of asking for a transfer to Homeworld. But what would become of me there? What services could I perform? I have shaped my life to one end: that of dwelling among the Earthfolk and reporting on their ways. If I give that up, I am nothing.

❋

Of course there is the physical pain. Which is considerable.

The gravitational pull of Earth is almost twice that of Homeworld. It makes for a leaden life for me. My inner organs always sagging against the lower rim of my carapace. My muscles cracking with strain. Every movement a willed effort. My heart in constant protest. In my eleven years I have as one might expect adapted somewhat to the conditions; I have toughened, I have thickened. I suspect if I were transported instantly to Homeworld now I would be quite giddy, baffled by the lightness of everything. I would leap and soar and stumble, and might even miss this crushing pull of Earth. Yet I doubt that. I suffer here; at all times the weight oppresses me. Not to sound too self-pitying about it. I knew the conditions in advance. I was placed in simulated Earth gravity when I volunteered, and was given a chance to withdraw, and I decided to go anyway. Not realizing that a week under double gravity is not the same thing as a lifetime. I could always have stepped out of the simulation chamber. Not here. The eternal drag on every molecule of me. The pressure. My flesh is always in mourning.

And the outer body I must wear. This cunning disguise. Forever to be swaddled in thick masses of synthetic flesh, smothering me, engulfing me. The soft slippery slap of it against the self within. The elaborate framework that holds it erect, by which I make it move; a forest of struts and braces and servoactuators and cables, in the midst of which I must unendingly huddle, atop my little platform in the gut. Adopting one or another of various uncomfortable positions, constantly shifting and squirming, now jabbing myself on some awkwardly placed projection, now trying to make my inflexible body flexibly to bend. Seeing the world by periscope through mechanical eyes. Enwombed in this mountain of meat. It is a clever thing; it must look convincingly human, since no one has ever doubted me, and it ages ever so slightly from year to year, graying a bit at the temples, thickening a bit at the paunch. It walks. It talks. It takes in food and drink, when it has to. (And deposits them in a removable pouch near my leftmost arm.) And I within it. The hidden chess player; the invisible rider. If I dared, I would periodically strip myself of this cloak of flesh and crawl around my room in my own guise. But it is forbidden. Eleven years now and I have not been outside my protoplasmic housing. I feel sometimes that it has come to adhere to me, that it is no longer merely around me but by now a part of me.

In order to eat I must unseal it at the middle, a process that takes many minutes. Three times a day I unbutton myself so that I can stuff the food concentrates into my true gullet. Faulty design, I call that. They could just as easily have arranged it so I could pop the food into my Earthmouth and have it land in my own digestive tract. I suppose the newer models have that. Excretion is just as troublesome for me; I unseal, reach in, remove the cubes of waste, seal my skin again. Down the toilet with them. A nuisance.

And the loneliness! To look at the stars and know Homeworld is out there somewhere! To think of all the others, mating, chanting, dividing, abstracting, while I live out my days in this crumbling hotel on an alien planet, tugged down by gravity and locked within a cramped counterfeit body—always alone, always pretending that I am not what I am and that I am what I am not, spying, questioning, recording, reporting, coping with the misery of solitude, hunting for the comforts of philosophy—

In all of this there is only one real consolation, aside, that is, from the pleasure of knowing that I am of service to Homeworld. The atmosphere of New York City grows grimier every year. The streets are full of crude vehicles belching undigested hydrocarbons. To the Earthfolk, this stuff is pollution, and they mutter worriedly about it. To me it is joy. It is the only touch of Homeworld here: that sweet soup of organic compounds adrift in the air. It intoxicates me. I walk down the street breathing deeply, sucking the good molecules through my false nostrils to my authentic lungs. The natives must think I'm insane. Tripping on auto exhaust! Can I get arrested for over-enthusiastic public breathing? Will they pull me in for a mental checkup?

Elizabeth Cooke continues to waft wistful attentions at me. Smiles in the hallway. Hopeful gleam of the eyes. "Perhaps we can have dinner together some night soon, Mr. Knecht. I know we'd have so much to talk about. And maybe you'd like to see the new poems I've been doing." She is trembling. Eyelids flickering tensely; head held rigid on long neck. I know she sometimes has men in her room, so it can't be out of loneliness or frustration that she's cultivating me. And I doubt that she's sexually attracted to my outer self. I believe I'm being accurate when I say that women don't consider me sexually magnetic. No, she loves me because she pities me. The sad shy bachelor at the end of the hall, dear unhappy Mr. Knecht; can I bring some brightness into his dreary life? And so forth. I think that's how it is. Will I be able to go on avoiding her? Perhaps I should move to another part of the city. But I've lived here so long I've grown accustomed to this hotel. Its easy ways do much to compensate for the hardships of my post. And my familiar room, The huge many-paned window; the cracked green floor tiles in the bathroom; the lumpy patterns of replastering on the wall above my bed. The high ceiling; the funny chandelier. Things that I love. But of course I can't let her try to start an affair with me. We are supposed to observe Earthfolk, not to get involved with them. Our disguise is not that difficult to penetrate at close range. I must keep her away somehow. Or flee.

Incredible! There is another of us in this very hotel! As I learned through accident. At one this afternoon, returning from my morning travels: Elizabeth in the lobby, as though lying in wait for me, chatting with the manager. Rides up with me in the elevator. Her eyes looking into mine. "Sometimes I think you're afraid of me," she begins. "You mustn't be. That's the great tragedy of human life, that people shut themselves up behind walls of fear and never let anyone through, anyone who might care about them and be warm to them. You've got no reason to be afraid of me." I do, but how to explain that to her? To sidestep prolonged conversation and possible entanglement I get off the elevator one floor below the right one. Let her think I'm visiting a friend. Or a mistress. I walk slowly down the hall to the stairs, using up time, waiting so she will be in her room before I go up. A maid bustles by me. She thrusts her key into a door on the left: a rare *faux pas* for the usually competent help here, she forgets to knock before going in to make up the room. The door opens and the occupant, inside, stands revealed. A stocky, muscular man, naked to the waist. "Oh, excuse me," the maid gasps, and backs out, shutting the door. But I have seen. My eyes are quick. The hairy chest is split, a dark gash three inches wide and some eleven inches long, beginning between the nipples and going past the navel. Visible within is the black shiny surface of a Homeworld carapace. My countryman, opening up for Second Feeding. Dazed, numbed, I stagger to the stairs and pull myself step by leaden step to my floor. No sign of Elizabeth. I stumble into my room and throw the bolt. Another of us here? Well, why not? I'm not the only one. There may be hundreds in New York alone. But in the same hotel? I remember, now, I've seen him occasionally: a silent, dour man, tense, hunted-looking, unsociable. No doubt I appear the same way to others. Keep the world at a distance. I don't know his name or what he is supposed to do for a living.

We are forbidden to make contact with fellow Homeworlders except in case of extreme emergency. Isolation is a necessary condition of our employment. I may not introduce myself to him; I may not seek his friendship. It is worse now for me, knowing that he is here, than when I was entirely alone. The things we could reminisce about! The friends we might have in common! We could reinforce one another's endurance of the gravity, the discomfort of our disguises, the vile climate. But no. I must pretend I know nothing. The rules. The harsh, unbending rules. I to go about my business, he his; if we meet, no hint of my knowledge must pass.

So be it. I will honor my vows. But it may be difficult.

He goes by the name of Swanson. Been living in the hotel eighteen months; a musician of some sort, according to the manager. "A very peculiar man. Keeps to himself; no small talk, never smiles. Defends his privacy. The other day a maid barged into his room without knocking and I thought he'd sue. Well, we get all sorts here." The manager thinks he may actually be a member of one of the old European royal families, living in exile, or something similarly romantic. The manager would be surprised.

I defend my privacy too. From Elizabeth, another assault on it.

In the hall outside my room. "My new poems," she said. "In case you're interested." And then: "Can I come in? I'd read them to you. I love reading out loud." And: "Please don't always seem so terribly afraid of me. I don't bite, David. Really I don't. I'm quite gentle."

"I'm sorry."

"So am I." Anger, now, lurking in her shiny eyes, her thin taut lips. "If you want me to leave you alone, say so, I will. But I want you to know how cruel you're being. I don't demand anything from you. I'm just offering some friendship. And you're refusing. Do I have a bad smell? Am I so ugly? Is it my poems you hate and you're afraid to tell me?"

"Elizabeth—"

"We're only on this world such a short time. Why can't we be kinder to each other while we are? To love, to share, to open up, Communication, soul to soul." Her tone changed, an artful shading. "For all I know, women turn you off. I wouldn't put anybody down for that. We've all got our ways. But it doesn't have to be a sexual thing, you and me. Just talk. Like, opening the channels. Please? Say no and I'll never bother you again, but don't say no, please. That's like shutting a door on life, David. And when you do that, you start to die a little."

Persistent. I should tell her to go to hell. But there is the loneliness. There is her obvious sincerity. Her warmth, her eagerness to pull me from my lunar isolation. Can there be harm in it? Knowing that Swanson is nearby, so close yet sealed from me by iron commandments, has intensified my sense of being alone. I can risk letting Elizabeth get closer to me. It will make her happy; it may make me happy; it could even yield information valuable to Homeworld. Of course I must still maintain certain barriers.

"I don't mean to be unfriendly. I think you've misunderstood, Elizabeth. I haven't really been rejecting you. Come in. Do come in." Stunned, she enters my room. The first guest ever. My few books; my modest furnishings; the ultrawave transmitter, impenetrably disguised as a piece of sculpture. She sits. Skirt far above the knees. Good legs, if I understand the criteria of quality correctly. I am determined to allow no sexual overtures. If she tries anything, I'll resort to—I don't know—hysteria. "Read me your new poems," I say. She opens her portfolio. Reads.

> In the midst of the hipster night of doubt and
> Emptiness, when the bad-trip god came to me with
> Cold hands, I looked up and shouted yes at the
> Stars. And yes and yes again. I groove on yes;
> The devil grooves on no. And I waited for you to
> Say yes, and at last you did. And the world said
> The stars said the trees said the grass said the
> Sky said the streets said yes and yes and yes—

She is ecstatic. Her face is flushed; her eyes are joyous. She has broken through to me. After two hours, when it becomes obvious that I am not going to ask her to go to bed with me, she leaves. Not to wear out her welcome. "I'm so glad I was wrong about you, David," she whispers. "I couldn't believe you were really a life-denier. And you're not." Ecstatic.

I am getting into very deep water.

We spend an hour or two together every night. Sometimes in my room, sometimes in hers. Usually she comes to me, but now and then, to be polite, I seek her out after Third Feeding. By now I've read all her poetry; we talk instead of the arts in general, politics, racial problems. She has a lively, well-stocked, disorderly mind. Though she probes constantly for information about me, she realizes how sensitive I am, and quickly withdraws when I parry her. Asking about my work; I reply vaguely that I'm doing research for a book, and when I don't amplify she drops it, though she tries again, gently, a few nights later. She drinks a lot of wine, and offers it to me. I nurse one glass through a whole visit. Often she suggests we go out together for dinner; I explain that I have digestive problems and prefer to eat alone, and she takes this in good grace but immediately resolves to help me overcome those problems, for soon she is asking me to eat with her again. There is an excellent Spanish restaurant right in the hotel, she says. She drops troublesome questions. Where was I born? Did I go to college? Do I have family somewhere? Have I ever been married? Have I published any of my writings? I improvise evasions. Nothing difficult about that, except that never before have I allowed anyone on Earth such sustained contact with me, so prolonged an opportunity to find inconsistencies in my pretended identity. What if she sees through?

And sex. Her invitations grow less subtle. She seems to think that we ought to be having a sexual relationship, simply because we've become such good friends. Not a matter of passion so much as one of communication: we talk, sometimes we take walks together, we should do *that* together too. But of course it's impossible. I have the external organs but not the capacity to use them. Wouldn't want her touching my false skin in any case. How to deflect her? If I declare myself impotent she'll demand a chance to try to cure me. If I pretend homosexuality she'll start some kind of straightening therapy. If I simply say she doesn't turn me on physically she'll be hurt. The sexual thing is a challenge to her, the way merely getting me to talk with her once was. She often wears the transparent pink shawl that reveals her breasts. Her skirts are hip-high. She doses herself with aphrodisiac perfumes. She grazes my body with hers whenever opportunity arises. The tension mounts; she is determined to have me.

I have said nothing about her in my reports to Homeworld. Though I do transmit some of the psychological data I have gathered by observing her.

"Could you ever admit you were in love with me?" she asked tonight.

And she asked, "Doesn't it hurt you to repress your feelings all the time? To sit there locked up inside yourself like a prisoner?"

And, "There's a physical side of life too, David. I don't mind so much the damage you're doing to me by ignoring it. But I worry about the damage you're doing to you."

Crossing her legs. Hiking her skirt even higher.

We are heading toward a crisis. I should never have let this begin. A torrid summer has descended on the city, and in hot weather my nervous system is always at the edge of eruption. She may push me too far. I might ruin everything. I should apply for transfer to Homeworld before I cause trouble. Maybe I should confer with Swanson. I think what is happening now qualifies as an emergency.

Elizabeth stayed past midnight tonight. I had to ask her finally to leave: work to do. An hour later she pushed an envelope under my door. Newest poems. Love poems. In a shaky hand: *"David you mean so much to me. You mean the stars and nebulas. Cant you let me show my love? Cant you accept happiness? Think about it. I adore you."*

What have I started?

103° F. today. The fourth successive day of intolerable heat. Met Swanson in the elevator at lunch time; nearly blurted the truth about myself to him. I must be more careful. But my control is slipping. Last night, in the worst of the heat, I was tempted to strip off my disguise. I could no longer stand being locked in here, pivoting and ducking to avoid all the machinery festooned about me. Resisted the temptation; just barely. Somehow I am more sensitive to the gravity too. I have the illusion that my carapace is developing cracks. Almost collapsed in the street this afternoon. All I need: heat exhaustion, whisked off to the hospital, routine fluoroscope exam. "You have a very odd skeletal structure, Mr. Knecht." Indeed. Dissecting me, next, with three thousand medical students looking on. And then the United Nations called in. Menace from outer space. Yes. I must be more careful. I must be more careful. I must be more—

Now I've done it. Eleven years of faithful service destroyed in a single wild moment. Violation of the Fundamental Rule. I hardly believe it. How was it possible that I—that I—with my respect for my responsibilities—that I could have—even considered, let alone actually done—

But the weather was terribly hot. The third week of the heat wave. I was stifling inside my false body. And the gravity: was New York having a gravity wave too? That terrible pull, worse than ever. Bending my internal organs out of shape. Elizabeth a tremendous annoyance: passionate, emotional, teary, poetic, giving me no rest, pleading for me to burn with a brighter flame. Declaring her love in sonnets, in rambling hip epics, in haiku. Spending two hours in my room, crouched at my feet, murmuring about the hidden beauty of my soul. "Open yourself and let love come in," she whispered. "It's like giving yourself to God. Making a commitment; breaking down all walls. Why not? For love's sake, David, why not?" I couldn't tell her why not, and she went away, but about midnight she was back knocking at my door. I let her in. She wore an ankle-length silk housecoat, gleaming, threadbare. "I'm stoned," she said hoarsely, voice an octave too deep. "I had to bust three joints to get up the nerve. But here I am. David, I'm sick of making the turnoff trip. We've been so wonderfully close, and then you won't go the last stretch of the way." A cascade of giggles. "Tonight you will. Don't fail me. Darling." Drops the housecoat. Naked underneath it: narrow waist, bony hips, long legs, thin thighs, blue veins crossing her breasts. Her hair wild and kinky. A sorceress. A seeress. Berserk. Approaching me, eyes slit-wide, mouth open, tongue flickering snakily. How fleshless she is! Beads of sweat glistening on her flat chest. Seizes my wrists; tugs me roughly toward the bed. We tussle a little. Within my false body I throw switches, nudge levers. I am stronger than she is. I pull free, breaking her hold with an effort. She stands flat-footed in front of me, glaring, eyes fiery. So vulnerable, so sad in her nudity. And yet so fierce. "David! David! David!" Sobbing. Breathless. Pleading with her eyes and the tips of her breasts. Gathering her strength; now she makes the next lunge, but I see it coming and let her topple past me. She lands on the bed, burying her face in the pillow, clawing at the sheet. "Why? Why why why WHY?" she screams.

In a minute we will have the manager in here. With the police.

"Am I so hideous? I love you, David, do you know what that word means? Love. Love." Sits up. Turns to me. Imploring. "Don't reject me," she whispers. "I couldn't take that. You know, I just wanted to make you happy, I figured I could be the one, only I didn't realize how unhappy you'd make me. And you just stand there. And you don't say anything. What are you, some kind of machine?"

"I'll tell you what I am," I said.

That was when I went sliding into the abyss. All control lost; all prudence gone. My mind so slathered with raw emotion that survival itself means nothing. I must make things clear to her, is all. I must show her. At whatever expense. I strip off my shirt. She glows, no doubt thinking I will let myself be seduced. My hands slide up and down my bare chest, seeking the catches and snaps. I go through the intricate, cumbersome process of opening my body. Deep within myself something is shouting NO NO NO NO NO, but I pay no attention. The heart has its reasons.

Hoarsely: "Look, Elizabeth. Look at me. This is what I am. Look at me and freak out. The reality trip."

My chest opens wide.

I push myself forward, stepping between the levers and struts, emerging halfway from the human shell I wear. I have not been this far out of it since the day they sealed me in, on Homeworld. I let her see my gleaming carapace. I wave my eyestalks around. I allow some of my claws to show. "See? See? Big black crab from outer space. That's what you love, Elizabeth. That's what I am. David Knecht's just a costume, and this is what's inside it." I have gone insane. "You want reality? Here's reality, Elizabeth. What good is the Knecht body to you? It's a fraud. It's a machine. Come on, come closer. Do you want to kiss me? Should I get on you and make love?"

During this episode her face has displayed an amazing range of reactions. Open-mouthed disbelief at first, of course. And frozen horror: gagging sounds in throat, jaws agape, eyes wide and rigid. Hands fanned across breasts. Sudden modesty in front of the alien monster?

But then, as the familiar Knecht-voice, now bitter and impassioned, continues to flow from the black thing within the sundered chest, a softening of her response. Curiosity. The poetic sensibility taking over. Nothing human is alien to me: Terence, quoted by Cicero. Nothing alien is alien to me. Eh? She will accept the evidence of her eyes. "What are you? Where did you come from?" And I say, "I've violated the Fundamental Rule. I deserve to be plucked and thinned. We're not supposed to reveal ourselves. If we get into some kind of accident that might lead to exposure, we're supposed to blow ourselves up. The switch is right here." She comes close and peers around me, into the cavern of David Knecht's chest. "From some other planet? Living here in disguise?" She understands the picture. Her shock is fading. She even laughs. "I've seen worse than you on acid," she says. "You don't frighten me now, David. David? Shall I go on calling you David?"

This is unreal and dreamlike to me. I have revealed myself, thinking to drive her away in terror; she is no longer aghast, and smiles at my strangeness. She kneels to get a better look. I move back a short way. Eyestalks fluttering: I am uneasy, I have somehow lost the upper hand in this encounter.

She says, "I knew you were unusual, but not like this. But it's all right. I can cope. I mean, the essential personality, that's what I fell in love with. Who cares that you're a crab-man from the Green Galaxy? Who cares that we can't ever be real lovers? I can make that sacrifice. It's your soul I dig, David. Go on. Close yourself up again. You don't look comfortable this way." The triumph of love. She will not abandon me, even now. Disaster. I crawl back into Knecht and lift his arms to his chest to seal it. Shock is glazing my consciousness: the enormity, the audacity. What have I done? Elizabeth watches, awed, even delighted. At last I am together again. She nods. "Listen," she tells me. "You can trust me. I mean, if you're some kind of spy, checking out the Earth, I don't care. *I don't care.* I won't tell anybody. Pour it all out, David. Tell me about yourself. Don't you see, this is the biggest thing that ever happened to me. A chance to show that love isn't just physical, isn't just chemistry, that it's a soul trip, that it crosses not just racial lines but the lines of the whole damned species, the planet itself—"

✸

It took several hours to get rid of her. A soaring, intense conversation, Elizabeth doing most of the talking. She putting forth theories of why I had come to Earth, me nodding, denying, amplifying, mostly lost in horror at my own perfidy and barely listening to her monologue. And the humidity turning me into rotting rags. Finally: "I'm down from the pot, David. And all wound up. I'm going out for a walk. Then back to my room to write for a while. To put this night into a poem before I lose the power of it. But I'll come to you again by dawn, all right? That's maybe five hours from now. You'll be here? You won't do anything foolish? Oh, I love you so much, David! Do you believe me? Do you?"

When she was gone I stood a long while by the window, trying to reassemble myself. Shattered. Drained. Remembering her kisses, her lips running along the ridge marking the place where my chest opens. The fascination of the abomination. She will love me even if I am crustaceous beneath.

I had to have help.

I went to Swanson's room. He was slow to respond to my knock; busy transmitting, no doubt. I could hear him within, but he didn't answer. "Swanson?" I called. "Swanson?" Then I added the distress signal in the Homeworld tongue. He rushed to the door. Blinking, suspicious. "It's all right," I said. "Look, let me in. I'm in big trouble." Speaking English, but I gave him the distress signal again.

"How did you know about me?" he asked.

"The day the maid blundered into your room while you were eating, I was going by. I saw."

"But you aren't supposed to—"

"Except in emergencies. This is an emergency." He shut off his ultrawave and listened intently to my story. Scowling. He didn't approve. But he wouldn't spurn me. I had been criminally foolish, but I was of his kind, prey to the same pains, the same lonelinesses, and he would help me.

"What do you plan to do now?" he asked. "You can't harm her. It isn't allowed."

"I don't want to harm her. Just to get free of her. To make her fall out of love with me."

"How? If showing yourself to her didn't—"

"Infidelity," I said. "Making her see that I love someone else. No room in my life for her. That'll drive her away. Afterwards it won't matter that she knows: who'd believe her story? The FBI would laugh and tell her to lay off the LSD. But if I don't break her attachment to me I'm finished."

"Love someone else? Who?"

"When she comes back to my room at dawn," I said, "she'll find the two of us together, dividing and abstracting. I think that'll do it, don't you?"

⁂

So I deceived Elizabeth with Swanson.

The fact that we both wore male human identities was irrelevant, of course. We went to my room and stepped out of our disguises—a bold, dizzying sensation!—and suddenly we were just two Homeworlders again, receptive to one another's needs. I left the door unlocked. Swanson and I crawled up on my bed and began the chanting. How strange it was, after these years of solitude, to feel those vibrations again! And how beautiful. Swanson's vibrissae touching mine. The interplay of harmonies. An underlying sternness to his technique—he was contemptuous of me for my idiocy, and rightly so—but once we passed from the chanting to the dividing all was forgiven, and as we moved into the abstracting it was truly sublime. We climbed through an infinity of climactic emptyings. Dawn crept upon us and found us unwilling to halt even for rest.

A knock at the door. Elizabeth.

"Come in," I said.

A dreamy, ecstatic look on her face. Fading instantly when she saw the two of us entangled on the bed. A questioning frown. "We've been mating," I explained. "Did you think I was a complete hermit?" She looked from Swanson to me, from me to Swanson. Hand over her mouth. Eyes anguished. I turned the screw a little tighter. "I couldn't stop you from falling in love with me, Elizabeth. But I really do prefer my own kind. As should have been obvious."

"To have her here now, though—when you knew I was coming back—"

"Not *her*, exactly. Not *him* exactly either, though."

"—so cruel, David! To ruin such a beautiful experience." Holding forth sheets of paper with shaking hands. "A whole sonnet cycle," she said. "About tonight. How beautiful it was, and all. And now—and now—" Crumpling the pages. Hurling them across the room. Turning.

Running out, sobbing furiously. Hell hath no fury like. "David!" A smothered cry. And slamming the door.

She was back in ten minutes. Swanson and I hadn't quite finished donning our bodies yet; we were both still unsealed. As we worked, we discussed further steps to take: he felt honor demanded that I request a transfer back to Homeworld, having terminated my usefulness here through tonight's indiscreet revelation. I agreed with him to some degree but was reluctant to leave. Despite the bodily torment of life on Earth I had come to feel I belonged here. Then Elizabeth entered, radiant.

"I mustn't be so possessive," she announced. "So bourgeois. So conventional. I'm willing to share my love." Embracing Swanson. Embracing me. "A menage a trois," she said. "I won't mind that you two are having a physical relationship. As long as you don't shut me out of your lives completely. I mean, David, we could never have been physical anyway, right, but we can have the other aspects of love, and we'll open ourselves to your friend also. Yes? Yes? Yes?"

Swanson and I both put in applications for transfer, he to Africa, me to Homeworld. It would be some time before we received a reply. Until then we were at her mercy. He was blazingly angry with me for involving him in this, but what choice had I had? Nor could either of us avoid Elizabeth. We were at her mercy. She bathed both of us in shimmering waves of tender emotion; wherever we turned, there she was, incandescent with love. Lighting up the darkness of our lives. You poor lonely creatures. Do you suffer much in our gravity? What about the heat? And the winters. Is there a custom of marriage on your planet? Do you have poetry?

A happy threesome. We went to the theater together. To concerts. Even to parties in Greenwich Village. "My friends," Elizabeth said, leaving no doubt in anyone's mind that she was living with both of us. Faintly scandalous doings; she loved to seem daring. Swanson was sullenly obliging, putting up with her antics but privately haranguing me for subjecting him to all this. Elizabeth got out another mimeographed booklet of poems, dedicated to both of us. *Triple Tripping,* she called it.

Flagrantly erotic. I quoted a few of the poems in one of my reports of Homeworld, then lost heart and hid the booklet in the closet. "Have you heard about your transfer yet?" I asked Swanson at least twice a week. He hadn't. Neither had I.

Autumn came. Elizabeth, burning her candle at both ends, looked gaunt and feverish. "I have never known such happiness," she announced frequently, one hand clasping Swanson, the other me. "I never think about the strangeness of you any more. I think of you only as people. Sweet, wonderful, lonely people. Here in the darkness of this horrid city." And she once said, "What if everybody here is like you, and I'm the only one who's really human? But that's silly. You must be the only ones of your kind here. The advance scouts. Will your planet invade ours? I do hope so! Set everything to rights. The reign of love and reason at last!"

"How long will this go on?" Swanson muttered.

*

At the end of October his transfer came through. He left without saying goodbye to either of us and without leaving a forwarding address. Nairobi? Addis Ababa? Kinshasa?

*

I had grown accustomed to having him around to share the burden of Elizabeth. Now the full brunt of her affection fell on me. My work was suffering; I had no time to file my reports properly. And I lived in fear of her gossiping. What was she telling her Village friends? ("You know David? He's not really a man, you know. Actually inside him there's a kind of crab-thing from another solar system. But what does that matter? Love's a universal phenomenon. The truly loving person doesn't draw limits around the planet.") I longed for my release. To go home; to accept my punishment; to shed my false skin. To empty my mind of Elizabeth.

My reply came through the ultrawave on November 13. Application denied. I was to remain on Earth and continue my work as before. Transfers to Homeworld were granted only for reasons of health.

I debated sending a full account of my treason to Homeworld and thus bringing about my certain recall. But I hesitated, overwhelmed with despair. Dark brooding seized me. "Why so sad?" Elizabeth asked. What could I say? That my attempt at escaping from her had failed? "I love you," she said. "I've never felt so real before." Nuzzling against my cheek. Fingers knotted in my hair. A seductive whisper. "David, open yourself up again. Your chest, I mean. I want to see the inner you. To make sure I'm not frightened of it. Please? You've only let me see you once." And then, when I had: "May I kiss you, David?" I was appalled. But I let her. She was unafraid. Transfigured by happiness. She is a cosmic nuisance, but I fear I'm getting to like her.

Can I leave her? I wish Swanson had not vanished. I need advice.

Either I break with Elizabeth or I break with Homeworld. This is absurd. I find new chasms of despondency every day. I am unable to do my work. I have requested a transfer once again, without giving details. The first snow of the winter today.

Application denied.

"When I found you with Swanson," she said, "it was a terrible shock. An even bigger blow than when you first came out of your chest. I mean, it was startling to find out you weren't human, but it didn't hit me in any emotional way, it didn't threaten me. But then, to come back a few hours later and find you with one of your own kind, to know that you wanted to shut me out, that I had no place in your life—Only we worked it out, didn't we?" Kissing me. Tears of joy in her eyes. How did this happen? Where did it all begin? Existence was once so simple. I have tried to trace the chain of events that brought me from there to here, and I cannot. I was outside of my false body for eight hours today. The longest spell so far. Elizabeth is talking of going to the islands with me for the winter. A secluded cottage that her friends will make available. Of course, I must not leave my post without permission. And it takes months simply to get a reply.

Let me admit the truth: I love her.

January 1. The new year begins. I have sent my resignation to Homeworld and have destroyed my ultrawave equipment. The links are broken. Tomorrow, when the city offices are open, Elizabeth and I will go to get the marriage license.

GOING

In the 1970s I assembled a number of "triplet" theme anthologies, in which some well-known science-fiction writer was asked to provide a provocative idea that would be used as the basis for a trio of novella-length stories by the chosen contributors. Sometimes I provided the theme idea myself, sometimes I asked other writers to set the theme.

The first of these books, Three for Tomorrow, *was based on a theme proposed by Arthur C. Clarke, and the stories were written by Roger Zelazny, James Blish, and me. It was so successful that I immediately organized a second such volume, this time working from an idea (actually, four of them) provided by Isaac Asimov.* Four Futures *was the name of the book; Asimov offered an assortment of scenarios dealing with life in the twenty-first century, which he pictured as a time of political stability, a leveling of population growth, and a significant increase in the human life-span. I invited three prominent writers of the period, R.A. Lafferty, Alexei Panshin, and Harry Harrison, to choose from this group of themes, and took the remaining one for myself.*

My story, "Going," was written in June, 1970, somewhat past the midpoint of that period of great creative fertility for me that had recently seen the production of the novels The World Inside, Tower of Glass, *and* Son of Man, *a host of short stories, and the early chapters of the Nebula-winning book* A Time of Changes. *Unlike most of those works, many of which were marked by great flamboyance of prose, all sorts of special effects, its tone is quiet, almost elegiac, as its theme seemed to require. I thought for a time afterward of expanding it into a novel, but ultimately decided against it: at any greater length it would probably have become even more introspective, and that was not the right direction for science fiction in that era. As is true of so many novellas, "Going" was just right at its own length, neither too long nor too short.*

One

In the early spring of 2095, with his one hundred thirty-sixth birthday coming on, Henry Staunt decided quite abruptly that the moment had arrived for him to Go. He would notify the Office of Fulfillment, get himself a congenial Guide, take a suite in one of the better Houses of Leavetaking. With the most pleasant season of the year about to unfurl, the timing would be ideal; he could make his farewells and renunciations during these cool green months and get decently out of the way before summer's blazing eye was open.

This was the first time that he had ever seriously considered Going, and he felt some surprise that the notion had stolen upon him so suddenly. Why, he wondered, was he willing to end it this morning, when he clearly had not been last week, last month, last year? What invisible watershed had he unknowingly crossed, what imperceptible valley of decision? Perhaps this was only a vagrant morning mood; perhaps by noon he would find himself eager to live another hundred years, after all. Eh? No, not likely. He was aware of the resolution, hard and firm, embedded, encapsulated, shining like a glittering pellet at the core of his soul. *Arrange for your Going, Henry.* Nothing equivocal about that. A tone of certainty. Of finality. Still, he thought, we must not hurry into this. First let me understand my own motives in coming to this decision. The unexamined death is not worth requesting.

He had heard that it was useful, when thoughts of Going first came into one's mind, to consult that book of Hallam's—the handbook of dying, the anatomy of world-renunciation. Very well. Staunt touched a bright enameled control stud and the screen opposite the window flowered into color. "Sir?" the library machine asked him.

Staunt said, "Hallam's book. The one about dying."

"*The Turning of the Wheel: Departure as Consolation*, sir?"

"Yes."

Instantly its title page was on the screen. Staunt picked up the scanning rod and pressed it here and there and there, randomly, bringing this page and that into view. He admired the clarity of the image. The type was bold and elegant, the margins were wide; not for several moments did he begin paying attention to the text.

> ...essential that the decision, when it is made, be made for the proper reasons. Although sooner or later we must all turn the wheel, abandoning the world to those who await a place in it, nevertheless no one should leave in resentment, thinking that he has been driven too soon from the worldly sphere. It is the task of the civilized man to bring himself, in the fullness of time, to an acceptance of the knowledge that his life has been completed; Going should not be undertaken by anyone who is not wholly ready, and attaining that state of readiness should be our lifelong goal. Too often we delude ourselves into thinking we are truly ready, when actually we have not reached readiness at all, and choose Going out of unworthy or shallow motives. How tragic it is to arrive at the actual moment of Leavetaking and to realize that one has deceived oneself, that one's motivations are false, that one is, in fact, not in the least ready to Go!
>
> There are many improper reasons for choosing to Go, but they all may be classified as expressions of the desire to escape. One who is experiencing emotional frustration, or difficulty with his work, or a deterioration of health, or intense fatigue, or disappointment of some kind, may, in a moment of dark whim, apply to a House of Leavetaking; but his real intention is a trivial one, that is, to punish the cruel world by escaping from it. One should never look upon Going as a way of getting even. I must point out again that Going is something more than mere suicide. Going is not a petulant, irrational, vindictive deed. It is a positive act, an act of willing renunciation, a deeply moral act; one does not enter into it lightly, solely to escape. One does not say: I loathe you, foul world, therefore I take my leave, and good riddance. One says: I love you, fair world, but I have experienced your joys to the fullest, and now remove myself so that others may know the same joys.

> When one first considers Going, therefore, one must strive to discover if one has attained true readiness—that is, the genuine willingness to put aside the world for the sake of others—or if one is simply seeking to satisfy the ego through the gesture of suicide—

There was much more in that vein. He would read it some other time. He turned the screen off.

So. To find the motive for wanting to Go. Walking slowly through the cool, spacious rooms of his old suburban house, Staunt searched for his reasons. His health? Perfect. He was tall, slender, still strong, with his own teeth and a full head of thick, close-cropped white hair. He hadn't had major surgery since the pancreas transplant nearly seventy years before. Each year he had his arteries retuned, his eyesight adjusted, and his metabolism enhanced, but at his age those were routine things; basically he was a very healthy man. With the right sort of medical care, and everyone nowadays had the right sort of medical care, his body would go on functioning smoothly for decades more.

What then? Emotional problems? Hardly. He had his friends; he had his family; his life had never been more serene than it was now. His work? Well, he rarely worked any longer: some sketches, some outlines for future compositions, but he knew he would never get around to finishing them. No matter. He had only happy thoughts about his work. Worries over the state of the world? No, the world was in fine shape. Rarely finer.

Boredom, perhaps. Perhaps. He had grown weary of his tranquil life, weary of being content, weary of his beautiful surroundings, weary of going through the motions of life. That could be it. He went to the thick clear window of the living room and peered out at the view that had given him so much delight for so many years. The lawn, still pale from winter, sloped evenly and serenely toward the brook, where stubby skunk cabbages clustered. The dogwoods held the first hints of color; the crocuses were not quite finished; the heavy buds of the daffodils would be bursting by Saturday. All was well outside. Lovely. As it always was, this time of year. Yet he was unmoved. It did not sadden him to think that he would probably not see another spring. There's the heart of it, Staunt thought: I must be ripe for Going, because I don't care to stay. It's that simple. I've done all I care to do, I've seen all I care to see; now I might just as well move along. The wheel has to turn.

Others are waiting to fill my place. It is a far, far better thing I do, et cetera, et cetera.

"Get me the Office of Fulfillment," he told his telephone.

A gentle female face appeared on the small screen.

Staunt smiled. "My name's Henry Staunt, and I think I'm ready to Go. Would you send a Guide over as soon as you can?"

Two

An hour later, as Staunt stood by the studio window listening to one of his favorites among his own compositions, the string quartet of 2038, a green-blue copter descended and came fluttering to a halt on his lawn, resting on a cushion of air a short distance above the tips of the grass. It bore on its hull the symbol of the Office of Fulfillment—a wheel and a set of enmeshed gears. The hatch of the copter lifted and, to Staunt's surprise, Martin Bollinger got out. Bollinger was a neighbor, a friend of long standing, possibly the closest friend Staunt had these days; he often came over for visits; lately there had been some talk of Staunt's setting a group of Bollinger's poems to music; but what was Bollinger doing riding around in a Fulfillment Office copter?

Jauntily Bollinger approached the house. He was short, compact, buoyant, with sparkling brown eyes and soft, wavy hair. Staunt supposed he must be seventy or so, eighty at most. Still a young man. Prime of life. It made Staunt feel youthful just to have Bollinger around, and yet he knew that to Bollinger, Bollinger was no youngster. Staunt hadn't felt like a boy when he was eighty, either. But living to one hundred thirty-six changes your perspective about what's old.

From outside Bollinger said, "Can I come in, Henry?"

"Let him in," Staunt murmured. One of the sensors in the studio wall picked up the command and relayed it to the front door, which opened. "Tell him I'm in the studio," Staunt said, and the house guided Bollinger in. With a flick of two fingers Staunt cut down the volume of the music.

Bollinger, as he entered, nodded and said pleasantly, "I've always loved that quartet."

Staunt embraced him. "So have I. How good to see you, Martin."

"I'm sorry it's been so long. Two weeks, isn't it?"

"I'm glad you've come. Although—to be really honest—I'm not going to be free this afternoon, Martin. I'm expecting someone else."

"Oh?"

"In fact, someone from the very organization whose vehicle you seem to have borrowed. How do you happen to come here in one of their copters, anyway?"

"Why not?" Bollinger asked.

"I can't understand why you should. It makes no sense."

"When I come on official business, I use an official copter, Henry."

"Official business?"

"You asked for a Guide."

Staunt was shaken. *"You?"*

"When they told me who had called, I insisted I be given the assignment, or I'd resign instantly. So I came. So here I am."

"I never realized you were with Fulfillment, Martin!"

"You never asked."

Staunt managed a baffled smile. "How long ago did you go into it?"

"Eight, ten years. A while ago."

"And why?"

"A sense of public duty. We all have to help out if the wheel's going to keep turning smoothly. Eh, Henry? Eh?" Bollinger came close to Staunt, looked up at him, staring straight into his eyes, and flashed an unexpectedly brilliant, somehow overpowering grin. Then he said in a crisp, aggressive tone, "What's all this about wanting to Go, Henry?"

"The idea came to me this morning. I was strolling around the house when suddenly I realized there was no further point in my staying here. I'm done: why not admit it? Turn the wheel. Clear a space."

"You're still relatively young."

Staunt laughed harshly. "Coming up on one hundred and thirty-six."

"I know men of one hundred sixty and one hundred seventy who haven't even dreamed of Going."

"That's their problem. I'm ready."

"Are you ill, Henry?"

"Never felt better."

"Are you in any kind of trouble, then?"

"None whatever. My life is unutterably tranquil. I have only the purest of motives in applying for Leavetaking."

Bollinger seemed agitated. He paced the studio, picked up and set down one of Staunt's Polynesian carvings, clasped his hands to his elbows, and said finally,

"We have to talk about this first, Henry. We have to talk about this!"

"I don't understand. Isn't it a Guide's function to speed me serenely on the way to oblivion? You sound as if you're trying to talk me out of Going!"

"It's the Guide's function," Bollinger said, "to serve the best interests of the Departing One, whatever those interests may be. The Guide may attempt to persuade the Departing One to delay his Going, or not to Go at all, if in his judgment that's the proper course to take."

Staunt shook his head. "There's a whole bustling world full of healthy young people out there who want to have more children, and who can't have them unless useless antiquities like myself get out of the way. I volunteer to make some space available. Are you telling me that you'd oppose my Going, Martin, if—"

"Maintaining the level of population at a consistent quantity is only one aspect of our work," Bollinger said. "We're also concerned with maintaining quality. We don't want useful older citizens taking themselves out of the world merely to make room for a newcomer whose capabilities we can't predict. If a man still has something important to give society—"

"I have nothing important left to give."

"If he does," Bollinger went on smoothly, "we will try to discourage him from Going until he's given it. In your case I think Going may be somewhat premature, and so I've wangled the assignment to be your Guide so that I can help you explore the consequences of what you propose to do, and perhaps—"

"What do you think I still can offer the world, Martin?"

"Your music."

"Haven't I written enough?"

"We can't be certain of that. You may have a masterpiece or two lurking in you." Bollinger began to pace again. "Henry, have you read Hallam's *Turning of the Wheel?*"

"I've glanced at it. This morning, in fact."

"Did you look at the section in which he explains why our society is unique in western civilization?"

"It may have slipped my mind."

Bollinger said, "Henry, ours is the first that accepts the concept of suicide as a virtuous act. In the past, you know, suicide was considered filthy and evil and cowardly; religions condemned it as an attack against the will of God, and even people who weren't religious tended to try to cover it up when a friend or a relative killed himself. Well, we're into a different concept. Since our medical skills are now so highly developed that almost no one ever dies naturally, even enlightened birth-limitation measures can't keep the world from filling up with people. So long as anyone is born at all, and no one dies, there's a constant and dangerous build-up of population, so that—"

"Yes, yes, but—"

"Let me finish. To cope with our population problem, we eventually decided to regard the voluntary ending of one's life as a noble sacrifice, and so forth. Hence the whole mystique of Going. Even so, we haven't entirely lost our old moral outlook on suicide. We still don't want valuable people to Go, because we feel they have no right to throw away their gifts, to deprive us of what they have to give. And so one of the functions of the Office of Fulfillment is to lead the old and useless toward the exit in a civilized and gentle way, but another of our functions is to keep the old and useful from Going too soon. Therefore—"

"I understand," Staunt said softly. "I agree with the philosophy. I merely deny that I'm useful any more."

"That's open to question."

"Can it be, Martin, that you're letting personal factors interfere with your judgment?"

"What do you mean? That I'd keep you from Going because I prize your friendship so dearly?"

"I mean my promise to set your poems to music."

Bollinger reddened faintly. "That's absurd. Do you believe that my ego is so bound up in those poems that I'd meddle with your Going, simply so that you'd live to—No. I like to think that my judgment is objective."

"You could be wrong. You might disqualify yourself from being my Guide. Simply on the chance that—"

"No. I'm your Guide."

"Are we going to fight, then, over whether I'll be allowed to Go?"

"Of course not, Henry. We just want you to understand the significance of the step you've asked to take."

"The significance is that I'll die. Is that such a complicated thing to understand?"

Bollinger looked disturbed by Staunt's blunt choice of words. One tried not to connect Going and dying. One was supposed to resort to the euphemisms.

He said, "Henry, I just want to follow orderly procedure."

"Which is?"

"We'll get you into a House of Leavetaking. Then we'll ask you to examine your soul and see if you're as truly ready to Go as you think you are. That's all. The final decision about when you Go will remain in your hands. If you insisted, you could Go this evening; we wouldn't stop you. Couldn't. But of course such haste would be unseemly."

"As you say."

"The House of Leavetaking I recommend for you," Bollinger said, "is known as Omega Prime. It's in Arizona—beautiful desert country rimmed with mountains—and the staff is superb. I could show you brochures on several others, but—"

"I'll trust your judgment."

"Fine. May I use the phone?"

It took less than a minute for Bollinger to book the reservation. For the first time, Staunt felt a sense of inexorability about the course of events. He was on his way out. There would be no turning back now. He would never have the audacity to cancel his Going once he had taken up residence at Omega Prime. But why, he wondered, was he showing even these faint tremors of hesitation? Had Bollinger already begun to undermine his resolution?

"There," Bollinger said. "They'll have your suite ready in an hour. Would you like to leave tonight?"

"Why not?"

"Under our procedures," Bollinger said, "your family will be notified as soon as you've arrived there. I'll do it myself. A custodian will be appointed for your house; it'll be sealed and placed under guard pending transfer of your property to your heirs. At the House of Leavetaking you'll have all the legal advice you'll require, assistance in making a distribution of assets, et cetera, et cetera. There'll be no loose ends left dangling. It'll all go quite smoothly."

"Splendid."

"And that completes the official part of my visit. You can stop thinking of me as your Guide for a while. Naturally, I'll be with you a good deal of the time at the House of Leavetaking, handling any queries you may have, doing whatever I can to make things easier for you. For the moment, though, I'm here simply as your friend, not as your Guide. Would you care to talk? Not about Going, I mean. About music, politics, the weather, anything you like."

Staunt said, "Somehow I don't feel very talkative."

"Shall I leave you alone?"

"I think that would be best. I'm starting to think of myself as a Departing One, Martin. I'd like a few hours to get accustomed to the idea."

Bollinger bowed awkwardly. "It must be a difficult moment for you. I don't want to intrude. I'll come back just before dinnertime, all right?"

"Fine," Staunt said.

Three

Afterward, feeling adrift, Staunt wandered aimlessly through his house, wondering how soon it would be before he changed his mind. He put no credence in Bollinger's flattering, hopeful hypothesis that he might yet have important works of art to give the world; Staunt knew better. If he had ever owed a debt of creativity to mankind, that debt had long since been paid in full, and civilization need not fear it would be losing anything significant by his Going. Even so, he might find it difficult, after all, to remove himself from all he loved. Would the sight of his familiar possessions shake his decision? Here were the memorabilia of a long, comfortable life: the African masks, the Pueblo pots, the Mozart manuscript, the little Elizabethan harpsichord, the lunar boulder, the Sung bowl, the Canopic jars, the Persian miniatures, the dueling pistols, the Greek coins, all the elegant things that he had collected him in his years of traveling. Once it had seemed unbearable to him that he might ever be parted from these precious objects. They had taken on life for him, so that when a clumsy cleaning machine knocked a Cypriote statuette to the floor and smashed it, he had wept not for the monetary loss, but for the pain he imagined the little clay creature was suffering, for the humiliation it must feel at being ruined. He imagined it hurling bitter reproaches at him: *I survived four thousand years so that I might become yours, and you let me get broken!* As a child might pretend that her dolls were alive, and talk to them, and apologize to them for fancied slights. It was, he had known all along, a foolish, sentimental, even contemptible attitude, this attachment he had to his inanimate belongings, this solemn fond concern for their "comfort" and "feelings," this way of speaking of them as "he" or "she" instead of "it," of worrying about whether some prized piece was receiving a place of display that was properly satisfying to its ego. He acknowledged the half-submerged notion that he had created a family, a special entity, by assembling this hodgepodge of artifacts from a hundred cultures and a hundred eras.

Now, though, he deliberately confronted himself with ugly reality: when he had Gone, his "family" would be scattered, his beloved things sold or given away, some of them surely lost or broken in transit, some ending up on the dusty shelves of ignorant people, none of them ever again to know the warmth of ownership he had lavished on them. And he did not care. Except in the most remote, abstract way, he simply did not care. Today the life was gone out of them, and they were merely masks and pots and bits of bone and pieces of paper—objects, interesting and valuable and attractive, but lacking all feeling. Objects. They needed no coddling. He was under no obligation to them to worry about their welfare. Somehow, without his noticing it, his possessions had ceased to be his pets, and he felt no pain at the thought of parting from them. I must indeed be ready to Go, he told himself.

Here, in the little alcove off the studio, was his *real* family. A stack of portrait cubes: his wife, his son, his daughter, his children's children, his children's children's children, each of them recorded in a gleaming plastic box a couple of inches high. There were so many of them—dozens! He had had only the socially approved two children, and so had his own children, and none of his grandchildren or great-grandchildren had had more than three, and yet look at the clutter of cubes! The multitude of them was the most vivid possible argument in favor of the idea of Going. One simply had to make room, or everyone would be overwhelmed by the tide of oncoming young ones. Of course in a world where practically no one ever died except voluntarily, and that only at a great old age, families did tend to accumulate amazingly as the generations came along. Even a small family, and these days there was no other kind, was bound to become immense over the course of eighty or ninety years through the compounding progressions of controlled but persistent fertility. All additions, no subtractions. Or very few. And so the numbers mounted. Look at all the cubes!

The cubes were clever things: computer-actuated personality simulations. Everyone got himself cubed at least once, and those who were particularly hungry for the odd sort of immortality that cubing conferred had new cubes made every few years. The process itself was a simple electronic transfer; it took about an hour to make a cube. The scanning machines recorded your voice and patterns of speech, your motion habits, your facial gestures, your whole set of standard reactions and responses. A battery of concise, cunningly perceptive personality tests yielded a character profile. This, too, went into the cube. They ended by having your soul in a box. Plug the cube into a receptor slot, and you came to life on a screen, smiling as you would smile, moving as you would move, sounding as you would sound, saying things you were likely to say. Of course, the thing on the screen was unreal, a mechanical mock-up, a counterfeit approximation of the person who had been cubed; but it was programmed to respond to conversation and to initiate its own conversational gambits without the stimulus of prior inputs, to absorb new data and change its outlook in the light of what it heard; in short, it behaved not like a frozen portrait but like a convincing imitation of the living person from whom it had been drawn.

Staunt studied the collection of cubes. He had five of his son, spanning Paul's life from early middle age to early old age; Paul faithfully sent his father a new cube at the beginning of each decade. Three cubes of his daughter. A number of the grandchildren. The proud parents sent him cubes of the young ones when they were ten or twelve years old, and the grandchildren themselves, when they were adults, sent along more mature versions of themselves. By now he had four or five cubes of some of them. Each year there were new cubes: an updating of someone's old one, or some great-great-grandchild getting immortalized for the first time, and everything landing on the patriarch's shelf. Staunt rather liked the custom.

He had only one cube of his wife. They had developed the process about fifty years ago, and Edith had been dead since '47, forty-eight years back. Staunt and his wife had been among the first to be cubed; just as well, for her time had been short, though they hadn't known it. Even now, not all deaths were voluntary. Edith had died in a copter crash, and Staunt, close to ninety, had not remarried. Having the cube of her had been a great comfort to him in the years just after her death. He rarely played it now, mainly because of its technical imperfections; since the process was so new when her cube had been made, the simulation was only approximate, and her movements were jerky and awkward, not much like those of the graceful Edith he had known. He had no idea how long it had been since he had last played her. Impulsively, he slipped her cube into the slot.

The screen brightened, and there was Edith. Supple, alert, aglow. Long creamy-white hair, a purple wrap, her favorite gold pin clasped to her shoulder. She had been in her late seventies when the cube was made; she looked hardly more than fifty. Their marriage had lasted half a century. Staunt had only recently realized that the span of his life without her was now nearly as long as the span of his life with her.

"You're looking well, Henry," she said as soon as her image appeared.

"Not bad for an old relic. It's 2095, Edith. I'll be one hundred thirty-six."

"You haven't switched me on in a while, then. Not for five years, in fact."

"No. But it isn't that I haven't thought of you, Edith. It's just that I've tended to drift away from everything I once loved. I've become a sleepwalker, in a way. Wandering through the days, filling in my time."

"Have you been well?"

"Well enough," Staunt said. "Healthy. Astonishingly healthy. I can't complain."

"Are you composing?"

"Very little, these days. Nothing, really. I've made some sketches for intended work, but that's all."

"I'm sorry. I was hoping you'd have something to play for me."

"No," he said. "Nothing."

Over the years, he had faithfully played each of his new compositions to Edith's cube, just as he had kept her up to date on the doings of their family and friends, on world events, on cultural fads. He had not wanted her cube to remain fixed forever in 2046. To have her constantly learning, growing, changing, helped to sustain his illusion that the Edith on the screen was the real Edith. He had even told her the details of her own death.

"How are the children?" she asked.

"Fine. I see them often. Paul's in fine shape, a tough old man just like his father. He's ninety-one, Edith. Does it puzzle you to be the mother of a son who's older than you are?"

She laughed. "Why should I think of it that way? If he's ninety-one, I'm one hundred twenty-five."

"Of course. Of course." If she wanted it like that.

"And Crystal's eighty-seven. Yes, that *is* a little strange. I can't help thinking of her as a young woman. Why, her children must be old themselves, and they were just babies!"

"Donna is sixty-one. David is fifty-eight. Henry is forty-seven."

"Henry?" Edith said, her face going blank. After a moment's confusion she recovered. "Oh, yes. The third child, the little accident. Your namesake. I forgot him for a moment." Henry had been born soon after Edith's death; Staunt had told her cube about him, but imprinting of post-cubing events never took as well as the original programming; she had lost the datum for a moment. As if to cover her embarrassment, Edith began asking him about all the other grandchildren, the great-grandchildren, the whole horde that had accumulated after her lifetime. She called forth names, assigned the right children to the right parents, scampered up and down the entire Staunt family tree, showing off to please him.

But he forced an abrupt switch of subject. "I want to tell you, Edith, that I've decided it's time for me to Go."

Again the blank look. "Go? Go where?"

"You know what I mean. *Going.*"

"No, I don't. Really, I don't."

"To a House of Leavetaking."

"I still don't follow."

He struggled against being impatient with her. "I've explained the idioms to you. Long ago. They've been in use at least thirty or forty years. It's voluntary termination of life, Edith. I've discussed it with you. Everyone comes to it sooner or later."

"You've decided to die?"

"To Go, yes, to die, to Go."

"Why?"

"Because of the boredom. The loneliness. I've outlived most of my early friends. I've outlived my own talent. I've outlived *myself*, Edith. A hundred thirty-six years. And I could go on another fifty. But why bother? To live just for the sake of living?"

"Poor Henry. You always had such a wonderful capacity for being interested in things. The day wasn't long enough for you, with your collections, and your books, and your music, and traveling around the world, and your friends—"

"I've read everything I want to read. I've seen the whole world. I'm tired of collecting things."

"Perhaps I was the lucky one, then. A decent number of years, a happy life, and then out. Quickly."

"No. I've enjoyed living on like this, Edith. I kept my health, I didn't go senile—it's been good, all of it. Except for not having you with me. But I've stopped enjoying things. Quite suddenly I've realized that there's no point in staying any longer. The wheel has to turn. The old have to clear themselves away. Somewhere there are people waiting to have a child, waiting for a vacancy in the world, and it's up to me to create that vacancy."

"Have you told Paul and Crystal?"

"Not yet. I made the decision just today. But I'll notify them—or it'll be done for me. They'll have most of my property. I'll give my cube of you to Paul. Everything's handled very efficiently for a Departing One."

"How soon will you—Go?"

Staunt shrugged. "I don't know yet. A month, two months—there's no rush about it."

"You sound as though you don't really want to do it."

He shook his head. "I want to, Edith. But in a civilized way. Taking my leave properly. I've lived a long time; I can't let go in a single day. But I won't stay here much longer."

"I'll miss you, Henry."

He pondered the intricacies of that. The cube missing the living man. Chuckling, he said, "Paul will play my cube to you, and yours to me. We'll talk to each other through the machinery. We'll always be there for each other."

The image of Edith reached a hand toward him. He cursed the clumsiness of the simulation. Gently he touched his fingertips to the screen, making a kind of contact with her across the decades, across the barriers separating them. He blew a kiss to her. Then, quickly, before sentimentality overcame him, he pulled her cube from the slot and set it beside those of his son and daughter. In haste, nearly stumbling, he went on into his studio.

The big room held the tangible residue of his long career. Over here, the music itself, in recorded performance: disks and cassettes for the early works, sparkling playback cubes for the later ones. Here were the manuscripts, uniformly bound in red half-morocco, one of his little vanities. Here were the scrapbooks of reviews and the programs of concerts. Here were the trophies. Here were the volumes of his critical writings. Staunt had been a busy man. He looked at the titles stamped on the bindings of the manuscripts: the symphonies, the string quartets, the concerti, the miscellaneous chamber works, the songs, the sonatas, the cantatas, the operas. So much. So much. He had tried his hand at virtually every form. His music was polite, agreeable, conservative, even a bit academic, yet he made no apologies for it: he had followed his own inner voices wherever they led, and if he had not been led to rebellion and fulminations, so be it. He had given pleasure through his work. He had added to the world's small stock of beauty. It was a respectable life's accomplishment. If he had had more passion, more turbulence, more dynamism, perhaps, he would have shaken the world as Beethoven had, as Wagner. Well, the great gesture had never been his to brandish; yet he had done his best, and in his way he had achieved enough. Some men heal the sick, some men soothe the souls of the troubled, some men invent wondrous machines—and some make songs and symphonies, because they must, and because it is all they can do to enrich the world into which they had been thrust. Even now, with his life's flame burning low, with everything suddenly seeming pointless and hollow to him, Staunt felt no sense of having wasted his time filling this room with what it held. Never in the past hundred years had a week gone by without a performance of one of his compositions somewhere. That was sufficient justification for having written, for having lived.

He turned on the synthesizer and rested his fingers lightly on the keys, and of their own will they played the opening theme of his *Venus* symphony of 1989, his first mature work. How far away all that seemed now—the glittering autumn of triumphs as he conducted it himself in a dozen capitals, the critics agog, everyone from the disgruntled Brahms-fanciers to the pundits of the avant-garde rushing to embrace him as the savior of serious music. Of course, there had been a reaction to that hysterical overpraise later, when the modernists decided that no one so popular could possibly be good and the conservatives began to find him too modern, but such things were only to be expected. He had gone his own way. Eventually others had recognized his genius—a limited and qualified genius, a small and tranquil genius, but genius nevertheless. As the world emerged from the storms of the twentieth century's bitter second half, as the new society of peace and harmony took shape on the debris of the old, Staunt created the music a quieter era needed, and became its lyric voice.

Here. He pushed a cube into a playback slot. The sweet outcry of his wind quintet. Here: *The Trials of Job*, his first opera. Here: *Three Orbits for Strings and Stasis Generator.* Here: *Polyphonies for Five Worlds.* He got them all going at once, bringing wild skeins of sound out of the room's assortment of speakers, and stood in the middle, trembling a little, accepting the sonic barrage and untangling everything in his mind.

After perhaps four minutes he cut off the sound. He did not need to play the music; it was all within his head, whenever he wanted it.

Lightly he caressed the smooth, glossy black backs of his scrapbooks, with all the documentation of his successes and his occasional failures neatly mounted. He ran his fingers along the rows of bound manuscripts. So much. So very much. Such a long productive life. He had no complaints.

He told his telephone to get him the Office of Fulfillment again.

"My Guide is Martin Bollinger," he said. "Would you let him know that I'd like to be transferred to the House of Leavetaking as soon as possible?"

Four

Bollinger, sitting beside him in the copter, leaned across him and pointed down.

"That's it," he said. "Omega Prime, right below."

The House of Leavetaking seemed to be a string of gauzy white tentlike pavilions, arranged in a U-shape around a courtyard garden. The late afternoon sun tinged the pavilions with gold and red. Bare fangs of purplish mountains rose on the north and east; on the other side of Omega Prime the fiat flat brown Arizona desert, pocked with cacti and palo verde, stretched toward the dark horizon.

The copter landed silently. When the hatch opened, Staunt felt the blast of heat. "We don't modulate the outdoor climate here," Bollinger explained. "Most Departing Ones seem to prefer it that way. Contact with the natural environment."

"I don't mind," Staunt said. "I've always loved the desert."

A welcoming party had gathered by the time he emerged from the copter. Three members of Omega Prime's staff, in smocks monogrammed with the Fulfillment insignia. Four withered oldsters, evidently awaiting their own imminent Going. A transport robot, with its wheelchair seat already in position. Staunt, picking his way carefully over the rough, pebble-strewn surface of the landing field, was embarrassed by the attention. He said in a low voice to Bollinger, "Tell them I don't need the chair. I can still walk. I'm no invalid."

They clustered around him, introducing themselves: Dr. James, Miss Elliot, Mr. Falkenbridge. Those were the staff people. The four Departing Ones croaked their names at him too, but Staunt was so astonished by their appearance that he forgot to pay attention. The shriveled faces, the palsied clawlike hands, the parchment skin—did he look like that, too? It was years since he had seen anyone his own age. He had the impression that he had come through his fourteen decades well preserved, but perhaps that was only an illusion born of vanity, perhaps he really was as much of a ruin as these four. Unless they were much older than he, one hundred seventy-five, one hundred eighty years old, right at the limits of what was now the human span of mortality. Staunt stared at them in wonder, awed and dismayed by their gummy grins.

Falkenbridge, a husky red-haired young man, apparently some sort of orderly, was trying to ease him into the wheelchair. Irritably Staunt shook him off, saying, "No. No. I'll manage. Martin, tell him I don't need it."

Bollinger whispered something to Falkenbridge. The young man shrugged and sent the transport robot away. Now they all began walking toward the House of Leavetaking, Falkenbridge on Staunt's right, Miss Elliot on his left, both of them staying close to him in case he should topple.

He found himself under unexpectedly severe strain. Possibly refusing the wheelchair had been foolish bravado. The fierce dry heat, the fatigue of his ninety-minute rocket journey across the continent, the coarse texture of the ground, all conspired to make his legs wobbly. Twice he came close to falling. The first time Miss Elliot gently caught his elbow and steadied him; the second, he managed to recover himself, after a short half-stumble that sent pain shooting through his left ankle.

Suddenly, all at once, he was feeling his age. In a single day he had begun to dodder, as though his decision to enter a House of Leavetaking had stripped him of all his late-staying vigor. No. No. He rejected the idea. He was merely tired, as a man his age had every right to be; with a little rest he'd be himself again. He walked faster, despite the effort it cost him. Sweat trickled down his cheeks. There was a stitch in his side. His entire left leg ached.

At last they reached the entrance to Omega Prime. He saw now that what had seemed to be gauzy tents, viewed from above, were in fact sturdy and substantial plastic domes, linked by an intricate network of covered passageways. The courtyard around which they were grouped, contained elaborate plantings of desert flora: giant stiff-armed cacti, looping white-whiskered succulents, odd and angular thorny things. The plants had been grouped with remarkable grace and subtleness around an assortment of strange boulders and sleek stone slabs; the effect was one of extraordinary beauty. Staunt stood a moment contemplating it. Bollinger said gently, "Why not go to your suite first? The garden will still be here this evening."

He had an entire dome to himself. Interior walls divided it into a bedroom, a sitting room, and a kind of utility room; everything was airy and tastefully simple, and the temperature was twenty-five degrees cooler than outside. A window faced the garden.

The staff people and the quartet of Departing Ones vanished, leaving Staunt alone with his Guide. Bollinger said, "Each of the residents has a suite like this. You can eat here, if you like, although there's a community dining room under the courtyard. There are recreational facilities there too—a library, a theater, a game room—but you can spend all of your time perfectly happily right where you are."

Staunt lowered himself gingerly into a webfoam hammock. As his weight registered, tiny Mechanical hands began to massage his back. Bollinger smiled.

"This is your data terminal," he said, handing Staunt a copper-colored rod about eight inches long. "It's a standard access unit. You can get any book in the library—and there are thousands of them—screened on request, and you can play whatever music you'd like, and it's also a telephone input. Ask it to connect you with anyone at all. Go on. Ask."

"My son Paul," Staunt said.

"Ask it," said Bollinger.

Staunt activated the terminal and gave it Paul's name and access number. Instantly a screen came to life just beside the hammock. Staunt's son appeared in its silvery depths. The screen could almost have been a mirror, a strange sort of time-softening mirror that was capable of taking the face of a very old man and reflecting it as that of a man who was merely old. Staunt beheld someone who was a younger version of himself, though far from young: cool gray eyes, thin lips, lean bony face, a dense mane of white hair.

Paul's face was deeply lined but still vigorous. At the age of ninety-one he had not yet retired from the firm of architects he headed. So long as a man's health was good and his mind was sound and he still found his career rewarding, there was no reason to retire; when mind or body failed or career lost its savor, that was the time to withdraw and make oneself ready to Go.

Staunt said, "I'm calling you from Omega Prime."

"What's that, Henry?"

"You've never heard of it? A House of Leavetaking in Arizona. It looks like a lovely place. Martin Bollinger brought me here this evening."

Paul looked startled. "Are you thinking of Going, Henry?"

"I am."

"You never told me you had any such thing in mind!"

"I'm telling you now."

"Are you in poor health?"

"I feel fine," Staunt said. "Everyone asks me that, and I say the same thing. My health is excellent."

"Then why—"

"Do I have to justify it? I've lived long enough. My life is over."

"But you've been so alert, so involved—"

"It's my decision to make. It's ungracious of you to quarrel with me over it."

"I'm not quarreling," Paul said. "I'm trying to adapt to it. You know, you've been part of my life for nine decades. I don't give a damn what the social conventions are: I can't simply smile and nod and say how sweet when my father announces he's going to die."

"To Go."

"To Go," Paul muttered. "Whatever. Have you told Crystal?"

"You're the first member of the family to know. Except for your mother, that is."

"My mother?"

"The cube," said Staunt.

"Oh. Yes. The cube." A thin, edgy laugh. "All right. I'll tell the others. I suppose I'll have to learn how to be head of the family, finally. You're not going to be doing this immediately, are you?"

"Naturally not. Where do you get such ideas? I'll have a proper Leavetaking. Graceful. Serene. A few weeks, a month or two—the usual thing."

"And we can visit you?"

"I'll expect you to," Staunt said. "That's part of the ritual."

"What about—pardon me—what about the legal aspects? Disposition of property, things like that?"

"It'll all be managed in the customary way. The Office of Fulfillment is supposed to help me. Don't worry: you'll get everything that's coming to you."

"That isn't a kind way to phrase it, Henry."

"I don't have to be kind any more. I don't even have to make sense. I'm just a crazy old man getting ready to Go."

"Henry—Father—"

"All right. I'm sorry. Somehow this conversation hasn't worked right at all. Shall we start it over?"

"I'd like to," Paul said.

Staunt realized he was quivering. The muscles of his face were drawn taut. He made a deliberate attempt to relax, and after a moment, said quietly, "It's a perfectly normal, desirable step to take. I'm old and tired and lonely and bored. I'm no use to myself or to anybody else, and there's really no sense troubling my doctors to keep me functioning any longer. So I'm going to Go. I'd rather Go now, when I'm still reasonably healthy and clear-witted, instead of trying to hang on another few decades until I've slid into senility. I've moved to Omega Prime, and you'll all come to visit me before my Leavetaking, and it'll be a peaceful and beautiful Going, I hope. That's all. There's nothing to weep about. In forty or fifty years you'll understand all this a lot better."

"I understand it now," Paul said. "You caught me by surprise when you called, but I understand. Of course. Of course. We don't want to lose you, but that's only our selfishness talking. You've lived a full life, and, well, the wheel has to turn."

How smoothly he does it, Staunt thought. How easily he slips into the jargon. How readily he agrees with me, after his first reflexive moment of shock. *Yes, Henry, certainly, Henry, it's wise of you to Go, Henry, you've lived long enough.* Staunt wondered which was the fraud: Paul's initial resistance to the idea of his Going, or his philosophical acquiescence. And what difference did it make? Why, Staunt asked himself, should I be offended if my son thinks it's right for me to Go when I was offended two minutes earlier by his trying to talk me out of it?

He was beginning to be unsure of his own ground. Perhaps he *did* want to be talked out of it.

I must read Hallam shortly, he told himself.

He said to Paul, "I have a great deal to do this evening. I'll call you tomorrow. Or you call me."

The screen went blank.

Bollinger said, "He took it rather well, I thought. The children don't always accept the idea that a parent is Going. They accept the theory of

Leavetaking, but they always assume that it's someone else's old folks who'll Go."

"They want their own parents to live forever, even if the parents don't feel like staying around any longer?"

"That's it."

"What if someone *does* feel like staying forever?" Staunt asked.

Bollinger shrugged. "We never try to force the issue. We hint a little, as subtly as we know how, if someone is one hundred forty or one hundred fifty or so, and really a wreck, but clinging to life anyway. For that matter, if he's eighty or ninety, even, and just going through the motions of living, held together by his doctors alone, we'll try to encourage Going. We have gentle ways of working through doctors or friends or relatives, trying to overcome the fear of dying in the ones who linger, trying to get across the idea that it's not only best for society for them to move on, it's best for themselves. If they don't take the hint, there's nothing we can do. Involuntary euthanasia just isn't part of our system."

"How old," Staunt asked, "are the oldest living people now?"

"I think the oldest ones known are something like one hundred seventy-five or one hundred eighty. Which means they were born in the early part of the twentieth century, around the time of the First World War. Anyone born before that simply spent too much of his life in the era of medieval medicine to hope for a really long span. But if you were born, say, in 1920, you were still only fifty-five or sixty when the era of organ transplants and computerized health services and laser surgery was beginning, and if you were lucky enough to be in good shape in the 1970's, the 1980's, why, you could be kept going just about indefinitely thereafter. Into the era of tissue regeneration and all the rest. A few from the early twentieth century did hang on into the era of total medicine, and some of them are still with us. Politely declining to Go."

"How much longer can they last?"

"Hard to say," Bollinger replied. "We just don't know what the practical limits of the human life-span are. Our experience with total medicine doesn't go back far enough. I've heard it said that two hundred or two hundred ten is the top figure, but in another twenty or thirty years we may have some people who've reached that figure, and we'll find that we can keep them going beyond it. Maybe there *is* no top limit, now that we can do the things we do to rebuild a decaying body. But how hideously antisocial it is of them to hang around for century after century just to test our medical skills!"

"But if they're making valuable contributions to society through all those hundreds of years—"

"*If,*" Bollinger said. "But the fact is that ninety, ninety-five percent of all people never make any contributions to society, even when they're young. They just occupy space, do jobs that could really be done better by machines, sire children who aren't any more gifted than they are—and hang on, living and living and living. We don't want to lose anyone who's valuable, Henry; I've been through that with you already. But most people aren't valuable to begin with, and get less valuable as they go along, and there's no reason in the universe why they should live past one hundred or one hundred ten, let alone to two hundred or three hundred or whatever."

"That's a harsh philosophy. Cynical, even."

"I know. But read Hallam. The wheel's got to turn. We've reached an average life-span that would have seemed wild fantasy as late as the time when you were a child, Henry, but that doesn't mean we have to strive to make everyone immortal. Not unless people are willing to give up having children, and they aren't. It's a finite planet. If there's inflow, there has to be outflow, and I like to think that those flowing out are the ones who have the least to offer to the rest of us. The decrepit, the feeble, the slow-witted, the mean-souled. Thank God, most old folks agree. For every one who absolutely won't give up his grip on life, there are fifty who are glad to go once they've hit one hundred or so. And as the remainder get even older, they change their minds about staying, just as you've done lately. Not many want to go on past one hundred fifty. The few who do, well, we'll look on them as experiments in geriatrics, and let them be."

"How old are those four who met my copter?" Staunt asked.

"I couldn't tell you. One hundred twenty, one hundred thirty, something like that. Most of those who arrange for Leavetaking now are people born between 1960 and 1980."

"Of my generation, then."

"I suppose, yes."

"Do I look as bad as they do? They're a bunch of walking mummies, Martin. I'd have guessed they were fifty years older than I am."

"I doubt that very much."

"But I'm not like them, am I? I've got my teeth. My hair. My real eyes. I look old, but not ancient. Or am I fooling myself, Martin? Am I really a dried-up nightmare too? Is it just that I've grown accustomed to the way I look, I haven't noticed the changes, decade after decade as I get older and older?"

"There's a mirror," Bollinger said. "Answer your own questions."

Staunt stared at himself. Lines and wrinkles, yes: a contour map of time, the valleys and ravines of a long life. Blotches on the skin. The glittering eyes deeply recessed; the cheeks fleshless, revealing the sharp outlines of the skull beneath. An old face, tremendously old. But yet not like their faces. He was no mummy yet. He imagined that a man of the twentieth century would guess him to be no more than eighty or eighty-five, just as a man of the twentieth century would guess Paul to be in his late sixties and Martin Bollinger in his late fifties. Those others, those four, showed their true ages. It must take all the magic at their doctors' command to keep them together. And now, weary of cheating death, they've come here to Go and be over with the farce. Whereas I am still strong, whereas I could continue easily, if only I wanted to continue.

"Well?" Bollinger asked.

"I'm in pretty good shape," Staunt said. "I'm quitting while I'm ahead. It's the right way to do it." He picked up the data terminal again. "I wonder if they have any of my music in storage here," he said, and opened the access node and made a request; and the room flooded with the first chords of his Twelfth Symphony. He was pleased. He closed his eyes and listened. When the movement ended, he looked around the room, and found that Bollinger had gone.

Five

Dr. James came to see him a little while later, as night was enfolding the desert. Staunt was standing by the window, watching the brilliant stars appear, when the room annunciator told him of his visitor.

The doctor was a youngish man—forty, fifty, Staunt was no longer good at guessing ages—with a long fragile-looking nose and a gentle, faintly unctuous, I-want-you-to-have-a-lovely-Going sort of manner. His first words to Staunt were, "I've been looking through your medical file. I really must congratulate you on the excellent state of your health."

"There's something about music that keeps people in good shape," Staunt said.

"Are you a conductor?"

"A composer. But I've conducted my own works quite often. Waving the baton—it's obviously good exercise."

"I don't know much about music, I'm afraid. Some afternoon you must program some of your favorite pieces for me." The doctor grinned shyly. "The simpler ones. Music for an unsophisticated medic, if you've written any." He was silent a moment. Then he said, "You really do have an excellent medical history. Your doctor's computer transferred your whole file to us this afternoon when your reservation was made. Naturally, while you're with us we want you to remain in perfect health and comfort. You'll receive the same kind of care here that you were getting at home—the muscle therapies, the ion-balance treatments, the circulatory clearances, and so forth. Including any special supportive therapy that may become necessary. Not that I anticipate someone like you to need a great deal of that."

"I could last another fifty years, eh?"

Dr. James looked abashed. His plump cheeks glowed. "That choice is entirely up to you, Mr. Staunt."

"Don't worry. I'm not about to change my mind."

"No one here will hurry you," the doctor said. "We've had people remain at Omega Prime for three, even four years. Each man's Leavetaking is the most important event in his life, after all; he's entitled to go about it at his own pace, to disengage himself from the world as gradually as he wants. You do understand that there is no cost to you for any part of your residence here. The government underwrites the whole business."

"I think Martin Bollinger explained that to me."

"Good. Let me discuss with you, then, some of your Leavetaking options. Many Departing Ones prefer to begin their withdrawal from the world by making a grand tour—a kind of farewell to all the great sights, the Pyramids, the Taj Mahal, Notre Dame, the Sahara, Antarctica, whatever. We can make any such travel arrangements you'd like. We have several organized tours, on which you'd travel with five or six or ten other Departing Ones and several Guides—a one-month tour of the most famous places, a two-month tour, or a three-month tour. These are packaged in advance, but we can make changes in itinerary by unanimous consent of the Departing Ones. Or, if you prefer, you could travel alone, that is, just you and your Guide, to any part of the world that—"

Staunt looked at him in astonishment. Was this man a doctor or a travel agent?

And did he want to take any such tour? It was vaguely tempting. At government expense to see the temples of Chichen Itza by moonlight, to float over the Andes and descend into Machu Picchu, to smell the scent of cloves on Zanzibar, to look up at a sequoia's distant blue-green crown, to see the hippos jostling in the Nile, to roam the crumbling dusty streets of Babylon, to drift above the baroque intricacies of the Great Barrier Reef, to see the red sandstone spires of Utah, to tramp along the Great Wall of China, to make his farewells to lakes and deserts and mountains and valleys, to cities and wastelands, to penguins, to polar bears—

But he had seen all those places. Why go back? Why bother to make a breathless pilgrimage, dragging his flimsy bones from place to place? Once was enough. He had his memories.

"No," he said. "If I had any desire to travel anywhere, I wouldn't have thought of Going in the first place. If you follow me. The flavor's gone out of everything, do you see? I don't have the motivation for hauling myself around. Not even to make sentimental gestures of farewell."

"As you wish, Mr. Staunt. Most Departing Ones do take advantage of the travel option. But you'll find no coercion here. If you feel no urge to travel, why, stay right where you are."

"Thank you. What are some of the other Leavetaking options?"

"It's customary for the Departing Ones to seek experiences they may have missed during their lifetimes, or to repeat ones that they found particularly rewarding. If there's some special type of food that you enjoy—"

"I was never a gourmet."

"Or works of music you want to hear again, masterpieces you'd like to live with one last time—"

"There are some," Staunt said. "Not many. Most of them bore me now. When Mozart and Bach and Beethoven begin to bore a man, he knows it's time to Go. Do you know, even Staunt has begun to seem less interesting to me lately?"

Dr. James did not smile.

He said, "In any event, you'll find that we're programmed for every imaginable work of music, and if there are any you know of that we don't have and ought to have, I hope you'll tell us. It's the same with books. Your screen can give you any work in any language—just put in the requisition. A number of Departing Ones use this opportunity at last to read *War and Peace,* or *Ulysses,* or *The Tale of Genji,* say."

"Or *The Encyclopœaedia Britannica,"* Staunt said, "from 'Aardvark' to 'Zwingli."'

"You think you're joking. We had a Departing One here five years ago who set out to do just that."

"How far did he get?" Staunt wanted to know. "'Antimony'? 'Betelgeuse'?"

"'Magnetism,' I think. He was quite dedicated to the job."

"Perhaps I'll do some reading, too, doctor. Not the *Britannica.* But Hallam, at least. Maybe Montaigne, and maybe Hobbes, and maybe Ben Jonson. For about sixty years I've been meaning to read my way through Ben Jonson. I suppose this is my last chance."

"Another option," Dr. James said, "is a memory jolt."

"Which is?"

"Chemical stimulation of the mnemonic centers. It stirs up the memories, awakens things you may not have thought about for eighty or ninety years, sends images and textures and odors and colors of past experiences through your mind in a remarkably vivid way. In a sense, it's a trip through your entire past. I don't know any Departing One who's done it and not come out of it in a kind of ecstasy, a radiant glow of joy."

Staunt frowned. "I'd guess that it could be a painful experience. Disturbing. Depressing."

"Not at all. Never. It's emotion recollected in tranquility: the experiences may have been painful originally, but the replay of them never is. The jolt allows you to come to terms with all that you've been and done. I've known people to ask to Go within an hour of coming out of the jolt, and not because they were depressed; they simply want to take their leave on a high note."

"I'll think about it," Staunt said.

"Other than the things I've mentioned, your period of Leavetaking is completely unstructured. You write the script. Your family will come to see you, and your friends; I think you'll get to know some of the other Departing Ones here; there'll be Leavetaking parties as one by one they opt to Go, and then there'll be Farewell ceremonies for them, and they'll Go; and eventually, a month, six months, as you choose, you'll request your own Leavetaking party and Farewell ceremony, and finally you'll Go. You know, Mr. Staunt, I feel a tremendous sense of exhilaration here every day, working with these wonderful Departing Ones, helping to make their last weeks beautiful, watching the serenity with which they Go. My own time of Going is still ninety or a hundred years away, I suppose, and yet in a way I look forward to it now; I feel a certain impatience, knowing that the happiest hours of my life will come at the very end of it. To Go when still healthy, to step voluntarily out of the world in an atmosphere of peace and fulfillment, to know that you cap a long and successful life by the noblest of all deeds, letting the wheel turn, giving younger people an opportunity to occupy your place—how marvelous it all is!"

"I wish," Staunt said, "that I could orchestrate your aria. Shimmering tremolos in the strings—the plaintive wail of the oboes—harps, six harps, making celestial noises—and then a great crescendo of trombones and French horns and bassoons, a sort of Valhalla music welling up—"

Looking baffled, Dr. James said, "I told you, I don't really know much about music."

"I'm sorry. I shouldn't mock, not at my age. I'm sure it is beautiful and marvelous. I'm very happy to be here."

"A pleasure to have you," said Dr. James.

Six

Staunt did not feel up to having dinner in the community dining room; he had had a long journey, crossing several time zones, and his appetite was awry. He ordered a light meal, juice and soup and fruit, and it arrived almost instantaneously via a subterranean conveyor system. He ate sparingly. Before I Go, he promised himself, I will have steak au poivre again, and escargots, and a curry of lamb, and all the other things I never cared much for while I was young enough to digest them. James offers me a chance; why not take it? I will become a preposthumous gourmet. Even if it kills me. Better to Go like that than by drinking whatever tasteless potion it is they give you at the end.

After dinner he asked where Bollinger was.

"Mr. Bollinger has gone home," Staunt was told. "But he'll be back the day after tomorrow. He'll spend three days a week with you while you're here."

Staunt supposed it was unreasonable of him to expect his Guide to devote all his time to him. But Bollinger might at least have stayed around for the first night. Unless the idea was to have the Departing One make his own adaptation to life in the House of Leavetaking.

He toyed with his data terminal, testing its resources. For a while he amused himself by pulling obscure music from the machine: medieval organs, Hummel sonatas, eighteenth-century German opera, odd electronic things from the middle of the twentieth century. But it was impossible to win that game; apparently, if the music had ever been recorded, the computer had access to it. Staunt turned next to books, asking for Hobbes and Hallam, Montaigne and Jonson—not screenings but actual print-out copies of his own, and within minutes after he placed the requisitions, the fresh crisp sheaves of pages began arriving on the same conveyor that had brought his dinner. He put the books aside without looking through them. Perhaps some telephone calls, he thought: my daughter, maybe, or a friend or two. But everyone he knew seemed to live in the East or in Europe, and it was some miserable early hour of the morning there. Staunt gave up the idea of talking to anyone. He dropped into a dull leaden mood. Why had he come to these three little plastic rooms in the desert, giving up his fine well-tended house, his treasures of art, his dogwoods, his books? Surrendering everything for this sterile halfway station on the road to death? I could call Dr. James, I suppose, and tell him I'd like to Go right now. Save the staff some trouble, save the taxpayers some money, save my family the bother of going through the Farewell rituals. How is Going managed, anyway? He believed it was a drug. Something sweet and pleasant, and then the body goes to sleep. A tranquil death, like Socrates', just a chill climbing quickly through the legs toward the heart. Tonight. Tonight. To Go tonight.

No.

I must play the game properly. I must do my Going with style.

He turned to the terminal and said, "I'd like someone to show me down to the recreation center."

Miss Elliot, the nurse, appeared, as though she had been stored waiting in a box just outside his suite. So far as Staunt still had the capacity to tell, she was a handsome girl, golden-haired and buxom, with fine clear skin and large glossy blue eyes, but there was something remote and impersonal and mechanical about her; she could almost have been a robot. "The recreation center? Certainly, Mr. Staunt." She offered her arm. He gestured as if to refuse it, but then, remembering his earlier struggle to walk, took it anyway, and leaned heavily on her as they went out. Thus I accept my mortality. Thus I speed my final decline.

A dropshaft took them into an immense, brightly lit area somewhere far underground. There was a moving slidewalk here; Miss Elliot guided him onto it and they trundled along a few hundred yards, to a step-off turntable that fed him smoothly into the recreation center.

It was a good-sized room, divided chapel-fashion at its far end into smaller rooms. Staunt saw screens, data terminals, playback units, and other access equipment, all of it duplicating what every Departing One had in his own suite. But of course they came here out of loneliness; it might be more comforting to do one's reading or listening in public, he thought. There also were games of various kinds suitable for the very old, nothing that required any great degree of stamina or coordination: stochastic chess, polyrhythmers, double-orbit, things like that. We slide into childhood on our way to the grave.

There were about fifty Departing Ones in the center, he guessed. Most of them looked as old as the four who had met his copter earlier in the day; a few, frighteningly, seemed even older. Some looked much younger, no more than seventy or eighty. Staunt thought at first they might be Guides, but he saw on their faces a certain placid slackness that seemed common to all these Departing Ones, a look of dim mindless content, of resignation, of death-in-life. Evidently, one did not have to be heavily stricken in years to feel the readiness to Go.

"Shall I introduce you to some of the other Departing Ones?" Miss Elliot asked.

"Please. Yes."

She took him around. This is Henry Staunt, she said again and again. The famous composer. And she told him their names. He recognized none of them. David Golding, Michael Green, Ella Freeman, Seymour Church, Katherine Parks. Names. Withered faces. Miss Elliot supplied no identifying tags for any of them, as she had done for him; no "Ella Freeman, the famous actress," no "David Golding, the famous astronaut," no "Seymour Church, the famous financier." They had not been actresses or astronauts or financiers. God alone knew what they had been; Miss Elliot wasn't saying, and Staunt found himself without the energy to ask. Accountants, stockbrokers, housewives, teachers, programmers. Anything. Nothing. Just people. Ordinary people. Survivors from previous geological epochs. So old, so old, so old. In hardly any of them could Staunt detect the glimmer of life, and he saw for the first time how fortunate he had been to reach this great old age of his intact. The walking dead. Seymour Church, the famous zombie. Katherine Parks, the famous somnambulist. None of them seemed ever to have heard of him. Staunt was not surprised at that; even a famous composer learns early in life that he will be famous only among a minority of his countrymen. But still, those blank looks, those unfocused eyes. Pleased to meet you, Mr. Stout. How d'ye do, Mr. Stint. Hello. Hello. Hello.

"Have you met some interesting people?" Miss Elliot said, passing close to Staunt half an hour later.

"I'm more tired than I thought," Staunt said. "Perhaps you should take me back to my suite."

Already the names of the other Departing Ones were slipping from his mind. He had had brief, fragmentary conversations with six or seven of them, but they could not keep their minds on what they were saying, and neither, he discovered, could he. A terrible fatigue that he had never known before was settling over him. Senility must be contagious, he decided. Thirty minutes among the Departing Ones and I am as they are. I must get away.

Miss Elliot guided him to his room. Mr. Falkenbridge, the orderly, appeared unbidden, helped him undress, and put him to bed. Staunt lay awake a long time in the unfamiliar bed, his tense mind ticking relentlessly. A time-zone problem, he thought. He was tempted to ask for a sedative, but as he searched for the strength to sit up and ring for Miss Elliot, sleep suddenly captured him and drew him down into a pit of darkness.

Seven

In the next few days he managed to get to know some of the others. It was a task he imposed on himself. Throughout his life Staunt had negotiated, sometimes with difficulty, the narrow boundary between reserve and snobbery, trying to keep to himself without seeming to reject the company of others, and he was particularly eager not to withdraw into self-sufficiency at this time of all times. So he sought out his fellow Departing Ones and did what he could to scale the barriers separating them from him.

It was late in life to be making new friends, though. He found it hard to communicate much about himself to them, or to draw from them anything of consequence beyond the bare facts of their lives. As he suspected, they were a dull lot, people who had never achieved anything in particular except longevity. Staunt did not hold that against them: he saw no reason why everyone had to bubble with creativity, and he had deeply loved many whose only gifts had been gifts of friendship. But these people, coming now to the end of their days, were hollowed by time's erosions, and there was so little left of them that even ordinary human warmth had been worn away. They answered his questions perfunctorily and rarely responded with questions of their own. "A composer? How nice. I used to listen to music sometimes." He succeeded in discovering that Seymour Church had been living in the House of Leavetaking for eight months at his son's insistence but did not want to Go; that Ella Freeman had had (or believed she had had) a love affair, more than a century ago, with a man who later became President; that David Golding had been married six times and was inordinately proud of it; that each of these Departing Ones clung to some such trifling biographical datum that gave him a morsel of individual identity. But Staunt was unable to penetrate beyond that one identifying datum; either nothing else was in them, or they could not or would not reveal themselves to him. A dull lot, but Staunt was no longer in a position to choose his companions for their merits.

During his first week in Arizona most of the members of his family came to see him, beginning with Paul and young Henry, Crystal's son. They stayed with him for two days. David, Crystal's other son, arrived a little later, along with his wife; their children, and one of their grandchildren; then Paul's two daughters showed up, and an assortment of youngsters. Everyone, even the young ones, wore sickly-sweet expressions of bliss, . They were determined to look upon Staunt's Going as a beautiful event. In their conversations with him they never spoke of Going at all, only of family gossip, music, springtime, flowers, reminiscences. Staunt played their game. He had no more wish for emotional turmoil than they did; he wanted to back amiably out of their lives, smiling and bowing. He was careful, therefore, not to imply in anything he said that he was shortly going to end his life. He pretended that he had merely come to this place in the desert for a brief vacation.

The only one who did not visit him, aside from a few great-grandchildren, was his daughter Crystal. When he tried to phone her, he got no reply. His callers avoided any mention of her. Was she ill, Staunt wondered? Dead, even? "What are you trying to hide from me?" he asked his son finally. "Where's Crystal?"

"Crystal's fine," Paul said.

"That's not what I asked. Why hasn't she come here?"

"Actually she hasn't been entirely well."

"As I suspected. She's seriously ill, and you think the shock of hearing about it will harm me."

Paul shook his head. "It isn't like that at all."

"What's wrong with her?" Visions of cancer, heart surgery, brain tumors. "Has she had some kind of transplant? Is she in a hospital?"

"It isn't a physical problem. Crystal's simply suffering from fatigue. She's gone to Luna Dome for a rest."

"I spoke to her last month," Staunt said. "She looked all right then. I want the truth, Paul."

"The truth."

"The truth, yes."

Paul's eyes closed wearily for a moment, and in that moment Staunt saw his son for what he was, an old man, though not so old a man as he. After a pause Paul said in a flat, toneless voice, "The trouble is that Crystal hasn't accepted your Going very well. I called her about it, right after you told me, and she became hysterical. She thinks you're being hoodwinked, that your Guide is part of a conspiracy to do away with you, that your decision is at least ten or fifteen years premature. And she can't speak calmly about it, so we felt it was best to get her away where she wasn't likely to speak to you, to keep her from disturbing you. There. That's the story. I wasn't going to tell you."

"Silly of you to hide it."

"We didn't want to spoil your Going with a lot of carrying on."

"My Going won't spoil that easily. I'd like to talk to her, Paul. She may benefit from whatever help I can give her. If I can make her see Going for what it really is—if I can convince her that her outlook is unhealthy—Paul, set up a call to Luna Dome for me, will you? The Fulfillment people will pay. Crystal needs me. I have to make her understand."

"If you insist," Paul said.

Somehow, though, technical problems prevented the placing of the call that day, and the next, and the one after that. And then Paul left the House of Leavetaking. When Staunt phoned him at home to find out where on the moon Crystal actually was, he became evasive and said that she had recently transferred from one sanatorium to another. It would be a few more days, Paul said, before the call could be placed. Seeing his son's agitation, Staunt ceased pressing the issue. They did not want him to talk to Crystal. Crystal's hysterics would ruin his Going, they felt. They would not give him the chance to soothe her. So be it. He could not fight them. This must be a difficult time for the whole family; if they wished to think that Crystal would upset him so terribly, he would let the matter drop, for a while. Perhaps he could speak to her later. There would be time before his Going. Perhaps. Perhaps.

Eight

Every Monday, Wednesday, and Friday, Martin Bollinger came to him, usually in midafternoon, an hour or so after lunch. Generally Staunt received his Guide in his suite, although sometimes, on the cooler days, they strolled together through the garden. Their meetings invariably fell into three well-defined segments. First, Bollinger would display lively interest in Staunt's current activities. What books are you reading? Have you been listening to music? Are there any interesting Departing Ones for you to talk with? Is the staff taking good care of you? Do your relatives visit you often enough? Has the urge to compose anything come over you? Is there anyone you'd especially like to see? Are you thinking of traveling at all? And so on and so on, the same questions surfacing frequently.

When the questions were over, Bollinger would glide into the second phase, a conversation with a quiet autumnal tone, a recollection of vanished days. Sometimes he spoke as though Staunt had already Gone; he talked of Staunt's compositions in the same way he might refer to those of some early master. The symphonies, Bollinger would say: what a testament, what a mighty cumulative structure, nothing like them since Mahler, surely. The quartets, obviously akin to Beethoven's, yet thoroughly contemporary, true expressions of their composer and his times. And Staunt would nod, solemnly accepting Bollinger's verdicts in curious, dreamy objectivity. They would talk of mutual friends in the same way, viewing them as closed books, as cubes rather than as living, evolving persons. Staunt saw that Bollinger was helping to place distance between him and the life he had lived. Already, he felt remote from that life. After several weeks in the House of Leavetaking, he was coming to look upon himself more as someone who had very carefully studied Henry Staunt's biography than as the actual living Staunt, the inhabitant of Staunt's body.

The third phase of each meeting saw Bollinger turn quite frankly to matters directly related to Staunt's Going. Constantly he pressed Staunt to examine his motives, and he avoided the false gentleness with which everyone else seemed to treat him. The Guide was pursuing truth. Do you truly wish to Go, Henry? If so, have you started to give thought to the date of your Leavetaking? Will you stay in the world another five weeks? Three months? Six? No, no one's rushing you. Stay a year, if you want. I merely wonder if you've looked realistically, yet, at what it means to Go. Whether you comprehend your purpose in asking for it. Get behind the euphemism, Henry. Going is dying. The termination of all. For you, the end of the universe. Is this what you want, Henry? Is it? Is it? Is it? I'm not trying to make it harder for you. I'm trying to make it more pure. A truly spiritual Going, the rarest kind. But only if you're ready. Are you aware that you can withdraw from the whole undertaking at any point? It isn't cowardly to turn away from Going. See Hallam: Going isn't suicide, it's a sweet renunciation, properly reserved only for those who fully understand their motives. Anyone can kill himself in a fit of gloom. A proper going requires spiritual strength. Some people enroll in a House of Leavetaking two, even three times before they can take that last step. Yes, they go through the entire ritual of Farewell, almost to the end—and then they say they want to go home, and we send them home. We never push. We are not interested in sending victims out of the world. Only volunteers whose eyes are open. Have you been reading Hallam, Henry? Our philosopher of death. Look into yourself before you leap. Ask yourself, Is this what I want?

"What I want is to Go," Staunt would reply. But he could not tell Bollinger how long it would actually be before he would find himself ready to take his leave.

There seemed to be some pattern in this thrice-weekly pas de deux of conversation with his Guide. Bollinger appeared to be maneuvering him patiently and circuitously toward some sort of apocalyptic burst of joyful insight, a radiant moment of comprehension in which he would be able to say, feeling worthy of Hallam as he did, "Now I shall Go." But the maneuvers did not seem successful. Often, Staunt came away from Bollinger confused and depressed, less certain than ever of his desire to Go.

By the fourth week, most of his time was being given over to reading. Music had largely palled for him. His family, having made the obligatory first round of visits, had stopped coming; they would not return to the House of Leavetaking until word reached them that he was in the final phase of his Going and ready for his Farewell ceremony. He had said all he cared to say to his friends. The recreation center bored him and the company of the other Departing Ones chilled him. Therefore he read. At the outset, he went about it dutifully, mechanically, taking it up solely as a chore for the improvement of his mind in its final hours. Like an old pharaoh trying to repair his looks before he must be delivered into the hands of the mummifiers, Staunt meant to polish his soul with philosophy while he still had the chance. It was in that spirit that he plodded through Hobbes, whose political ideas had set him ablaze when he was nineteen, and who merely seemed crabbed and sour now. *It may seem strange to some man, that has not well weighed these things; that nature should thus dissociate, and render men apt to invade, and destroy one another: and he may therefore, not trusting to this inference, made from the passions, desire perhaps to have the same confirmed by experience. Let him therefore consider with himself:, when taking a journey, he arms himself, and seeks to go well accompanied; when going to sleep, he locks his doors; when even in his house he locks his chests; and this when he knows there be laws, and public officers, armed, to revenge all injuries shall be done him; what opinion he has of his fellow-subjects, when he rides armed; of his fellow citizens, when he locks his doors; and of his children, and servants, when he locks his chests. Does he not there as much accuse mankind by his actions, as I do by my words?* Growing up in a tense, bleak world of peace that was really war, Staunt had found it easy to accept Hobbes' dark teachings. Now he was not so sure that the natural condition of mankind was a state of conflict, every man at war with every other man. Something had changed in the world, it seemed. Or in Staunt. He put Hobbes away in displeasure.

He was almost afraid to turn to Montaigne, fearing that that other great guide of his youth might also have soured over the long decades. But no. Instantly the old charm claimed him. *I cannot accept the way in which we fix the span of our lives. I have observed that the sages hold it to be much shorter than is commonly supposed. "What!" said the younger Cato to those who would prevent him from killing himself, "am I now of an age to be reproached with yielding up my life too soon?" And yet he was but forty-eight years of age. He thought that age very ripe and well advanced, considering how few men reach it.* Yes. Yes. And: *Wherever your life ends, it is all there. The profit of life is not in its length but in the use we put it to: many a man has lived long, who has lived little; see to it as long as you are here. It lies in your will, not in the number of years, to make the best of life. Did you think never to arrive at a place you were incessantly making for? Yet there is no road but has an end. And if society is any comfort to you, is not the world going the selfsame way as you?* Yes. Perfect. Staunt read deep into the night, and sent for a bottle of Chateau d'Yquem from the House of Leavetaking's well-stocked cellars, and solemnly toasted old Montaigne in his own sleek wine, and read on until morning. *There is no road but has an end.*

When he was done with Montaigne, he turned to Ben Jonson, first the familiar works, *Volpone* and *The Silent Woman* and *The Case is Altered,* then the black, explosive plays of later years, *Bartholomew Fair* and *The New Inn* and *The Devil Is an Ass.* Staunt had always felt a strong affinity for the Elizabethans, and particularly for Jonson, that crackling, hissing, scintillating man, whose stormy, sprawling plays blazed with a nightmarish intensity that Shakespeare, the greater poet, seemed to lack. As he had always vowed he would, Staunt submerged himself in Jonson, until the sound and rhythm of Jonson's verse echoed and reechoed like thunder in his overloaded brain, and the texture of Jonson's mind seemed inlaid on his own. *The Magnetic Lady, Cynthia's Revels, Catiline his Conspiracy*—no play was too obscure, too hermetic, for Staunt in his gluttony. And one afternoon during this period he found himself doing an unexpected thing. From his data terminal he requested a print-out of the final pages of *The New Inn*'s first act, with an inch of blank space between each line. At the top of the sheet he wrote carefully, *The New Inn, an Opera by Henry Staunt, from the play of Ben Jonson.* Then, turning to Lovel's long speech, "O thereon hangs a history, mine host," Staunt began to pencil musical notations beneath the words, idly at first, then with sudden earnest fervor as the proper contours of the vocal line suggested themselves to him. Within minutes he had turned the entire speech into an aria and had. even scribbled some preliminary marginal notes to himself about orchestration. The style of the music was strange to him, a spare, lean, angular sort of melodiousness, thorny and complex, with a curiously archaic flavor. It was the sort of music Alban Berg might have written during an extended visit to the early seventeenth century. It did not sound much like Staunt's own kind of thing. My late style, he thought. Probably the aria was impossible to sing. No matter: this was how the muse had called it forth. It was the first sustained composing Staunt had done in years. He stared at the completed aria in wonder, astonished that music could still flow from him like that, welling up without conscious command from the gushing spring within.

For an instant he was tempted to feed what he had written into a synthesizer and get back a rough orchestration. To hear the sound of it, with the baritone riding tensely over the swooping strings, might carry him on to set down the next page of the score, and the next, and the next. He resisted. The world already had enough operas that no one listened to. Shaking his head, smiling sadly, he dated the page, initialed it in his customary way, jotted down an opus number—by guesswork, for he was far from his ledgers—and, folding the sheet, put it away among his papers. Yet the music went on unfolding in his mind.

Nine

In his ninth week at the House of Fulfillment, finding himself stranded in stagnant waters, Staunt sought Dr. James and applied for the memory-jolt treatment. It seemed to be the only option left, short of Going, and he rarely contemplated Going these days. He was done with Jonson, and the impulse to request other books had not come to him; he peeked occasionally at his single page of *The New Inn,* but did not resume work on it; he was guarded and aloof in his conversations with Bollinger and with his occasional visitors; he realized that he was sliding imperceptibly into a deathlike passivity, without actually coming closer to his exit. He would not return to his former life, and he could not yet surrender and Go. Possibly the memory jolt would nudge him off dead center.

"It'll take six hours to prepare you," Dr. James said, his long nose twitching with enthusiasm for Staunt's project. "The brain has to be cleared of all fatigue products, and the autonomic nervous system needs a tuning. When would you like to begin?"

"Now," Staunt said.

They cleansed and tuned him, and took him back to his suite and put him to bed, and hooked him into his metabolic monitor. "If you get overexcited," Dr. James explained, "the monitor will automatically adjust the intensity of your emotional flow downward." Staunt was willing to take his chances with the intensity of his emotional flow, but the medic was insistent. The monitor stayed on. "It isn't psychic pain we're worried about," Dr. James said. "There's never any of that. But. sometimes—an excess of remembered love, do you know?—a burst of happiness—it could be too much, we've found." Staunt nodded. He would not argue the point. The doctor produced a hypodermic and pressed its ultrasonic snout against Staunt's arm. Briefly Staunt wondered whether this was all a trick, whether the drug would really send him to his Going rather than for a trip along his time-track, but he pushed the irrational notion aside, and the snout made its brief droning sound and the mysterious dark fluid leaped into his veins.

Ten

He hears the final crashing chords of *The Trials of Job,* and the curtain, a sheet of dense purple light, springs up from the floor of the stage. Applause. Curtain calls for the singers. The conductor on stage, now, bowing, smiling. The chorus master, even. Cascades of cheers. All about him swirl the glittering mobile chandeliers of the Haifa Opera House. Someone is shouting incomprehensible jubilant words in his ear: the language is Hebrew, Staunt realizes. He says, Yes, yes, thank you so very much. They want him to stand and acknowledge the applause. Edith sits beside him, flushed with excitement, her eyes sparkling. His mind supplies the date: September 9, 1999. "Let them see you," Edith whispers through the tumult. A hand claps his shoulder. Wild eyes blazing into his own: Mannheim, the critic. "The opera of the century!" he cries. Staunt forces himself to rise. They are screaming his name. Staunt! Staunt! Staunt! The audience is his. Two thousand berserk Israelis, his to command. What shall he say to them? *Sieg! Heil! Sieg! Heil!* He chokes on his own appalling unvoiced joke. In the end he can do nothing but wave and grin and topple back into his seat. Edith rubs his arm lovingly. His glowing bride. His night of triumph. To write an opera at all these days is a mighty task; to enjoy a premiere like this is heavenly. Now the audience wants an encore. The conductor at his station. The curtain fades. Job alone on stage: his final scene, the proud bass voice crying, "Behold, I am vile," and the voice of the Lord replying to him out of a thousand loudspeakers, filling all the world with sound: "Deck thyself now with majesty and excellency." Staunt weeps at his own music. If I live a hundred years, I will never forget this night, he tells himself.

Eleven

"The copter went down so suddenly, Mr. Staunt. They had it on the stabilizer beam all through the storm, but you know it isn't always possible—"

"And my wife? And my wife?"

"We're so sorry, Mr. Staunt."

Twelve

He sits at the keyboard fretting over the theory and harmony. His legs are not yet long enough to reach the piano's pedals: a nuisance, but temporary. He closes his eyes and strikes the keyboard. This is the key of C major, the easy one. The tonic chord. The dominant. Why did they wait so long to tell him about these things? He builds chord after chord. *I will now moderate into the key of D minor. Modulate. I do this and this and this.* He is nine years old. All this long hot Sunday afternoon he has explored this wondrous other language of sounds. While his family sits frozen by the television set. "Henry? Henry, they're going to be coming out of the module any minute!" He shrugs. What does the moonwalk matter to him? The moon is dead and far away. And this is the world of D minor. He has his own exploring to do today. "Henry, he's out! He came down the ladder!" Fine. Tonic. Dominant. And the diminished seventh. The words are strange. But how easy it is to go deeper and deeper into the maze of sound.

Thirteen

"The faculty and students take great pleasure, Mr. Staunt, to present you on the occasion of your one-hundredth birthday with this memorial of a composer who shared your divine productivity if not your blessed longevity: the original manuscript of Mozart's 'Divertimento in B,' Köchel number—"

Fourteen

"A boy, yes. We're calling him Paul, after Edith's father. And what an odd feeling it is to tell myself I have a son. You know, I'm forty-five years old. More than half my life gone, I suppose. And now a son."

Fifteen

The sun is huge in the sky, and the beach is ablaze with shimmering heat-furies, and beyond the crescent of pink sand the green Caribbean rests against its bed like water in a quiet tub. These are the hours when he remains under cover, in some shady hammock, reading, perhaps making notes for an essay or his next composition. But there is the girl again, crouched by the shore, gently poking at the creatures of the tidal pool, the shy anemones and the little sea-slugs and the busy hermit crabs. So he must expose his vulnerable skin, for tomorrow he will fly back to New York, and this may be his last chance to introduce himself to her. He has watched her through this whole week of vacation. Not a girl, exactly. Surely at least twenty-five years old. Very much her own person: self-contained, coolly precise, alert, elegant. Tempting. He has rarely felt so drawn toward anyone. Preserving his bachelorhood has been no chore for him; he glides as easily from woman to woman as he does from city to city. But there is something about the eyes of this Edith, something about her smile, that pulls him. He knows he is being foolish. All this is pure fantasy: he has no idea what she is like, where her interests lie. That look of intelligence and sympathy may be all his own invention; the girl inside the face may in truth be drab and empty, some programmer on holiday, her soul a dull haze of daydreams about glamorous holovision stars. Yet he must approach. The sun pounds his sensitive skin. She looks up, smiling, from the tidal pool. A purple sea-slug crawls lightly across her palm. He kneels beside her. She offers him the sea-slug, and he lets it crawl on his hand, and they laugh, and she points out limpets and periwinkles and barnacles for him, until there is a kind of contact between them through the creatures of this salty pond, and at last he says, feeling clumsy about it, "We haven't even introduced ourselves. I'm Henry Staunt."

"I know," Edith says. "The composer."

And it all becomes so much easier.

Sixteen

"—and the gold medal for the outstanding work in extended symphonic form by a student under sixteen years of age goes, as I'm sure everyone has already realized, to Henry Staunt, who—"

Seventeen

"And my wife? And my wife?"
"We're so sorry, Mr. Staunt."

Eighteen

"As long as we're getting into that end of the evening, Henry, I'll allow myself the privilege of delivering a little analysis, too. Do you know what the real trouble with you is? With your music, with your soul, with everything? You don't suffer. You've never been touched by pain, or, if you have, it doesn't sink in. Look, you're forty years old, and you've never known anything but success, and your music is played everywhere, an incredible achievement for a living composer, and you could pass for thirty. Or even twenty-seven. Time doesn't claw you. I don't recommend suffering, mind you, but I do say it tempers an artist's soul; it adds a richness of texture that—forgive me—you lack, Henry. You know, you could live to be a very old man, considering the way you don't seem to age, and someday, when you're ninety-seven or one hundred five or something like that, you may realize that you've never really intersected reality, that you've kept yourself insulated, and that in a sense you haven't really lived at all or created anything at all or—forgive me, Henry. I take it all back, even if you are still smiling. Not even a friend should say things like that. Not even a friend."

Nineteen

"The Pulitzer Prize for Music for the year 2002—"

Twenty

"I Edith do take thee Henry to be my lawful wedded husband—"

Twenty-One

"It isn't as if she was a bride, Henry. God knows it's terrible to lose her that way, but she was yours for fifty years, Henry, *fifty years,* the kind of marriage most people hardly dare to dream of having, and if she's gone, well, be content that you had the fifty, at least."

"I wish we had crashed together, though."

"Don't be childish. You're—what?—eighty-five, eighty-seven years old? You've got fifteen or twenty healthy and productive years ahead of you. More, if you're lucky. People live to fantastic ages nowadays. You might see one hundred ten or one hundred fifteen."

"Without Edith, what good is that?"

Twenty-Two

"Put your hands in the middle of the keyboard. Spread the fingers out as wide as you can. Wider. Wider. That's the boy! Now, Henry, this is what we call middle C—"

Twenty-Three

In haste, stumbling, he goes on into his studio. The big room holds the tangible residue of his long career. Over here, the music itself, in recorded performance: disks and cassettes for the early works, sparkling playback cubes for the later ones. Here are the manuscripts, uniformly bound in red half-morocco, one of his little vanities. Here are the scrapbooks of reviews and the programs of concerts. Here are the trophies. Here are the volumes of his critical writings. Staunt has been a busy man. He looks at the titles stamped on the bindings of the manuscripts: the symphonies, the string quartets, the concerti, the miscellaneous chamber works, the songs, the sonatas, the cantatas, the operas. So much. So much. Staunt feels no sense of having wasted his time, though, filling this room with what it holds. Never in the past hundred years has a week gone by without a performance of one of his compositions somewhere. That is sufficient justification for having written, for having lived. And yet, one hundred thirty-six years is such a long time.

He pushes cubes into playback slots, getting three of his works going at once, bringing wild skeins of sound out of the room's assortment of speakers, and stands in the middle, trembling a little, accepting the sonic barrage. After perhaps four minutes he cuts off the sound and orders his telephone to ring up the Office of Fulfillment.

"My Guide is Martin Bollinger," he says. "Would you let him know that I'd like to be transferred to the House of Leavetaking as soon as possible?"

Twenty-Four

Dr. James had told him, long before, that Departing Ones invariably came out of memory jolts in a state of ecstasy, and that frequently they were in such raptures that they insisted on Going immediately, before the high could ebb. Emerging from the drug, Staunt searched in vain for the ecstasy. Where? He was wholly calm. For some hours past, or maybe just a few minutes—he had no idea how long the memory jolt has lasted—he had tasted morsels of his past, scraps of conversation, bits of scenery, random textures of contact, a stew of incidents, nonchronological, unsorted. His music and his wife. His wife and his music. A pretty thin gruel for one hundred thirty-six years of life. Where were the storms? Where were the tempests? A single great tragedy, yes, and otherwise everything tranquil. Too orderly a life, too sane, too empty, and now, permitted to review it, he found himself with nothing to grasp but applause, which slipped through his fingers, and his love of Edith, and even that had lost its magic. Where was that excess of remembered love that Dr. James had said could be dangerous? Perhaps they had monitored him too closely, tuning down the intensity of his spirit. Or perhaps it was his spirit that was at fault. Old and dry, pale and lean.

Unlike the others he had heard about, he did not request immediate Going after his voyage. Without that terminal ecstasy, why Go? He felt not exactly depressed but certainly lowered; his tour of his yesterdays had thrust him into a sort of stasis, a paralysis of the will, that left him hung up as before, enmeshed by the strands of his own quiet past.

But if Staunt remained unready to Go, not so with others. "You are invited to the Farewell ceremony of David Golding," Miss Elliot told him the day after his memory jolt.

Golding was the man who had had six wives—outliving some, divorcing some, being divorced by some. His heroic husbandry was no longer apparent: now he was small and gnarled and fleshless, and because he was nearly blind, his pinched ungenerous face was disfigured by the jutting cones of two optical transducers. They said he was one hundred twenty-five years old, but to Staunt he looked at least two hundred. For the Farewell ceremony, though, the technicians of the House of Leavetaking had transformed the little old man into something sublime. His face gleamed with make-up that obliterated the crevices of decades; he held himself buoyantly upright, no doubt inflated into a semblance of his ancient virility by some drug; he was clad in a radiant, shimmering gown. Scores of relatives and friends surrounded him in the Chambers of Farewell, a brightly decorated underground suite opposite the recreation center. Staunt, as he entered, was dismayed by the size of the crowd. So many, so young, so noisy.

Ella Freeman sidled up to him and touched her shriveled hand to Staunt's arm. "Look there: two of his wives. He hadn't seen one in sixty years. And his sons. All of them, his sons. Two or three by each wife!"

The ceremony, conducted by the relatively young man who was Golding's Guide, was elegiac in tone, brief, sweet. Standing under the emblem of the Office of Fulfillment, the wheel and the gears, the Guide spoke briefly of the philosophy of making room for others, of the beauty of a willing departure. Then he praised the Departing One in vague, general terms; one of his sons delivered a more specific eulogy; lastly, Seymour Church, chosen to represent Golding's companions at the House of Leavetaking, croaked out a short, almost incoherent speech of farewell. To this the Departing One, who seemed transfigured with joy and already at least halfway into the next world, made reply in a few faint syllables, blurrily expressing gratitude for his long and happy life. Golding barely appeared to comprehend what was going on; he sat beaming in a kind of throne, dreamy, distant. Staunt wondered if he had been drugged into a stupor.

When the speeches were done, refreshments were served. Then, accompanied only by his closest kin, fifteen or twenty people, Golding was ushered into the innermost room of the Chambers of Farewell. The door slid shut behind him, and in his absence the Leavetaking party proceeded merrily.

There were four such events in the next five weeks At two of them—the Goings of Michael Green and Katherine Parks—Staunt was asked to give the speech of farewell. It was a task that he performed gracefully, serenely, and, he thought, with a good deal of eloquence. He spoke for ten minutes about Michael Green, for close to fifteen about Katherine Parks, talking not so much about the Departing Ones, whom he had scarcely come to know well, but about the entire philosophy of Going, the beauty and wonder of the act of world-renunciation. It was not customary for the giver of the speech of farewell to manage such sustained feats, and his audience listened in total fascination; if the occasion had permitted it, Staunt suspected, they would have applauded.

So he had a new vocation, and several Departing Ones whom he did not know at all accelerated their own Goings so that they would not fail to have Staunt speak at the rites. It was summer now, and Arizona was caught in glistening tides of heat. Staunt never went outdoors any longer; he spent much of his time mingling in the recreation center, doing research, so to speak, for future oratory. He rarely read these days. He never listened to music. He had settled into a pleasing, quiet routine. This was his fourth month at the House of Leavetaking. Except for Seymour Church, who still refused to be nudged into Going, Staunt was now the senior Departing One in point of length of residence. And at the end of July, Church at last took his leave. Staunt, of course, spoke, touching on the Departing One's slow journey toward Going, and it was difficult for him to avoid self-conscious references to his own similar reluctance. Why do I tarry here? Staunt wondered. Why do I not say the word?

Every few weeks his son Paul visited him. Staunt found their meetings difficult. Paul, showing signs of strain and anxiety, always seemed on the verge of blurting out, "Why don't you. Go, already?" And Staunt would have no answer, for he did not know the answer. He had read Hallam four times. Philosophically and psychologically he was prepared to Go. Yet he remained.

Twenty-Five

In mid-August Martin Bollinger entered his suite, held out a sheet of paper, and said, "What's this, Henry?"

Staunt glanced at it. It was a photocopy of the aria from *The New Inn*. "Where did you find that?" he asked.

"One of the staff people came across it while tidying your room."

"I thought we were entitled to privacy."

"This isn't an inquisition, Henry. I'm just curious. Have you started to compose again?"

"That scrap is all I wrote. It was months ago."

"It's fascinating music," Bollinger said.

"Is it, now? I thought it was rather harsh and forced, myself."

"No. No. Not at all. You always talked about a Ben Jonson opera, didn't you? And now you've begun it."

"I was enlivening a dull day," said Staunt. "Mere scribbling."

"Henry, would you like to get out of this place?"

"Are we back to *that?*"

"Obviously you still have music in you. Perhaps a great opera."

"Which you mean to squeeze out of me, eh? Don't talk nonsense. There's nothing left in me, Martin. I'm here to Go."

"You haven't Gone, though."

"You've noticed that," Staunt said.

"It was made clear to you at the beginning that you wouldn't be rushed. But I've begun to suspect, Henry, that you aren't interested in Going at all, that you're marking time here, perhaps incubating this opera, perhaps coming to terms with something indigestible in your soul. Whatever. You don't have to Go. We'll send you home. Finish *The New Inn*. Think the thoughts you want to think. Reapply for Going next year or the year after."

"You want that opera out of me, don't you?"

"I want you to be happy," said Bollinger. "I want your Going to be *right*. The bit of music here is just a clue to your inner state."

"There won't be any opera, Martin. And I don't plan to leave Omega Prime alive. To have put my family through this ordeal, and then to come home, to tell them it's' all been just a holiday lark out here—no. No."

"As you wish," Bollinger said. He smiled and turned away, leaving an unspoken question hanging like a sword between them: *If you want to Go, Henry, why don't you Go?*

Twenty-Six

Staunt realized that he had taken on the status of a permanent Departing One, a kind of curator emeritus of the House of Fulfillment. Here he was, enjoying this life of ease and dignity, accepting the soft-voiced attentions of those who meant to slide him gently from the world, playing his role of patriarch among the shattered hulks that were the other Departing Ones here. Each week new ones came; he greeted them solemnly, helped them blend with those already in residence, and, in time, presided over their Goings. And he stayed on. Why? Why? Surely not out of fear of dying. Why, then, was he making a career out of his Going?

So that he might have the prestige of being a hero of his time, possibly—an exponent of noble renunciation, a practitioner of joyful departure. Making much glib talk of turning the wheel and creating a place for those to come—a twenty-first-century Sydney Carton, standing by the guillotine and praising the far, far better thing that he will do, only he finds himself enjoying the part so much that he forgets to kneel and present his neck to the blade.

Or maybe he is only interrupting the boredom of a too-bland life with a feigned fling at dying. The glamour of becoming a Departing One injecting interesting complexities into a static existence. But diversion and not death his real object. Yes? If that's it, Henry, go home and write your opera; the holiday should have ended by now.

He came close to summoning Bollinger and asking to be sent home. But he fought the impulse down. To leave Omega Prime now would be the true cowardice. He owed the world a death. He had occupied this body long enough. His place was needed; soon he would Go. Soon. Soon. Soon.

Twenty-Seven

At the beginning of September there were four days in a row of rain, an almost unknown occurrence in that part of Arizona. Miss Elliot said that the Hopi, doing their annual snake dances on their mesas far to the north, had overdone things this year and sent rain clouds all through the state. Staunt, to the horror of the staff, went out each day to stand in the rain, letting the cool drops soak his thin gown, watching the water sink swiftly into the parched red soil. "You'll catch your death of cold," Mr. Falkenbridge told him sternly. Staunt laughed.

He requested another wide-spaced print-out of *The New Inn* and tried to set the opening scene. Nothing came. He could not find the right vocal line, nor could he recapture the strange color of the earlier aria. The tones and textures of Ben Jonson were gone from his head. He gave the project up without regret.

There were three Farewell ceremonies in eight days. Staunt attended them all, and spoke at two of them.

Arbitrarily, he chose September 19 as the day of his own Going. But he told no one about his decision, and September 19 came and went with Staunt unchanged.

At the end of the month he told Martin Bollinger, "I'm a fraud. I haven't gotten an inch closer to Going in all the time I've been here. I never wanted to Go at all. I still want to live, to see and do things, to experience things. I came here out of desperation, because I was stale, I was bored, I needed novelty. To toy with death, to live a little scenario of dying—that was all I was after. Excitement. An event in an eventless life: Henry Staunt Prepares to Die. I've been using all you people as players in a cynical charade."

Bollinger said quietly, "Shall I arrange for you to go home, then, Henry?"

"No. No. Get me Dr. James. And notify my family that my Farewell ceremony will be held a week from today. It's time for me to Go."

"But if you still want to live—"

"What better time to Go?" Staunt asked.

Twenty-Eight

They were all here, close around him. Paul had come, and Crystal, too, back from the moon and looking feeble, and all the grandchildren and the great-grandchildren, and the friends, the conductors and the younger composers and some critics, more than a hundred people in all coming to see him off. Staunt, undrugged but already beginning to ascend, had moved coolly among them, thanking them for attending his Leavetaking party, welcoming them to his Farewell ceremony. He was amazed at how calm he was. Seated now in the throne of honor, he listened to the final orations and endured without objection a scrambled medley of his most famous compositions, obviously assembled hastily by someone inexpert in such matters. Martin Bollinger, giving the main eulogy, quoted heavily from Hallam: "Too often we delude ourselves into thinking we are truly ready, when actually we have not reached readiness at all, and choose Going out of unworthy or shallow motives. How tragic it is to arrive at the actual moment of Leavetaking and to realize that one has deceived oneself, that one's motivations are false, that one is, in fact, not in the least ready to Go!"

How true, Staunt told himself. And yet how false. For here I am ready to Go and yet not in the least ready, and in my unreadiness lies my readiness.

Bollinger finished what he had to say, and one of the Departing Ones, a man named Bradford who had come to Omega Prime in August, began to fumble through the usual final speech. He stammered and coughed and lost the thread of his words, for he was one hundred forty years old and due for Going himself next week, but somehow he made it to the end. Staunt, paying little attention, beamed at his son and his daughter, his horde of descendants, his admirers, his doctors. He understood now why Departing Ones generally seemed detached from their own Farewell ceremonies: the dreary drone of the speeches launched them early into the shores of paradise.

And then they were serving the refreshments, and now they were about to wheel him into the innermost room. And Staunt said, "May I speak also?"

They looked at him, appalled, frightened, obviously fearing he would wreck the harmony of the occasion with this unconventional, ill-timed intrusion. But they could not refuse. He had delivered so many eulogies for others—now he would speak for himself.

Softly Staunt said, making them strain their ears to hear it, "I accept the concept of the turning wheel, and I gladly yield my place to those who are to come. But let me tell you that this is not an ordinary Going. You know, when I came here I thought I was weary of the world and ready to Go, but yet I stayed, I held back from the brink, I delayed, I pretended. I even—Martin knows this—began another opera. I was told I could go home, and I refused. Hallam forgive me, but I refused. For his way is not the only way of Going. Because life still seems sweet, I give it up today. And so I take my final pleasure: that of relinquishing the only thing left to me worth keeping."

They were whispering. They were staring.

I have said all the wrong things, he thought. I have spoiled the day for them. But whose Going is it? Why should I care about them?

Martin Bollinger, bending low, murmured, "It's still not too late, Henry. We can stop everything right now."

"The final temptation," Staunt said. "And I withstand it. Bring down the curtain. I'm ready to Go."

They wheeled him to the innermost chamber. When they offered him the cup, he seized it, winked at Martin Bollinger, and drained it in a single gulp.

CALIBAN

Now and then I write a story that strikes me as a comic one, although I'm usually chagrined to discover that most other people don't see it as particularly funny. This is one of that sort. It makes its comic effects not through jokes or farcical horseplay, but through unexpected reversals. ("In the country of the beautiful people, the ugly man is king.") But perhaps the comic nature of the piece lies in its verbal play ("I am the latest Thing") rather than in any inherently funny action.

I wrote it in November, 1970, toward the end of that annus mirabilis *that saw me producing a slew of short stories and at least three major novels. (Novels tended to be shorter in those days than they run now, and I wrote faster.) Aside from that hefty fictional output, I managed also in 1970 to write three of the non-fictional books on archaeological and historical themes that I was doing back then—*Clocks for the Ages, The Pueblo Revolt, *and* The Realm of Prester John. *The last was quite a major project indeed, running to some 120,000 words and involving a great deal of research. The year's total output came to more than half a million words, which I've never equaled since, nor would I want to try. How I managed to get that much done in a mere twelve months is a mystery to my present self; but being half as old as I am now may have had something to do with it.*

They have all changed their faces to a standard model. It is the latest thing, which should not be confused with the latest Thing. The latest Thing is me. The latest thing, the latest fad, the latest rage, is for them all to change their faces to a standard model. I have no idea how it is done but I think it is genetic, with the RNA, the DNA, the NDA. Only retroactive. They all come out with blond wavy hair and sparkling blue eyes. And long straight faces with sharp cheekbones. And notched chins and thin lips curling in ironic smiles. Even the black ones: thin lips, blue eyes, blond wavy hair. And pink skins. They all look alike now. The sweet Aryanized world. Our entire planet. Except me. Meee.

I am imperfect. I am blemished. I am unforgiving. I am the latest Thing.

Louisiana said, Would you like to copulate with me? You are so strange. You are so beautiful. Oh, how I desire you, strange being from a strange time. My orifices are yours.

It was a thoughtful offer. I considered it a while, thinking she might be trying to patronize me. At length I notified her of my acceptance. We went to a public copulatorium. Louisiana is taller than I am and her hair is a torrent of spun gold. Her eyes are blue and her face is long and straight. I would say she is about twenty-three years old. In the copulatorium she dissolved her clothes and stood naked before me. She was wearing gold pubic hair that day and her belly was flat and taut. Her breasts were round and slightly elongated and the nipples were very small. Go on, she said, now you dissolve your clothes.

I said, I am afraid to because my body is ugly and you will mock me.

Your body is not ugly, she said. Your body is strange but it is not ugly.

My body is ugly, I insisted. My legs are short and they curve outward and my thighs have bulging muscles and I have black hairy hair all over me. Like an ape. And there is this hideous scar on my belly.

A scar?

Where they took out my appendix, I told her.

This aroused her beyond all probability. Her nipples stood up tall and her face became flushed.

Your appendix? Your appendix was removed?

Yes, I said, it was done when I was fourteen years old, and I have a loathsome red scar on my abdomen.

She asked, What year was it when you were fourteen?

I said, It was 1967, I think.

She laughed and clapped her hands and began to dance around the room. Her breasts bounced up and down, but her long flowing silken hair soon covered them, leaving only the stubby pinkish nipples poking through like buttons. 1967! she cried. Fourteen! Your appendix was removed! 1967!

Then she turned to me and said, My grandfather was born in 1967, I think. How terribly ancient you are. My helix-father's father on the countermolecular side. I didn't realize you were so very ancient.

Ancient and ugly, I said.

Not ugly, only strange, she said.

Strange and ugly, I said. Strangely ugly.

We think you are beautiful, she said. Will you dissolve your clothes now? It would not be pleasing to me to copulate with you if you keep your clothes on.

There, I said, and boldly revealed myself. The bandy legs. The hairy chest. The scarred belly. The bulging shoulders. The short neck. She has seen my lopsided face, she can see my dismal body as well. If that is what she wants.

She threw herself upon me, gasping and making soft noises.

What did Louisiana look like before the change came? Did she have dull stringy hair thick lips a hook nose bushy black eyebrows no chin foul breath one breast bigger than the other splay feet crooked teeth little dark hairs around her nipples a bulging navel too many dimples in her buttocks skinny thighs blue veins in her calves protruding ears? And then did they give her the homogenizing treatment and make her the golden creature she is today? How long did it take? What were the costs? Did the government subsidize the process? Were the large corporations involved? How were these matters handled in the socialist countries? Was there anyone who did not care to be changed? Perhaps Louisiana was born this way. Perhaps her beauty is natural. In any society there are always a few whose beauty is natural.

Dr. Habakkuk and Senator Mandragore spent a great deal of time questioning me in the Palazzo of Mirrors. They put a green plastic dome over my head so that everything I said would be recorded with the proper nuance and intensity. Speak to us, they said. We are fascinated by your antique accent. We are enthralled by your primitive odors. Do you realize that you are our sole representative of the nightmare out of which we have awakened? Tell us, said the Senator, tell us about your brutally competitive civilization. Describe in detail the fouling of the environment. Explain the nature of national rivalry. Compare and contrast methods of political discourse in the Soviet Union and in the United States. Let us have your analysis of the sociological implications of the first voyage to the moon. Would you like to see the moon? Can we offer you any psychedelic drugs? Did you find Louisiana sexually satisfying? We are so glad to have you here. We regard you as a unique spiritual treasure. Speak to us of yesterday's yesterdays, while we listen entranced and enraptured.

Louisiana says that she is eighty-seven years old. Am I to believe this? There is about her a springtime freshness. No, she maintains, I am eighty-seven years old. I was born on March-alternate 11, 2022. Does that depress you? Is my great age frightening to you? See how tight my skin is. See how my teeth gleam. Why are you so disturbed? I am, after all, much younger than you.

I understand that in some cases making the great change involved elaborate surgery. Cornea transplants and cosmetic adjustment of the facial structure. A great deal of organ-swapping went on. There is not much permanence among these people. They are forever exchanging segments of themselves for new and improved segments. I am told that among some advanced groups the use of mechanical limb-interfaces has come to be common, in order that new arms and legs may be plugged in with a minimum of trouble. This is truly an astonishing era. Even so, their women seem to copulate in the old ways: knees up thighs apart, lying on the right side left leg flexed, back to the man and knees slightly bent, etc., etc., etc. One might think they would have invented something new by this time. But perhaps the possibilities for innovation in the sphere of erotics are not extensive. Can I suggest anything? What if the woman unplugs both arms and both legs and presents her mere torso to the man? Helpless! Vulnerable! Quintessentially feminine! I will discuss it with Louisiana. But it would be just my luck that her arms and legs don't come off.

On the first para-Wednesday of every month Lieutenant Hotchkiss gives me lessons in fluid-breathing. We go to one of the deepest sublevels of the Extravagance Building, where there is a special hyperoxygenated pool, for the use of beginners only, circular in shape and not at all deep. The water sparkles like opal. Usually the pool is crowded with children, but Lieutenant Hotchkiss arranges for me to have private instruction since I am shy about revealing my body. Each lesson is much like the one before. Lieutenant Hotchkiss descends the gentle ramp that leads one into the pool. He is taller than I am and his hair is golden and his eyes are blue. Sometimes I have difficulties distinguishing him from Dr. Habakkuk and Senator Mandragore. In a casual moment the lieutenant confided that he is ninety-eight years old and therefore not really a contemporary of Louisiana's, although Louisiana has hinted that on several occasions in the past she has allowed the lieutenant to fertilize her ova. I doubt this inasmuch as reproduction is quite uncommon in this era and what probability is there that she would have permitted him to do it more than once? I think she believes that by telling me such things she will stimulate emotions of jealousy in me, since she knows that the primitive ancients were frequently jealous. Regardless of all this Lieutenant Hotchkiss proceeds to enter the water. It reaches his navel, his broad hairless chest, his throat, his chin, his sensitive thin-walled nostrils. He submerges and crawls about on the floor of the pool. I see his golden hair glittering through the opal water. He remains totally submerged for eight or twelve minutes, now and again lifting his hands above the surface and waggling them as if to show me where he is. Then he comes forth. Water streams from his nostrils but he is not in the least out of breath. Come on, now, he says. You can do it. It's as easy as it looks. He beckons me toward the ramp. Any child can do it, the lieutenant assures me. It's a matter of control and determination. I shake my head. No, I say, genetic modification has something to do with it. My lungs aren't equipped to handle water, although I suppose yours are. The lieutenant merely laughs. Come on, come on, into the water. And I go down the ramp. How the water glows and shimmers! It reaches my navel, my black-matted chest, my throat, my chin, my wide thick nostrils. I breathe it in and choke and splutter; and I rush up the ramp, struggling for air. With the water a leaden weight in my lungs, I throw myself exhausted to the marble floor and cry out, No, no, no, it's impossible. Lieutenant Hotchkiss stands over me. His body is without flaw. He says, You've got to try to cultivate the proper attitudes. Your mental set determines everything. Let's think more positively about this business of breathing under water. Don't you realize that it's a major evolutionary step, one of the grand and glorious things separating our species from the australopithecines? Don't you want to be part of the great leap forward? Up, now. Try again. Thinking positively all the time. Carrying in your mind the distinction between yourself and our bestial ancestors. Go in. In. In. And I go in. And moments later burst from the water, choking and spluttering. This takes place on the first para-Wednesday of every month. The same thing, every time.

When you are talking on the telephone and your call is abruptly cut off, do you worry that the person on the other end will think you have hung up on him? Do you suspect that the person on the other end has hung up on you? Such problems are unknown here. These people make very few telephone calls. We are beyond mere communication in this era, Louisiana sometimes remarks.

Through my eyes these people behold their shining plastic epoch in proper historical perspective. They must see it as the present, which is always the same. But to me it is the future and so I have the true observer's parallax: I can say, it once was like that and now it is like *this*. They prize my gift. They treasure me. People come from other continents to run their fingers over my face. They tell me how much they admire my asymmetry. And they ask me many questions. Most of them ask about their own era rather than about mine. Such questions as:

Does suspended animation tempt you?

Was the fusion plant overwhelming in its implications of contained might?

Can you properly describe interconnection of the brain with a computer as an ecstatic experience?

Do you approve of modification of the solar system?

And also there are those who make more searching demands on my critical powers, such as Dr. Habakkuk and Senator Mandragore. They ask such questions as:

Was the brevity of your life span a hindrance to the development of the moral instincts?

Do you find our standardization of appearance at all abhorrent?

What was your typical emotional response to the sight of the dung of some wild animal in the streets?

Can you quantify the intensity of your feelings concerning the transience of human institutions?

I do my best to serve their needs. Often it is a strain to answer them in meaningful ways, but I strive to do so. Wondering occasionally if it would not have been more valuable for them to interrogate a Neanderthal. Or one of Lieutenant Hotchkiss's australopithecines. I am perhaps not primitive enough, though I do have my own charisma, nevertheless.

The first day it was pretty frightening to me. I saw one of them, with his sleek face and all, and I could accept that, but then another one came into the room to give me an injection, and he looked just like the first one. Twins, I thought, my doctors are twins. But then a third and a fourth and a fifth arrived. The same face, the very same fucking face. Imagine my chagrin, me with my blob of a nose, with my uneven teeth, with my eyebrows that meet in the middle, with my fleshy pockmarked cheeks, lying there beneath this convocation of the perfect. Let me tell you I felt out of place. I was never touchy about my looks before—I mean, it's an imperfect world, we all have our flaws—but these bastards didn't have flaws, and that was a hard acceptance for me to relate to. I thought I was being clever: I said, You're all multiples of the same gene pattern, right? Modern advances in medicine have made possible an infinite reduplication of genetic information and the five of you belong to one clone, isn't that it? And several of them answered, No, this is not the case, we are in fact wholly unrelated but within the last meta-week we have independently decided to standardize our appearance according to the presently favored model. And then three or four more of them came into my room to get a look at me.

In the beginning I kept telling myself: *In the country of the beautiful the ugly man is king.*

Louisiana was the first one with whom I had a sexual liaison. We often went to public copulatoria. She was easy to arouse and quite passionate although her friend Calpurnia informed me some months later that Louisiana takes orgasm-inducing drugs before copulating with me. I asked Calpurnia why and she became embarrassed. Dismayed, I bared my body to her and threw myself on top of her. Yes, she cried, rape me, violate me! Calpurnia's vigorous spasms astonished me. The following morning Louisiana asked me if I had noticed Calpurnia swallowing a small purple spansule prior to our intercourse. Calpurnia's face is identical to Louisiana's but her breasts are farther apart. I have also had sexual relations with Helena, Amniota, Drusilla, Florinda, and Vibrissa. Before each episode of copulation I ask them their names so that there will be no mistakes.

At twilight they programmed an hour of red and green rainfall and I queried Senator Mandragore about the means by which I had been brought to this era. Was it bodily transportation through time? That is, the physical lifting of my very self out of then and into now? Or was my body dead and kept on deposit in a freezer vault until these people resuscitated and refurbished it? Am I, perhaps, a total genetic reconstruct fashioned from a few fragments of ancient somatic tissue found in a baroque urn? Possibly I am only a simulated and stylized interpretation of twentieth-century man produced by a computer under intelligent and sympathetic guidance. How was it done, Senator? How was it done? The rain ceased. Leaving elegant puddles of blurred hue in the puddle-places.

Walking with Louisiana on my arm down Venus Avenue I imagined that I saw another man with a face like mine. It was the merest flash: a dark visage, thick heavy brows, stubble on the cheeks, the head thrust belligerently forward between the massive shoulders. But he was gone, turning a sudden corner, before I could get a good look. Louisiana suggested I was overindulging in hallucinogens. We went to an underwater theatre and she swam below me like a golden fish, revolving lights glinting off the upturned globes of her rump.

This is a demonstration of augmented mental capacity, said Vibrissa. I wish to show you what the extent of human potentiality can be. Read me any passage of Shakespeare of your own choice and I will repeat it verbatim and then offer you textual analysis. Shall we try this? Very well, I said and delicately put my fingernail to the Shakespeare cube and the words formed and I said out loud, What man dare, I dare: Approach thou like the rugged Russian bear, the arm'd rhinoceros, or the Hyrcan tiger, Take any shape but that, and my firm nerves Shall never tremble. Vibrissa instantly recited the lines to me without error and interpreted them in terms of the poet's penis envy, offering me footnotes from Seneca and Strindberg. I was quite impressed. But then I was never what you might call an intellectual.

On the day of the snow-gliding events I distinctly and beyond any possibilities of ambiguity or misapprehension saw two separate individuals who resembled me. Are they importing more of my kind for their amusement? If they are I will be resentful. I cherish my unique status.

I told Dr. Habakkuk that I wished to apply for transformation to the facial norm of society. Do it, I said, the transplant thing or the genetic manipulation or however you manage it. I want to be golden-haired and have blue eyes and regular features. I want to look like you. Dr. Habakkuk smiled genially and shook his youthful golden head. No, he told me. Forgive us, but we like you as you are.

Sometimes I dream of my life as it was in the former days. I think of automobiles and pastrami and tax returns and marigolds and pimples and mortgages and the gross national product. Also I indulge in recollections of my childhood my parents my wife my dentist my younger daughter my desk my toothbrush my dog my umbrella my favorite brand of beer my wristwatch my answering service my neighbors my phonograph my ocarina. All of these things are gone. Grinding my flesh against that of Drusilla in the copulatorium I wonder if she could be one of my descendants. I must have descendants somewhere in this civilization, and why not she? She asks me to perform an act of oral perversion with her and I explain that I couldn't possibly engage in such stuff with my own great-grandchild.

I think I remain quite calm at most times considering the extraordinary nature of the stress that this experience has imposed on me. I am still self-conscious about my appearance but I pretend otherwise. Often I go naked just as they do. If they dislike bodily hair or disproportionate limbs, let them look away.

Occasionally I belch or scratch under my arms or do other primitive things to remind them that I am the authentic man from antiquity. For now there can be no doubt that I have my imitators. There are at least five. Calpurnia denies this, but I am no fool.

Dr. Habakkuk revealed that he was going to take a holiday in the Carpathians and would not return until the 14th of June-surrogate. In the meantime Dr. Clasp would minister to my needs. Dr. Clasp entered my suite and I remarked on his startling resemblance to Dr. Habakkuk. He asked, What would you like? and I told him I wanted him to operate on me so that I looked like everybody else. I am tired of appearing bestial and primordial, I said. To my surprise Dr. Clasp smiled warmly and told me that he'd arrange for the transformation at once, since it violated his principles to allow any organism needlessly to suffer. I was taken to the operating room and given a sour-tasting anaesthetic. Seemingly without the passing of time I awakened and was wheeled into a dome of mirrors to behold myself. Even as I had requested they had redone me into one of them, blond-haired, blue-eyed, with a slim, agile body and a splendidly symmetrical face. Dr. Clasp came in after a while and we stood side by side: we might have been twins. How do you like it? he asked. Tears brimmed in my eyes and I said that this was the most wonderful moment of my life. Dr. Clasp pummeled my shoulder jovially and said, You know, I am not Dr. Clasp at all, I am really Dr. Habakkuk and I never went to the Carpathians. This entire episode has been a facet of our analysis of your pattern of responses.

Louisiana was astonished by my changed appearance. Are you truly he? she kept asking. Are you truly he? I'll prove it, I said and mounted her with my old prehistoric zeal, snorting and gnawing her breasts. But she shook me free with a deft flip of her pelvis and rushed from the chamber. You'll never see me again she shouted but I merely shrugged and called after her, So what I can see lots of others just like you. I never saw her again.

So now they have all changed themselves again to the new standard model. It happened gradually over a period of months but the transition is at last complete. Their heavy brows, their pockmarked cheeks, their hairy chests. It is the latest thing. I make my way through the crowded streets and wherever I turn I see faces that mirror my own lopsidedness. Only I am not lopsided myself any more, of course. I am symmetrical and flawless, and I am the only one. I cannot find Dr. Habakkuk, and Dr. Clasp is in the Pyrenees; Senator Mandragore was defeated in the primary. So I must remain beautiful. Walking among them. They are all alike. Thick lips uneven teeth noses like blobs. How I despise them! I the only golden one. And all of them mocking me by their metamorphosis. All of them. Mocking me. Meee.

GOOD NEWS FROM THE VATICAN

Ever since I read Baron Corvo's remarkable novel Hadrian the Seventh *in 1955 I have amused myself with the fantasy of being elected Pope—an ambition complicated to some degree by the fact that I am not in holy orders, nor a Roman Catholic, nor, indeed, any kind of Christian at all. As my friends know, I duly submit an application whenever a vacancy occurs at the Vatican, but as of this date the Church has not yet seen fit to make use of my services.*

All the same, I keep close watch over events in the Holy City as I bide my time, and in the pursuit of this not entirely serious career plan I've learned a good deal about the rituals and tensions surrounding the elections of a pontiff. This led me, one chilly but cheery day in February, 1971, to produce this sly, playful story of the accession of the first robot to the Holy See. (The robot is, in fact, meant to be my own successor, though the point is made only through an oblique private reference in the final paragraph.)

At the time I wrote this story a year and a half had passed since the completion of rebuilding work on my New York house, and it was even more handsome than it had been before the fire. I assumed I would live there for the rest of my life. But some sort of uneasiness was stirring in my soul even then, for the winter of 1970-71 was unusually snowy in New York, and as the white drifts piled up outside the door I began to tell people that I yearned for some warmer climate. On the February day when Terry Carr called to ask me to write a story for Universe, *his new anthology of previously unpublished short stories, I was, as a matter of fact, at work on* The Book of Skulls, *a novel set in the torrid Arizona desert.*

Carr, then at the peak of his distinguished career as a science-fiction editor for Ace Books, told me that he was approaching the deadline for delivery of the first volume of Universe *and was badly in need of fiction by authors with recognizable names. He had been asking me for a story for weeks, but I was busy with my novel, and I put him off; now, though, he appealed bluntly to me to help him out. Since Terry was a persuasive man and a close friend besides, I agreed to interrupt the novel and do a quick short story for him.*

What to write about? Well, I thought, hastily casting about for an idea, suppose they elect a robot as Pope? That ought to be worth 3000 words or so of amiable foolery, right? My own pretense of interest in attaining the Papacy and my knowledge of the mechanics of Papal elections would help me make the story reasonably convincing. A couple of hours' work and Terry and his new anthology would be off my conscience.

So I sat down and wrote "Good News from the Vatican" just about as fast as I could type it out. Terry was amused by its cool, detached, tongue-in-cheek mode of irony (which I was beginning to employ more and more, as I entered my third decade as a writer) and published it in the first issue of Universe *with a brief introduction noting that although my stories were usually quite serious in tone, this one was a bit on the silly side, although nevertheless quite thoughtful and ingenious, et cetera, et cetera.*

A couple of unexpected ironies proceeded from this enterprise. The little story I had written so quickly that snowy February day caught everybody's attention, was nominated for a Nebula award, and won the trophy for me—the second of, ultimately, five Nebulas—the following spring. (I won my third the same night, for the novel A Time of Changes.*) I collected my awards not in New York but at a ceremony held in California, for, much to my astonishment, the inner uneasiness of February had culminated by late summer in a series of explosive personal upheavals that had caused me to sell my New York house and move westward, a few months after Terry Carr himself had done the very same thing.*

And also—rather sadly, actually—a decade and a half after I had helped Terry get Universe *started by hastily writing an award—winning story for his first issue, I found myself taking his place as its editor, when his publisher decided to continue the anthology as a memorial to him following his untimely death in 1987.*

GOOD NEWS FROM THE VATICAN

This is the morning everyone has waited for, when at last the robot cardinal is to be elected pope. There can no longer be any doubt of the outcome. The conclave has been deadlocked for many days between the obstinate advocates of Cardinal Asciuga of Milan and Cardinal Carciofo of Genoa, and word has gone out that a compromise is in the making. All factions now are agreed on the selection of the robot. This morning I read in *Osservatore Romano* that the Vatican computer itself has taken a hand in the deliberations. The computer has been strongly urging the candidacy of the robot. I suppose we should not be surprised by this loyalty among machines. Nor should we let it distress us. We *absolutely must not* let it distress us.

"Every era gets the pope it deserves," Bishop FitzPatrick observed somewhat gloomily today at breakfast. "The proper pope for our times is a robot, certainly. At some future date it may be desirable for the pope to be a whale, an automobile, a cat, a mountain." Bishop FitzPatrick stands well over two meters in height and his normal facial expression is a morbid, mournful one. Thus it is impossible for us to determine whether any particular pronouncement of his reflects existential despair or placid acceptance. Many years ago he was a star player for the Holy Cross championship basketball team. He has come to Rome to do research for a biography of St. Marcellus the Righteous.

We have been watching the unfolding drama of the papal election from an outdoor café several blocks from the Square of St. Peter's. For all of us, this has been an unexpected dividend of our holiday in Rome; the previous pope was reputed to be in good health and there was no reason to suspect that a successor would have to be chosen for him this summer.

Each morning we drive across by taxi from our hotel near the Via Veneto and take up our regular positions around "our" table. From where we sit, we all have a clear view of the Vatican chimney through which the smoke of the burning ballots rises: black smoke if no pope has been elected, white if the conclave has been successful. Luigi, the owner and headwaiter, automatically brings us our preferred beverages: Fernet Branca for Bishop FitzPatrick, Campari and soda for Rabbi Mueller, Turkish coffee for Miss Harshaw, lemon squash for Kenneth and Beverly, and Pernod on the rocks for me. We take turns paying the check, although Kenneth has not paid it even once since our vigil began. Yesterday, when Miss Harshaw paid, she emptied her purse and found herself 350 lire short; she had nothing else except hundred-dollar travelers' checks. The rest of us looked pointedly at Kenneth but he went on calmly sipping his lemon squash. After a brief period of tension Rabbi Mueller produced a 500-lire coin and rather irascibly slapped the heavy silver piece against the table. The rabbi is known for his short temper and vehement style. He is twenty-eight years old, customarily dresses in a fashionable plaid cassock and silvered sunglasses, and frequently boasts that he has never performed a bar mitzvah ceremony for his congregation, which is in Wicomico County, Maryland. He believes that the rite is vulgar and obsolete, and invariably farms out all his bar mitzvahs to a franchised organization of itinerant clergymen who handle such affairs on a commission basis. Rabbi Mueller is an authority on angels.

Our group is divided over the merits of electing a robot as the new pope. Bishop FitzPatrick, Rabbi Mueller, and I are in favor of the idea. Miss Harshaw, Kenneth, and Beverly are opposed. It is interesting to note that both of our gentlemen of the cloth, one quite elderly and one fairly young, support this remarkable departure from tradition. Yet the three "swingers" among us do not.

I am not sure why I align myself with the progressives. I am a man of mature years and fairly sedate ways. Nor have I ever concerned myself with the doings of the Church of Rome. I am unfamiliar with Catholic dogma and unaware of recent currents of thought within the Church. Still, I have been hoping for the election of the robot since the start of the conclave.

Why, I wonder? Is it because the image of a metal creature upon the Throne of St. Peter stimulates my imagination and tickles my sense of the incongruous? That is, is my support of the robot purely an aesthetic matter? Or is it, rather, a function of my moral cowardice? Do I secretly think that this gesture will buy the robots off? Am I privately saying, Give them the papacy and maybe they won't want other things for a while? No. I can't believe anything so unworthy of myself. Possibly I am for the robot because I am a person of unusual sensitivity to the needs of others.

"If he's elected," says Rabbi Mueller, "he plans an immediate time-sharing agreement with the Dalai Lama and a reciprocal plug-in with the head programmer of the Greek Orthodox Church, just for starters. I'm told he'll make ecumenical overtures to the Rabbinate as well, which is certainly something for all of us to look forward to."

"I don't doubt that there'll be many corrections in the customs and practices of the hierarchy," Bishop FitzPatrick declares. "For example we can look forward to superior information-gathering techniques as the Vatican computer is given a greater role in the operations of the Curia. Let me illustrate by—"

"What an utterly ghastly notion," Kenneth says. He is a gaudy young man with white hair and pink eyes. Beverly is either his wife or his sister. She rarely speaks. Kenneth makes the sign of the Cross with offensive brusqueness and murmurs, "In the name of the Father, the Son, and the Holy Automaton." Miss Harshaw giggles but chokes the giggle off when she sees my disapproving face.

Dejectedly, but not responding at all to the interruption, Bishop FitzPatrick continues, "Let me illustrate by giving you some figures I obtained yesterday afternoon. I read in the newspaper *Oggi* that during the last five years, according to a spokesman for the *Missiones Catholicae,* the Church has increased its membership in Yugoslavia from 19,381,403 to 23,501,062. But the government census taken last year gives the total population of Yugoslavia at 23,575,194. That leaves only 74,132 for the other religious and irreligious bodies. Aware of the large Moslem population of Yugoslavia, I suspected an inaccuracy in the published statistics and consulted the computer in St. Peter's, which informed me"—the bishop, pausing, produces a lengthy printout and unfolds it across much of the table—"that the last count of the Faithful in Yugoslavia, made a year and a half ago, places our numbers at 14,206,198. Therefore an overstatement of 9,294,864 has been made. Which is absurd. And perpetuated. Which is damnable."

"What does he look like?" Miss Harshaw asks. "Does anyone have any idea?"

"He's like all the rest," says Kenneth. "A shiny metal box with wheels below and eyes on top."

"You haven't seen him," Bishop FitzPatrick interjects. "I don't think it's proper for you to assume that—"

"They're all alike," Kenneth says. "Once you've seen one, you've seen all of them. Shiny boxes. Wheels. Eyes. And voices coming out of their bellies like mechanized belches. Inside, they're all cogs and gears." Kenneth shudders delicately. "It's too much for me to accept. Let's have another round of drinks, shall we?"

Rabbi Mueller says, "It so happens that I've seen him with my own eyes."

"You *have?*" Beverly exclaims.

Kenneth scowls at her. Luigi, approaching, brings a tray of new drinks for everyone. I hand him a 5,000-lire note. Rabbi Mueller removes his sunglasses and breathes on their brilliantly reflective surfaces. He has small, watery grey eyes and a bad squint. He says, "The cardinal was the keynote speaker at the Congress of World Jewry that was held last fall in Beirut. His theme was 'Cybernetic Ecumenicism for Contemporary Man'. I was there. I can tell you that His Eminency is tall and distinguished, with a fine voice and a gentle smile. There's something inherently melancholy about his manner that reminds me greatly of our friend the bishop, here. His movements are graceful and his wit is keen."

"But he's mounted on wheels, isn't he?" Kenneth persists.

"On treads," replies the rabbi, giving Kenneth a fiery, devastating look and resuming his sunglasses. "Treads, like a tractor has. But I don't think that treads are spiritually inferior to feet, or, for that matter, to wheels. If I were a Catholic I'd be proud to have a man like that as my pope."

"Not a man," Miss Harshaw puts in. A giddy edge enters her voice whenever she addresses Rabbi Mueller. "A robot," she says. "He's not a man, remember?"

"A robot like that as my pope, then," Rabbi Mueller says, shrugging at the correction. He raises his glass. "To the new pope!"

"To the new pope!" cries Bishop FitzPatrick.

Luigi comes rushing from his cafe. Kenneth waves him away. "Wait a second," Kenneth says. "The election isn't over yet. How can you be so sure?"

"The *Osservatore Romano,*" I say, "indicates in this morning's edition that everything will be decided today. Cardinal Carciofo has agreed to withdraw in his favor, in return for a larger realtime allotment when the new computer hours are decreed at next year's consistory."

"In other words, the fix is in," Kenneth says.

Bishop FitzPatrick sadly shakes his head. "You state things much too harshly, my son. For three weeks now we have been without a Holy Father. It is God's Will that we shall have a pope. The conclave, unable to choose between the candidacies of Cardinal Carciofo and Cardinal Asciuga, thwarts that Will. If necessary, therefore, we must make certain accommodations with the realities of the times so that His Will shall not be further frustrated. Prolonged politicking within the conclave now becomes sinful. Cardinal Carciofo's sacrifice of his personal ambitions is not as self-seeking an act as you would claim."

Kenneth continues to attack poor Carciofo's motives for withdrawing. Beverly occasionally applauds his cruel sallies. Miss Harshaw several times declares her unwillingness to remain a communicant of a Church whose leader is a machine. I find this dispute distasteful and swing my chair away from the table to have a better view of the Vatican. At this moment the cardinals are meeting in the Sistine Chapel. How I wish I were there! What splendid mysteries are being enacted in that gloomy, magnificent room! Each prince of the Church now sits on a small throne surmounted by a violet-hued canopy. Fat wax tapers glimmer on the desk before each throne. Masters of ceremonies move solemnly through the vast chamber, carrying the silver basins in which the blank ballots repose. These basins are placed on the table before the altar. One by one the cardinals advance to the table, take ballots, return to their desks. Now, lifting their quill pens, they begin to write. "I, Cardinal—, elect to the Supreme Pontificate the Most Reverend Lord my Lord Cardinal—." What name do they fill in? Is it Carciofo? Is it Asciuga? Is it the name of some obscure and shriveled prelate from Madrid or Heidelberg, some last-minute choice of the anti-robot faction in its desperation? Or are they writing *his* name? The sound of scratching pens is loud in the chapel. The cardinals are completing their ballots, sealing them at the ends, folding them, folding them again and again, carrying them to the altar, dropping them into the great gold chalice. So have they done every morning and every afternoon for days, as the deadlock has prevailed.

"I read in the *Herald-Tribune* a couple of days ago," says Miss Harshaw, "that a delegation of two hundred and fifty young Catholic robots from Iowa is waiting at the Des Moines airport for news of the election. If their man gets in, they've got a chartered flight ready to leave, and they intend to request that they be granted the Holy Father's first public audience."

"There can be no doubt," Bishop FitzPatrick agrees, "that his election will bring a great many people of synthetic origin into the fold of the Church."

"While driving out plenty of flesh and blood people!" Miss Harshaw says shrilly.

"I doubt that," says the bishop. "Certainly there will be some feelings of shock, of dismay, of injury, of loss, for some of us at first. But these will pass. The inherent goodness of the new pope, to which Rabbi Mueller alluded, will prevail. Also I believe that technologically minded young folk everywhere will be encouraged to join the Church. Irresistible religious impulses will be awakened throughout the world."

"Can you imagine two hundred and fifty robots clanking into St. Peter's?" Miss Harshaw demands.

I contemplate the distant Vatican. The morning sunlight is brilliant and dazzling, but the assembled cardinals, walled away from the world, cannot enjoy its gay sparkle. They all have voted, now. The three cardinals who were chosen by lot as this morning's scrutators of the vote have risen. One of them lifts the chalice and shakes it, mixing the ballots. Then he places it on the table before the altar; a second scrutator removes the ballots and counts them. He ascertains that the number of ballots is identical to the number of cardinals present. The ballots now have been transferred to a ciborium, which is a goblet ordinarily used to hold the consecrated bread of the Mass. The first scrutator withdraws a ballot, unfolds it, reads its inscription; passes it to the second scrutator, who reads it also; then it is given to the third scrutator, who reads the name aloud. Asciuga? Carciofo? Some other? *His?*

Rabbi Mueller is discussing angels. "Then we have the Angels of the Throne, known in Hebrew as *arelim* or *ophanim*. There are seventy of them, noted primarily for their steadfastness. Among them are the angels Orifiel, Ophaniel, Zabkiel, Jophiel, Ambriel, Tychagar, Barael, Quelamia, Paschar, Boel, and Raum. Some of these are no longer found in Heaven and are numbered among the fallen angels in Hell."

"So much for their steadfastness," says Kenneth.

"Then, too," the rabbi goes on, "there are the Angels of the Presence, who apparently were circumcised at the moment of their creation. These are Michael, Metatron, Suriel, Sandalphon, Uriel, Saraqael, Astanphaeus, Phanuel, Jehoel, Zagzagael, Yefefiah, and Akatriel. But I think my favorite of the whole group is the Angel of Lust, who is mentioned in Talmud *Bereshith Rabba* 85 as follows, that when Judah was about to pass by—"

They have finished counting the votes by this time, surely. An immense throng has assembled in the Square of St. Peter's. The sunlight gleams off hundreds if not thousands of steel-jacketed craniums. This must be a wonderful day for the robot population of Rome. But most of those in the piazza are creatures of flesh and blood: old women in black, gaunt young pickpockets, boys with puppies, plump vendors of sausages, and an assortment of poets, philosophers, generals, legislators, tourists, and fishermen. How has the tally gone? We will have our answer shortly. If no candidate has had a majority, they will mix the ballots with wet straw before casting them into the chapel stove, and black smoke will billow from the chimney. But if a pope has been elected, the straw will be dry, the smoke will be white.

The system has agreeable resonances. I like it. It gives me the satisfactions one normally derives from a flawless work of art: the Tristan chord, let us say, or the teeth of the frog in Bosch's *Temptation of St. Anthony.* I await the outcome with fierce concentration. I am certain of the result; I can already feel the irresistible religious impulses awakening in me. Although I feel, also, an odd nostalgia for the days of flesh and blood popes. Tomorrow's newspapers will have no interviews with the Holy Father's aged mother in Sicily, nor with his proud younger brother in San Francisco. And will this grand ceremony of election ever be held again? Will we need another pope, when this one whom we will soon have can be repaired so easily?

Ah. The white smoke! The moment of revelation comes!

A figure emerges on the central balcony of the facade of St. Peter's, spreads a web of cloth-of-gold, and disappears. The blaze of light against that fabric stuns the eye. It reminds me perhaps of moonlight coldly kissing the sea at Castellamare, or, perhaps even more, of the noonday glare rebounding from the breast of the Caribbean off the coast of St. John. A second figure, clad in ermine and vermilion, has appeared on the balcony. "The cardinal-archdeacon," Bishop FitzPatrick whispers. People have started to faint. Luigi stands beside me, listening to the proceedings on a tiny radio, Kenneth says, "It's all been fixed." Rabbi Mueller hisses at him to be still. Miss Harshaw begins to sob. Beverly softly recites the Pledge of Allegiance, crossing herself throughout. This is a wonderful moment for me. I think it is the most truly contemporary moment I have ever experienced.

The amplified voice of the cardinal-archdeacon cries, "I announce to you great joy. We have a pope."

Cheering commences, and grows in intensity as the cardinal-archdeacon tells the world that the newly chosen pontiff is indeed that cardinal, that noble and distinguished person, that melancholy and austere individual, whose elevation to the Holy See we have all awaited so intensely for so long. "He has imposed upon himself," says the cardinal-archdeacon, "the name of—"

Lost in the cheering, I turn to Luigi. "Who? What name?"

"Sisto Settimo," Luigi tells me.

Yes, and there he is, Pope Sixtus the Seventh, as we now must call him. A tiny figure clad in the silver and gold papal robes, arms outstretched to the multitude, and, yes! the sunlight glints on his cheeks, his lofty forehead, there is the brightness of polished steel. Luigi is already on his knees. I kneel beside him. Miss Harshaw, Beverly, Kenneth, even the rabbi, all kneel, for beyond doubt this is a miraculous event. The pope comes forward on his balcony. Now he will deliver the traditional apostolic benediction to the city and to the world. "Our help is in the Name of the Lord," he declares gravely. He activates the levitator jets beneath his arms; even at this distance I can see the two small puffs of smoke. White smoke, again. He begins to rise into the air. "Who hath made heaven and earth," he says. "May Almighty God, Father, Son, and Holy Ghost, bless you." His voice rolls majestically toward us. His shadow extends across the whole piazza. Higher and higher he goes, until he is lost to sight. Kenneth taps Luigi. "Another round of drinks," he says, and presses a bill of high denomination into the innkeeper's fleshy palm. Bishop FitzPatrick weeps. Rabbi Mueller embraces Miss Harshaw. The new pontiff, I think, has begun his reign in an auspicious way.

THOMAS THE PROCLAIMER

This story comes from another of the series of "triplet" theme anthologies that I edited in the 1970s. As with the volume called Four Futures, *from which "Going" was drawn, I turned to a well–known science-fiction writer to provide a challenging concept that would be used as the basis for novella-length stories by the three invited contributors.*

For the 1972 book I invited Lester del Rey to set the theme. In much of his own work del Rey had taken iconoclastic views of conventional religious ideas, and that was precisely what he did here. We read in the Book of Joshua how the Israelite warrior Joshua, not wanting night to fall while he was in the midst of battle, cried out, "Sun, stand thou still," and the Lord complied: "The sun stood still in the midst of heaven, and hasted not to go down about a whole day," and Joshua was victorious.

What del Rey asked was what would happen if in our own era of widespread disbelief the same miracle were to take place: that a great leader would appear and cry out to God for a sign in the heavens so that the unbelieving should heed, and God would comply, so that "for a day and a night the Earth moved not around the Sun, neither did it rotate. And the laws of momentum were confounded." And the question that Lester propounded to the three writers was, "What kind of world might exist were the basis of faith replaced by certain knowledge?"

I named the anthology The Day the Sun Stood Still *(though of course it was the Earth that would cease to move), asked those experienced old professionals, Poul Anderson and Gordon R. Dickson, to write stories for the book, and chose to write the third one myself. They came through magnificently, Anderson with a splendid novella called "A Chapter of Revelation," and Dickson with his very fine "Things Which Are Caesar's."*

My own story, which I wrote in April of 1971, was "Thomas the Proclaimer," which is reprinted here. I was still being swept along on an irresistible tide of creative energy, which had another couple of years to run. Stories were pouring out of me as fast as I could get them down on paper: I had just finished the novel The Book of Skulls *and the short story "Good News from the Vatican," which would win a Nebula, and in a few months I would start on* Dying Inside. *I chose to set "Thomas the Proclaimer" at the very edge of what we later would come to call Y2K: the miracle occurs on June 6, 1999, and the story moves inexorably along to the apocalyptic end of December.*

I've never felt that science fiction should be taken as literal prophecy, and that belief is confirmed again here. The future era that I imagined for "Thomas the Proclaimer" has by this time receded into the past: we know now that neither the Sun nor the Earth stood still on June 6, 1999, and no wild-eyed hordes of religious fanatics were rampaging through our cities as December 31 approached. Nor did such events as the Children's Crusade for Sanity, the Nine Weeks' War, or the Night of the Lasers occur during the 1980s. But the future looked very chaotic indeed to me in 1971 as I wrote the story, and much of that chaos did unfold in one form and another in the years that followed, and though "Thomas the Proclaimer" is in no way literally prophetic, I think you will find that it quite accurately prefigured much of what would occur in the world in the generation just ended.

One
Moonlight, Starlight, Torchlight

How long will this night last? The blackness, though moon-pierced, star-pierced, torch-pierced, is dense and tangible. They are singing and chanting in the valley. Bitter smoke from their firebrands rises to the hilltop where Thomas stands, flanked by his closest followers. Fragments of old hymns dance through the trees. "Rock of Ages, Cleft for Me." "O God, Our Help in Ages Past." "Jesus, Lover of My Soul, Let Me to Thy Bosom Fly." Thomas is the center of all attention. A kind of invisible aura surrounds his blocky, powerful figure, an unseen crackling electrical radiance. Saul Kraft, at his side, seems eclipsed and obscured, a small, fragile-looking man, overshadowed now but far from unimportant in the events of this night. "Nearer, My God, to Thee." Thomas begins to hum the tune, then to sing. His voice, though deep and magical, the true charismatic voice, tumbles randomly from key to key: the prophet has no ear for music. Kraft smiles sourly at Thomas' dismal sounds.

"Watchman, tell us of the night,
What its signs of promise are.
Traveler, o'er yon mountain's height,
See that glory-beaming star!"

Ragged shouts from below. Occasional sobs and loud coughs. What is the hour? The hour is late. Thomas runs his hands through his long, tangled hair, tugging, smoothing, pulling the strands down toward his thick shoulders. The familiar gesture, beloved by the multitudes. He wonders if he should make an appearance. They are calling his name; he hears the rhythmic cries punching through the snarl of clashing hymns. *Tho-mas! Tho-mas! Tho-mas!* Hysteria in their voices. They want him to come forth and stretch out his arms and make the heavens move again, just as he caused them to stop. But Thomas resists that grand but hollow gesture. How easy it is to play the prophet's part! He did not cause the heavens to stop, though, and he knows that he cannot make them move again. Not of his own will alone, at any rate.

"What time is it?" he asks.

"Quarter to ten," Kraft tells him. Adding, after an instant's thought: "P.M."

So the twenty-four hours are nearly up. And still the sky hangs frozen. Well, Thomas? It this not what you asked for? Go down on your knees, you cried, and beg Him for a Sign, so that we may know He is still with us, in this our time of need. And render up to Him a great shout. And the people knelt throughout all the lands. And begged. And shouted. And the Sign was given. Why, then, this sense of foreboding? Why these fears? Surely this night will pass. Look at Kraft. Smiling serenely. Kraft has never known any doubts. Those cold eyes, those thin wide lips, the fixed expression of tranquility.

"You ought to speak to them," Kraft says.

"I have nothing to say."

"A few words of comfort for them."

"Let's see what happens, first. What can I tell them now?"

"Empty of words, Thomas? You, who have had so much to proclaim?"

Thomas shrugs. There are times when Kraft infuriates him: the little man needling him, goading, scheming, never letting up, always pushing this Crusade toward some appointed goal grasped by Kraft alone. The intensity of Kraft's faith exhausts Thomas. Annoyed, the prophet turns away from him. Thomas sees scattered fires leaping on the horizon. Prayer meetings? Or are they riots? Peering at those distant blazes, Thomas jabs idly at the tuner of the radio before him.

"...rounding out the unprecedented span of twenty-four hours of continuous daylight in much of the Eastern Hemisphere, an endless daybreak over the Near East and an endless noon over Siberia, eastern China, the Philippines, and Indonesia. Meanwhile western Europe and the Americas remain locked in endless night..."

"...then spake Joshua to the Lord in the day when the Lord delivered up the Amorites before the children of Israel, and he said in the sight of Israel, Sun, stand thou still upon Gibeon; and thou, Moon, in the valley of Ajalon. And the sun stood still, and the moon stayed, until the people had avenged themselves upon their enemies. Is this not written in the book of Jasher? So the sun stood still in the midst of heaven, and hasted not to go, down about a whole day..."

"...an astonishing culmination, apparently, to the campaign led by Thomas Davidson of Reno, Nevada, known popularly as Thomas the Proclaimer. The shaggy-bearded, long-haired, self-designated Apostle of Peace brought his Crusade of Faith to a climax yesterday with the world-wide program of simultaneous prayer that appears to have been the cause of..."

"Watchman, does its beauteous ray
Aught of joy or hope foretell?
Traveler, yes; it brings the day,
Promised day of Israel."

Kraft says sharply, "Do you hear what they're singing, Thomas? You've got to speak to them. You got them into this; now they want you to tell them you'll get them out of it."

"Not yet, Saul."

"You mustn't let your moment slip by. Show them that God still speaks through you!"

"When God is ready to speak again," Thomas says frostily, "I'll let His words come forth. Not before." He glares at Kraft and punches for another change of station.

"...continued meetings in Washington, but no communiqué as yet. Meanwhile, at the United Nations..."

"...Behold, He cometh with clouds; and every eye shall see Him, and they also which pierced Him: and all kindreds of the Earth shall wail because of Him. Even so, Amen..."

"...outbreaks of looting in Caracas, Mexico City, Oakland, and Vancouver. But in the daylight half of the world, violence and other disruption has been slight, though an unconfirmed report from Moscow..."

"...and when, brethren, when did the sun cease in its course? At six in the morning, brethren, six in the morning, Jerusalem time! And on what day, brethren? Why, the sixth of June, the sixth day of the sixth month! *Six—six—six!* And what does Holy Writ tell us, my dearly beloved ones, in the thirteenth chapter of Revelations? That a beast shall rise up out of the sea, having seven heads and ten horns, and upon his horns ten crowns, and upon his heads the name of blasphemy. And the Holy Book tells us the number of the beast, beloved, and the number is six hundred three score and six, wherein we see again the significant digits, *six—six—six!* Who then can deny that these are the last days, and that the Apocalypse must be upon us? Thus in this time of woe and fire as we sit upon this stilled planet awaiting His judgment, we must..."

"...latest observatory report confirms that no appreciable momentum effects could be detected as the Earth shifted to its present period of rotation. Scientists agree that the world's abrupt slowing on its axis should have produced a global catastrophe leading, perhaps, to the destruction of all life. However, nothing but minor tidal disturbances have been recorded so far. Two hours ago, we interviewed Presidential Science Adviser Raymond Bartell, who made this statement:

"'Calculations now show that the Earth's period of rotation and its period of revolution have suddenly become equal; that is, the day and the year now have the same length. This locks the Earth into its present position relative to the sun, so that the side of the Earth now enjoying daylight will continue indefinitely to do so, while the other side will remain permanently in night. Other effects of the slowdown that might have been expected include the flooding of coastal areas, the collapse of most buildings, and a series of earthquakes and volcanic eruptions, but none of these things seem to have happened. For the moment we have no rational explanation of all this, and I must admit it's a great temptation to say that Thomas the Proclaimer must have managed to get his miracle, because there isn't any other apparent way of...'"

"...I am Alpha and Omega, the beginning and the ending, saith the Lord, which is, and which was, and which is to come, the Almighty..."

With a fierce fingerthrust Thomas silences all the radio's clamoring voices. Alpha and Omega! Apocalyptist garbage! The drivel of hysterical preachers pouring from a thousand transmitters, poisoning the air! Thomas despises all these criers of doom. None of them knows anything. No one understands. His throat fills with a turbulence of angry incoherent words, almost choking him. A coppery taste of denunciations. Kraft again urges him to speak. Thomas glowers. Why doesn't Kraft do the speaking himself, for once? He's a truer believer than I am. He's the real prophet. But of course the idea is ridiculous. Kraft has no eloquence, no fire. Only ideas and visions. He'd bore everybody to splinters. Thomas succumbs. He beckons with his fingertips. "The microphone," he mutters. "Let me have the microphone."

Among his entourage there is fluttery excitement. "He wants the mike!" they murmur. "Give him the mike!" Much activity on the part of the technicians.

Kraft presses a plaque of cold metal into the Proclaimer's hand. Grins, winks. "Make their hearts soar," Kraft whispers. "Send them on a trip!" Everyone waits. In the valley the torches bob and weave; have they begun dancing down there? Overhead the pocked moon holds its corner of the sky in frosty grasp. The stars are chained to their places. Thomas draws a deep breath and lets the air travel inward, upward, surging to the recesses of his skull. He waits for the good lightheadedness to come upon him, the buoyancy that liberates his tongue. He thinks he is ready to speak. He hears the desperate chanting: *"Tho-mas! Tho-mas! Tho-mas!* It is more than half a day since his last public statement. He is tense and hollow; he has fasted throughout this Day of the Sign, and of course he has not slept. No one has slept.

"Friends," he begins. "Friends, this is Thomas."

The amplifiers hurl his voice outward. A thousand loudspeakers drifting in the air pick up his words and they bounce across the valley, returning as jagged echoes. He hears cries, eerie shrieks; his own name ascends to him in blurry distortions. *Too-mis! Too-mis! Too-mis!*

"Nearly a full day has passed," he says, "since the Lord gave us the Sign for which we asked. For us it has been a long day of darkness, and for others it has been a day of strange light, and for all of us there has been fear. But this I say to you now: BE...NOT...AFRAID. For the Lord is good and we are the Lord's."

Now he pauses. Not only for effect; his throat is raging. He signals furiously and Kraft, scowling, hands him a flask. Thomas takes a deep gulp of the good red wine, cool, strong. Ah. He glances at the screen beside him: the video pickup relayed from the valley. What lunacy down there! Wild-eyed, sweaty madmen, half-naked and worse, jumping up and down! Crying out his name, invoking him as though he were divine. *Too-mis! Too-mis!*

"There are those who tell you now," Thomas goes on, "that the end of days is at hand, that judgment is come. They talk of apocalypses and the wrath of God. And what do I say to that? I say: BE...NOT... AFRAID. The Lord God is a God of mercy. We asked Him for a Sign, and a Sign was given. Should we not therefore rejoice? Now we may be certain of His presence and His guidance. Ignore the doom-sayers. Put away your fears. We live now in God's love!"

Thomas halts again. For the first time in his memory he has no sense of being in command of his audience. Is he reaching them at all? Is he touching the right chords? Or has he begun already to lose them? Maybe it was a mistake to let Kraft nag him into speaking so soon. He thought he was ready; maybe not. Now he sees Kraft staring at him, aghast, pantomiming the gestures of speech, silently telling him, *Get with it, you've got to keep talking now!* Thomas' self-assurance momentarily wavers, and terror floods his soul, for he knows that if he falters at this point he may well be destroyed by the forces he has set loose. Teetering at the brink of an abyss, he searches frantically for his customary confidence. Where is that steely column of words that ordinarily rises unbidden from the depths of him? Another gulp of wine, fast. Good. Kraft, nervously rubbing hands together, essays a smile of encouragement. Thomas tugs at his hair. He pushes back his shoulders, thrusts out his chest. Be not afraid! He feels control returning after the frightening lapse. They are his, all those who listen. They have always been his. What are they shouting in the valley now? No longer his name, but some new cry. He strains to hear. Two words. What are they? *De-dum! De-dum! De-dum!* What? *De-dum! De-dum! De-dum, too-mis, de-dum!* What? What? "The sun," Kraft says. The sun? Yes. They want the sun. "The sun! The sun! The sun!"

"The sun," Thomas says. "Yes. This day the sun stands still, as our Sign from Him. BE NOT AFRAID! A long dawn over Jerusalem has He decreed, and a long night for us, but not so very long, and soon sped." Thomas feels the power surging at last. Kraft nods to him, and Thomas nods back and spits a stream of wine at Kraft's feet. He is aware of that consciousness of risk in which the joy of prophecy lies: I will bring forth what I see, and trust to God to make it real. That feeling of risk accepted, of triumph over doubt. Calmly he says, "The Day of the Sign will end in a few minutes. Once more the world will turn, and moon and stars will move across the sky. So put down your torches, and go to your homes, and offer up joyful prayers of thanksgiving to Him, for this night will pass, and dawn will come at the appointed hour."

How do you know, Thomas? Why are you so sure?

He hands the microphone to Saul Kraft and calls for more wine. Around him are tense faces, rigid eyes, clamped jaws. Thomas smiles. He goes among them, slapping backs, punching shoulders, laughing, embracing, winking ribaldly, poking his fingers playfully into their ribs. Be of good cheer, ye who follow my way! Share ye not my faith in Him? He asks Kraft how he came across. Fine, Kraft says, except for that uneasy moment in the middle. Thomas slaps Kraft's back hard enough to loosen teeth. Good old Saul. My inspiration, my counselor, my beacon. Thomas pushes his flask toward Kraft's face. Kraft shakes his head. He is fastidious about drinking, about decorum in general, as fastidious as Thomas is disreputable. You disapprove of me, don't you, Saul? But you need my charisma. You need my energy and my big loud voice. Too bad, Saul, that prophets aren't as neat and housebroken as you'd like them to be. "Ten o'clock," someone says. "It's now been going on for twenty-four hours."

A woman says, "The moon! Look! Didn't the moon just start to move again?"

From Kraft: "You wouldn't be able to see it with the naked eye. Not possibly. No way."

"Ask Thomas! Ask him!"

One of the technicians cries, "I can feel it! The Earth is turning!"

"Look, the stars!"

"Thomas! Thomas!"

They rush to him. Thomas, benign, serene, stretching forth his huge hands to reassure them, tells them that he has felt it too. Yes. There is motion in the universe again. Perhaps the turnings of the heavenly bodies are too subtle to be detected in a single glance, perhaps an hour or more will be needed for verification, and yet he knows, he is sure, he is absolutely sure. The Lord has withdrawn His Sign. The Earth turns. "Let us sleep now," Thomas says joyfully, "and greet the dawn in happiness."

Two
The Dance of the Apocalyptists

In late afternoon every day a band of Apocalyptists gathers by the stinking shore of Lake Erie to dance the sunset in. Their faces are painted with grotesque nightmare stripes; their expressions are wild; they fling themselves about in jerky, lurching steps, awkward and convulsive, the classic death-dance. Two immense golden loudspeakers, mounted like idols atop metal spikes rammed into the soggy soil, bellow abstract rhythms at them from either side. The leader of the group stands thigh-deep in the fouled waters, chanting, beckoning, directing them with short blurted cries: "People...holy people...chosen people... blessed people...persecuted people...Dance!...Dance!...The end...is near..." And they dance. Fingers shooting electrically into the air, elbows ramming empty space, knees rising high, they scramble toward the lake, withdraw, advance, withdraw, advance, three steps forward and two steps back, a will-you-won't-you-will-you-won't-you approach to salvation.

They have been doing this seven times a week since the beginning of the year, this fateful, terminal year, but only in the week since the Day of the Sign have they drawn much of an audience. At the outset, in frozen January, no one would bother to come to watch a dozen madmen capering on the windswept ice. Then the cult began getting sporadic television coverage, and that brought a few curiosity seekers. On the milder nights of April perhaps thirty dancers and twenty onlookers could be found at the lake. But now it is June, apocalyptic June, when the Lord in all His Majesty has revealed Himself, and the nightly dances are an event that brings thousands out of Cleveland's suburbs. Police lines hold the mob at a safe distance from the performers. A closed-circuit video loop relays the action to those on the outskirts of the crowd, too far away for a direct view. Network copters hover, cameras ready in case something unusual happens—the death of a dancer, the bursting loose of the mob, mass conversions, another miracle, anything. The air is cool tonight. The sun, delicately blurred and purpled by the smoky haze that perpetually thickens this region's sky, drops toward the breast of the lake. The dancers move in frenzied patterns, those in the front rank approaching the water, dipping their toes, retreating. Their leader, slapping the lake, throwing up fountaining spumes, continues to exhort them in a high, strained voice.

"People...holy people...chosen people..."

"Hallelujah! Hallelujah!"

"Come and be sealed! Blessed people...persecuted people...Come! Be! Sealed! Unto! The! Lord!"

"Hallelujah!"

The spectators shift uneasily. Some nudge and snigger. Some, staring fixedly, lock their arms and glower. Some move their lips in silent prayer or silent curses. Some look tempted to lurch forward and join the dance. Some will. Each night, there are a few who go forward. Each night, also, there are some who attempt to burst the police lines and attack the dancers. In June alone seven spectators have suffered heart seizures at the nightly festival: five fatalities.

"Servants of God!" cries the man in the water.

"Hallelujah!" reply the dancers.

"The year is speeding! The time is coming!"

"Hallelujah!"

"The trumpet shall sound! And we shall be saved!"

"Yes! Yes! Yes! Yes!"

Oh, the fervor of the dance! The wildness of the faces! The painted stripes swirl and run as sweat invades the thick greasy pigments. One could strew hot coals on the shore, now, and the dancers would advance all the same, oblivious, blissful. The choreography of their faith absorbs them wholly at this moment and they admit of no distractions. There is so little time left, after all, and such a great output of holy exertion is required of them before the end! June is almost half-spent. The year itself is almost half-spent. January approaches: the dawning of the new millennium, the day of the final trump, the moment of apocalypse. January 1, 2000: six and a half months away. And already He has given the Sign that the end of days is at hand. They dance. Through ecstatic movement comes salvation.

"Fear God, and give glory to Him; for the hour of His Judgment is come!"

"Hallelujah! Amen!"

"And worship Him that made heaven, and earth, and the sea, and the fountains of waters!"

"Hallelujah! Amen!"

They dance. The music grows more intense: prickly blurts of harsh tone flickering through the air. Spectators begin to clap hands and sway. Here comes the first convert of the night, now, a woman, middle-aged, plump, beseeching her way through the police cordon. An electronic device checks her for concealed weapons and explosive devices; she is found to be harmless; she passes the line and runs, stumbling, to join the dance.

"For the great day of His wrath is come; and who shall be able to stand?"

"Amen!"

"Servants of God! Be sealed unto Him, and be saved!"

"Sealed...sealed...We shall be sealed...We shall be saved..."

"And I saw four angels standing on the four corners of the Earth, holding the four winds of the Earth, that the wind should not blow on the Earth, nor on the sea, nor on any tree," roars the man in the water. "And I saw another angel ascending from the east, having the seal of the living God: and he cried with a loud voice to the four angels, to whom it was given to hurt the Earth and the sea, saying, Hurt not the Earth, neither the sea, nor the trees, till we have sealed the servants of our God in their foreheads."

"Sealed! Hallelujah! Amen!"

"And I heard the number of them which were sealed: and there were sealed an hundred and forty and four thousand of all the tribes of the children of Israel."

"Sealed! Sealed!"

"Come to me and be sealed! Dance and be sealed!"

The sun drops into the lake. The purple stain of sunset spreads across the horizon. The dancers shriek ecstatically and rush toward the water. They splash one another; they offer frantic baptisms in the murky lake; they drink, they spew forth what they have drunk, they drink again. Surrounding their leader. Seeking his blessing. An angry thick mutter from the onlookers. They are disgusted by this hectic show of faith. A menagerie, they say. A circus sideshow. These freaks. These godly freaks. Whom we have come to watch, so that we may despise them.

And if they are right? And if the world *does* end next January 1, and we go to hellfire, while *they* are saved? Impossible. Preposterous.

Absurd. But yet, who's to say? Only last week the Earth stood still a whole day. We live under His hand now. We always have, but now we have no liberty to doubt it. We can no longer deny that He's up there, watching us, listening to us, thinking about us. And if the end is really coming, as the crazy dancers think, what should I do to prepare for it? Should I join the dance? God help me. God help us all. Now the darkness falls. Look at the lunatics wallowing in the lake.

"Hallelujah! Amen!"

Three
The Sleep of Reason Produces Monsters

When I was about seven years old, which is to say somewhere in the late 1960's, I was playing out in front of the house on a Sunday morning, perhaps stalking some ladybirds for my insect collection, when three freckle-faced Irish kids who lived on the next block came wandering by. They were on their way home from church. The youngest one was my age, and the other two must have been eight or nine. To me they were Big Boys: ragged, strong, swaggering, alien. My father was a college professor and theirs was probably a bus conductor or a coal-miner, and so they were as strange to me as a trio of tourists from Patagonia would have been. They stopped and watched me for a minute, and then the biggest one called me out into the street, and he asked me how it was that they never saw me in church on Sundays.

The simplest and most tactful thing for me to tell them would have been that I didn't happen to be Roman Catholic. That was true. I think that all they wanted to find out was what church I did go to, since I obviously didn't go to theirs. Was I Jewish, Moslem, Presbyterian, Baptist, what? But I was a smug little snot then, and instead of handling the situation diplomatically, I cheerfully told them that I didn't go to church because I didn't believe in God.

They looked at me as though I had just blown my nose on the American flag.

"Say that again?" the biggest one demanded.

"I don't believe in God," I said. "Religion's just a big fake. My father says so, and I think he's right."

They frowned and backed off a few paces and conferred in low, earnest voices, with many glances in my direction. Evidently I was their first atheist. I assumed we would now have a debate on the existence of the Deity: they would explain to me the motives that led them to use up so many valuable hours on their knees inside the Church of Our Lady of the Sorrows, and then I would try to show them how silly it was to worry so much about an invisible old man in the sky. But a theological disputation, wasn't their style. They came out of their huddle and strolled toward me, and I suddenly detected menace in their eyes, and just as the two smaller ones lunged at me I slipped past them and started to run. They had longer legs, but I was more agile; besides, I was on my home block and knew the turf better. I sprinted halfway down the street, darted into an alley, slipped through the open place in the back of the Allertons' garage, doubled back up the street via the rear lane, and made it safely into our house by way of the kitchen door. For the next couple of days I stayed close to home after school and kept a wary watch, but the pious Irish lads never came around again to punish the blasphemer. After that I learned to be more careful about expressing my opinions on religious matters.

But I never became a believer. I had a natural predisposition toward skepticism. *If you can't measure it, it isn't there.* That included not only Old Whiskers and His Only Begotten Son, but all the other mystic baggage that people liked to carry around in those tense credulous years: the flying saucers, Zen Buddhism, the Atlantis cult, Hare Krishna, macrobiotics, telepathy and other species of extrasensory perception, theosophy, entropy-worship, astrology, and such. I was willing to accept neutrinos, quasars, the theory of continental drift, and the various species of quarks, because I respected the evidence for their existence; I couldn't buy the other stuff, the irrational stuff, the assorted opiates of the masses. When the Moon is in the seventh house, etc., etc.—sorry, no. I clung to the path of reason as I made my uneasy journey toward maturity, and hardheaded little Billy Gifford, smartypants bug collector, remained unchurched as he ripened into Professor William F. Gifford, Ph.D., of the Department of Physics, Harvard. I wasn't *hostile* to organized religion, I just ignored it, as I might ignore a newspaper account of a jai-alai tournament in Afghanistan.

I envied the faithful their faith, oh, yes. When the dark times got darker, how sweet it must have been to be able to rush to Our Lady of the Sorrows for comfort! They could pray, they had the illusion that a divine plan governed this best of all possible worlds, while I was left in bleak, stormy limbo, dismally aware that the universe makes no sense and that the only universal truth there is, is that Entropy Eventually Wins.

There were times when I wanted genuinely to be able to pray, when I was weary of operating solely on my own existential capital, when I wanted to grovel and cry out, *Okay, Lord, I give up, You take it from here.* I had favors to ask of Him: God, let my little girl's fever go down. Let my plane not crash. Let them not shoot *this* President too. Let the races learn how to live in peace before the blacks get around to burning down my street. Let the peace-loving enlightened students not bomb the computer center this semester. Let the next kindergarten drug scandal not erupt in my boy's school. Let the lion lie down with the lamb. As we zoomed along on the Chaos Express, I was sometimes tempted toward godliness the way the godly are tempted toward sin. But my love of divine reason left me no way to opt for the irrational. Call it stiff-neckedness, call it rampant egomania: no matter how bad things got, Bill Gifford wasn't going to submit to the tyranny of a hobgoblin. Even a benevolent one. Even if I had favors to ask of Him. So much to ask; so little faith. Intellectual, honesty *über alles,* Gifford! While every year things were a little worse than the last.

When I was growing up, in the 1970's, it was fashionable for educated and serious-minded people to get together and tell each other that western civilization was collapsing. The Germans had a word for it, *Schadenfreude,* the pleasure one gets from talking about catastrophes. And the 1970's were shadowed by catastrophes, real or expected: the pollution escalation, the population explosion, Vietnam and all the little Vietnams, the supersonic transport, black separatism, white backlash, student unrest, extremist women's lib, the neofascism of the New Left, the neonihilism of the New Right, a hundred other varieties of dynamic irrationality going full blast, yes, ample fuel for the *Schadenfreude* syndrome. Yes, my parents and their civilized friends said solemnly, sadly, gleefully, it's all blowing up, it's all going smash, it's all whooshing down the drain. Through the fumes of the Saturday-night pot came the inevitable portentous quotes from Yeats: *Things fall apart; the center cannot hold; mere anarchy is loosed upon the world.* Well, that shall we do about it? Perhaps it's really beyond our control now. Brethren, shall we pray? Lift up your voices unto Him! But I can't. I'd feel like a damned fool. Forgive me, God, but I must deny You! *The best lack all conviction, while the worst are full of passionate intensity.*

And of course everything got much more awful than the doomsayers of the 1970's really expected. Even those who most dearly relished enumerating the calamities to come still thought, beneath their grim joy, that somehow reason ultimately would triumph. The most gloomy Jeremiah entertained secret hopes that the noble ecological resolutions would eventually be translated into meaningful environmental action, that the crazy birth spiral would be checked in time, that the strident rhetoric of the innumerable protest groups would be tempered and modulated as time brought them the beginning of a fulfillment of their revolutionary goals—but no. Came the 1980's, the decade of my young manhood, and all the hysteria jumped to the next-highest energy level. That was when we began having the Gas Mask Days. The programmed electrical shutdowns. The elegantly orchestrated international chaos of the Third World People's Prosperity Group. The airport riots. The black rains. The Computer Purge. The Brazilian Pacification Program. The Claude Harkins Book List with its accompanying library-burnings. The Ecological Police Action. The Genetic Purity League and its even more frightening black counterpart. The Children's Crusade for Sanity. The Nine Weeks' War. The Night of the Lasers. The center had long ago ceased to hold; now we were strapped to a runaway wheel. Amidst the furies I studied, married, brought forth young, built a career, fought off daily terror, and like everyone else, waited for the inevitable final calamity.

Who could doubt that it would come? Not you, not I. And not the strange wild-eyed folk who emerged among us like dark growths pushing out of rotting logs, the Apocalyptists, who raised *Schadenfreude* to the sacramental level and organized an ecstatic religion of doom. The end of the world, they told us, was scheduled for January 1, A.D. 2000, and upon that date, 144,000 elite souls, who had "sealed" themselves unto God by devotion and good works, would be saved; the rest of us poor sinners would be hauled before the Judge. I could see their point. Although I rejected their talk of the Second Coming, having long ago rejected the First, and although I shared neither their confidence in the exact date of the apocalypse nor their notions of how the survivors would be chosen, I agreed with them that the end was close at hand. The fact that for a quarter of a century we had been milking giddy cocktail-party chatter out of the impending collapse of western civilization didn't of itself guarantee that western civilization wasn't going to collapse; some of the things people like to say at cocktail parties can hit the target. As a physicist with a decent understanding of the entropic process, I found all the signs of advanced societal decay easy to identify: for a century we had been increasing the complexity of society's functions so that an ever-higher level of organization was required in order to make things run, and for much of that time we had simultaneously been trending toward total universal democracy, toward a world consisting of several billion self-governing republics with a maximum of three citizens each. Any closed system which experiences simultaneous sharp increases in mechanical complexity and in entropic diffusion is going to go to pieces long before the maximum distribution of energy is reached. The pattern of consents and contracts on which civilization is based is destroyed; every social interaction, from parking your car to settling an international boundary dispute, becomes a problem that can be handled only by means of force, since all "civilized" techniques of reconciling disagreement have been suspended as irrelevant; when the delivery of mail is a matter of private negotiation between the citizen and his postman, what hope is there for the rule of reason? Somewhere, somehow, we had passed a point of no return—in 1984, 1972, maybe even that ghastly day in November of 1963—and nothing now could save us from plunging over the brink.

Nothing?

Out of Nevada came Thomas, shaggy Thomas, Thomas the Proclaimer, rising above the slot machines and the roulette wheels to cry, If ye have faith, ye shall be saved! An anti-Apocalyptist prophet, no less, whose message was that civilization still might be preserved, that it was not yet too late. The voice of hope, the enemy of entropy, the new Apostle of Peace. Though to people like me he looked just as wild-eyed and hairy and dangerous and terrifyingly psychotic as the worshippers of the holocaust, for he, like the Apocalyptists, dealt in forces operating outside the realm of sanity. By rights he should have come out of the backwoods of Arkansas or the crazier corners of California, but he didn't, he was a desert rat, a Nevadan, a sand-eating latter-day John the Baptist. A true prophet for our times, too: seedy, disreputable, a wine-swiller, a cynic. Capable of beginning a global telecast sermon with a belch. An ex-soldier who had happily napalmed whole provinces during the Brazilian Pacification Program. A part-time dealer in bootlegged hallucinogens. An expert at pocket-picking and computer-jamming. He had gone into the evangelism business because he thought he could make an easy buck that way, peddling the Gospels and appropriating the collection box, but a funny thing had happened to him, he claimed: he had seen the Lord, he had discovered the error of his ways, he had become inflamed with righteousness. Hiding not his grimy past, he now offered himself as a walking personification of redemption: *Look ye, if I can be saved from sin, there's hope for everyone!* The media picked him up. That magnificent voice of his, that great mop of hair, those eyes, that hypnotic self-confidence—perfect. He walked from California to Florida to proclaim the coming millennium. And gathered followers, thousands, millions, all those who weren't yet ready to let Armageddon begin, and he made them pray and pray and pray; he held revival meetings that were beamed to Karachi and Katmandu and Addis Ababa and Shanghai, he preached no particular theology and no particular scripture, but only a smooth ecumenical theism that practically anybody could swallow, whether he be Confucianist or Moslem or Hindu. Listen, Thomas said, there *is* a God, some kind of all-powerful being out there whose divine plan guides the universe, and He watches over us, and don't you believe otherwise! And He is good and will not let us come to harm if we hew to His path. And He has tested us with all these troubles, in order to measure the depth of our faith in Him. So let's show Him, brethren! Let's all pray together and send up a great shout unto Him! For He would certainly give a Sign, and the unbelievers would at last be converted, and the epoch of purity would commence. People said, Why not give it a try? We've got a lot to gain and nothing to lose. A vulgar version of the old Pascal wager: if He's really there, He may help us, and if He's not, we've only wasted a little time. So the hour of beseeching was set.

In faculty circles we had a good deal of fun with the whole idea, we brittle worldly rational types, but sometimes there was a nervous edge to our jokes and a forced heartiness to our laughter, as if some of us suspected that Pascal might have been offering pretty good odds, or that Thomas might just have hit on something. Naturally I was among the skeptics, though as usual I kept my doubts to myself. (The lesson learned so long ago, the narrow escape from the Irish lads.) I hadn't really paid much attention to Thomas and his message, any more than I did to football scores or children's video programs: not my sphere, not my concern. But as the day of prayer drew near, the old temptation beset me. *Give in at last, Gifford. Bow your head and offer homage. Even if He's the myth you've always known He is, do it. Do it!* I argued with myself. I told myself not to be an idiot, not to yield to the age-old claims of superstition. I reminded myself of the holy wars, the Inquisition, the lascivious Renaissance popes, all the crimes of the pious. *So what, Gifford? Can't you be an ordinary humble God-fearing human being for once in your life? Down on your knees beside your brethren? Read your Pascal. Suppose He exists and is listening, and suppose your refusal is the one that tips the scales against mankind? We're not asking so very much.* Still I fought the sly inner voice. To believe is absurd, I cried. I must not let despair stampede me into the renunciation of reason, even in this apocalyptic moment. Thomas is a cunning ruffian and his followers are hysterical grubby fools. *And you're an arrogant elitist, Gifford. Who may live long enough to repent his arrogance.* It was psychological warfare, Gifford vs. Gifford, reason vs. faith.

In the end reason lost. I was jittery, off balance, demoralized. The most astonishing people were coming out in support of Thomas the Proclaimer, and I felt increasingly isolated, a man of ice, heart of stone, the village atheist scowling at Christmas wreaths. Up until the final moment I wasn't sure what I was going to do, but then the hour struck and I found myself in my study, alone, door locked, safely apart from wife and children—who had already, all of them, somewhat defiantly announced their intentions of participating—and there I was on my knees, feeling foolish, feeling preposterous, my cheeks blazing, my lips moving, saying the swords. *Saying the words.* Around the world the billions of believers prayed, and I also. I too prayed, embarrassed by my weakness, and the pain of my shame was a stone in my throat.

And the Lord heard us, and He gave a Sign. And for a day and a night (less 1×12^{-4} sidereal day) the Earth moved not around the sun, neither did it rotate. And the laws of momentum were confounded, as was I. Then Earth again took up its appointed course, as though nothing out of the ordinary had occurred. Imagine my chagrin. I wish I knew where to find those Irish boys. I have some apologies to make.

Four
Thomas Preaches in the Marketplace

I hear what you're saying. You tell me I'm a prophet. You tell me I'm a saint. Some of you even tell me I'm the Son of God come again. You tell me I made the sun stand still over Jerusalem. Well, no, I didn't do that, the Lord Almighty did that, the Lord of Hosts. Through His divine

Will, in response to your prayers. And I'm only the vehicle through which your prayers were channeled. I'm not any kind of saint, folks. I'm not the Son of God reborn, or any of the other crazy things you've been saying I am. I'm only Thomas.

Who am I?

I'm just a voice. A spokesman. A tool through which His will was made manifest. I'm not giving you the old humility act, friends, I'm trying to make you see the truth about me.

Who am I?

I'll tell you who I was, though you know it already. I was a bandit, I was a man of evil, I was a defiler of the law. A killer, a liar, a drunkard, a cheat! I did what I damned pleased. I was a law unto myself. If I ever got caught, you bet I wouldn't have whined for mercy. I'd have spit in the judge's face and taken my punishment with my eyes open. Only I never got caught, because my luck was running good and because this is a time when a really bad man can flourish, when the wicked are raised high and the virtuous are ground into the mud. Outside the law, that was me! Thomas the criminal! Thomas the brigand, thumbing his nose! Doing bad was my religion, all the time—when I was down there in Brazil with those flamethrowers, or when I was free-lancing your pockets in our cities, or when I was ringing up funny numbers on the big computers. I belonged to Satan if ever a man did, that's the truth, and then what happened? The Lord came along to Satan and said to him, Satan, give me Thomas, I have need of him. And Satan handed me over to Him, because Satan is God's servant too.

And the Lord took me and shook me and knocked me around and said, Thomas, you're nothing but trash!

And I said, I know that, Lord, but who was it who made me that way?

And the Lord laughed and said, You've got guts, Thomas, talking back to me like that. I like a man with guts. But you're wrong, fellow. I made you with the potential to be a saint or a sinner, and you chose to be a sinner, yes, of your own free will! You think I'd bother to create people to be wicked? I'm not interested in creating puppets, Thomas, I set out to make me a race of human beings. I gave you your options and you opted for evil, eh, Thomas? Isn't that the truth?

And I said, Well, Lord, maybe it is; I don't know.

And the Lord God grew annoyed with me and took me again and shook me again and knocked me around some more, and when I picked myself up I had a puffed lip and a bloody nose, and He asked me how

I would do things if I could live my life over again from the start. And I looked Him right in the eye and said, Well, Lord, I'd say that being evil paid off pretty well for me. I lived a right nice life and I had all my happies and I never spent a day behind bars, oh, no. So tell me, Lord, since I got away with everything the first time, why shouldn't I opt to be a sinner again?

And he said, Because you've done that already, and now it's time for you to do something else.

I said, What's that, Lord?

He said, I want you to do something important for me, Thomas. There's a world out there full of people who've lost all faith, people without hope, people who've made up their minds it's no use trying any more, the world's going to end. I want to reach those people somehow, Thomas, and tell them that they're wrong, And show them that they can shape their own destiny, that if they have faith in themselves and in me they can build a good world.

I said, That's easy, Lord. Why don't You just appear in the sky and say that to them, like You just did to me?

He laughed again and said, Oh, no, Thomas, that's much too easy. I told you, I don't run a puppet show. They've got to *want* to lift themselves up out of despair. They've got to take the first step by themselves. You follow me, Thomas?

Yes, Lord, but where do I come in?

And He said, You go to them, Thomas, and you tell them all about your wasted, useless, defiant life, and then tell them how the Lord gave you a chance to do something worthwhile for a change, and how you rose up above your evil self and accepted the opportunity. And then tell them to gather and pray and restore their faith, and ask for a Sign from on high. Thomas, if they listen to you, if they pray and it's sincere prayer, I promise you I will give them a Sign, I *will* reveal myself to them, and all doubt will drop like scales from their eyes. Will you do that thing for me, Thomas?

Friends, I listened to the Lord, and. I discovered myself shaking and quivering and bursting into sweat, and in a moment, in the twinkling of an eye, I wasn't the old filthy Thomas any more, I was somebody new and clean, I was a man with a high purpose, a man with a belief in something bigger and better than his own greedy desires. And I went down among you, changed as I was, and I told my tale, and all of you know the rest of the story, how we came freely together and offered up our hearts to Him, and how He vouchsafed us a miracle these two and a half weeks past, and gave us a Sign that He still watches over us.

But what do I see now, in these latter days after the giving of the Sign? What do I see?

Where is that new world of faith? Where is that new dream of hope? Where is mankind shoulder to shoulder, praising Him and working together to reach the light?

What do I see? I see this rotting planet turning black inside and splitting open at the core. I see the cancer of doubt. I see the virus of confusion. I see His Sign misinterpreted on every hand, and its beauty trampled on and destroyed.

I still see painted fools dancing and beating on drums and screaming that the world is going to be destroyed at the end of this year of nineteen hundred and ninety-nine. What madness is this? Has God not spoken? Has He not told us joyful news? God is with us! God is good! Why do these Apocalyptists not yet accept the truth of His Sign?

Even worse! Each day new madnesses take form! What are these cults sprouting up among us? Who are these people who demand of God that He return and spell out His intentions, as though the Sign wasn't enough for them? And who are these cowardly blasphemers who say we must lie down in fear and weep piteous tears, because we have invoked not God but Satan, and destruction is our lot? Who are these men of empty souls who bleat and mumble and snivel in our midst? And look at your lofty churchmen, in their priestly robes and glittering tiaras, trying to explain away the Sign as some accident of nature! What talk is this from God's own ministers? And behold the formerly godless ones, screeching like frightened monkeys now that their godlessness has been ripped from them! What do I see? I see madness and terror on all sides, where I should see only joy abounding!

I beg you, friends, have care, take counsel with your souls. I beg you, think clearly now if you ever have thought at all. Choose a wise path, friends, or you will throw away all the glory of the Day of the Sign and lay waste to our great achievement. Give no comfort to the forces of darkness. Keep away from these peddlers of lunatic creeds. Strive to recapture the wonder of that moment when all mankind spoke with a single voice. I beg you—how can you have doubt of Him now?—I beg you—faith—the triumph of faith—let us not allow—let us—not allow—not—allow—

(Jesus, my throat! All this shouting, it's like swallowing fire. Give me that bottle, will you? Come on, give it here! The wine. The wine.

Now. Ah. Oh, that's better! Much better, oh, yes. No, wait, give it back—good, good—stop looking at me like that, Saul. Ah. *Ah.)*

And so I beseech you today, brothers and sisters in the Lord—brothers and sisters (what was I saying, Saul? what did I start to say?)—I call upon you to rededicate yourselves—to pledge yourselves to—to (is that it? I can't remember)—to a new Crusade of Faith, that's what we need, a purging of all our doubts and all our hesitations and all our (oh, Jesus, Saul, I'm lost, I don't remember where the hell I'm supposed to be. Let the music start playing. Quick. That's it. Good and louder. Louder.) Folks, let's all sing! Raise your voices joyously unto Him!

I *shall praise the Lord my God,*
Fountain of all power…

That's the way! Sing! Everybody sing!

Five
Ceremonies of Innocence

Throughout the world the quest for an appropriate response to the event of June 6 continues. No satisfactory interpretation of that day's happenings has yet been established, though many have been proposed. Meanwhile passions run high; tempers easily give way; a surprising degree of violence has entered the situation. Clearly the temporary slowing of the earth's axial rotation must have imposed exceptional emotional stress on the entire global population, creating severe strains that have persisted and even intensified in the succeeding weeks. Instances of seemingly motiveless crimes, particularly arson and vandalism, have greatly increased. Government authorities in Brazil, India, the United Arab Republic, and Italy have suggested that clandestine revolutionary or counterrevolutionary groups are behind much of this activity, taking advantage of the widespread mood of uncertainty to stir discontent. No evidence of this has thus far been made public. Much hostility has been directed toward the organized religions, a phenomenon for which there is as yet no generally accepted explanation, although several sociologists have asserted that this pattern of violent anticlerical behavior is a reaction to the failure of most established religious bodies as of this time to provide official interpretations of the so-called miracle of June 6. Reports of the destruction by mob action of houses of worship of various faiths, with accompanying injuries or fatalities suffered by ecclesiastical personnel, have come from Mexico, Denmark, Burma, Puerto Rico, Portugal, Hungary, Ethiopia, the Philippines, and, in the United States, Alabama, Colorado, and New York. Statements are promised shortly by leaders of most major faiths. Meanwhile a tendency has developed in certain ecclesiastical quarters toward supporting a mechanistic or rationalistic causation for the June 6 event; thus on Tuesday the Archbishop of York, stressing that he was speaking as a private citizen and not as a prelate of the Church of England, declared that we should not rule out entirely the possibility of a manipulation of the Earth's movements by superior beings native to another planet, intent on spreading confusion preparatory to conquest. Modern theologians, the Archbishop said, see no inherent impossibility in the doctrine of a separate act of creation that brought forth an intelligent species on some extraterrestrial or extragalactic planet, nor is it inconceivable, he went on, that it might be the Lord's ultimate purpose to cause a purging of sinful mankind at the hands of that other species. Thus the slowing of the Earth's rotation may have been an attempt by these enemies from space to capitalize on the emotions generated by the recent campaign of the so-called prophet Thomas the Proclaimer. A spokesman for the Coptic Patriarch of Alexandria, commenting favorably two days later on the Archbishop's theory, added that in the private view of the Patriarch it seems less implausible that such an alien species should exist than that a divine miracle of the June 6 sort could be invoked by popular demand. A number of other religious leaders, similarly speaking unofficially, have cautioned against too rapid acceptance of the divine origin of the June 6 event, without as yet going so far as to embrace the Archbishop of York's suggestion. On Friday Dr. Nathan F. Scharf, President of the Central Conference of American Rabbis, urgently appealed to American and Israeli scientists to produce a computer-generated mathematical schema capable of demonstrating how a unique but natural conjunction of astronomical forces might have resulted in the June 6 event. The only reply to this appeal thus far has come from Ssu-ma Hsiang, Minister of Science of the People's Republic of China, who has revealed that a task force of several hundred Chinese astronomers is already at work on such a project. But his Soviet counterpart, Academician N. V. Posilippov, has on the contrary called for a revision of Marxist-Leninist astronomical theory to take into account what he terms "the possibility of intervention by as yet undefined forces, perhaps of supernatural aspect, in the motions of the heavenly bodies." We may conclude, therefore, that the situation remains in flux. Observers agree that the chief beneficiaries of the June 6 event at this point have been the various recently founded apocalyptic sects, who now regard the so-called Day of the Sign as an indication of the imminent destruction of life on Earth. Undoubtedly much of the current violence and the other irrational behavior can be traced to the increased activity of such groups. A related manifestation is the dramatic expansion in recent weeks of older millenarian sects, notably the Pentecostal churches. The Protestant world in general has experienced a rebirth of the Pentecostal-inspired phenomenon known as glossolalia, or "speaking in tongues," a technique for penetrating to revelatory or prophetic levels by means of unreined ecstatic outbursts *illalum gha ghollim ve illalum ghollim ghaznim kroo! Aiha! Kroo illalum nildaz sitamon ghaznim* of seemingly random syllables in no language known to the speaker; the value of this practice has *mehigioo camaleelee honistar zam* been a matter of controversy in religious circles for many centuries.

Six
The Woman Who Is Sore at Heart Reproaches Thomas

I knew he was in our county and I had to get to see him because he was the one who made all this trouble for me. So I went to his headquarters, the place where the broadcasts were being made that week, and I saw him standing in the middle of a group of his followers. A very handsome man, really, somewhat too dirty and wild-looking for my tastes, but you give him a shave and a haircut and he'd be quite attractive in my estimation. Big and strong he is, and when you see him you want to throw yourself into his arms, though of course I was in no frame of mind to do any such thing just then and in any case I'm not that sort of woman. I went right toward him. There was a tremendous crowd in the street, but I'm not discouraged easily, my husband likes to call me his "little bulldog" sometimes, and I just bulled my way through that mob, a little kicking and some elbowing and I think I bit someone's arm once and I got through. There was Thomas and next to him that skinny little man who's always with him, that Saul Kraft, who I guess is his press agent or something. As l I got close, three of his bodyguards looked at me and then at each other, probably saying oh-oh, here comes another crank dame, and they started to surround me and move me away, and Thomas wasn't even looking at me, and I began to yell, saying I had to talk to Thomas, I had something important to say. And then this Saul Kraft told them to let go of me and bring me forward. They checked me out for concealed weapons and then Thomas asked me what I wanted.

I felt nervous before him. Such a famous man. But I planted my feet flat on the ground and stuck my jaw up the way Dad taught me, and I said, "You did all this. You've wrecked me, Thomas. You've got me so I don't know if I'm standing on my head or right side up."

He gave me a funny sideways smile. "I did?"

"Look," I said, "I'll tell you how it was. I went to Mass every week, my whole family, Church of the Redeemer on Wilson Avenue. We put money in the plate, we did everything the fathers told us to do, we tried to live good Christian lives, right? Not that we really thought much about God. Whether He was actually up there listening to me saying my paternoster. I figured He was too busy to worry much about me, and I couldn't be too concerned about Him, because He surpasses my understanding, you follow? Instead I prayed to the fathers. To me Father McDermott was like God Himself, in a way, not meaning any disrespect. What I'm trying to say is that the average ordinary person, they don't have a very close relationship with God, you follow? With the church, yes, with the fathers, but not with God. Okay. Now you come along and say the world is in a mess, so let's pray to God to show Himself like in the olden times. I ask Father McDermott about it and he says it's all right, it's permitted even though it isn't an idea that came from Rome, on such-and-such day we'll have this world moment of prayer. So I pray, and the sun stands still. June 6, you made the sun stand still."

"Not me. *Him.*" Thomas was smiling again. And looking at me like he could read everything in my soul.

I said, "You know what I mean. It's a miracle, anyway. The biggest miracle since, I don't know, since, the Resurrection. The next day we need help, guidance, right? My husband and I, we go to church. *The church is closed.* Locked tight. We go around back and try to find the fathers. Nobody there but a housekeeper and she's scared. Won't open up. Why is the church shut? They're afraid of rioters, she says. Where's Father McDermott? He's gone to the Archdiocese for a conference. So have all the other fathers. Go away, she says. Nobody's here. You follow me, Thomas? Biggest miracle since the Resurrection, *and they close the church the next day.*"

Thomas said, "They got nervous, I guess."

"Nervous? Sure they were nervous. That's my whole point. Where were the fathers when we needed them? Conferring at the Archdiocese. The Cardinal was holding a special meeting about the crisis. *The crisis,* Thomas! God Himself works a miracle, and to the church it's a crisis! What am I supposed to do? Where does it leave me? I need the church, the church has always been telling me that, and all of a sudden the church locks its doors and says to me, Go figure it out by yourself, lady, we won't have a bulletin for a couple of days. The church was scared! I think they were afraid the Lord was going to come in and say we don't need priests any more, we don't need churches, all this organized-religion stuff hasn't worked out so well anyway, so let's forget it and move right into the Millennium."

"Anything big and strange always upsets the people in power," Thomas said, shrugging. "But the church opened again, didn't it?"

"Sure, four days later. Business as usual, except we aren't supposed to ask any questions about June 6 yet. Because they don't have The Word from Rome yet, the interpretation, the official policy." I had to laugh. "'Three weeks, almost, since it happened, and the College of Cardinals is still in special consistory, trying to decide what position the church ought to take. Isn't that crazy, Thomas? If the Pope can't recognize a miracle when he sees one, what good is the whole church?"

"All right," Thomas said, "but why blame me?"

"Because you took my church away from me. I can't trust those people any more. I don't know what to believe. We've got God right here beside us, and the church isn't giving any leadership. What do we do now? How do we handle this thing?"

"Have faith, my child," he said, "and pray for salvation, and remain steadfast in your righteousness." He said a lot of other stuff like that too, rattling it off like he was a computer programmed to deliver blessings. I could tell he wasn't sincere. He wasn't trying to answer me, just to calm me down and get rid of me.

"No," I said, breaking in on him. "That stuff isn't good enough. *Have faith. Pray a lot.* I've been doing that all my life. Okay, we prayed and we got God to show Himself. What now? What's your program, Thomas? Tell me that. What do you want us to do? You took our church away—what will you give us to replace it?"

I could tell he didn't have any answers.

His face turned red and he tugged on the ends of his hair and looked at Saul Kraft in a sour way, almost like he was saying I-told-you-so with his eyes. Then he looked back at me and I saw either sorrow or fear in his face, I don't know which, and I realized right then that this Thomas is just a human being like you and me, a human being, who doesn't really understand what's happening and doesn't know how to go on from this point. He tried to fake it. He told me again to pray, never underestimate the power of prayer, et cetera, et cetera, but his heart wasn't in his words. He was stuck. *What's your program, Thomas?* He doesn't have any. He hasn't thought things through past the point of getting the Sign from God. He can't help us now. There's your Thomas for you, the Proclaimer, the prophet. He's scared. We're all scared, and he's just one of us, no different, no wiser. And last night the Apocalyptists burned the shopping center. You know, if you had asked me six months ago how I'd feel if God gave us a Sign that He was really watching over us, I'd have told you that I thought it would be the most wonderful thing that had ever happened since Jesus in the manger. But now it's happened. And I'm not so sure how wonderful it is. I walk around feeling that the ground might open up under my feet any time. I don't know what's going to happen to us all. God has come, and it ought to be beautiful, and instead it's just scary. I never imagined it would be this way. Oh, God. God I feel so lost. God I I feel so empty.

Seven
An Insight of Discerners

Speaking before an audience was nothing new for me, of course. Not after all the years I've spent in classrooms, patiently instructing each season's hairy new crop of young in the mysteries of tachyon theory, anterior-charge particles, and time-reversal equations. Nor was this audience a particularly alien or frightening one: it was made up mainly of faculty people from Harvard and M.I.T., some graduate students, and a sprinkling of lawyers, psychologists, and other professional folk from Cambridge and the outskirts. All of us part of the community of scholarship, so to speak. The sort of audience that might come together to protest the latest incident of ecological rape or of preventive national liberation. But one aspect of my role this evening was unsettling to me. This was in the truest sense a religious gathering; that is, we were meeting to discuss the nature of God and to arrive at some comprehension of our proper relationship to Him. And I was the main speaker, me, old

Bill Gifford, who for nearly four decades had regarded the Deity as an antiquated irrelevance. I was this flock's pastor. How strange that felt.

"But I believe that many of you are in the same predicament," I told them. "Men and women to whom the religious impulse has been something essentially foreign. Whose lives were complete and fulfilled although prayer and ritual were wholly absent from them. Who regarded the concept of a supreme being as meaningless and who looked upon the churchgoing habits of those around them as nothing more than lower-class superstitiousness on the one hand and middle-class pietism on the other. And then came the great surprise of June 6—forcing us to reconsider doctrines we had scorned, forcing us to reexamine our basic philosophical constructs, forcing us to seek an acceptable explanation of a phenomenon that we had always deemed impossible and implausible. All of you, like myself, suddenly found yourselves treading very deep metaphysical waters."

The nucleus of this group had come together on an ad hoc basis the week after It happened, and since then had been meeting two or three times a week. At first there was no formal organizational structure, no organizational name, no policy; it was merely a gathering of intelligent and sophisticated New Englanders who felt unable to cope individually with the altered nature of reality and who needed mutual reassurance and reinforcement. That was why I started going, anyway. But within ten days we were groping toward a more positive purpose: no longer simply to learn how to *accept* what had befallen humanity, but to find some way of turning it to a useful purpose. I had begun articulating some ideas along those lines in private conversation, and abruptly I was asked by several of the leaders of the group to make my thoughts public at the next meeting.

"An astonishing event has occurred," I went on. "A good many ingenious theories have been proposed to account for it—as, for example, that the Earth was brought to a halt through the workings of an extrasensory telekinetic force generated by the simultaneous concentration of the entire world population. We have also heard the astrological explanations—that the planets or the stars were lined up in a certain once-in-a-universe's-lifetime way to bring about such a result. And there have been the arguments, some of them coming from quite surprising places, in favor of the notion that the June 6 event was the doing of malevolent creatures from outer space. The telekinesis hypothesis has a certain superficial plausibility, marred only by the fact that experimenters in the past have never been able to detect even an iota of telekinetic ability in any human being or combination of human beings. Perhaps a simultaneous world-wide effort might generate forces not to be found in any unit smaller than the total human population, but such reasoning requires an undesirable multiplication of hypotheses. I believe that most of you here agree with me that the other explanations of the June 6 event beg one critical question: Why did the slowing of the Earth occur so promptly, in seemingly direct response to Thomas the Proclaimer's campaign of global prayer? Can we believe that a unique alignment of astrological forces just happened to occur the day after that hour of prayer? Can we believe that the extragalactic fiends just happened to meddle with the Earth's rotation on that particular day? The element of coincidence necessary to sustain these and other arguments is fatal to them, I think.

"What are we left with, then? Only with the explanation that the Lord Almighty, heeding mankind's entreaties, performed a miracle so that we should be confirmed in our faith in Him.

"So I conclude. So do many of you. But does it necessarily follow that mankind's sorry religious history, with all its holy wars, its absurd dogmas, its childish rituals, its fastings and flagellations, is thereby justified? Because you and you and you and I were bowled over on June 6, blasted out of our skepticism by an event that has no rational explanation, should we therefore rush to the churches and synagogues and mosques and enroll immediately in the orthodoxy of our choice? I think not. I submit that our attitudes of skepticism and rationalism were properly held, although our aim was misplaced. In scorning the showy, trivial trappings of organized faith, in walking past the churches where our neighbors devoutly knelt, we erred by turning away also from the matter that underlay, their faith: the existence of a supreme being whose divine plan guides the universe. The spinning of prayer wheels and the mumbling of credos seemed so inane to us that, in our revulsion for such things, we were led to deny all notions of a higher order, of a teleological universe, and we embraced the concept of a wholly random cosmos. And then the Earth stood still for a day and a night.

"How did it happen? We admit it was God's doing, you and I, amazed though we are to find ourselves saying so. We have been hammered into a posture of belief by that inexplicable event. But what do we mean by 'God'? Who is He? An old man with long white whiskers?

Where is He to be found? Somewhere between the orbits of Mars and Jupiter? Is He a supernatural being, or merely an extraterrestrial one? Does He too acknowledge a superior authority? And so on, an infinity of new questions. We have no valid knowledge of His nature, though now we have certain knowledge of His existence.

"Very well. A tremendous opportunity now exists for us the discerning few, for us who are in the habit of intellectual activity. All about us we see a world in frenzy. The Apocalyptists swoon with joy over the approaching catastrophe, the glossolaliacs chatter in maniac glee, the heads of entrenched churchly hierarchies are aghast at the possibility that the Millennium may really be at hand; everything is in flux, everything is new and strange. New cults spring up. Old creeds dissolve. And this is our moment. Let us step in and replace credulity and superstition with reason. An end to cults; an end to theology; an end to blind faith. Let it be our goal to relate the events of that awesome day to some principle of reason, and develop a useful, dynamic, *rational* movement of rebirth and revival—not a religion per se but rather a cluster of belief, based on the concept that a divine plan exists, that we live under the authority of a supreme or at least superior being, and that we must strive to come to some kind of rational relationship with this being.

"We've already had the moral strength to admit that our old intuitive skepticism was an error. Now let us provide an attractive alternate for those of us who still find ritualistic orthodoxy unpalatable, but who fear a total collapse into apocalyptic disarray if no steps are taken to strengthen mankind's spiritual insight. Let us create, if we can, a purely secular movement, a nonreligious religion, which offers the hope of establishing a meaningful dialogue between Us and Him. Let us make plans. Let us find powerful symbols with which we may sway the undecided and the confused. Let us march forth as crusaders in a dramatic effort to rescue humanity from unreason and desperation."

And so forth. I think it was a pretty eloquent speech, especially coming from someone who isn't in the habit of delivering orations. A transcript of it got into the local paper the next day and was reprinted all over. My "us the discerning few" line drew a lot of attention, and spawned an instant label for our previously unnamed movement. We became known as the Discerners. Once we had a name, our status was different. We weren't simply a group of concerned citizens any longer. Now we constituted a cult—a skeptical, rational, anti-superstitious cult, true, but nevertheless a cult, a sect, the newest facet of the world's furiously proliferating latter-day craziness.

Eight
An Expectation of Awaiters

I know it hasn't been fashionable to believe in God these last twenty thirty forty years people haven't been keeping His path much but I always did even when I was a little boy I believed truly and I loved Him and I wanted to go to church all the time even in the middle of the week I'd say to Mother let's go to church I genuinely enjoyed kneeling and praying and feeling Him near me but she'd say no Davey you've got to wait till Sunday for that it's only Wednesday now. So as they say I'm no stranger to His ways and of course when they called for that day of prayer I prayed with all my heart that he might give us a Sign but even so I'm no fool I mean I don't accept everything on a silver platter I ask questions I have doubts I test things and probe a little I'm not one of your ordinary country bumpkins that takes everything on faith. In a way I suppose I could be said to belong to the discerning few although I don't want any of you to get the idea I'm a Discerner oh no I have no sympathy whatever with that atheistic bunch. Anyway we all prayed and the Sign came and my first reaction was joy I don't mind telling you I wept for joy when the sun stood still feeling that all the faith of a lifetime had been confirmed and the godless had better shiver in their boots but then a day or so later I began to think about it and I asked myself how do we know that the Sign really came from God? How can we be sure that the being we have invoked is really on our side I asked myself and of course I had no good answer to that. For all I knew we had conjured up Satan the Accursed and what we imagined was a miracle was really a trick out of the depths of hell designed to lead us all to perdition. Here are these Discerners telling us that they repent their atheism because they know now that God is real and God is with us but how naive they are they aren't even allowing for the possibility that the Sign is a snare and a delusion I tell you we can't be sure the thing is we absolutely *can't be sure*. The Sign might have been from God or from the Devil and we don't know we won't know until we receive a second Sign which I await which I believe will be coming quite soon. And what will that second Sign tell us? I maintain that that has not yet been decided on high it may be a Sign announcing our utter damnation or it may be a Sign welcoming us to the Earthly Paradise and we must await it humbly and prayerfully my friends we must pray and purify ourselves and prepare for the worst as well as for the best. I like to think that in a short while God Himself will present Himself to us not in any indirect way like stopping the sun but rather in a direct manifestation either as God the Father or as God the Son and we will all be saved but this will come about *only if we remain righteous.* If we succumb to error and evil we will bring it to pass that the Devil's advent will descend on us for as Thomas has said himself our destiny is in our hands as well as in His and I believe the first Sign was only the start of a process that will be decided for good or for evil in the days just ahead. Therefore I Davey Strafford call upon you my friends to keep the way of the faith for we must not waver in our hope that He Who Comes will be lovingly inclined toward us and I say that this is our time of supreme test and if we fail it we may discover that it is Satan who shows up to claim our souls. I say once more we cannot interpret the first Sign we can only have faith that it is truly from God and we must pray that this is so while we await the ultimate verdict of heaven therefore we have obtained the rental of a vacant grocery store on Coshocton Avenue which we have renamed the First Church of the Awaiters of Redemption and we will pray round the clock there are seventeen of us now and we will pray in three-hour shifts five of us at a time in rotation the numbers increasing as our expected rapid growth takes place I trust you will come to us and swell our voices for we must pray we've got to there's no other hope now just pray a lot in order that He Who Comes may be benevolent and I ask you to keep praying and have a trusting heart in this our time of waiting.

Nine
A Crying of Proclaimers

Kraft enters the room as Thomas puts down the telephone. "Who were you talking to?" Kraft asks.

"Gifford the Discerner, calling from Boston."

"Why are you answering the phone yourself?"

"There was no one else here."

"There were three apostles in the outer office who could have handled the call, Thomas."

Thomas shrugs. "They would have had to refer it to me eventually. So I answered. What's wrong with that?"

"You've got to maintain distance between yourself and ordinary daily routines. You've got to stay up there on your pedestal and not go around answering telephones."

"I'll try, Saul," says Thomas heavily.

"What did Gifford want?"

"He'd like to merge his group and ours."

Kraft's eyes flash. "To merge? *To merge?* What are we, some sort of manufacturing company? We're a movement. A spiritual force. To talk mergers is nonsense."

"He means that we should start working together, Saul. He says we should join forces because we're both on the side of sanity."

"Exactly what is that supposed to mean?"

"That we're both anti-Apocalyptist. That we're both working to preserve society instead of to bury it."

"An oversimplification," Kraft says. "We deal in faith and he deals in equations. We believe in a Divine Being and he believes in the sanctity of reason. Where's the meeting point?"

"The Cincinnati and Chicago fires are our meeting point, Saul. The Apocalyptists are going crazy. And now these Awaiters too, these spokesmen for Satan—no. We have to act. If I put myself at Gifford's disposal—"

"At his *disposal?*"

"He wants a statement from me backing the spirit if not the substance of the Discerner philosophy. He thinks it'll serve to calm things a little."

"He wants to co-opt you for his own purposes."

"For the purposes of mankind, Saul."

Kraft laughs harshly. "How naive you can be, Thomas! Where's your sense? You can't make an alliance with atheists. You can't let them turn you into a ventriloquist's dummy who—"

"They believe in God just as much as—"

"You have power, Thomas. It's in your voice, it's in your eyes. They have none. They're just a bunch of professors. They want to borrow your power and make use of it to serve their own ends. They don't want you, Thomas, they want your charisma. I forbid this alliance."

Thomas is trembling. He towers over Kraft, but his entire body quivers and Kraft remains steady. Thomas says, "I'm so tired, Saul."

"Tired?"

"The uproar. The rioting. The fires. I'm carrying too big a burden. Gifford can help me. With planning, with ideas. That's a clever bunch, those people."

"I can give you all the help you need."

"No, Saul! What have you been telling me all along? That prayer is sufficient unto every occasion! Faith! Faith! Faith! Faith moves mountains! Well? You were right, yes, you channeled your faith through me and I spoke to the people and we got ourselves a miracle, but what now? What have we really accomplished? Everything's falling apart, and we need strong souls to build and rebuild, and you aren't offering anything new. You—"

"The Lord will provide for—"

"Will He? Will He, Saul? How many thousands dead already, since June 6? How much property damage? Government paralyzed. Transportation breaking down. New cults. New prophets. Here's Gifford saying, Let's join hands, Thomas, let's try to work together, and you tell me—"

"I forbid this," Kraft says.

"It's all agreed. Gifford's going to take the first plane west, and—"

"I'll call him. He mustn't come. If he does I won't let him see you. I'll notify the apostles to bar him."

"No, Saul."

"We don't need him. We'll be ruined if we let him near you."

"Why?"

"Because he's godless and our movement's strength proceeds from the Lord!" Kraft shouts. "Thomas, what's happened to you? Where's your fire? Where's your zeal? Where's my old swaggering Thomas who talked back to God? Belch, Thomas. Spit on the floor, scratch your belly, curse a little. I'll get you some wine. It shocks me to see you sniveling like this. Telling me how tired you are, how scared."

"I don't feel like swaggering much these days, Saul."

"Damn you, swagger anyway! The whole world is watching you! Here, listen—I'll rough out a new speech for you that you'll deliver on full hookup tomorrow night. We'll outflank Gifford and his bunch. We'll co-opt him. What you'll do, Thomas, is call for a new act of faith, some kind of mass demonstration, something symbolic and powerful, something to turn people away from despair and destruction. We'll follow the Discerner line plus our own element of faith. You'll denounce all the false new cults and urge everyone to—to—let me think—to make a pilgrimage of some kind?—a coming together—a mass baptism, that's it, a march to the sea, everybody bathing in God's own sea, washing away doubt and sin. Right? A rededication to faith." Kraft's face is red. His forehead gleams. Thomas scowls at him. Kraft goes on, "Stop pulling those long faces. You'll do it and it'll work. It'll pull people back from the abyss of Apocalypticism. Positive goals, that's our approach. Thomas the Proclaimer cries out that we must work together under God. Yes? Yes. We'll get this thing under control in ten days, I promise you. Now go have yourself a drink. Relax. I've got to call Gifford, and then I'll start blocking in your new appeal. Go on. And stop looking so glum, Thomas! We hold a mighty power in our hands. We're wielding the sword of the Lord. You want to turn all that over to Gifford's crowd? Go. Go. Get some rest, Thomas."

Ten
A Prostration of Propitiators

ALL PARISH CHAIRMEN PLEASE COPY AND DISTRIBUTE. The Reverend August Hammacher to his dearly beloved brothers and sisters in Christ, members of the Authentic Church of the Doctrine of Propitiation, this message from Central Shrine: greetings and blessings. Be you hereby advised that we have notified Elder Davey Strafford of the First Church of the Awaiters of Redemption that as of this date we no longer consider ourselves in communion with his church, on grounds of irremediable doctrinal differences. It is now forbidden for members of the Authentic Church to participate in the Awaiter rite or to have any sacramental contact with the instrumentalities of the Awaiter creed, although we shall continue to remember the Awaiters in our prayers and to strive for their salvation as if they were our own people.

The schism between ourselves and the Awaiters, which has been in the making for more than a week, arises from a fundamental disagreement over the nature of the Sign. It is of course our belief, greatly strengthened by the violent events of recent days, that the Author of the Sign was Satan and that the Sign foretells a coming realignment in heaven, the probable beneficiaries of which are to be the Diabolical Forces. In expectation of the imminent establishment of the Dark Powers on Earth, we therefore direct our most humble homage to Satan the Second

Incarnation of Christ, hoping that when He comes among us He will take cognizance of our obeisance and spare us from the ultimate holocaust.

Now the Awaiters hold what is essentially an agnostic position, saying that we cannot know whether the Sign proceeds from God or from Satan, and that pending further revelation we must continue to pray as before to the Father and the Son, so that perhaps through our devotions we may stave off the advent of Satan entirely. There is one point of superficial kinship between their ideas and ours, which is an unwillingness to share the confidence of Thomas the Proclaimer on the one hand, and the Discerners on the other, that the Sign is God's work. But it may be seen that a basic conflict of doctrine exists between ourselves and the Awaiters, for they refuse to comprehend our teachings concerning the potential benevolence of Satan, and cling to an attitude that may be deemed dangerously offensive by Him. Unwilling to commit themselves finally to one side or the other, they hope to steer a cautious middle course, not realizing that when the Dark One comes He will chastise all those who failed to accept the proper meaning of the revelation of June 6. We have hoped to sway the Awaiters to our position, but their attitude has grown increasingly abusive as we have exposed their doctrinal inconsistencies, and now we have no option but to pronounce excommunication upon them. For what does Revelation say? "I know thy works, that thou art neither cold nor hot: I would thou wert cold or hot. So then because thou art lukewarm, and neither cold nor hot, I will spue thee out of my mouth." We cannot risk being tainted by these lukewarm Awaiters who will not bow the knee to the Dark One, though they admit the possibility (but not the inevitability) of His Advent.

However, dearly loved friends in Christ, I am happy to reveal that we have this day established preliminary communion with the United Diabolist Apocalyptic Pentecostal Church of the United States, the headquarters of which is in Los Angeles, California. I need not here recapitulate the deep doctrinal chasms separating us from the Apocalyptist sects in general; but although we abhor certain teachings even of this Diabolist faction, we recognize large areas of common belief linking us, and hope to wean the United Diabolist Apocalyptics entirely from their errors in the course of time. This is by no means to be interpreted as presently authorizing communicants of the Authentic Church of the Doctrine of Propitiation to take part in Apocalyptist activities, even those which are nondestructive, but I do wish to advise you of the possibility of a deeper relationship with at least one Apocalyptist group even as we sever our union with the Awaiters. Our love goes out to all of you, from all of us at Central Shrine. We prostrate ourselves humbly before the Dark One whose triumph is ordained. In the name of the Father, the Son, the Holy Ghost, and Him Who Comes. Amen.

Eleven
The March to the Sea

It was the most frightening thing ever. Like an army invading us. Like a plague of locusts. They came like the locusts came upon the land of Egypt when Moses stretched out his hand. Exodus 10:15 tells it: *For they covered the face of the whole earth, so that the land was darkened; and they did eat every herb of the land, and all the fruit of the trees which the hail had left: and there remained not any green thing in the trees, or in the herbs of the field, through all the land of Egypt.* Like a nightmare. Lucy and me were the Egyptians and all of Thomas' people, they were the locusts.

Lucy wanted to be in the middle of it all along. To her, Thomas was like a holy prophet of God from the moment he first started to preach, although I tried to tell her back then that he was a charlatan and a dangerous lunatic with a criminal record. Look at his face, I said, look at those eyes! A lot of good it did me. She kept a scrapbook of him like he was a movie star and she was a fifteen-year-old girl instead of a woman of seventy-four. Pictures of him, texts of all his speeches. She got angry at me when I called him crazy or unscrupulous: we had our worst quarrel in maybe thirty years when she wanted to send him $500 to help pay for his television expenses and I absolutely refused. Naturally after the Day of the Sign she came to look upon him as being right up there in the same exalted category as Moses and Elijah and John the Baptist, one of the true anointed voices of the Lord, and I guess I was starting to think of him that way too, despite myself. Though I didn't like him or trust him I sensed he had a special power. When everybody was praying for the Sign I prayed too, not so much because I thought it would come about but just to avoid trouble with Lucy, but I did put my heart into the prayer, and when the Earth stopped turning a shiver ran all through me and I got such a jolt of amazement that I thought I might be having a stroke. So I apologized to Lucy for all I had said about Thomas. I still suspected he was a madman and a charlatan, but I couldn't deny that he had something of the saint and prophet about him too. I suppose it's possible for a man to be a saint and a charlatan both. Anything's possible. I understand that one of these new religions is saying that Satan is actually an incarnation of Jesus, or the fourth member of the Trinity, or something like that. Honestly.

Well then all the riotings and burnings began when the hot weather came and the world seemed to be going crazy with things worse not better after God had given His Sign, and Thomas called for this Day of Rededication, everybody to go down to the sea and wash off his sins, a real old-time total-immersion revival meeting where we'd all get together and denounce the new cults and get things back on the right track again.

And Lucy came to me all aglow and said, Let's go, let's be part of it. I think there were supposed to be ten gathering-places all around the United States, New York and Houston and San Diego and Seattle and Chicago and I don't remember which else, but Thomas himself was going to attend the main one at Atlantic City, which is just a little ways down the coast from us, and the proceedings would be beamed by live telecast to all the other meetings being held here and overseas. She hadn't ever seen Thomas in person. I told her it was crazy for people our age to get mixed up in a mob of the size Thomas always attracts. We'd be crushed, we'd be trampled, we'd die sure as anything. Look, I said, we live right here by the seashore anyway, the ocean is fifty steps from our front porch; so why ask for trouble? We'll stay here and watch the praying on television, and then when everybody goes down into the sea to be purified we can go right here on our own beach and we'll be part of things in a way without taking the risks. I could see that Lucy was disappointed about not seeing Thomas in person but after all she's a sensible woman and I'm going to be eighty next November and there had already been some pretty wild scenes at each of Thomas' public appearances.

The big day dawned and I turned on the television and then of course we got the news that Atlantic City had banned Thomas' meeting at the last minute on the grounds of public safety. A big oil tanker had broken up off shore the night before and an oil slick was heading toward the beach, the mayor said. If there was a mass meeting on the beach that day it would interfere with the city's pollution-prevention procedures, and also the oil would endanger the health of anybody who went into the water, so the whole Atlantic City waterfront was being cordoned off, extra police brought in from out of town, laser lines set up, and so forth. Actually the oil slick wasn't anywhere near Atlantic City and was drifting the other way, and when the mayor talked about public safety he really meant the safety of his city, not wanting a couple of million people ripping up the boardwalk and breaking windows. So there was Atlantic City sealed off and Thomas had this immense horde of people already collected, coming from Philadelphia and Trenton and Wilmington and even Baltimore, a crowd so big it couldn't be counted, five, six, maybe ten million people. They showed it from a helicopter view and everybody was standing shoulder to shoulder for about twenty miles in this direction and fifty miles in that direction, that's how it seemed, anyway, and about the only open place was where Thomas was, a clearing around fifty yards across with his apostles forming a tight ring protecting him.

Where was this mob going to go, since it couldn't get into Atlantic City? Why, Thomas said, everybody would just march up the Jersey coast and spread out along the shore from Long Beach Island to Sandy Hook. When I heard that I wanted to jump into the car and start heading for maybe Montana, but it was too late: the marchers were already on their way, all the mainland highways were choked with them. I went up on the sundeck with our binoculars and I could see the first of them coming across the causeway, walking seventy or eighty abreast, and a sea of faces behind them going inland on and on back toward Manahawkin and beyond. Well it was like the Mongol hordes of Genghis Khan. One swarm went south toward Beach Haven and the other came up through Surf City and Loveladies and Harvey Cedars in our direction. Thousands and thousands and thousands of them. Our island is long and skinny like any coastal sandspit, and it's pretty well built up both on the beach side and on the bay side, no open space except the narrow streets, and there wasn't room for all those people. But they kept on coming, and as I watched through the binoculars I thought I was getting dizzy because I imagined some of the houses on the beach side were moving too, and then I realized that the houses *were* moving, some of the flimsier ones, they were being pushed right off their foundations by the press of humanity. Toppling and being ground underfoot, entire houses, can you imagine? I told Lucy to pray, but she was already doing it, and I got my shotgun ready because I felt I had to try at least to protect us, but I said to her that this was probably going to be our last day alive and I kissed her and we told each other how good it had been, all of it, fifty-three years together. And then the mob came spilling through our part of the island. Rushing down to the beach. A berserk crazy multitude.

And Thomas was there, right close to our place. Bigger than I thought he'd be, and his hair and beard were all tangled up, and his face was red and peeling some from sunburn—he was that close, I could see the sunburn—and he was still in the middle of his ring of apostles, and he was shouting through a bullhorn, but no matter how much amplification they gave him from the copter-borne speakers overhead it was impossible to understand anything he was saying. Saul Kraft was next to him. He looked pale and frightened. People were rushing into the water, some of them fully clothed and some stark naked, until the whole shoreline was packed right out to where the breakers begin. As more and more people piled into the water the ones in front were pushed beyond their depth, and I think this was when the drownings started. I know I saw a number of people waving and kicking and yelling for help and getting swept out to sea. Thomas remained on shore, shouting through the bullhorn. He must have realized it was all out of control, but there was nothing he could do. Until this point the thrust of the mob was all forward, toward the sea, but now there was a change in the flow: some of those in the water tried to force their way back up onto land, and smashed head on into those going the other way. I thought they were coming up out of the water to avoid being drowned, but then I saw the black smears on their clothing and I thought, *the oil slick!* and yes, there it was, not down by Atlantic City but up here by us, right off the beach and moving shoreward. People in the water were getting bogged down in it, getting it all over their hair and faces, but they couldn't reach the shore because of the rush still heading in the opposite direction. This was when the tramplings started as the ones coming out of the water, coughing and choking and blinded with oil, fell under the feet of those still trying to get into the sea.

I looked at Thomas again and he was like a maniac. His face was wild and he had thrown the bullhorn away and he was just screaming, with angry cords standing out on his neck and forehead. Saul Kraft went up to him and said something and Thomas turned like the wrath of God, turned and rose up and brought his hands down like two clubs on Saul Kraft's head, and you know Kraft is a small man and he went down like he was dead, with blood all over his face. Two or three apostles picked him up and carried him into one of the beachfront houses. Just then somebody managed to slip through the cordon of apostles and went running toward Thomas. He was a short, plump man wearing the robes of one of the new religions, an Awaiter or Propitiator or I don't know what, and he had a laser-hatchet in his hand. He shouted something at Thomas and lifted the hatchet. But Thomas moved toward him and stood so tall that the assassin almost seemed to shrink, and the man was so afraid that he couldn't do a thing. Thomas reached out and plucked the hatchet from his hand and threw it aside. Then he caught the man and started hitting him, tremendous close-range punches, slam slam slam, all but knocking the man's head off his shoulders. Thomas didn't look human while he was doing that. He was some kind of machine of destruction. He was bellowing and roaring and running foam from his mouth, and he was into this terrible deadly rhythm of punching, slam slam slam. Finally he stopped and took the man by both hands and flung him across the beach, like you'd fling a rag doll. The man flew maybe twenty feet and landed and didn't move. I'm certain Thomas beat him to death. There's your holy prophet for you, your saint of God. Suddenly Thomas' whole appearance changed: he became terribly calm, almost frozen, standing there with his arms dangling and his shoulders hunched up and his chest heaving from all that hitting. And he began to cry. His face broke up like winter ice on a spring pond and I saw the tears. I'll never forget that: Thomas the Proclaimer all alone in the middle of that madhouse on the beach, sobbing like a new widow.

I didn't see anything after that. There was a crash of glass from downstairs and I grabbed my gun and went down to see, and I found maybe fifteen people piled up on the livingroom floor who had been pushed right through the picture window by the crowd outside. The window had cut them all up and some were terribly maimed and there was blood on everything, and more and more and more people kept flying through the place where the window had been, and I heard Lucy screaming and my gun went off and I don't know what happened after that. Next I remember it was the middle of the night and I was sitting in our completely wrecked house and I saw a helicopter land on the beach, and a tactical squad began collecting bodies. There were hundreds of dead just on our strip of beach. Drowned, trampled, choked by oil, heart attacks, everything. The corpses are gone now but the island is a ruin. We're asking the government for disaster aid. I don't know: is a religious meeting a proper disaster? It was for us. That was your Day of Rededication, all right: a disaster. Prayer and purification to bring us all together under the banner of the Lord. May I be struck dead for saying this if I don't mean it with all my heart: I wish the Lord and all his prophets would disappear and leave us alone. We've had enough religion for one season.

Twelve
The Voice from the Heavens

Saul Kraft, hidden behind nine thousand dollars' worth of security devices, an array of scanners and sensors and shunt-gates and trip-vaults, wonders why everything is going so badly. Perhaps his choice of Thomas as the vehicle was an error. Thomas, he has come to realize, is too complicated, too unpredictable—a dual soul, demon and angel inextricably merged. Nevertheless the Crusade had begun promisingly enough. Working through Thomas, he had coaxed God Almighty into responding to the prayers of mankind, hadn't he? How much better than that do you need to do?

But now. This nightmarish carnival atmosphere everywhere. These cults, these other prophets. A thousand interpretations of an event whose meaning should have been crystal-clear. The bonfires. Madness crackling like lightning across the sky. Maybe the fault was in Thomas. The Proclaimer had been deficient in true grace all along. Possibly any mass movement centered on a prophet who had Thomas' faults of character was inherently doomed to slip into chaos.

Or maybe the fault was mine, O Lord.

Kraft has been in seclusion for many days, perhaps for several weeks; he is no longer sure when he began this retreat. He will see no one, not even Thomas, who is eager to make amends. Kraft's injuries have healed and he holds no grievance against Thomas for striking him: the fiasco of the Day of Rededication had driven all of them a little insane there on the beach, and Thomas' outburst of violence was understandable if not justifiable. It may even have been of divine inspiration, God inflicting punishment on Kraft through the vehicle of Thomas for his sins. The sin of pride, mainly. To turn Gifford away, to organize the Day of Rededication for such cynical motives—

Kraft fears for his soul, and for the soul of Thomas.

He dares not see Thomas now, not until he has regained his own spiritual equilibrium; Thomas is too turbulent, too tempestuous, emits such powerful emanations of self-will; Kraft must first recapture his moral strength. He fasts much of the time. He tries to surrender himself fully in prayer. But prayer will not come: he feels cut off from the Almighty, separated from Him as he has never been before. By bungling this holy Crusade he must have earned the Lord's displeasure. A gulf, a chasm, parts them; Kraft is earthbound and helpless. He abandons his efforts to pray. He prowls his suite restlessly, listening for intruders, constantly running security checks. He switches on his closed-circuit video inputs, expecting to see fires in the streets, but all is calm out there. He listens to news bulletins on the radio: chaos; turmoil, everywhere. Thomas is said to be dead; Thomas is reported on the same day to be in Istanbul, Karachi, Johannesburg, San Francisco; the Propitiators have announced that on the twenty-fourth of November, according to their calculations, Satan will appear on Earth to enter into his sovereignty; the Pope, at last breaking his silence, has declared that he has no idea what power might have been responsible for the startling happenings of June 6, but thinks it would be rash to attribute the event to God's direct intervention without some further evidence. So the Pope has become an Awaiter too. Kraft smiles. Marvelous! Kraft wonders if the Archbishop of Canterbury is attending Propitiator services. Or the Dalai Lama consorting with the Apocalyptists. Anything can happen now. Gog and Magog are let loose upon the world. Kraft no longer is surprised by anything. He feels no astonishment even when he turns the radio on late one afternoon and finds that God Himself seems to be making a broadcast.

God's voice is rich and majestic. It reminds Kraft somewhat of the voice of Thomas, but God's tone is less fervid, less evangelical; He speaks in an easy but serious-minded way, like a senator campaigning for election to his fifth term of office. There is a barely perceptible easternness to God's accent: He could be a senator from Pennsylvania, maybe, or Ohio. He has gone on the air, He explains, in the hope of restoring order to a troubled world. He wishes to reassure everyone: no apocalypse is planned, and those who anticipate the imminent destruction of the world are most unwise. Nor should you pay heed to those who claim that the recent Sign was the work of Satan. It certainly was not, God says, not at all, and propitiation of the Evil One is uncalled for. By all means let's give the Devil his due, but nothing beyond that. All I intended when I stopped the Earth's rotation, God declares, was to let you know that I'm here, looking after your interests.

I wanted you to be aware that in the event of really bad trouble down there I'll see to it—

Kraft, lips clamped tautly, changes stations. The resonant baritone voice pursues him.

—that peace is maintained and the forces of justice are strengthened in—

Kraft turns on his television set. The screen shows nothing but the channel insignia. Across the top of the screen gleams a bright-green title:

ALLEGED VOICE OF GOD

and across the bottom, in frantic scarlet, is a second caption:

BY LIVE PICKUP FROM THE MOON

The Deity, meanwhile, has moved smoothly on to new themes. All the problems of the world, He observes, can be attributed to the rise and spread of atheistic socialism. The false prophet Karl Marx, aided by the Antichrist Lenin and the subsidiary demons Stalin and Mao, have set loose in the world a plague of godlessness that has tainted the entire twentieth century and, here at the dawn of the twenty-first, must at last be eradicated. For a long time the zealous godly folk of the world resisted the pernicious Bolshevik doctrines, God continues, His voice still lucid and reasonable; but in the past twenty years an accommodation with the powers of darkness has come into effect, and this has allowed spreading corruption to infect even such splendidly righteous lands as Japan, Brazil, the German Federal Republic, and God's own beloved United States of America. The foul philosophy of coexistence has led to a step-by-step entrapment of the forces of good, and as a result—

Kraft finds all of this quite odd. Is God speaking to every nation in English, or is He speaking Japanese to the Japanese, Hebrew to the Israelis, Croatian to the Croats, Bulgarian to the Bulgars? And when did God become so staunch a defender of the capitalist ethic? Kraft recalls something about driving money-changers out of the temple, long ago. But now the voice of God appears to be demanding a holy war against communism. Kraft hears Him calling on the legions of the sanctified to attack the Marxist foe wherever the red flag flies. Sack embassies and consulates, burn the houses of ardent left-wingers, destroy libraries and other sources of dangerous propaganda, the Lord advises. He says everything in a level, civilized tone.

Abruptly, in midsentence, the voice of the Almighty vanishes from the airwaves. A short time later an announcer, unable to conceal his chagrin, declares that the broadcast was a hoax contrived by bored technicians in a satellite relay station. Investigations have begun to determine how so many radio and television stations let themselves be persuaded to transmit it as a public-interest item. But for many godless Marxists the revelation comes too late. The requested sackings and lootings have occurred in dozens of cities. Hundreds of diplomats, guards, and clerical workers have been slain by maddened mobs bent on doing the Lord's work. Property losses are immense. An international crisis is developing, and there are scattered reports of retribution against American citizens in several eastern European countries. We live in strange times, Kraft tells himself. He prays. For himself. For Thomas. For all mankind. Lord have mercy. Amen. Amen. Amen.

Thirteen
The Burial of Faith

The line of march begins at the city line and runs westward out of town into the suburban maze. The marchers, at least a thousand of them, stride vigorously forward even though a dank, oppressive heat enfolds them. On they go, past the park dense with the dark-green leaves of late summer, past the highway cloverleaf, past the row of burned motels and filling stations, past the bombed reservoir, past the cemeteries, heading for the municipal dumping-grounds.

Gifford, leading the long sober procession, wears ordinary classroom clothes: a pair of worn khaki trousers, a loose-fitting gray shirt, and old leather sandals. Originally there had been some talk of having the most important Discerners come garbed in their academic robes, but Gifford had vetoed that on the grounds that it wasn't in keeping with the spirit of the ceremony. Today all of the old superstitions and pomposities were to be laid to rest; why then bedeck the chief iconoclasts in hieratic costume as though they were priests, as though this new creed were going to be just as full of mummery as the outmoded religions it hoped to supplant?

Because the marchers are so simply dressed, the contrast is all the more striking between the plain garments they wear and the elaborate, rich-textured ecclesiastical paraphernalia they carry. No one is empty-handed; each has some vestment, some sacred artifact, some work of scripture. Draped over Gifford's left arm is a large white linen alb, ornately embroidered, with a dangling silken cincture. The man behind him carries a deacon's dalmatic; the third marcher has a handsome chasuble; the fourth, a splendid cope. The rest of the priestly gear is close behind: amice, stole, maniple, vimpa. A frosty-eyed woman well along in years waves a crozier aloft; the man beside her wears a mitre at a mockingly rakish angle. Here are cassocks, surplices, hoods, tippets, cottas, rochets, mozettas, mantellettas, chimeres, and much more: virtually everything, in fact, save the papal tiara itself. Here are chalices, crucifixes, thuribles, fonts; three men struggle beneath a marvelously carved fragment of a pulpit; a little band of marchers displays Greek Orthodox outfits, the rhason and the sticharion, the epitrachelion and the epimanikia, the sakkos, the epigonation, the zone, the omophorion; they brandish ikons and enkolpia, dikerotrikera and dikanikion. Austere Presbyterian gowns may be seen, and rabbinical yarmulkes and tallithim and tfilin. Farther back in the procession one may observe more exotic holy objects, prayer wheels and tonkas, sudras and kustis, idols of fifty sorts, things sacred to Confucianists, Shintoists, Parsees, Buddhists both Mahayana and Hinayana, Jains, Sikhs, animists of no formal rite, and others. The marchers have shofars, mezuzahs, candelabra, communion trays, even collection plates; no portable element of faith has been ignored. And of course the holy books of the world are well represented: an infinity of Old and New Testaments, the Koran, the Bhagavad-Gita, the Upanishads, the Tao Te Ching, the Vedas, the Vedanta Sutra, the Talmud, the Book of the Dead, and more. Gifford has been queasy about destroying books, for that is an act with ugly undertones; but these are extreme times, and extreme measures are required. Therefore he has given his consent even for that.

Much of the material the marchers carry was freely contributed, mostly by disgruntled members of congregations, some of it given by disaffected clergymen themselves. The other objects come mostly from churches or museums plundered during the civil disturbances. But the Discerners have done no plundering of their own; they have merely accepted donations and picked up some artifacts that rioters had scattered in the streets. On this point Gifford was most strict: acquisition of material. by force was prohibited. Thus the robes and emblems of the newly founded creeds are seen but sparsely today, since Awaiters and Propitiators Propritiators and their like would hardly have been inclined to contribute to Gifford's festival of destruction.

They have reached the municipal dump now. It is a vast fiat wasteland, surprisingly aseptic-looking: there are large areas of meadow, and the unreclaimed regions of the dump have been neatly graded and mulched, in readiness for the scheduled autumn planting of grass. The marchers put down their burdens and the chief Discerners come forward to take spades and shovels from a truck that has accompanied them. Gifford looks up; helicopters hover and television cameras bristle in the sky. This event will have extensive coverage. He turns to face the others and intones, "Let this ceremony mark the end of all ceremonies. Let this rite usher in a time without rites. Let reason rule forevermore."

Gifford lifts the first shovelful of soil himself. Now the rest of the diggers set to work, preparing a trench three feet deep, ten to twelve feet wide. The topsoil comes off easily, revealing strata of cans, broken toys, discarded television sets, automobile tires, and garden rakes. A mound of debris begins to grow as the digging team does its task; soon a shallow opening gapes. Though it is now late afternoon, the heat has not diminished, and those who dig stream with sweat. They rest frequently, panting, leaning on their tools. Meanwhile those who are not digging stand quietly, not putting down that which they carry.

Twilight is near before Gifford decides that the trench is adequate. Again he looks up at the cameras, again he turns to face his followers.

He says, "On this day we bury a hundred thousand years of superstition. We lay to rest the old idols, the old fantasies, the old errors, the old lies. The time of faith is over and done with; the era of certainty opens. No longer do we need theologians to speculate on the proper way of worshiping the Lord; no longer do we need priests to mediate between ourselves and Him; no longer do we need man-made scriptures that pretend to interpret His nature. We have all of us felt His hand upon our world, and the time has come to approach Him with clear eyes, with an alert, open mind. Hence we give to the earth these relics of bygone epochs, and we call upon discerning men and women everywhere to join us in this ceremony of renunciation."

He signals. One by one the Discerners advance to the edge of the pit. One by one they cast their burdens in: albs, chasubles, copes, miters, Korans, Upanishads, yarmulkes, crucifixes. No one hurries; the Burial of Faith is serious business. As it proceeds, a drum roll of dull distant thunder reverberates along the horizon. A storm on the way? Just heat lightning, perhaps, Gifford decides. The ceremony continues. In with the maniple. In with the shofar. In with the cassock. Thunder again: louder, more distinct. The sky darkens. Gifford attempts to hasten the tempo of the ceremony, beckoning the Discerners forward to drop their booty. A blade of lightning slices the heavens and this time the answering thunderclap comes almost instantaneously, *ka-thock*. A few drops of rain. The forecast had been in error. A nuisance, but no real harm. Another flash of lightning. A tremendous crash. That one must have struck only a few hundred yards away. There is some nervous laughter. "We've annoyed Zeus," someone says. "He's throwing thunderbolts." Gifford is not amused; he enjoys ironies, but not now, not now. And he realizes that he has become just credulous enough, since the sixth of June, to be at least marginally worried that the Almighty might indeed be about to punish this sacrilegious band of Discerners. A flash again. *Ka-thock!* The clouds now split asunder and torrents of rain abruptly descend. In moments, shirts are pasted to skins, the floor of the pit turns to mud, rivulets begin to stream across the dump.

And then, as though they had scheduled the storm for their own purposes, a mob of fierce-faced people in gaudy robes burst into view. They wield clubs, pitchforks, rake handles, cleavers, and other improvised weapons; they scream incoherent, unintelligible slogans; and they rush into the midst of the Discerners, laying about them vigorously. "Death to the godless blasphemers!" is what they are shrieking, and similar phrases. Who are they, Gifford wonders? Awaiters. Propitiators. Diabolists. Apocalyptists. Perhaps a coalition of all cultists. The television helicopters descend to get a better view of the melee, and hang just out of reach, twenty or thirty feet above the struggle. Their powerful floodlights provide apocalyptic illumination. Gifford finds hands at his throat: a crazed woman, howling, grotesque. He pushes her away and she tumbles into the pit, landing on a stack of mud-crusted Bibles. A frantic stampede has begun; his people are rushing in all directions, followed by the vengeful servants of the Lord, who wield their weapons with vindictive glee. Gifford sees his friends fall, wounded, badly hurt, perhaps slain. Where are the police? Why are they giving no protection? "Kill all the blasphemers!" a maniac voice shrills near him. He whirls, ready to defend himself. A pitchfork. He feels a strange cold clarity of thought and moves swiftly in, feinting, seizing the handle of the pitchfork, wresting it from his adversary. The rain redoubles its force; a sheet of water comes between Gifford and the other, and when he can see again, he is alone at the edge of the pit. He hurls the pitchfork into the pit and instantly wishes he had kept it, for three of the robed ones are coming toward him. He breaks into a cautious trot, tries to move past them, puts on a sudden spurt of speed, and slips in the mud. He lands in a puddle; the taste of mud is in his mouth; he is breathless, terrified, unable to rise. They fling themselves upon him. "Wait," he says. "This is madness!" One of them has a club. "No," Gifford mutters. "No. No. No. No."

Fourteen
The Seventh Seal

1. And when he had opened the seventh seal, there was silence in heaven about the space of half an hour.

2. And I saw the seven angels which stood before God; and to them were given seven trumpets.

3. And another angel came and stood at the altar, having a golden censer; and there was given unto him much incense, that he should offer it with the prayers of all saints upon the golden altar which was before the throne.

4. And the smoke of the incense, which came with the prayers of the saints, ascended up before God out of the angel's hand.

5. And the angel took the censer, and filled it with fire of the altar, and cast it into the earth: and there were voices, and thunderings, and lightnings, and an earthquake.

6. And the seven angels which had the seven trumpets prepared themselves to sound.

7. The first angel sounded, and there followed hail and fire mingled with blood, and they were cast upon the earth: and the third part of trees was burnt up, and all green grass was burnt up.

8. And the second angel sounded, and as it were a great mountain burning with fire was cast into the sea: and the third part of the sea became blood;

9. And the third part of the creatures which were in the sea, and had life, died; and the third part of the ships were destroyed.

10. And the third angel sounded, and there fell a great star from heaven, burning as it were a lamp, and it fell upon the third part of the rivers, and upon the fountains of waters;

11. And the name of the star is called Wormwood: and the third part of the waters became wormwood; and many men died of the waters, because they were made bitter.

12. And the fourth angel sounded, and the third part of the sun was smitten, and the third part of the moon, and the third part of the stars; so as the third part of them was darkened, and the day shone not for a third part of it, and the night likewise.

13. And I beheld, and heard an angel flying through the midst of heaven, saying with a loud voice, Woe, woe, woe, to the inhabiters of the earth by reason of the other voices of the trumpet of the three angels, which are yet to sound!

Fifteen
The Flight of the Prophet

All, all over. Thomas weeps. The cities burn. The very lakes are afire. So many thousands dead. The Apocalyptists dance, for though the year is not yet sped the end seems plainly in view. The Church of Rome has pronounced anathema on Thomas, denying his miracle: he is the Antichrist, the Pope has said. Signs and portents are seen everywhere. This is the season of two-headed calves and dogs with cats' faces. New prophets have arisen. God may shortly return, or He may not; revelations differ. Many people now pray for an end to all such visitations and miracles. The Awaiters no longer Await, but now ask that we be spared from His next coming; even the Diabolists and the Propitiators cry, Come not, Lucifer. Those who begged a Sign from God in June would be content now only with God's renewed and prolonged absence. Let Him neglect us; let Him dismiss us from His mind. It is a time of torches and hymns. Rumors of barbaric warfare come from distant continents. They say the neutron bomb has been used in Bolivia. Thomas' last few followers have asked him to speak with God once more, in the hope that things can still be set to rights, but Thomas refuses. The lines of communication to the Deity are closed. He dares not reopen them: see, see how many plagues and evils he has let loose as it is! He renounces his prophethood. Others may dabble in charismatic mysticism if they so please. Others may kneel before the burning bush or sweat in the glare of the pillar of fire. Not Thomas. Thomas' vocation is gone. All over. All, all, all over.

He hopes to slip into anonymity. He shaves his beard and docks his hair; he obtains a new wardrobe, bland and undistinguished; he alters the color of his eyes; he practices walking in a slouch to lessen his great height. Perhaps he has not lost his pocket-picking skills. He will go silently into the cities, head down, fingers on the ready, and thus he will make his way. It will be a quieter life.

Disguised, alone, Thomas goes forth. He wanders unmolested from place to place, sleeping in odd corners, eating in dim rooms. He is in Chicago for the Long Sabbath, and he is in Milwaukee for the Night of Blood, and he is in St. Louis for the Invocation of Flame. These events leave him unaffected. He moves on. The year is ebbing. The leaves have fallen. If the Apocalyptists tell us true, mankind has but a few weeks left. God's wrath, or Satan's, will blaze over the land as the year 2000 sweeps in on December's heels. Thomas scarcely minds. Let him go unnoticed and he will not mind if the universe tumbles about him.

"What do you think?" he is asked on a street corner in Los Angeles. "Will God come back on New Year's Day?"

A few idle loungers, killing time. Thomas slouches among them. They do not recognize him, he is sure. But they want an answer. "Well? What do you say?"

Thomas makes his voice furry and thick, and mumbles, "No, not a chance. He's never going to mess with us again. He gave us a miracle and look what we made out of it."

"That so? You really think so?"

Thomas nods. "God's turned His back on us. He said, Here, I give you proof of My existence, now pull yourselves together and get somewhere. And instead we fell apart all the faster. So that's it. We've had it. The end is coming."

"Hey, you might be right!" Grins. Winks.

This conversation makes Thomas uncomfortable. He starts to edge away, elbows out, head bobbing clumsily, shoulders hunched. His new walk, his camouflage.

"Wait," one of them says. "Stick around. Let's talk a little."

Thomas hesitates.

"You know, I think you're right, fellow. We made a royal mess. I tell you something else: we never should have started all that stuff. Asking for a Sign. Stopping the Earth. Would have been a lot better off if that Thomas had stuck to picking pockets, let me tell you."

"I agree three hundred percent," Thomas says, flashing a quick smile, on-off. "If you'll excuse me—"

Again he starts to shuffle away. Ten paces. An office building's door opens. A short, slender man steps out. *Oh, God! Saul!* Thomas covers his face with his hand and turns away. Too late. No use. Kraft recognizes him through all the alterations. His eyes gleam. "Thomas!" he gasps.

"No. You're mistaken. My name is—"

"Where have you been?" Kraft demands. "Everyone's searching for you, Thomas. Oh, it was wicked of you to run away, to shirk your responsibilities. You dumped everything into our hands, didn't you? But you were the only one with the strength to lead people. You were the only one who—"

"Keep your voice down," Thomas says hoarsely. No use pretending. "For the love of God, Saul, stop yelling at me! Stop saying my name! Do you want everyone to know that I'm—"

"That's exactly what I want," Kraft says. By now a fair crowd has gathered, ten people, a dozen. Kraft points. "Don't you know him? That's Thomas the Proclaimer! He's shaved and cut his hair, but can't you see his face all the same? There's your prophet! There's the thief who talked with God!"

"No, Saul!"

"Thomas?" someone says. And they all begin to mutter it. "Thomas? Thomas? Thomas?" They nod heads, point, rub chins, nod heads again. "Thomas? Thomas?"

Surrounding him. Staring. Touching him. He tries to push them away. Too many of them, and no apostles, now. Kraft is at the edge of the crowd, smiling, the little Judas! "Keep back," Thomas says. "You've got the wrong man. I'm not Thomas. I'd like to get my hands on him myself. I-I-" *Judas! Judas!* "Saul!" he screams. And then they swarm over him.

WHEN WE WENT TO SEE THE END OF THE WORLD

As I indicated in the introductions to "In Entropy's Jaws" and "Good News from the Vatican," the early 1970s was a time when I was beginning to ask myself whether there was any point to writing science fiction at all, even as I was reaching my own peak of creativity in the field. Looking back now on that period, I see my attitudes then as analogous to that of the baseball player who, after devoting most of his life to attaining and sustaining a major-league career, suddenly begins wondering whether it really made any sense for a grown man to spend his days swinging a wooden stick at a small horsehide-covered ball. It was a phase I was going through, born, I suppose, out of the weariness that the fire in my house in 1968 had engendered in me, out of the different sort of weariness brought about by having written so many million words of fiction over so many years, and, also, by the fact that I was entering my dangerous midlife years at a time when all of American society seemed to be questioning the fundamental assumptions of our entire political and cultural system.

For those and perhaps other reasons, I found myself writing stories in which, one by one, the basic themes of science fiction were called up and looked at with a jaundiced eye, and then turned into sly, subversive, tongue-in-cheek stories that plainly indicated I could no longer take those themes seriously as a platform for fiction. "Good News from the Vatican" is a case in point: I scarcely expected that a day would actually come when a robot would be elected Pope, nor did I think my readers would put any literal credence in that story's playful theme. Another good example of this deliberately flip, even nihilistic, mode is this one, written in June of 1971, once again for Terry Carr's Universe *and published in the second issue of that distinguished anthology series.*

Nick and Jane were glad that they had gone to see the end of the world, because it gave them something special to talk about at Mike and Ruby's party. One always likes to come to a party armed with a little conversation. Mike and Ruby give marvelous parties.

Their home is superb, one of the finest in the neighborhood. It is truly a home for all seasons, all moods. Their very special corner of the world. With more space indoors and out…more wide-open freedom. The living room with its exposed ceiling beams is a natural focal point for entertaining. Custom-finished, with a conversation pit and fireplace. There's also a family room with beamed ceiling and wood paneling…plus a study. And a magnificent master suite with twelve-foot dressing room and private bath. Solidly impressive exterior design. Sheltered courtyard. Beautifully wooded -acre grounds. Their parties are highlights of any month. Nick and Jane waited until they thought enough people had arrived. Then Jane nudged Nick and Nick said gaily, "You know what we did last week? Hey, we went to see the end of the world!"

"The end of the world?" Henry asked.

"You went to see it?" said Henry's wife Cynthia.

"How did you manage that?" Paula wanted to know.

"It's been available since March," Stan told her. "I think a division of American Express runs it."

Nick was put out to discover that Stan already knew. Quickly, before Stan could say anything more, Nick said, "Yes, it's just started. Our travel agent found out for us. What they do is they put you in this machine, it looks like a tiny teeny submarine, you know, with dials and levers up front behind a plastic wall to keep you from touching anything, and they send you into the future. You can charge it with any of the regular credit cards."

"It must be very expensive," Marcia said.

"They're bringing the costs down rapidly," Jane said. "Last year only millionaires could afford it. Really, haven't you heard about it before?"

"What did you see?" Henry asked.

"For a while, just greyness outside the porthole," said Nick. "And a kind of flickering effect." Everybody was looking at him. He enjoyed the attention. Jane wore a rapt, loving expression. "Then the haze cleared and a voice said over a loudspeaker that we had now reached the very end of time, when life had become impossible on Earth. Of course, we were sealed into the submarine thing. Only looking out. On this beach, this empty beach. The water a funny grey color with a pink sheen. And then the sun came up. It was red like it sometimes is at sunrise, only it stayed red as it got to the middle of the sky, and it looked lumpy and saggy at the edges. Like a few of us, hah hah. Lumpy and sagging at the edges. A cold wind blowing across the beach."

"If you were sealed in the submarine, how did you know there was a cold wind?" Cynthia asked.

Jane glared at her. Nick said, "We could see the sand blowing around. And it looked cold. The grey ocean. Like winter."

"Tell them about the crab," said Jane.

"Yes, the crab. The last life-form on Earth. It wasn't really a crab, of course, it was something about two feet wide and a foot high, with thick shiny green armor and maybe a dozen legs and some curving horns coming up, and it moved slowly from right to left in front of us. It took all day to cross the beach. And toward nightfall it died. Its horns went limp and it stopped moving. The tide came in and carried it away. The sun went down. There wasn't any moon. The stars didn't seem to be in the right places. The loudspeaker told us we had just seen the death of Earth's last living thing."

"How eerie!" cried Paula.

"Were you gone very long?" Ruby asked.

"Three hours," Jane said. "You can spend weeks or days at the end of the world, if you want to pay extra, but they always bring you back to a point three hours after you went. To hold down the babysitter expenses."

Mike offered Nick some pot. "That's really something," he said. "To have gone to the end of the world. Hey, Ruby, maybe we'll talk to the travel agent about it."

Nick took a deep drag and passed the joint to Jane. He felt pleased with himself about the way he had told the story. They had all been very impressed. That swollen red sun, that scuttling crab. The trip had cost more than a month in Japan, but it had been a good investment.

He and Jane were the first in the neighborhood who had gone. That was important. Paula was staring at him in awe. Nick knew that she regarded him in a completely different light now. Possibly she would meet him at a motel on Tuesday at lunchtime. Last month she had turned him down but now he had an extra attractiveness for her. Nick winked at her. Cynthia was holding hands with Stan. Henry and Mike both were crouched at Jane's feet. Mike and Ruby's twelve-year-old son came into the room and stood at the edge of the conversation pit. He said, "There just was a bulletin on the news. Mutated amoebas escaped from a government research station and got into Lake Michigan. They're carrying a tissue-dissolving virus and everybody in seven states is supposed to boil their water until further notice." Mike scowled at the boy and said, "It's after your bedtime, Timmy." The boy went out. The doorbell rang. Ruby answered it and returned with Eddie and Fran.

Paula said, "Nick and Jane went to see the end of the world. They've just been telling us about it."

"Gee," said Eddie, "We did that too, on Wednesday night."

Nick was crestfallen. Jane bit her lip and asked Cynthia quietly why Fran always wore such flashy dresses. Ruby said, "You saw the whole works, eh? The crab and everything?"

"The crab?" Eddie said. "What crab? We didn't see the crab."

"It must have died the time before," Paula said. "When Nick and Jane were there."

Mike said, "A fresh shipment of Cuernavaca Lightning is in. Here, have a toke."

"How long ago did you do it?" Eddie said to Nick.

"Sunday afternoon. I guess we were about the first."

"Great trip, isn't it?" Eddie said. "A little somber, though. When the last hill crumbles into the sea."

"That's not what we saw," said Jane. "And you didn't see the crab? Maybe we were on different trips."

Mike said, "What was it like for you, Eddie?"

Eddie put his arms around Cynthia from behind. He said, "They put us into this little capsule, with a porthole, you know, and a lot of instruments and—"

"We heard that part," said Paula. "What did you see?"

"The end of the world," Eddie said. "When water covers everything. The sun and the moon were in the sky at the same time—"

"We didn't see the moon at all," Jane remarked. "It just wasn't there."

"It was on one side and the sun was on the other," Eddie went on. "The moon was closer than it should have been. And a funny color, almost like bronze. And the ocean creeping up. We went halfway around the world and all we saw was ocean. Except in one place, there was this chunk of land sticking up, this hill, and the guide told us it was the top of Mount Everest." He waved to Fran. "That was groovy, huh, floating in our tin boat next to the top of Mount Everest. Maybe ten feet of it sticking up. And the water rising all the time. Up, up, up. Up and over the top. Glub. No land left. I have to admit it was a little disappointing, except of course the idea of the thing. That human ingenuity can design a machine that can send people billions of years forward in time and bring them back, wow! But there was just this ocean."

"How strange," said Jane. "We saw the ocean too, but there was a beach, a kind of nasty beach, and the crab-thing walking along it, and the sun—it was all red, was the sun red when you saw it?"

"A kind of pale green," Fran said.

"Are you people talking about the end of the world?" Tom asked. He and Harriet were standing by the door taking off their coats. Mike's son must have let them in. Tom gave his coat to Ruby and said, "Man, what a spectacle!"

"So you did it, too?" Jane asked, a little hollowly.

"Two weeks ago," said Tom. "The travel agent called and said, Guess what we're offering now, the end of the goddamned world! With all the extras it didn't really cost so much. So we went right down there to the office, Saturday, I think—was it a Friday?—the day of the big riot, anyway, when they burned St Louis—"

"That was a Saturday," Cynthia said. "I remember I was coming back from the shopping center when the radio said they were using nuclears—"

"Saturday, yes," Tom said. "And we told them we were ready to go, and off they sent us."

"Did you see a beach with crabs," Stan demanded, "or was it a world full of water?"

"Neither one. It was like a big ice age. Glaciers covered everything. No oceans showing, no mountains. We flew clear around the world and it was all a huge snowball. They had floodlights on the vehicle because the sun had gone out."

"I was sure I could see the sun still hanging up there," Harriet put in. "Like a ball of cinders in the sky. But the guide said no, nobody could see it."

"How come everybody gets to visit a different kind of end of the world?" Henry asked. "You'd think there'd be only one kind of end of the world. I mean, it ends, and this is how it ends, and there can't be more than one way."

"Could it be fake?" Stan asked. Everybody turned around and looked at him. Nick's face got very red. Fran looked so mean that Eddie let go of Cynthia and started to rub Fran's shoulders. Stan shrugged. "I'm not suggesting it is," he said defensively. "I was just wondering."

"Seemed pretty real to me," said Tom. "The sun burned out. A big ball of ice. The atmosphere, you know, frozen. The end of the goddamned world."

The telephone rang. Ruby went to answer it. Nick asked Paula about lunch on Tuesday. She said yes. "Let's meet at the motel," he said, and she grinned. Eddie was making out with Cynthia again. Henry looked very stoned and was having trouble staying awake. Phil and Isabel arrived. They heard Tom and Fran talking about their trips to the end of the world and Isabel said she and Phil had gone only the day before yesterday. "Goddamn," Tom said, "everybody's doing it! What was your trip like?"

Ruby came back into the room. "That was my sister calling from Fresno to say she's safe. Fresno wasn't hit by the earthquake at all."

"Earthquake?" Paula asked.

"'In California," Mike told her. "This afternoon. You didn't know? Wiped out most of Los Angeles and ran right up the coast practically to Monterey. They think it was on account of the underground bomb test in the Mohave Desert."

"California's always having such awful disasters," Marcia said.

"Good thing those amoebas got loose back east," said Nick. "Imagine how complicated it would be if they had them in LA now too."

"They will," Tom said . "Two to one they reproduce by airborne spores."

"Like the typhoid germs last November," Jane said.

"That was typhus," Nick corrected.

"Anyway," Phil said, "I was telling Tom and Fran about what we saw at the end of the world. It was the sun going nova. They showed it very cleverly, too. I mean, you can't actually sit around and experience it, on account of the heat and the hard radiation and all. But they give it to you in a peripheral way, very elegant in the McLuhanesque sense of the word. First they take you to a point about two hours before the blowup, right? It's I don't know how many jillion years from now, but a long way, anyhow, because the trees are all different, they've got blue scales and ropy branches, and the animals are like things with one leg that jump on pogo sticks—"

"Oh, I don't *believe* that," Cynthia drawled.

Phil ignored her gracefully. "And we didn't see any sign of human beings, not a house, not a telephone pole, nothing, so I suppose we must have been extinct a long time before. Anyway, they let us look at that for a while. Not getting out of our time machine, naturally, because they said the atmosphere was wrong. Gradually the sun started to puff up. We were nervous—weren't we, Iz?—I mean, suppose they miscalculated things? This whole trip is a very new concept and things might go wrong. The sun was getting bigger and bigger, and then this thing like an arm seemed to pop out of its left side, a big fiery arm reaching out across space, getting closer and closer. We saw it through smoked glass, like you do an eclipse. They gave us about two minutes of the explosion, and we could feel it getting hot already. Then we jumped a couple of years forward in time. The sun was back to its regular shape, only it was smaller, sort of like a little white sun instead of a big yellow one. And on Earth everything was ashes."

"Ashes," Isabel said, with emphasis.

"It looked like Detroit after the union nuked Ford," Phil said. "Only much, much worse. Whole mountains were melted. The oceans were dried up. Everything was ashes." He shuddered and took a joint from Mike. "'Isabel was crying."

"The things with one leg," Isabel said. "I mean, they must have all been wiped out." She began to sob. Stan comforted her. "I wonder why it's a different way for everyone who goes," he said. "Freezing. Or the oceans. Or the sun blowing up. Or the thing Nick and Jane saw."

"I'm convinced that each of us had a genuine experience in the far future," said Nick. He felt he had to regain control of the group somehow. It had been so good when he was telling his story, before those others had come. "That is to say, the world suffers a variety of natural calamities, it doesn't just have one end of the world, and they keep mixing things up and sending people to different catastrophes. But never for a moment did I doubt that I was seeing an authentic event."

"We have to do it," Ruby said to Mike. "It's only three hours. What about calling them first thing Monday and making an appointment for Thursday night?"

"Monday's the President's funeral," Tom pointed out. "The travel agency will be closed."

"Have they caught the assassin yet?" Fran asked.

"They didn't mention it on the four o'clock news," said Stan. "I guess he'll get away like the last one."

"Beats me why anybody wants to be President," Phil said.

Mike put on some music. Nick danced with Paula. Eddie danced with Cynthia. Henry was asleep. Dave, Paula's husband, was on crutches because of his mugging, and he asked Isabel to sit and talk with him. Tom danced with Harriet even though he was married to her. She hadn't been out of the hospital more than a few months since the transplant and he treated her extremely tenderly. Mike danced with Fran. Phil danced with Jane. Stan danced with Marcia. Ruby cut in on Eddie and Cynthia. Afterward Tom danced with Jane and Phil danced with Paula. Mike and Ruby's little girl woke up and came out to say hello. Mike sent her back to bed. Far away there was the sound of an explosion. Nick danced with Paula again, but he didn't want her to get bored with him before Tuesday, so he excused himself and went to talk with Dave. Dave handled most of Nick's investments. Ruby said to Mike, "The day after the funeral, will you call the travel agent?" Mike said he would, but Tom said somebody would probably shoot the new President too and there'd be another funeral. These funerals were demolishing the gross national product, Stan observed, on account of how everything had to close all the time. Nick saw Cynthia wake Henry up and ask him sharply if he would take her on the end-of-the-world trip. Henry looked embarrassed. His factory had been blown up at Christmas in a peace demonstration and everybody knew he was in bad shape financially. "You can *charge* it," Cynthia said, her fierce voice carrying above the chitchat. "And it's so *beautiful,* Henry. The ice. Or the sun exploding. I want to go."

"Lou and Janet were going to be here tonight, too," Ruby said to Paula. "But their younger boy came back from Texas with that new kind of cholera and they had to cancel."

Phil said, "I understand that one couple saw the moon come apart. It got too close to the Earth and split into chunks and the chunks fell like meteors. Smashing everything up, you know. One big piece nearly hit their time machine."

"I wouldn't have liked that at all," Marcia said.

"Our trip was very lovely," said Jane. "No violent things at all. Just the big red sun and the tide and that crab creeping along the beach. We were both deeply moved."

"It's amazing what science can accomplish nowadays," Fran said.

Mike and Ruby agreed they would try to arrange a trip to the end of the world as soon as the funeral was over. Cynthia drank too much and got sick. Phil, Tom, and Dave discussed the stock market. Harriet told Nick about her operation. Isabel flirted with Mike, tugging her neckline lower. At midnight someone turned on the news. They had some shots of the earthquake and a warning about boiling your water if you lived in the affected states. The President's widow was shown visiting the last President's widow to get some pointers for the funeral. Then there was an interview with an executive of the time-trip company. "Business is phenomenal," he said. "Time-tripping will be the nation's number one growth industry next year." The reporter asked him if his company would soon be offering something besides the end-of-the-world trip. "Later on, we hope to," the executive said. "We plan to apply for Congressional approval soon. But meanwhile the demand for our present offering is running very high. You can't imagine. Of course, you have to expect apocalyptic stuff to attain immense popularity in times like these." The reporter said, "What do you mean, times like these?" but as the time-trip man started to reply, he was interrupted by the commercial. Mike shut off the set. Nick discovered that he was extremely depressed. He decided that it was because so many of his friends had made the journey, and he had thought he and Jane were the only ones who had. He found himself standing next to Marcia and tried to describe the way the crab had moved, but Marcia only shrugged. No one was talking about time-trips now. The party had moved beyond that point. Nick and Jane left quite early and went right to sleep, without making love. The next morning the Sunday paper wasn't delivered because of the Bridge Authority strike, and the radio said that the mutant amoebas were proving harder to eradicate than originally anticipated. They were spreading into Lake Superior and everyone in the region would have to boil all their drinking water. Nick and Jane discussed where they would go for their next vacation. "What about going to see the end of the world all over again?" Jane suggested, and Nick laughed quite a good deal.

PUSH NO MORE

Among the many anthologies of previously unpublished science-fiction stories that were launched in 1971, two dealt specifically with erotic themes—something that would have been unthinkable only a decade earlier, before Philip Jose Farmer's taboo–smashing 1952 novella "The Lovers" made it possible to regard sexual issues as something appropriate to consider within the speculative framework of science fiction. The first of these anthologies was Thomas N. Scortia's Strange Bedfellows; *the other was Joseph Elder's* Eros in Orbit. *I had stories in both of them.*

Scortia, a space engineer turned science-fiction writer, was an earthy, jovial, extraverted guy, big and loud, the perfect stereotype of the Middle American businessman—except that despite all those traits he happened to be gay and didn't really fit any stereotypes at all. I had known him in a glancing way since the late 1950s, but after he left the Midwest for the San Francisco Bay Area about 1969, something that I would do myself (for very different reasons) a few years later, he and I became much closer friends in our new California incarnations. But I was still in my last months as a New Yorker when he asked me, in September, 1971, to do a story for his anthology of s-f erotica.

I was getting ready, that month, to write Dying Inside, *a novel about the problems of a middle-aged telepath, and so the whole topic of extrasensory powers was much on my mind. For my contribution to* Strange Bedfellows *I chose to write about a different extrasensory manifestation—the poltergeist phenomenon—and that required me to use a younger protagonist than I had in mind for* Dying Inside, *since the standard poltergeist theory maintains that most carriers of that ability are adolescents who have not yet had their first sexual experience. So in place of the balding, world–weary David Selig of* Dying Inside, *we have the lively, quirky, very horny Harry Blaufeldt of "Push No More."*

But—seeing now that I wrote those two stories consecutively in the autumn of 1971—I realize now, suddenly and with some surprise, that both stories had precisely the same structure: the first-person narrative of a bright Jewish boy with ESP who eventually has to come to terms with the loss of his special power. So "Push No More" can be considered a warm-up for Dying Inside *in more ways than one. It's odd that I never noticed that until this moment—but neither, apparently, has anyone else.*

I push…and the shoe moves. Will you look at that? It really moves! All I have to do is give a silent inner nudge, no hands, just reaching from the core of my mind, and my old worn-out brown shoe, the left one, goes sliding slowly across the floor of my bedroom. Past the chair, past the pile of beaten-up textbooks (Geometry, Second Year Spanish, Civic Studies, Biology, etc.), past my sweaty heap of discarded clothes. Indeed the shoe obeys me. Making a little swishing sound as it snags against the roughness of the elderly linoleum floor tiling. Look at it now, bumping gently into the far wall, tipping edge-up, stopping. Its voyage is over. I bet I could make it climb right up the wall. But don't bother doing it, man. Not just now. This is hard work. Just relax, Harry. Your arms are shaking. You're perspiring all over. Take it easy for a while. You don't have to prove everything all at once.

What have I proven, anyway?

It seems that I can make things move with my mind. How about that, man? Did you ever imagine that you had freaky powers? Not until this very night. This very lousy night. Standing there with Cindy Klein and finding that terrible knot of throbbing tension in my groin, like needing to take a leak only fifty times more intense, a zone of anguish spinning off some kind of fearful energy like a crazy dynamo implanted in my crotch. And suddenly, without any conscious awareness, finding a way of tapping that energy, drawing it up through my body to my head, amplifying it, and…*using* it. As I just did with my shoe. As I did a couple of hours earlier with Cindy. So you aren't just a dumb gawky adolescent schmuck, Harry Blaufeld. You are somebody very special.

You have power. You are potent.

How good it is to lie here in the privacy of my own musty bedroom and be able to make my shoe slide along the floor, simply by looking at it in that special way. The feeling of strength that I get from that! Tremendous. I am potent. I have power. That's what potent means, to have power, out of the Latin *potentia,* derived from *posse.* To be able. I am able. I can do this most extraordinary thing. And not just in fitful unpredictable bursts. It's under my conscious control. All I have to do is dip into that reservoir of tension and skim off a few watts of *push.* Far out! What a weird night this is.

Let's go back three hours. To a time when I know nothing of this *potentia* in me. Three hours ago I know only from horniness. I'm standing outside Cindy's front door with her at half past ten. We have done the going-to-the-movies thing, we have done the cappuccino-afterward thing, now I want to do the makeout thing. I'm trying to get myself invited inside, knowing that her parents have gone away for the weekend and there's nobody home except her older brother, who is seeing his girl in Scarsdale tonight and won't be back for hours, and once I'm past Cindy's front door I hope, well, to get invited inside. (What a coy metaphor! You know what I mean.) So three cheers for Casanova Blaufeld, who is suffering a bad attack of inflammation of the cherry. Look at me, stammering, fumbling for words, shifting my weight from foot to foot, chewing on my lips, going red in the face. All my pimples light up like beacons when I blush. Come on, Blaufeld, pull yourself together. Change your image of yourself. Try this on for size: you're twenty-three years old, tall, strong, suave, a man of the world, veteran of so many beds you've lost count. Bushy beard that girls love to run their hands through. Big drooping handlebar mustachios. And you aren't asking her for any favors. You aren't whining and wheedling and saying please, Cindy, let's do it, because you know you don't need to say please. It's no boon you seek: you give as good as you get, right, so it's a mutually beneficial transaction, right? Right? Wrong. You're as suave as a pig. You want to exploit her for the sake of your own grubby needs. You know you'll be inept. But let's pretend, at least. Straighten the shoulders, suck in the gut, inflate the chest. Harry Blaufeld, the devilish seducer. Get your hands on her sweater for starters. No one's around; it's a dark night. Go for the boobs, get her hot. Isn't that what Jimmy the Greek told you to do? So you try it. Grinning stupidly, practically apologizing with your eyes. Reaching out. The grabby fingers connecting with the fuzzy purple fabric.

Her face, flushed and big-eyed. Her mouth, thin-lipped and wide. Her voice, harsh and wire-edged. She says, "Don't be disgusting, Harry. Don't be *silly.*" Silly. Backing away from me like I've turned into a monster with eight eyes and green fangs. Don't be disgusting. She tries to slip into the house fast, before I can paw her again. I stand there watching her fumble for her key, and this terrible rage starts to rise in me. Why disgusting? Why silly? All I wanted was to show her my love, right? That I really care for her, that I *relate* to her. A display of affection through physical contact. Right? So I reached out. A little caress. Prelude to tender intimacy. "Don't be disgusting," she said. "Don't be *silly.*" The trivial little immature bitch. And now I feel the anger mounting. Down between my legs there's this hideous pain, this throbbing sensation of anguish, this purely sexual tension, and it's pouring out into my belly, spreading upward along my gut like a stream of flame. A dam has broken somewhere inside me. I feel fire blazing under the top of my skull. And there it is! The power! The strength! I don't question it. I don't ask myself what it is or where it came from. I just push her, hard, from ten feet away, a quick furious shove. It's like an invisible hand against her breasts—I can see the front of her sweater flatten out—and she topples backward, clutching at the air, and goes over on her ass. I've knocked her sprawling without touching her. "Harry," she mumbles. "Harry?"

My anger's gone. Now I feel terror. What have I done? How? How? Down on her ass, *boom.* From ten feet away!

I run all the way home, never looking back.

Footsteps in the hallway, *clickety-clack.* My sister is home from her date with Jimmy the Greek. That isn't his name. Aristides Pappas is who he really is. Ari, she calls him. Jimmy the Greek, I call him, but not to his face. He's nine feet tall with black greasy hair and a tremendous beak of a nose that comes straight out of his forehead. He's twenty-seven years old and he's laid a thousand girls. Sara is going to marry him next year. Meanwhile they see each other three nights a week and they screw a lot. She's never said a word to me about that, about the screwing, but I know. Sure they screw. Why not? They're going to get married, aren't they? And they're adults. She's nineteen years old, so it's legal for her to screw. I won't be nineteen for four years and four months. It's legal for me to screw now, I think. If only. If only I had somebody. If only.

Clickety-clickety-clack. There she goes, into her room. *Blunk*. That's her door closing. She doesn't give a damn if she wakes the whole family up. Why should she care? She's all turned on now. Soaring on her memories of what she was just doing with Jimmy the Greek. That warm feeling. The afterglow, the book calls it.

I wonder how they do it when they do it.

They go to his apartment. Do they take off all their clothes first? Do they talk before they begin? A drink or two? Smoke a joint? Sara claims she doesn't smoke it. I bet she's putting me on. They get naked. Christ, he's so tall, he must have a dong a foot long. Doesn't it scare her? They lie down on the bed together. Or on a couch. The floor, maybe? A thick fluffy carpet? He touches her body. Doing the foreplay stuff. I've read about it. He strokes the breasts, making the nipples go erect. I've seen her nipples. They aren't any bigger than mine. How tall do they get when they're erect? An inch? Three inches? Standing up like a couple of pink pencils? And his hand must go down below, too. There's this thing you're supposed to touch, this tiny bump of flesh hidden inside there. I've studied the diagrams and I still don't know where it is. Jimmy the Greek knows where it is, you can bet your ass. So he touches her there. Then what? She must get hot, right? How can he tell when it's time to go inside her? The time arrives. They're finally doing it. You know, I can't visualize it. He's on top of her and they're moving up and down, sure, but I still can't imagine how the bodies fit together, how they really move, how they do it.

She's getting undressed now, right across the hallway. Off with the shirt, the slacks, the bra, the panties, whatever the hell she wears. I can hear her moving around. I wonder if her door is really closed tight. It's a long time since I've had a good look at her. Who knows, maybe her nipples are still standing up. Even if her door's open only a few inches, I can see into her room from mine, if I hunch down here in the dark and peek.

But her door's closed. What if I reach out and give it a little nudge? From here. I pull the power up into my head, yes...reach...*push*... ah...yes! Yes! It moves! One inch, two, three. That's good enough. I can see a slice of her room. The light's on. Hey, there she goes! Too fast, out of sight. I think she was naked. Now she's coming back. Naked, yes. Her back is to me. You've got a cute ass, Sis, you know that? Turn around, turn around, turn around...ah. Her nipples look the same as always. Not standing up at all. I guess they must go back down after it's all over.

Thy two breasts are like two young roes that are twins, which feed among the lilies. (I don't really read the Bible a lot, just the dirty parts.) Cindy's got bigger ones than you, Sis, I bet she has. Unless she pads them. I couldn't tell tonight. I was too excited to notice whether I was squeezing flesh or rubber.

Sara's putting her housecoat on. One last flash of thigh and belly, then no more. Damn. Into the bathroom now. The sound of water running. She's getting washed. Now the tap is off. And now…*tinkle, tinkle, tinkle.* I can picture her sitting there, grinning to herself, taking a happy piss, thinking cozy thoughts about what she and Jimmy the Greek did tonight. Oh, Christ, I hurt! I'm jealous of my own sister! That she can do it three times a week while I…am nowhere…with nobody…no one…nothing…

Let's give Sis a little surprise.

Hmm. Can I manipulate something that's out of my direct line of sight? Let's try it. The toilet seat is in the right-hand corner of the bathroom, under the window. And the flush knob is—let me think—on the side closer to the wall, up high—yes. Okay, reach out, man. Grab it before she does. *Push*…down…*push.* Yeah! Listen to that, man! You flushed it for her without leaving your own room!

She's going to have a hard time figuring that one out.

Sunday: a rainy day, a day of worrying. I can't get the strange events of last night out of my mind. This power of mine—where did it come from, what can I use it for? And I can't stop fretting over the awareness that I'll have to face Cindy again first thing tomorrow morning, in our Biology class. What will she say to me? Does she realize I actually wasn't anywhere near her when I knocked her down? If she knows I have a power, is she frightened of me? Will she report me to the Society for the Prevention of Supernatural Phenomena, or whoever looks after such things? I'm tempted to pretend I'm sick, and stay home from school tomorrow. But what's the sense of that? I can't avoid her forever.

The more tense I get, the more intensely I feel the power surging within me. It's very strong today. (The rain may have something to do with that. Every nerve is twitching. The air is damp and maybe that makes me more conductive.) When nobody is looking, I experiment. In the bathroom, standing far from the sink, I unscrew the top of the toothpaste tube. I turn the water taps on and off. I open and close the window. How fine my control is! Doing these things is a strain: I tremble, I sweat, I feel the muscles of my jaws knotting up, my back teeth ache. But I can't resist the kick of exercising my skills. I get riskily mischievous. At breakfast, my mother puts four slices of bread in the toaster; sitting with my back to it, I delicately work the toaster's plug out of the socket, so that when she goes over to investigate five minutes later, she's bewildered to find the bread still raw. "How did the plug slip out?" she asks, but of course no one tells her. Afterward, as we all sit around reading the Sunday papers, I turn the television set on by remote control, and the sudden blaring of a cartoon show makes everyone jump. And a few hours later I unscrew a light bulb in the hallway, gently, gently, easing it from its fixture, holding it suspended close to the ceiling for a moment, then letting it crash to the floor. "What was that?" my mother says in alarm. My father inspects the hall. "Bulb fell out of the fixture and smashed itself to bits." My mother shakes her head. "How could a bulb fall out? It isn't possible." And my father says, "It must have been loose." He doesn't sound convinced. It must be occurring to him that a bulb loose enough to fall to the floor couldn't have been lit. And this bulb had been lit.

How soon before my sister connects these incidents with the episode of the toilet that flushed by itself?

Monday is here. I enter the classroom through the rear door and skulk to my seat. Cindy hasn't arrived yet. But now here she comes. God, how beautiful she is! The gleaming, shimmering red hair, down to her shoulders. The pale flawless skin. The bright, mysterious eyes. The purple sweater, same one as Saturday night. My hands have touched that sweater. I've touched that sweater with my power, too.

I bend low over my notebook. I can't bear to look at her. I'm a coward.

But I force myself to look up. She's standing in the aisle, up by the front of the room, staring at me. Her expression is strange—edgy, uneasy, the lips clamped tight. As if she's thinking of coming back here to talk to me but is hesitating. The moment she sees me watching her, she glances away and takes her seat. All through the hour I sit hunched forward, studying her shoulders, the back of her neck, the tips of her ears. Five desks separate her from me. I let out a heavy romantic sigh.

Temptation is tickling me. It would be so easy to reach across that distance and touch her. Gently stroking her soft cheek with an invisible fingertip. Lightly fondling the side of her throat. Using my special power to say a tender hello to her. See, Cindy? See what I can do to show my love? Having imagined it, I find myself unable to resist doing it. I summon the force from the churning reservoir in my depths; I pump it upward and simultaneously make the automatic calculations of intensity of push. Then I realize what I'm doing. Are you crazy, man? She'll scream. She'll jump out of her chair like she was stung. She'll roll on the floor and have hysterics. Hold back, hold back, you lunatic! At the last moment I manage to deflect the impulse. Gasping, grunting, I twist the force away from Cindy and hurl it blindly in some other direction. My random thrust sweeps across the room like a whiplash and intersects the big framed chart of the plant and animal kingdoms that hangs on the classroom's left-hand wall. It rips loose as though kicked by a tornado and soars twenty feet on a diagonal arc that sends it crashing into the blackboard. The frame shatters. Broken glass sprays everywhere. The class is thrown into panic. Everybody yelling, running around, picking up pieces of glass, exclaiming in awe, asking questions. I sit like a statue. Then I start to shiver. And Cindy, very slowly, turns and looks at me. A chilly look of horror freezes her face.

She knows, then. She thinks I'm some sort of freak. She thinks I'm some sort of monster.

Poltergeist. That's what I am. That's me.

I've been to the library. I've done some homework in the occultism section. So: Harry Blaufeld, boy poltergeist. From the German, *poltern,* "to make a noise", and *geist,* "spirit". Thus, poltergeist = "noisy spirit". Poltergeists make plates go smash against the wall, pictures fall suddenly to the floor, doors bang when no one is near them, rocks fly through the air.

I'm not sure whether it's proper to say that I *am* a poltergeist, or that I'm merely the host for one. It depends on which theory you prefer. True-blue occultists like to think that poltergeists are wandering demons or spirits that occasionally take up residence in human beings, through whom they focus their energies and play their naughty tricks. On the other hand, those who hold a more scientific attitude toward paranormal extrasensory phenomena say that it's absurdly medieval to believe in wandering demons; to them, a poltergeist is simply someone who's capable of harnessing a paranormal ability within himself that allows him to move things without touching them. Myself, I incline toward the latter view. It's much more flattering to think that I have an extraordinary psychic gift than that I've been possessed by a marauding demon. Also less scary.

Poltergeists are nothing new. A Chinese book about a thousand years old called *Gossip from the Jade Hall* tells of one that disturbed the peace of a monastery by flinging crockery around. The monks hired an exorcist to get things under control, but the noisy spirit gave him the works: "His cap was pulled off and thrown against the wall, his robe was loosed, and even his trousers pulled off, which caused him to retire precipitately." Right on, poltergeist! "Others tried where he had failed, but they were rewarded for their pains by a rain of insolent missives from the air, upon which were written words of malice and bitter odium."

The archives bulge with such tales from many lands and many eras. Consider the Clarke case, Oakland, California, 1874. On hand: Mr. Clarke, a successful businessman of austere and reserved ways, and his wife and adolescent daughter and eight-year-old son, plus two of Mr. Clarke's sisters and two male house guests. On the night of April 23, as everyone prepares for bed, the front doorbell rings. No one there. Rings again a few minutes later. No one there. Sound of furniture being moved in the parlor. One of the house guests, a banker named Bayley, inspects, in the dark, and is hit by a chair. No one there. A box of silverware comes floating down the stairs and lands with a bang. (Poltergeist = "noisy spirit".) A heavy box of coal flies about next. A chair hits Bayley on the elbow and lands against a bed. In the dining room a massive oak chair rises two feet in the air, spins, lets itself down, chases the unfortunate Bayley around the room in front of three witnesses. And so on. Much spooked, everybody goes to bed, but all night they hear crashes and rumbling sounds; in the morning they find all the downstairs furniture in a scramble. Also the front door, which was locked and bolted, has been ripped off its hinges. More such events the next night. Likewise on the next, culminating in a female shriek out of nowhere, so terrible that it drives the Clarkes and guests to take refuge in another house. No explanation for any of this ever offered.

A man named Charles Fort, who died in 1932, spent much of his life studying poltergeist phenomena and similar mysteries. Fort wrote four fat books which so far I've only skimmed. They're full of newspaper accounts of strange things like the sudden appearance of several young crocodiles on English farms in the middle of the nineteenth century, and rainstorms in which the earth was pelted with snakes, frogs, blood, or stones. He collected clippings describing instances of coal-heaps and houses and even human beings suddenly and spontaneously bursting into flame. Luminous objects sailing through the sky. Invisible hands that mutilate animals and people. "Phantom bullets" shattering the windows of houses. Inexplicable disappearances of human beings, and equally inexplicable reappearances far away. Et cetera, et cetera, et cetera. I gather that Fort believed that most of these phenomena were the work of beings from interplanetary space who meddle in events on our world for their own amusement. But he couldn't explain away everything like that. Poltergeists in particular didn't fit into his bogeymen-from-space fantasy, and so, he wrote, "Therefore I regard poltergeists as evil or false or discordant or absurd..." Still, he said, "I don't care to deny poltergeists, because I suspect that later, when we're more enlightened, or when we widen the range of our credulities, or take on more of that increase of ignorance that is called knowledge, poltergeists may become assimilable. Then they'll be as reasonable as trees."

I like Fort. He was eccentric and probably very gullible, but he wasn't foolish or crazy. I don't think he's right about beings from interplanetary space, but I admire his attitude toward the inexplicable.

Most of the poltergeist cases on record are frauds. They've been exposed by experts. There was the 1944 episode in Wild Plum, North Dakota, in which lumps of burning coal began to jump out of a bucket in the one-room schoolhouse of Mrs. Pauline Rebel. Papers caught fire on the pupils' desks and charred spots appeared on the curtains. The class dictionary moved around of its own accord. There was talk in town of demonic forces. A few days later, after an assistant state attorney general had begun interrogating people, four of Mrs. Rebel's pupils confessed that they had been tossing the coal around to terrorize their teacher. They'd done most of the dirty work while her back was turned or when she had had her glasses off. A prank. A hoax. Some people would tell you that all poltergeist stories are equally phony. I'm here to testify that they aren't.

One pattern is consistent in all genuine poltergeist incidents: an adolescent is invariably involved, or a child on the edge of adolescence. This is the "naughty child" theory of poltergeists, first put forth by

Frank Podmore in 1890 in the *Proceedings of the Society for Psychical Research*. (See, I've done my homework very thoroughly.) The child is usually unhappy, customarily over sexual matters, and suffers either from a sense of not being wanted or from frustration, or both. There are no statistics on the matter, but the lore indicates that teenagers involved in poltergeist activity are customarily virgins.

The 1874 Clarke case, then, becomes the work of the adolescent daughter, who—I would guess—had a yen for Mr. Bayley. The multitude of cases cited by Fort, most of them dating from the nineteenth century, show a bunch of poltergeist kids flinging stuff around in a sexually repressed era. That seething energy had to go somewhere. I discovered my own poltering power while in an acute state of palpitating lust for Cindy Klein, who wasn't having any part of me. Especially *that* part. But instead of exploding from the sheer force of my bottled-up yearnings I suddenly found a way of channeling all that drive outward. And pushed...

Fort again: "Wherein children are atavistic, they may be in rapport with forces that most human beings have outgrown." Atavism: a strange recurrence to the primitive past. Perhaps in Neanderthal times we were all poltergeists, but most of us lost it over the millennia. But see Fort, also: "There are of course other explanations of the 'occult power' of children. One is that children, instead of being atavistic, may occasionally be far in advance of adults, foreshadowing coming human powers, because their minds are not stifled by conventions. After that, they go to school and lose their superiority. Few boy-prodigies have survived an education."

I feel reassured, knowing I'm just a statistic in a long-established pattern of paranormal behavior. Nobody likes to think he's a freak, even when he is a freak. Here I am, virginal, awkward, owlish, quirky, precocious, edgy, uncertain, timid, clever, solemn, socially inept, stumbling through all the standard problems of the immediately post-pubescent years. I have pimples and wet dreams and the sort of fine fuzz that isn't worth shaving, only I shave it anyway. Cindy Klein thinks I'm silly and disgusting. And I've got this hot core of fury and frustration in my gut, which is my great curse and my great supremacy. I'm a poltergeist, man. Go on, give me a hard time, make fun of me, call me silly and disgusting. The next time I may not just knock you on your ass. I might heave you all the way to Pluto.

An unavoidable humiliating encounter with Cindy today. At lunchtime I go into Schindler's for my usual bacon-lettuce-tomato; I take a seat in one of the back booths and open a book and someone says, "Harry," and there she is at the booth just opposite, with three of her friends. What do I do? Get up and run out? Poltergeist her into the next county? Already I feel the power twitching in me. Mrs. Schindler brings me my sandwich. I'm stuck. I can't bear to be here. I hand her the money and mutter, "Just remembered, got to make a phone call." Sandwich in hand, I start to leave, giving Cindy a foolish hot-cheeked grin as I go by. She's looking at me fiercely. Those deep green eyes of hers terrify me.

"Wait," she says. "Can I ask you something?"

She slides out of her booth and blocks the aisle of the luncheonette. She's nearly as tall as I am, and I'm tall. My knees are shaking. God in heaven, Cindy, don't trap me like this, I'm not responsible for what I might do.

She says in a low voice, "Yesterday in Bio, when that chart hit the blackboard. You did that, didn't you?"

"I don't understand."

"You made it jump across the room."

"That's impossible," I mumble. "What do you think I am, a magician?"

"I don't know. And Saturday night, that dumb scene outside my house—"

"I'd rather not talk about it."

"I would. How did you do that to me, Harry? Where did you learn the trick?"

"Trick? Look, Cindy, I've absolutely got to go."

"You pushed me over. You just looked at me and I felt a push."

"You tripped," I say. "You just fell down."

She laughs. Right now she seems about nineteen years old and I feel about nine years old. "Don't put me on," she says, her voice a deep sophisticated drawl. Her girlfriends are peering at us, trying to overhear. "Listen, this interests me. I'm involved. I want to know how you do that stuff."

"There isn't any stuff," I tell her, and suddenly I know I have to escape. I give her the tiniest push, not touching her, of course, just a wee mental nudge, and she feels it and gives ground, and I rush miserably past her, cramming my sandwich into my mouth. I flee the store. At the door I look back and see her smiling, waving to me, telling me to come back.

I have a rich fantasy life. Sometimes I'm a movie star, twenty-two years old with a palace in the Hollywood hills, and I give parties that Peter Fonda and Dustin Hoffman and Julie Christie and Faye Dunaway come to, and we all turn on and get naked and swim in my pool and afterward I make it with five or six starlets all at once. Sometimes I'm a famous novelist, author of the book that really gets it together and speaks for My Generation, and I stand around in Brentano's in a glittering science-fiction costume signing thousands of autographs, and afterward I go to my penthouse high over First Avenue and make it with a dazzling young lady editor. Sometimes I'm a great scientist, four years out of Harvard Medical School and already acclaimed for my pioneering research in genetic reprogramming of unborn children, and when the phone rings to notify me of my Nobel Prize I'm just about to reach my third climax of the evening with a celebrated Metropolitan Opera soprano who wants me to design a son for her who'll eclipse Caruso. And sometimes—

But why go on? That's all fantasy. Fantasy is dumb because it encourages you to live a self-deluding life, instead of coming to grips with reality. Consider reality, Harry. Consider the genuine article that is Harry Blaufeld. The genuine article is something pimply and ungainly and naive, something that shrieks with every molecule of his skinny body that he's not quite fifteen and has never made it with a girl and doesn't know how to go about it and is terribly afraid that he never will. Mix equal parts of desire and self-pity. And a dash of incompetence and a dollop of insecurity. Season lightly with extrasensory powers. You're a long way from the Hollywood hills, boy.

Is there some way I can harness my gift for the good of mankind? What if all these ghastly power plants, belching black smoke into the atmosphere, could be shut down forever, and humanity's electrical needs were met by a trained corps of youthful poltergeists, volunteers living a monastic life and using their sizzling sexual tensions as the fuel that keeps the turbines spinning? Or perhaps NASA wants a poltergeist-driven spaceship. There I am, lean and bronzed and jaunty, a handsome figure in my white astronaut suit, taking my seat in the command capsule of the *Mars One*. T minus thirty seconds and counting. An anxious world awaits the big moment. Five. Four. Three. Two. One. Lift-off. And I grin my world-famous grin and coolly summon my power and open the mental throttle and push, and the mighty vessel rises, hovering serenely a moment above the launching pad, rises and climbs, slicing like a giant glittering needle through the ice-blue Florida sky, soaring up and away on man's first voyage to the red planet...

Another experiment is called for. I'll try to send a beer can to the moon. If I can do that, I should be able to send a spaceship. A simple Newtonian process, a matter of attaining escape velocity; and I don't think thrust is likely to be a determining quantitative function. A push is a push is a push, and so far I haven't noticed limitations of mass, so if I can get it up with a beer can, I ought to succeed in throwing anything of any mass into space. I think. Anyway, I raid the family garbage and go outside clutching a crumpled Schlitz container. A mild misty night; the moon isn't visible. No matter. I place the can on the ground and contemplate it. Five. Four. Three. Two. One. Lift-off. I grin my world-famous grin. I coolly summon my power and open the mental throttle. *Push.* Yes, the beer can rises. Hovering serenely a moment above the pavement. Rises and climbs, end over end, slicing like a crumpled beer can through the muggy air. Up. Up. Into the darkness. Long after it disappears, I continue to push. Am I still in contact? Does it still climb? I have no way of telling. I lack the proper tracking stations. Perhaps it does travel on and on through the lonely void, on a perfect lunar trajectory. Or maybe it has already tumbled down, a block away, skulling some hapless cop. I shot a beer can into the air, it fell to earth I know not where. Shrugging, I go back into the house. So much for my career as a spaceman. Blaufeld, you've pulled off another dumb fantasy. Blaufeld, how can you stand being such a silly putz?

Clickety-clack. Four in the morning, Sara's just coming in from her date. Here I am lying awake like a worried parent. Notice that the parents themselves don't worry: they're fast asleep, I bet, giving no damns about the hours their daughter keeps. Whereas I brood. She got laid again tonight, no doubt of it. Possibly twice. Grimly I try to reconstruct the event in my imagination. The positions, the sounds of flesh against flesh, the panting and moaning. How often has she done it now? A hundred times? Three hundred? She's been doing it at least since she was sixteen. I'm sure of that. For girls it's so much easier; they don't need to chase and coax, all they have to do is say yes. Sara says yes a lot. Before Jimmy the Greek there was Greasy Kid Stuff, and before him there was the Spade Wonder, and before him…

Out there tonight in this city there are three million people at the very minimum who just got laid. I detest adults and their easy screwing. They devalue it by doing it so much. They just have to roll over and grab some meat, and away they go, in and out, oooh oooh oooh ahhh. Christ, how boring it must get! If they could only look at it from the point of view of a frustrated adolescent again. The hungry virgin, on the outside peering in. Excluded from the world of screwing. Feeling that delicious sweet tension of wanting and not knowing how to get. The fiery knot of longing, sitting like a ravenous tapeworm in my belly, devouring my soul. I magnify sex. I exalt it. I multiply its wonders. It'll never live up to my anticipations. But I love the tension of anticipating and speculating and not getting. In fact, I think sometimes I'd like to spend my whole life on the edge of the blade, looking forward always to being deflowered but never quite taking the steps that would bring it about. A dynamic stasis, sustaining and enhancing my special power. Harry Blaufeld, virgin and poltergeist. Why not? Anybody at all can screw. Idiots, morons, bores, uglies. Everybody does it. There's magic in renunciation. I f I keep myself aloof, pure, unique…

Push…

I do my little poltergeisty numbers. I stack and restack my textbooks without leaving my bed. I move my shirt from the floor to the back of the chair. I turn the chair around to face the wall. Push… push…push…

Water running in the john. Sara's washing up. What's it like, Sara? How does it feel when he puts it in you? We don't talk much, you and I. You think I'm a child; you patronize me, you give me cute winks, your voice goes up half an octave. Do you wink at Jimmy the Greek like that? Like hell. And you talk husky contralto to him. Sit down and talk to me some time, Sis. I'm teetering on the brink of manhood. Guide me out of my virginity. Tell me what girls like guys to say to them. Sure. You won't tell me shit, Sara. You want me to stay your baby brother forever, because that enhances your own sense of being grown up. And you screw and screw and screw, you and Jimmy the Greek, and you don't even understand the mystical significance of the act of intercourse. To you it's just good sweaty fun, like going bowling. Right? Right? Oh, you miserable bitch! Screw you, Sara!

A shriek from the bathroom. Christ, what have I done now? I better go see.

Sara, naked, kneels on the cold tiles. Her head is in the bathtub and she's clinging with both hands to the bathtub's rim and she's shaking violently.

"You okay?" I ask. "What happened?"

"Like a kick in the back," she says hoarsely. "I was at the sink, washing my face, and I turned around and something hit me like a kick in the back and knocked me halfway across the room."

"You okay, though? You aren't hurt?"

"Help me up."

She's upset but not injured. She's so upset that she forgets that she's naked, and without putting on her robe she cuddles up against me, trembling. She seems small and fragile and scared. I stroke her bare back where I imagine she felt the blow. Also I sneak a look at her nipples, just to see if they're still standing up after her date with Jimmy the Greek. They aren't. I soothe her with my fingers. I feel very manly and protective, even if it's only my cruddy dumb sister I'm protecting.

"What could have happened?" she asks. "You weren't pulling any tricks, were you?"

"I was in bed," I say, totally sincere.

"A lot of funny things been going on around this house lately," she says.

Cindy, catching me in the hallway between Geometry and Spanish: "How come you never call me any more?"

"Been busy."

"Busy how?"

"Busy."

"I guess you must be," she says. "Looks to me like you haven't slept in a week. What's her name?"

"Her? No her. I've just been busy." I try to escape. Must I push her again? "A research project."

"You could take some time out for relaxing. You should keep in touch with old friends."

"Friends? What kind of friend are you? You said I was silly. You said I was disgusting. Remember, Cindy?"

"The emotions of the moment. I was off balance. I mean, psychologically. Look, let's talk about all this some time, Harry. Some time soon."

"Maybe."

"If you're not doing anything Saturday night—"

I look at her in astonishment. She's actually asking me for a date! Why is she pursuing me? What does she want from me? Is she itching for another chance to humiliate me? Silly and disgusting, disgusting and silly. I look at my watch and quirk up my lips. Time to move along.

"I'm not sure," I tell her. "I may have some work to do."

"Work?"

"Research," I say. "I'll let you know."

A night of happy experiments. I unscrew a light bulb, float it from one side of my room to the other, return it to the fixture, and efficiently *screw it back in.* Precision control. I go up to the roof and launch another beer can to the moon, only this time I loft it a thousand feet, bring it back, kick it up even higher, bring it back, send it off a third time with a tremendous accumulated kinetic energy, and I have no doubt it'll cleave through space. I pick up trash in the street from a hundred yards away and throw it in the trash basket. Lastly—most scary of all—I polt *myself.* I levitate a little, lifting myself five feet into the air. That's as high as I dare go. (What if I lose the power and fall?) If I had the courage, I could fly. I can do anything. Give me the right fulcrum and I'll move the world. O, *potentia!* What a fantastic trip this is!

After two awful days of inner debate I phone Cindy and make a date for Saturday. I'm not sure whether it's a good idea. Her sudden new aggressiveness turns me off, slightly, but nevertheless it's a novelty to have a girl chasing me, and who am I to snub her? I wonder what she's up to, though. Coming on so interested in me after dumping me mercilessly on our last date. I'm still angry with her about that, but I can't hold a grudge, not with *her.* Maybe she wants to make amends. We did have a pretty decent relationship in the nonphysical sense, until that one stupid evening. Jesus, what if she really *does* want to make amends, all the way? She scares me. I guess I'm a little bit of a coward. Or a lot of a coward. I don't understand any of this, man. I think I'm getting into something very heavy.

I juggle three tennis balls and keep them all in the air at once, with my hands in my pockets. I see a woman trying to park her car in a space that's too small, and as I pass by I give her a sneaky little assist by pushing against the car behind her space; it moves backward a foot and a half, and she has room to park. Friday afternoon, in my gym class, I get into a basketball game and on five separate occasions when Mike Kisiak goes driving in for one of his sure-thing lay-ups I flick the ball away from the hoop. He can't figure out why he's off form and it really kills him. There seem to be no limits to what I can do. I'm awed at it myself. I gain skill from day to day. I might just be an authentic superman.

Cindy and Harry, Harry and Cindy, warm and cozy, sitting on her living-room couch. Christ, I think I'm being seduced! How can this be happening? To me? Christ. Christ. Christ. Cindy and Harry. Harry and Cindy. Where are we heading tonight?

In the movie house Cindy snuggles close. Midway through the flick I take the hint. A big bold move: slipping my arm around her shoulders. She wriggles so that my hand slides down through her armpit and comes to rest grasping her right breast. My cheeks blaze. I do as if to pull back, as if I've touched a hot stove, but she clamps her arm over my forearm. Trapped. I explore her yielding flesh. No padding there, just authentic Cindy. She's so eager and easy that it terrifies me. Afterward we go for sodas. In the shop she turns on the body language something frightening—gleaming eyes, suggestive smiles, little steamy twistings of her shoulders. I feel like telling her not to be so obvious about it. It's like living one of my own wet dreams.

Back to her place, now. It starts to rain. We stand outside, in the very spot where I stood when I polted her the last time. I can write the script effortlessly. "Why don't you come inside for a while, Harry?" "I'd love to." "Here, dry your feet on the doormat. Would you like some hot chocolate?" "Whatever you're having, Cindy." "No, whatever you'd like to have." "Hot chocolate would be fine, then." Her parents aren't home. Her older brother is fornicating in Scarsdale. The rain hammers at the windows. The house is big, expensive-looking, thick carpets, fancy draperies. Cindy in the kitchen, puttering at the stove. Harry in the living room, fidgeting at the bookshelves. Then Cindy and Harry, Harry and Cindy, warm and cozy, together on the couch. Hot chocolate: two sips apiece. Her lips near mine. Silently begging me. Come on, dope, bend forward. Be a *mencsh*. We kiss. We've kissed before, but this time it's with tongues. Christ. Christ. I don't believe this. Suave old Casanova Blaufeld swinging into action like a well-oiled seducing machine. Her perfume in my nostrils, my tongue in her mouth, my hand on her sweater, and then, unexpectedly, my hand is *under* her sweater, and then, astonishingly, my other hand is on her knee, and up under her skirt, and her thigh is satiny and cool, and I sit there having this weird two-dimensional feeling that I'm not an autonomous human being but just somebody on the screen in a movie rated X, aware that thousands of people out there in the audience are watching me with held breath, and I don't dare let them down. I continue, not letting myself pause to examine what's happening, not thinking at all, turning off my mind completely, just going forward step by step. I know that if I ever halt and back off to ask myself if this is real, it'll all blow up in my face. She's helping me. She knows much more about this than I do. Murmuring softly. Encouraging me. My fingers scrabbling at our undergarments. "Don't rush it," she whispers. "We've got all the time in the world." My body pressing urgently against hers. Somehow now I'm not puzzled by the mechanics of the thing. So this is how it happens. What a miracle of evolution that we're designed to fit together this way! "Be gentle," she says, the way girls always say in the novels, and I want to be gentle, but how can I be gentle when I'm riding a runaway chariot? I push, not with my mind but with my body, and suddenly I feel this wondrous velvety softness enfolding me, and I begin to move fast, unable to hold back, and she moves too and we clasp each other and I'm swept helter-skelter along into a whirlpool. Down and down and down. "Harry!" she gasps and I explode uncontrollably and I know it's over. Hardly begun, and it's over. Is that it? That's it. That's all there is to it, the moving, the clasping, the gasping, the explosion. It felt good, but not *that* good, not as good as in my feverish virginal hallucinations I hoped it would be, and a backwash of let-down rips through me at the realization that it isn't transcendental after all, it isn't a mystic thing, it's just a body thing that starts and continues and ends. Abruptly I want to pull away and be alone to think. But I know I mustn't, I have to be tender and grateful now, I hold her in my arms, I whisper soft things to her, I tell her how good it was, she tells me how good it was. We're both lying, but so what? It *was* good. In retrospect it's starting to seem fantastic, overwhelming, all the things I wanted it to be. The *idea* of what we've done blows my mind. If only it hadn't been over so fast. No matter. Next time will be better. We've crossed a frontier; we're in unfamiliar territory now.

Much later she says, "I'd like to know how you make things move without touching them."

I shrug. "Why do you want to know?"

"It fascinates me. *You* fascinate me. I thought for a long time you were just another fellow, you know, kind of clumsy, kind of immature. But then this gift of yours. It's ESP, isn't it, Harry? I've read a lot about it. I know. The moment you knocked me down, I knew what it must have been. Wasn't it?"

Why be coy with her?

"Yes," I say, proud in my new manhood. "As a matter of fact, it's a classic poltergeist manifestation. When I gave you that shove, it was the first I knew I had the power. But I've been developing it. You wouldn't believe some of the things I've been able to do lately." My voice is deep; my manner is assured. I have graduated into my own fantasy self tonight.

"Show me," she says. "Poltergeist something, Harry!"

"Anything. You name it."

"That chair."

"Of course." I survey the chair. I reach for the power. It does not come. The chair stays where it is. What about the saucer, then? No. The spoon? No. "Cindy, I don't understand it, but—it doesn't seem to be working right now..."

"You must be tired."

"Yes. That's it. Tired. A good night's sleep and I'll have it again. I'll phone you in the morning and give you a real demonstration." Hastily buttoning my shirt. Looking for my shoes. Her parents will walk in any minute. Her brother. "Listen, a wonderful evening, unforgettable, tremendous—"

"Stay a little longer."

"I really can't."

Out into the rain.

Home. Stunned. I push...and the shoe sits there. I look up at the light fixture. Nothing. The bulb will not turn. The power is gone. What will become of me now? Commander Blaufeld, space hero! No. No. Nothing. I will drop back into the ordinary rut of mankind. I will be...*a husband.* I will be...*an employee.* And push no more. And push no more. Can I even lift my shirt and flip it to the floor? No. No. Gone. Every shred, gone. I pull the covers over my head. I put my hands to my deflowered maleness. That alone responds. There alone am I still potent. Like all the rest. Just one of the common herd, now. Let's face it: I'll push no more. I'm ordinary again. Fighting off tears, I coil tight against myself in the darkness, and, sweating, moaning a little, working hard, I descend numbly into the quicksand, into the first moments of the long colorless years ahead.

THE WIND AND THE RAIN

The modern-day excitement—bordering on hysteria—over Saving the Planet is actually nothing new. Conservationist movements go back into the nineteenth century. The fervor of the recent converts might lead us to believe that ecological awareness was unknown prior to, say, 1982 or thereabouts; but in fact the very rhetoric used today is old stuff, first espoused by the likes of Theodore Roosevelt and Gifford Pinchot before the grandparents of the modern environmentalists were born.

I will not raise my voice in support of the reduction of ancient redwood trees to toilet tissue and the turning of national parks into freeway interchanges, and I do think that global warming (which was not much of an issue when I wrote the stories included in this book) is a very serious problem indeed. But I have an innate dislike of hysteria, rhetoric, and hysterical rhetoric, and so my sympathy with the current eco-terrorist groups who seem to demand an immediate return to the pre-Homeric pastoral age is rather limited, and I'm speaking euphemistically when I say that. But although I did resign from the Sierra Club many years back in protest against its extremist positions, I do regard myself as preferring natural beauty to urban pollution, and have demonstrated that over the years by supporting organizations that seem to me to strike a reasonable balance between the need to protect our environment and the realities of modern-day high-population-density life.

And so when Roger Elwood and Virginia Kidd announced in 1971 that they were editing an anthology of stories devoted to enhancing our ecological awareness, I was happy to take part. (I probably wouldn't do so today;

the whole subject has become a cliché, and I hate to be part of a herd. And too much science fiction has been written in the past twenty years that is designed to enhance our awareness of this or that special cause; I don't want to add to the supply.)

"The Wind and the Rain," which I wrote in November, 1971 for the Elwood-Kidd book Saving Worlds, is, I suppose, more of a sermon than a story. But it does have characters, of a sort, and a plot, of a sort, and some verbal special effects of a kind that I enjoyed experimenting with in those days.

Its basic theme—that 20th-century mankind made a big mess out of its only planet—is still valid here in the 21st, and should come as no great surprise to any reader, which is why stories of this kind now seem to me to be mere flogging of the obvious. But I call the attention of modern-day eco-worriers to the story's opening sentence, which states a powerful countertheme that should never be forgotten:

The planet cleanses itself.

Indeed so. The world is a big, solid place, and it can look after itself. Our petty depredations will be undone, in time, by the natural actions of the global ecology. People who go around saying that the planet is endangered don't know what they're saying. The planet will survive in fine shape, given enough time for it to undo the mess we have made. We're the ones who are placed in jeopardy by our wastrel ways. Pious moaning about Saving the Planet disguises the main issue and defeats the purpose of the conservationists. The planet doesn't care whether the mean global temperature rises five or six degrees and all low-lying cities are drowned—but we will. The planet doesn't even give a damn whether we become extinct: it won't be the first time that a species has been kiboshed. The rain forests will come back, a couple of million years hence, even if we clear-cut every last sapling next month. Seal-like creatures will re-evolve even if we turn the whole present population of them into fur coats. The thing for us to remember is that if we don't mend our ways we will make the world uninhabitable for ourselves. If the Save-the-Planet folks would only stop talking about saving the planet and focus on saving Us, its current dominant inhabitants, we might stand a much better chance of still being the dominant inhabitants fifty thousand years from now.

The planet cleanses itself. That is the important thing to remember, at moments when we become too pleased with ourselves. The healing process is a natural and inevitable one. The action of the wind and the rain, the ebbing and flowing of the tides, the vigorous rivers flushing out the choked and stinking lakes—these are all natural rhythms, all healthy manifestations of universal harmony. Of course, we are here too. We do our best to hurry the process along. But we are only auxiliaries, and we know it. We must not exaggerate the value of our work. False pride is worse than a sin: it is a foolishness. We do not deceive ourselves into thinking we are important. If we were not here at all, the planet would repair itself anyway within twenty to fifty million years. It is estimated that our presence cuts that time down by somewhat more than half.

The uncontrolled release of methane into the atmosphere was one of the most serious problems. Methane is a colorless, odorless gas, sometimes known as "swamp gas". Its components are carbon and hydrogen. Much of the atmosphere of Jupiter and Saturn consists of methane. (Jupiter and Saturn have never been habitable by human beings.) A small amount of methane was always normally present in the atmosphere of Earth. However, the growth of human population produced a consequent increase in the supply of methane. Much of the methane released into the atmosphere came from swamps and coal mines. A great deal of it came from Asian rice fields fertilized with human or animal waste; methane is a byproduct of the digestive process.

The surplus methane escaped into the lower stratosphere, from ten to thirty miles above the surface of the planet, where a layer of ozone molecules once existed. Ozone, formed of three oxygen atoms, absorbs the harmful ultraviolet radiation that the sun emits. By reacting with free oxygen atoms in the stratosphere, the intrusive methane reduced the quantity available for ozone formation. Moreover, methane reactions in the stratosphere yielded water vapor that further depleted the ozone. This methane-induced exhaustion of the ozone content of the stratosphere permitted the unchecked ultraviolet bombardment of the Earth, with a consequent rise in the incidence of skin cancer.

A major contributor to the methane increase was the flatulence of domesticated cattle. According to the US Department of Agriculture, domesticated ruminants in the late twentieth century were generating more than eighty-five million tons of methane a year. Yet nothing was done to check the activities of these dangerous creatures. Are you amused by the idea of a world destroyed by herds of farting cows? It must not have been amusing to the people of the late twentieth century. However, the extinction of domesticated ruminants shortly helped to reduce the impact of this process.

Today we must inject colored fluids into a major river. Edith, Bruce, Paul, Elaine, Oliver, Ronald, and I have been assigned to this task. Most members of the team believe the river is the Mississippi, although there is some evidence that it may be the Nile. Oliver, Bruce, and Edith believe it is more likely to be the Nile than the Mississippi, but they defer to the opinion of the majority. The river is wide and deep and its color is black in some places and dark green in others. The fluids are computer-mixed on the east bank of the river in a large factory erected by a previous reclamation team. We supervise their passage into the river. First we inject the red fluid, then the blue, then the yellow; they have different densities and form parallel stripes running for many hundreds of kilometers in the water. We are not certain whether these fluids are active healing agents—that is, substances which dissolve the solid pollutants lining the riverbed—or merely serve as markers permitting further chemical analysis of the river by the orbiting satellite system. It is not necessary for us to understand what we are doing, so long as we follow instructions explicitly. Elaine jokes about going swimming. Bruce says, "How absurd. This river is famous for deadly fish that will strip the flesh from your bones." We all laugh at that. Fish? Here? What fish could be as deadly as the river itself? This water would consume our flesh if we entered it, and probably dissolve our bones as well. I scribbled a poem yesterday and dropped it in, and the paper vanished instantly.

In the evenings we walk along the beach and have philosophical discussions. The sunsets on this coast are embellished by rich tones of

purple, green, crimson, and yellow. Sometimes we cheer when a particularly beautiful combination of atmospheric gases transforms the sunlight. Our mood is always optimistic and gay. We are never depressed by the things we find on this planet. Even devastation can be an art form, can it not? Perhaps it is one of the greatest of all art forms, since an art of destruction consumes its medium, it devours its own epistemological foundations, and in this sublimely nullifying doubling-back upon its origins it far exceeds in moral complexity those forms which are merely productive. That is, I place a higher value on transformative art than on generative art. Is my meaning clear? In any event, since art ennobles and exalts the spirits of those who perceive it, we are exalted and ennobled by the conditions on Earth. We envy those who collaborate to create those extraordinary conditions. We know ourselves to be small-souled folk of a minor latter-day epoch; we lack the dynamic grandeur of energy that enabled our ancestors to commit such depredations. This world is a symphony. Naturally you might argue that to restore a planet takes more energy than to destroy it, but you would be wrong. Nevertheless, though our daily tasks leave us weary and drained, we also feel stimulated and excited, because by restoring this world, the mother-world of mankind, we are in a sense participating in the original splendid process of its destruction. I mean in the sense that the resolution of a dissonant chord participates in the dissonance of that chord.

Now we have come to Tokyo, the capital of the island empire of Japan. See how small the skeletons of the citizens are? That is one way we have of identifying this place as Japan. The Japanese are known to have been people of small stature. Edward's ancestors were Japanese. He is of small stature. (Edith says his skin should be yellow as well. His skin is just like ours. Why is his skin not yellow?) "See?" Edward cries. "There is Mount Fuji!" It is an extraordinarily beautiful mountain, mantled in white snow. On its slopes one of our archaeological teams is at work, tunneling under the snow to collect samples from the twentieth century strata of chemical residues, dust, and ashes. "Once there were over 75,000 industrial smokestacks around Tokyo," says Edward proudly, "from which were released hundreds of tons of sulfur, nitrous oxides, ammonia, and carbon gases every day. We should not forget that this city had more than 1,500,000 automobiles as well." Many of the automobiles are still visible, but they are very fragile, worn to threads by the action of the atmosphere. When we touch them they collapse in puffs of grey smoke. Edward, who has studied his heritage well, tells us, "It was not uncommon for the density of carbon monoxide in the air here to exceed the permissible levels by factors of 250 per cent on mild summer days. Owing to atmospheric conditions, Mount Fuji was visible only one day of every nine. Yet no one showed dismay." He conjures up for us a picture of his small, industrious yellow ancestors toiling cheerfully and unremittingly in their poisonous environment. The Japanese, he insists, were able to maintain and even increase their gross national product at a time when other nationalities had already begun to lose ground in the global economic struggle because of diminished population owing to unfavorable ecological factors. And so on and so on. After a time we grow bored with Edward's incessant boasting. "Stop boasting," Oliver tells him, "or we will expose you to the atmosphere." We have much dreary work to do here. Paul and I guide the huge trenching machines; Oliver and Ronald follow, planting seeds. Almost immediately, strange angular shrubs spring up. They have shiny bluish leaves and long crooked branches. One of them seized Elaine by the throat yesterday and might have hurt her seriously had Bruce not uprooted it. We were not upset. This is merely one phase in the long, slow process of repair. There will be many such incidents. Some day cherry trees will blossom in this place.

This is the poem that the river ate:

Destruction

I. Nouns. Destruction, desolation, wreck, wreckage, ruin, ruination, rack and ruin, smash, smashup, demolition, demolishment, ravagement, havoc, ravage, dilapidation, decimation, blight, breakdown, consumption, dissolution, obliteration, overthrow, spoilage; mutilation, disintegration, undoing, pulverization; sabotage, vandalism; annulment, damnation, extinguishment, extinction; invalidation, nullification, shatterment, shipwreck; annihilation, disannulment, discreation, extermination, extirpation, obliteration, perdition, subversion.

II. Verbs. Destroy, wreck, ruin, ruinate, smash, demolish, raze, ravage, gut, dilapidate, decimate, blast, blight, break down, consume, dissolve, overthrow; mutilate, disintegrate, unmake, pulverize; sabotage, vandalize, annul, blast, blight, damn, dash, extinguish, invalidate, nullify, quell, quench, scuttle, shatter, shipwreck, torpedo, smash, spoil, undo, void; annihilate, devour, disannul, discreate, exterminate, obliterate, extirpate, subvert; corrode, erode, sap, undermine, waste, waste away, whittle away (or down); eat away, canker, gnaw; wear away, abrade, batter, excoriate, rust.

III. Adjectives. Destructive, ruinous, vandalistic, baneful, cutthroat, fell, lethiferous, pernicious, slaughterous, predatory, sinistrous, nihilistic; corrosive, erosive, cankerous, caustic, abrasive.

"I validate," says Ethel.

"I unravage," says Oliver.

"I integrate," says Paul.

"I devandalize," says Elaine.

"I unshatter," says Bruce.

""I unscuttle," says Edward.

"I discorrode," says Ronald.

"I undesolate," says Edith.

"I create," say I.

We reconstitute. We renew. We repair. We reclaim. We refurbish. We restore. We renovate. We rebuild. We reproduce. We redeem. We reintegrate. We replace. We reconstruct. We retrieve. We revivify. We resurrect. We fix, overhaul, mend, put in repair, retouch, tinker, cobble, patch, darn, staunch, caulk, splice. We celebrate our successes by energetic and lusty singing. Some of us copulate.

Here is an outstanding example of the dark humour of the ancients. At a place called Richland, Washington, there was an installation that manufactured plutonium for use in nuclear weapons. This was done in the name of "national security", that is, to enhance and strengthen the safety of the United States of America and render its inhabitants carefree and hopeful. In a relatively short span of time these activities produced approximately fifty-five million gallons of concentrated radioactive waste. This material was so intensely hot that it would boil spontaneously for decades, and would retain a virulently toxic character for many thousands of years. The presence of so much dangerous waste posed a severe environmental threat to a large area of the United States. How, then, to dispose of this waste? An appropriately comic solution was devised. The plutonium installation was situated in a seismically unstable area located along the earthquake belt that rings the Pacific Ocean. A storage site was chosen nearby, directly above a fault line that had produced a violent earthquake half a century earlier. Here 140 steel and concrete tanks were constructed just below the surface of the ground and some 240 feet above the water table of the Columbia River, from which a densely populated region derived its water supply. Into these tanks the boiling radioactive wastes were poured: a magnificent gift to future generations. Within a few years the true subtlety of the jest became apparent when the first small leaks were detected in the tanks. Some observers predicted that no more than ten to twenty years would pass before the great heat caused the seams of the tanks to burst, releasing radioactive gases into the atmosphere or permitting radioactive fluids to escape into the river. The designers of the tanks maintained, though, that they were sturdy enough to last at least a century. It will be noted that this was something less than one percent of the known half-life of the materials placed in the tanks. Because of discontinuities in the records, we are unable to determine which estimate was more nearly correct. It should be possible for our decontamination squads to enter the affected regions in 800 to 1300 years. This episode arouses tremendous admiration in me. How much gusto, how much robust wit, those old ones must have had!

We are granted a holiday so we may go to the mountains of Uruguay to visit the site of one of the last human settlements, perhaps the very last. It was discovered by a reclamation team several hundred years ago and has been set aside, in its original state, as a museum for the tourists who one day will wish to view the mother-world. One enters through a lengthy tunnel of glossy pink brick. A series of airlocks prevents the outside air from penetrating. The village itself, nestling between two craggy spires, is shielded by a clear shining dome. Automatic controls maintain its temperature at a constant mild level. There were a thousand inhabitants. We can view them in the spacious plazas, in the taverns, and in places of recreation. Family groups remain together, often with their pets. A few carry umbrellas. Everyone is in an unusually fine state of preservation. Many of them are smiling. It is not yet known why these people perished. Some died in the act of speaking, and scholars have devoted much effort, so far without success, to the task of determining and translating the last words still frozen on their lips. We are not allowed to touch anyone, but we may enter their homes and inspect their possessions and toilet furnishings. I am moved almost to tears, as are several of the others. "Perhaps these are our very ancestors," Ronald exclaims. But Bruce declares scornfully, "You say ridiculous things. Our ancestors must have escaped from here long before the time these people lived." Just outside the settlement I find a tiny glistening bone, possibly the shinbone of a child, possibly part of a dog's tail. "May I keep it?" I ask our leader. But he compels me to donate it to the museum.

The archives yield much that is fascinating. For example, this fine example of ironic distance in ecological management. In the ocean off a place named California were tremendous forests of a giant seaweed called kelp, housing a vast and intricate community of maritime creatures. Sea urchins lived on the ocean floor, 100 feet down, amid the holdfasts that anchored the kelp. Furry aquatic mammals known as sea otters fed on the urchins. The Earth people removed the otters because they had some use for their fur. Later, the kelp began to die. Forests many square miles in diameter vanished. This had serious commercial consequences, for the kelp was valuable and so were many of the animal forms that lived in it. Investigation of the ocean floor showed a great increase in sea urchins. Not only had their natural enemies, the otters, been removed, but the urchins were taking nourishment from the immense quantities of organic matter in the sewage discharges dumped into the ocean by the Earth people. Millions of urchins were nibbling at the holdfasts of the kelp, uprooting the huge plants and killing them. When an oil tanker accidentally released its cargo into the sea, many urchins were killed and the kelp began to reestablish itself. But this proved to be an impractical means of controlling the urchins. Encouraging the otters to return was suggested, but there was not a sufficient supply of living otters. The kelp foresters of California solved their problem by dumping quicklime into the sea from barges. This was fatal to the urchins; once they were dead, healthy kelp plants were brought from other parts of the sea and embedded to become the nucleus of a new forest. After a while the urchins returned and began to eat the kelp again. More quicklime was dumped. The urchins died and new kelp was planted. Later, it was discovered that the quicklime was having harmful effects on the ocean floor itself, and other chemicals were dumped to counteract those effects. All of this required great ingenuity and a considerable outlay of energy and resources. Edward thinks there was something very Japanese about these maneuvers. Ethel points out that the kelp trouble would never have happened if the Earth people had not originally removed the otters. How naive Ethel is! She has no understanding of the principles of irony. Poetry bewilders her also. Edward refuses to sleep with Ethel now.

In the final centuries of their era the people of Earth succeeded in paving the surface of their planet almost entirely with a skin of concrete and metal. We must pry much of this up so that the planet may start to breathe again. It would be easy and efficient to use explosives or acids, but we are not overly concerned with ease and efficiency; besides, there is great concern that explosives or acids may do further ecological harm here. Therefore we employ large machines that inset prongs in the great cracks that have developed in the concrete. Once we have lifted the paved slabs they usually crumble quickly. Clouds of concrete dust blow freely through the streets of these cities, covering the stumps of the buildings with a fine, pure coating of grayish-white powder. The effect is delicate and refreshing. Paul suggested yesterday that we may be doing ecological harm by setting free this dust. I became frightened at the idea and reported him to the leader of our team. Paul will be transferred to another group.

Toward the end here they all wore breathing suits, similar to ours but even more comprehensive. We find these suits lying around everywhere like the discarded shells of giant insects. The most advanced models were complete individual housing units. Apparently it was not necessary to leave one's suit except to perform such vital functions as sexual intercourse and childbirth. We understand that the reluctance of the Earth people to leave their suits even for those functions, near the close, immensely hastened the decrease in population.

Our philosophical discussions. God created this planet. We all agree on that, in a manner of speaking, ignoring for the moment definitions of such concepts as "God" and "created". Why did He go to so much trouble to bring Earth into being, if it was His intention merely to have it rendered uninhabitable? Did He create mankind especially for this purpose, or did they exercise free will in doing what they did here? Was mankind God's way of taking vengeance against His own creation? Why would He want to take vengeance against His own creation? Perhaps it is a mistake to approach the destruction of Earth from the moral or ethical standpoint. I think we must see it in purely aesthetic terms, i.e., a self-contained artistic achievement, like a *fouetté en tournant* or an *entrechat-dix,* performed for its own sake and requiring no explanations. Only in this way can we understand how the Earth people were able to collaborate so joyfully in their own asphyxiation.

My tour of duty is almost over. It has been an overwhelming experience; I will never be the same. I must express my gratitude for this opportunity to have seen Earth almost as its people knew it. Its rusted streams, its corroded meadows, its purpled skies, its bluish puddles. The debris, the barren hillsides, the blazing rivers. Soon, thanks to the dedicated work of reclamation teams such as ours, these superficial but beautiful emblems of death will have disappeared. This will be just another world for tourists, of sentimental curiosity but no unique value to the sensibility. How dull that will be: a green and pleasant Earth once more, why, why? The universe has enough habitable planets; at present it has only one Earth. Has all our labor here been an error, then? I sometimes do think it was misguided of us to have undertaken this project. But on the other hand I remind myself of our fundamental irrelevance. The healing process is a natural and inevitable one. With us or without us, the planet cleanses itself. The wind, the rain, the tides. We merely help things along.

A rumor reaches us that a colony of live Earthmen has been found on the Tibetan plateau. We travel there to see if this is true. Hovering above a vast red empty plain, we see large figures moving slowly about. Are these Earthmen, inside breathing suits of a strange design? We descend. Members of other reclamation teams are already on hand. They have surrounded one of the large creatures. It travels in a wobbly circle, uttering indistinct cries and grunts. Then it comes to a halt, confronting us blankly as if defying us to embrace it. We tip it over; it moves its massive limbs dumbly but is unable to arise. After a brief conference we decide to dissect it. The outer plates lift easily. Inside we find nothing but gears and coils of gleaming wire. The limbs no longer move, although things click and hum within it for quite some time. We are favorably impressed by the durability and resilience of these machines. Perhaps in the distant future such entities will wholly replace the softer and more fragile life forms on all worlds, as they seem to have done on Earth.

The wind. The rain. The tides. All sadnesses flow to the sea.

SOME NOTES ON THE PRE-DYNASTIC EPOCH

There were so many anthologies of previously unpublished science fiction stories in the early 1970s that themes kept overlapping: two anthologies of erotic science fiction, two or three books of environmental-crisis stories, etc., etc. "Some Notes on the Pre-Dynastic Epoch" was written in December, 1971, right after "The Wind and the Rain," for one of the several minatory save-our-disintegrating-society-through-science-fiction books, Thomas M. Disch's Bad Moon Rising. *I am, as you probably know by now, skeptical of the possibility of saving a disintegrating society through science fiction, but American society really did seem to be disintegrating then, just as it seems to be today, and despite my skepticism about the worth of the enterprise I wrote the story anyway. (It's important to note that even though things looked really terrible in 1971, somehow we managed to survive and get from there to here anyway, and perhaps it'll be possible to say the same thing thirty years from today.)*

In "Some Notes on the Pre-Dynastic Epoch" I made use of the fragmentary non-narrative mode that I was fond of employing around that time, and which seemed particularly appropriate for a story dealing with the ruins of a vanished civilization. My interest in archaeology and my readings in incomplete archaic texts suggested the use of poems with built-in lacunae. Of the three in the story, one is Babylonian in origin, one is a fragmentized version of a well-known Bob Dylan song, and one is an original Silverberg. No prizes will be given for correct guesses about which is which.

We understand some of their languages, but none of them completely. That is one of the great difficulties. What has come down from their epoch to ours is spotted and stained and eroded by time, full of lacunae and static; and so we can only approximately comprehend the nature of their civilization and the reasons for its collapse. Too often, I fear, we project our own values and assumptions back upon them and deceive ourselves into thinking we are making valid historic judgments.

On the other hand there are certain aesthetic rewards in the very incompleteness of the record. Their poetry, for example, is heightened and made more mysterious, more strangely appealing, by the tantalizing gaps that result from our faulty linguistic knowledge and from the uncertainties we experience in transliterating their fragmentary written texts, as well as in transcribing their surviving spoken archives. It is as though time itself has turned poet, collaborating belatedly with the ancients to produce something new and fascinating by punching its own inexorable imprint into their work. Consider the resonances and implications of this deformed and defective song, perhaps a chant of a ritual nature, dating from the late pre-dynastic:

Once upon a time you........so fine,
You threw the (?) a (? small unit of currency?) in your prime,
Didn't you?
People'd call, say "Beware........to fall,"
You........kidding you.
You........laugh........
Everybody........
Now you don't........so loud,
Now you don't........so proud
About........for your next meal.
How does it feel, how does it feel
To be........home........unknown
...........a rolling stone?

Or examine this, which is an earlier pre-dynastic piece, possibly of Babylonian-American origin:

In my wearied........, me......
In my inflamed nostril, me......

Punishment, sickness, trouble......me
A flail which wickedly afflicts,......me
A lacerating rod......me
A......hand......me
A terrifying message......me
A stinging whip........me
....
...........in pain I *faint* (?)

The Center for Pre-Dynastic Studies is a comfortingly massive building fashioned from blocks of some greasy green synthetic stone and laid out in three spokelike wings radiating from a common center. It is situated in the midst of the central continental plateau, near what may have been the site of the ancient metropolis of Omahaha. On clear days we take to the air in small solar-powered flying machines and survey the outlines of the city, which are still visible as indistinct white scars on the green breast of the earth. There are more than two thousand staff members. Many of them are women and some are sexually available, even to me. I have been employed here for eleven years. My current title is Metalinguistic Archaeologist, Third Grade. My father before me held that title for much of his life. He died in a professional quarrel while I was a child, and my mother dedicated me to filling his place. I have a small office with several data terminals, a neatly beveled viewing screen, and a modest desk. Upon my desk I keep a collection of artifacts of the so-called twentieth century. These serve as talismans, spurring me on to greater depth of insight. They include:

One grey communications device ("telephone").

One black inscribing device ("typewriter"?) which has been exposed to high temperatures and is somewhat melted.

One metal key, incised with the numerals 1714 and fastened by a rusted metal ring to a small white plastic plaque that declares, in red letters, IF CARRIED AWAY INADVERTENTLY///DROP IN ANY MAIL BOX///SHERATON BOSTON HOTEL///BOSTON, MASS. 02199.

One coin of uncertain denomination.

It is understood that these items are the property of the Center for Pre-Dynastic Studies and are merely on loan to me. Considering their great age and the harsh conditions to which they must have been exposed after the collapse of twentieth-century civilization, they are in remarkably fine condition. I am proud to be their custodian.

I am thirty-one years of age, slender, blue-eyed, austere in personal habits, and unmarried. My knowledge of the languages and customs of the so-called twentieth century is considerable, although I strive constantly to increase it. My work both saddens and exhilarates me. I see it as a species of poetry, if poetry may be understood to be the imaginative verbal reconstruction of experience; in my case the experiences I reconstruct are not my own, are in fact alien and repugnant to me, but what does that matter? Each night when I go home my feet are moist and chilled, as though I have been wading in swamps all day. Last summer the Dynast visited the Center on Imperial Unity Day, examined our latest findings with care and an apparently sincere show of interest, and said, "'We must draw from these researches a profound lesson for our times.'"

None of the foregoing is true. I take pleasure in deceiving. I am an extremely unreliable witness.

The heart of the problem, as we have come to understand it, is a pervasive generalized dislocation of awareness. Nightmares break into the fabric of daily life, and we no longer notice, or, if we do notice, we fail to make appropriate response. Nothing seems excessive any longer, nothing perturbs our dulled, numbed minds. Predatory giant insects, the products of pointless experiments in mutation, escape from laboratories and devastate the countryside. Rivers are contaminated by lethal micro-organisms released accidentally or deliberately by civil servants. Parts of human foetuses obtained from abortions are kept alive in hospital research units; human fetal toes and fingers grow up to four times as fast under controlled conditions as they do *in utero,* starting from single rods of cartilage and becoming fully jointed digits in seven to ten days. These are used in the study of the causes of arthritis. Zoos are vandalized by children, who stone geese and ducks to death and shoot lions in their cages. Sulfuric acid, the result of a combination of rain, mist, and sea spray with sulfurous industrial effluents, devours the statuary of Venice at a rate of five percent a year. The nose is the first part to go when this process, locally termed "marble cancer", strikes. Just off the shores of Manhattan Island, a thick, stinking mass of floating sludge transforms a twenty-square-mile region of the ocean into a dead sea, a sterile soup of dark, poisonous wastes; this pocket of coagulated pollutants has been formed over a forty-year period by the licensed dumping each year of millions of cubic yards of treated sewage, towed by barge to the site, and by the unrestrained discharge of 365 million gallons per day of raw sewage from the Hudson River.

All these events are widely deplored but the causative factors are permitted to remain uncorrected, which means a constant widening of their operative zone. (There are no static negative phases; the laws of expansive deterioration decree that bad inevitably becomes worse.) Why is nothing done on any functional level? Because no one believes anything can be done. Such a belief in collective impotence is, structurally speaking, identical in effect to actual impotence; one does not need to be helpless, merely to think that one is helpless, in order to reach a condition of surrender to accelerating degenerative conditions. Under such circumstances a withdrawal of attention is the only satisfactory therapy. Along with this emptying of reactive impulse comes a corresponding semantic inflation and devaluation which further speeds the process of general dehumanization. Thus the roving gangs of adolescents who commit random crimes in the streets of New York City say they have "blown away" a victim whom they have in fact murdered, and the President of the United States, announcing an adjustment in the par value of his country's currency made necessary by the surreptitious economic mismanagement of the previous administration, describes it as "the most significant monetary agreement in the history of the world."

Some of the topics urgently requiring detailed analysis:

1. Their poetry
2. Preferred positions of sexual intercourse
3. The street plans of their major cities
4. Religious beliefs and practices
5. Terms of endearment, heterosexual and homosexual
6. Ecological destruction, accidental and deliberate
7. Sports and rituals

8. Attitudes toward technological progress
9. Forms of government, political processes
10. Their visual art forms
11. Means of transportation
12. Their collapse and social decay
13. Their terrible last days

One of our amusements here—no, let me be frank, it's more than an amusement, it's a professional necessity—is periodically to enter the vanished pre-dynastic world through the gate of dreams. A drug that leaves a sour, salty taste on the tongue facilitates these journeys. Also we make use of talismans: I clutch my key in my left hand and carry my coin in my right-hand pocket. We never travel alone, but usually go in teams of two or three. A special section of the Center is set aside for those who make these dream-journeys. The rooms are small and brightly lit, with soft rubbery pink walls, rather womblike in appearance, tuned to a bland heat and an intimate humidity. Alexandra, Jerome, and I enter such a room. We remove our clothing to perform the customary ablutions. Alexandra is plump, but her breasts are small and far apart. Jerome's body is hairy, and his muscles lie in thick slabs over his bones. I see them both looking at me. We wash and dress; Jerome produces three hexagonal grey tablets and we swallow them. Sour, salty. We lie side by side on the triple couch in the centre center of the room. I clutch my key, I touch my coin. Backward, backward, backward we drift. Alexandra's soft forearm presses gently against my thin shoulder. Into the dark, into the old times. The pre-dynastic epoch swallows us. This is the kingdom of earth, distorted, broken, twisted, maimed, perjured. The kingdom of hell. A snowbound kingdom. Bright lights on the grease-speckled airstrip. A rusting vehicle jutting from the sand. The eyes and lips of madmen. My feet are sixteen inches above the surface of the ground. Mists curl upward, licking at my soles. I stand before a bleak hotel, and women carrying glossy leather bags pass in and out. Toward us come automobiles, berserk, driverless, with blazing headlights. A blurred column of song rises out of the darkness. Home...........unknown...........a rolling stone? These ruins are inhabited.

LIFE-SYNTHESIS PIONEER URGES
POLICING OF RESEARCH
Buffalo Doctor Says New Organisms Could Be Peril

USE OF PRIVATE PATROLMEN
ON CITY STREETS INCREASING

MACROBIOTIC COOKING—LEARNING THE
SECRETS OF YANG AND YIN

PATMAN WARNS U.S. MAY CHECK
GAMBLING "DISEASE" IN THE STATES

SOME AREAS SEEK TO HALT GROWTH

NIXON DEPICTS HIS WIFE
AS STRONG AND SENSITIVE

PSYCHIATRIST IN BELFAST FINDS CHILDREN
ARE DEEPLY DISTURBED BY THE VIOLENCE

GROWING USE OF MIND-AFFECTING
DRUGS STIRS CONCERN

Saigon, Sept. 5—United States Army psychologists said today they are working on a plan to brainwash enemy troops with bars of soap that reveal a new propaganda message practically every time the guerrillas lather up. As the soap is used, gradual wear reveals eight messages embedded in layers.

"The Beatles, and their mimicking rock-and-rollers, use the Pavlovian techniques to produce artificial neuroses in our young people," declared Rep. James B. Utt R-Calif). "Extensive experiments in hypnosis and rhythm have shown how rock and roll music leads to a destruction of the normal inhibitory mechanism of the cerebral cortex and permits easy acceptance of immorality and disregard of all moral norms."

Taylor said the time has come for police "to study and apply so far as possible all the factors that will in any way promote better understanding and a better relationship between citizens and the law enforcement officer, even if it means attempting to enter into the learning and cultural realms of unborn children."

Secretary of Defense Melvin R. Laird formally dedicated a small room in the Pentagon today as a quiet place for meditation and prayer. "In a sense, this ceremony marks the completion of the Pentagon, for until now this building lacked a place where man's inner spirit could find quiet expression," Mr. Laird said.

The meditation room, he said, "is an affirmation that, though we cling to the principle that church and state should be separate, we do not propose to separate man from God."

Moscow, June 19—Oil industry expert says Moses and Joshua were among earth's original polluters, criticizes regulations inhibiting inventiveness and progress.

Much of the interior of the continent lies submerged in a deep sea of radioactive water. The region was deliberately flooded under the policy of "compensating catastrophe" promulgated by the government toward the close of the period of terminal convulsions. Hence, though we come in dreams, we do not dare enter this zone unprotected, and we make use of aquatic robots bearing brain-coupled remote-vision cameras. Without interrupting our slumber we don the equipment, giggling self-consciously as we help one another with the harnesses and snaps. The robots stride into the green, glistening depths, leaving trails of shimmering fiery bubbles. We turn and tilt our heads and our cameras obey, projecting what they see directly upon our retinas. This is a magical realm. Everything sleeps here in a single grave, yet everything throbs and bursts with terrible life. Small boys, glowing, play marbles in the street. Thieves glide on mincing feet past beefy, stolid shopkeepers. A syphilitic whore displays her thighs to potential purchasers.

A giant blue screen mounted on the haunch of a colossal glossy-skinned building shows us the face of the President, jowly, earnest, energetic. His eyes are extraordinarily narrow, almost slits. He speaks but his words are vague and formless, without perceptible syllabic intervals. We are unaware of the pressure of the water. Scraps of paper flutter past us as though driven by the wind. Little girls dance in a ring: their skinny bare legs flash like pistons. Alexandra's robot briefly touches its coppery hand to mine, a gesture of delight, of love. We take turns entering an automobile, sitting at its wheel, depressing its pedals and levers. I am filled with an intense sense of the reality of the pre-dynastic, of its oppressive imminence, of the danger of its return. Who says the past is dead and sealed? Everything comes around at least twice, perhaps even more often, and the later passes are always more grotesque, more deadly, and more comical. Destruction is eternal. Grief is cyclical. Death is undying. We walk the drowned face of the murdered earth and we are tormented by the awareness that past and future lie joined like a lunatic serpent. The sorrows of the pharaohs will be our sorrows. Listen to the voice of Egypt.

The high-born are full of lamentation but the poor are jubilant. Every town sayeth, "Let us drive out the powerful"...The splendid judgment-hall has been stripped of its documents...The public offices lie open and their records have been stolen. Serfs have become the masters of serfs...Behold, they that had clothes are now in rags...He who had nothing is now rich and the high official must court the parvenu...Squalor is throughout the land: no clothes are white these days...The Nile is in flood yet no one has the heart to plough...Corn has perished everywhere...Everyone says, "There is no more"...The dead are thrown into the river...Laughter has perished. Grief walks the land. A man of character goes in mourning because of what has happened in the land...Foreigners have become people everywhere. There is no man of yesterday.

Alexandra, Jerome, and I waltz in the pre-dynastic streets. We sing the Hymn to the Dynast. We embrace. Jerome couples with Alexandra. We take books, phonograph records, kitchen appliances, and postage stamps, and we leave without paying, for we have no money of this epoch. No one protests. We stare at the clumsy bulk of an aeroplane soaring over the tops of the buildings. We cup our hands and drink at a public fountain. Naked, I show myself to the veiled green sun. I couple with Jerome. We peer into the pinched, dead faces of the pre-dynastic people we meet outside the grand hotel. We whisper to them in gentle voices, trying to warn them of their danger. Some sand blows across the pavement. Alexandra tenderly kisses an old man's withered cheek and he flees her warmth. Jewelery finer than any our museums own glitters in every window. The great wealth of this epoch is awesome to us. Where did these people go astray? How did they lose the path? What is the source of their pain? Tell us, we beg. Explain yourselves to us. We are historians from a happier time. We seek to know you. What can you reveal to us concerning your poetry, your preferred positions of sexual intercourse, the street plans of your major cities, your religious beliefs and practices, your terms of endearment, heterosexual and homosexual, your ecological destruction, accidental and deliberate, your sports and rituals, your attitudes toward technical progress, your forms of government, your political processes, your visual art forms, your means of transportation, your collapse and social decay, your terrible last days? For your last days will be terrible. There is no avoiding that now. The course is fixed; the end is inevitable. The time of the Dynast must come.

I see myself tied into the totality of epochs. I am inextricably linked to the pharaohs, to Assurnasirpal, to Tiglath-Pileser, to the beggars in Calcutta, to Yuri Gagarin and Neil Armstrong, to Caesar, to Adam, to the dwarfed and pallid scrabblers on the bleak shores of the enfamined future. All time converges on this point of now. My soul's core is the universal focus. There is no escape. The swollen reddened moon perpetually climbs the sky. The moment of the Dynast is eternally at hand. All of time and space becomes a cage for now. We are condemned to our own company until death do us part, and perhaps even afterward. Where did we go astray? How did we lose the path? Why can't we escape? Ah. Yes. There's the catch. There is no escape.

They drank wine, and praised the gods of gold, and of silver, of brass, of iron, of wood, and of stone.

In the same hour came forth fingers of a man's hand, and wrote over against the candlestick upon the plaister of the wall of the king's palace: and the king saw the part of the hand that wrote.

Then the king's countenance was changed, and his thoughts troubled him, so that the joints of his loins were loosed, and his knees smote one against another.

And this is the writing that was written, MENE, MENE, TEKEL, UPHARSIN.

This is the interpretation of the thing: MENE; God hath numbered thy kingdom, and finished it.

TEKEL; Thou art weighed in the balances, and art found wanting.

PERES; Thy kingdom is divided, and given to the Medes and Persians.

In that night was Belshazzar the king of the Chaldeans slain.

And Darius the Median took the kingdom, being about threescore and two years old.

We wake. We say nothing to one another as we leave the room of dreams; we avert our eyes from each other's gaze. We return to our separate offices. I spend the remainder of the afternoon analyzing shards of pre-dynastic poetry. The words are muddled and will not cohere. My eyes fill with tears. Why have I become so involved in the fate of these sad and foolish people?

Let me unmask myself. Let me confess everything. There is no Center for Pre-Dynastic Studies. I am no Metalinguistic Archaeologist, Third Grade, living in a remote and idyllic era far in your future and passing my days in pondering the wreckage of the twentieth century. The time of the Dynast may be coming, but he does not yet rule. I am your contemporary. I am your brother. These notes are the work of a pre-dynastic man like yourself, a native of the so-called twentieth century, who, like you, has lived through dark hours and may live to see darker ones. That much is true. All the rest is fantasy of my own invention. Do you believe that? Do I seem reliable now? Can you trust me, just this once?

All time converges on this point of now.

✹

My……hurts me sorely.
The……of my……is decaying.
This is the path that the bison took.
This is the path that the moa took.
This is the……of the dying (beasts?)
Let us not……that dry path.
Let us not……that bony path.
Let us……another path……
O my brother, sharer of my mother's (womb?)
O my sister, whose……I…………
Listen……close……the wall……
Now the cold winds come.
Now the heavy snows fall.
Now……………………
…………the suffering…………
…………the solitude…………
……blood…………sleep……blood…………
……………………blood…………
……………………
…………the river, the sea…………
……me…………

THE FEAST OF ST. DIONYSUS

We were still in the very weird year of 1971 when I began this novella, a year when we all wore our hair in strange ways, dressed in odd-colored clothing, and experimented with varying degrees of boldness with conscious-altering chemical substances. And I was in the process of leaving my identity as a New Yorker behind and reinventing myself as a Californian, which meant that by the time I had finished "The Feast of St. Dionysus" I was well on my way toward the very capital of all the weirdness, the San Francisco Bay Area. That was a place where even Republicans, that year, would shyly admit that they were dabbling a bit in Buddhism, meditation, and Tantric sex.

It could not fail to happen that our immersion in psychedelia, Eastern philosophies, far-out music, and other phenomena of the moment would have its effect on the sort of science fiction that we were writing at the time. There was a Day-Glo splendor to the world in those days, and science fiction is nothing if not a reflection of the era in which it is written. One editor who knew that very well was my friend and neighbor Terry Carr, who was, I think, the preeminent science-fiction editor just then, the man who helped bring into print such classic novels as Ursula Le Guin's The Left Hand of Darkness *and (in a later, very different era) William Gibson's* Neuromancer*).*

Terry was not only a book editor; he also edited anthologies, some containing reprints, others featuring material written specifically for that collection. One of his projects in 1971 was a book called An Exaltation of Stars, *subtitled* Transcendental Adventures in Science Fiction, *for which he invited three writers to do novellas embodying the excitingly mind-expanding concepts many of us were grappling with at the time. "Science fiction has always been fascinated by the irrational, the numinous and transcendental," Terry wrote in his introduction to the book. "I suppose this is because science fiction likes to ask large questions: not simply* How? *but* Why? *And what are the implications?" He cited such books as Walter Miller's* A Canticle for Leibowitz *and James Blish's* A Case of Conscience *as examples of what he meant.*

The writers he chose for An Exaltation of Stars *were all seriously involved in the cultural manifestations of the* Zeitgeist *that had exploded around us, although they could hardly be called revolutionaries, let alone hippies. Roger Zelazny was a former employee of the Social Security Administration; his novella, with a name so complicated I refuse to reproduce it here, dealt with spiritual ecstasy as it might be experienced by alien life-forms. Edgar Pangborn, a quiet, elderly man of a philosophical nature, examined the religious beliefs of a far-future civilization. And I, who had been making an extensive study of the Dionysiac cults, provided Terry in January of 1972 with "The Feast of St. Dionysus," a novella that dealt with, of all unlikely things, an unhappy astronaut who becomes entangled in a transcendental cult in the California desert.*

It was a wild and wonderful time. I wouldn't want to be doing today a lot of the things I did back then, but I don't have to, because I was there the first time around. And the era left some interesting artifacts behind, such as the story you are about to read.

> *Sleepers, awake. Sleep is separateness; the cave of solitude is the cave of dreams, the cave of the passive spectator. To be awake is to participate, carnally and not in fantasy, in the feast; the great communion.*
>
> NORMAN O. BROWN: *Love's Body*

This is the dawn of the day of the Feast. Oxenshuer knows roughly what to expect, for he has spied on the children at their catechisms; he has had hints from some of the adults; he has spoken at length with the high priest of this strange apocalyptic city; and yet, for all his patiently gathered knowledge, he really knows nothing at all of today's event. What will happen? They will come for him, Matt who has been appointed his brother, and Will and Nick, who are his sponsors. They will lead him through the labyrinth to the place of the saint, to the god-house at the city's core. They will give him wine until he is glutted, until his cheeks and chin drip with it and his robe is stained with red. And he and Matt will struggle, will have a contest of some sort, a wrestling match, an agon: whether real or symbolic, he does not yet know. Before the whole community they will contend. What else, what else? There will be hymns to the saint, to the god—god and saint, both are one, Dionysus and Jesus, each an aspect of the other. Each a manifestation of the divinity we carry within us, so the Speaker has said. Jesus and Dionysus, Dionysus and Jesus, god and saint, saint and god, what do the terms matter? He had heard the people singing:

> This is the god who burns like fire
> This is the god whose name is music
> This is the god whose soul is wine

Fire. Music. Wine. The healing fire, the joining fire, in which all things will be made one. By its leaping blaze he will drink and drink and drink, dance and dance and dance. Maybe there will be some sort of sexual event, an orgy, perhaps, for sex and religion are closely bound among these people: a communion of the flesh opening the way toward communality of spirit.

> I go to the god's house and his fire consumes me
> I cry the god's name and his thunder deafens me
> I take the god's cup and his wine dissolves me

And then? And then? How can he possibly know what will happen, until it has happened? "You will enter into the ocean of Christ," they have told him. An ocean? Here in the Mojave Desert? Well, a figurative ocean, a metaphorical ocean. All is metaphor here. "Dionysus will carry you to Jesus," they say. Go, child, swim out to God. Jesus waits. The saint, the mad saint, the boozy old god who is their saint, the mad saintly god who abolishes walls and makes all things one, will lead you to bliss, dear John, dear tired John. Give your soul gladly to Dionysus the Saint. Make yourself whole in his blessed fire. You've been divided too long. How can you lie dead on Mars and still walk alive on Earth?

Heal yourself, John. This is the day.

From Los Angeles the old San Bernardino Freeway rolls eastward through the plastic suburbs, through Alhambra and Azusa, past the Covina Hills branch of Forest Lawn Memorial-Parks, past the mushroom sprawl of San Bernardino, which is becoming a little Los Angeles, but not so little. The highway pushes onward into the desert like a flat, grey cincture holding the dry, brown hills asunder. This was the road by which John Oxenshuer finally chose to make his escape. He had had no particular destination in mind but was seeking only a parched place, a sandy place, a place where he could be alone: he needed to re-create, in what might well be his last weeks of life, certain aspects of barren Mars. After considering a number of possibilities he fastened upon this route, attracted to it by the way the freeway seemed to lose itself in the desert north of the Salton Sea. Even in this overcivilized epoch a man could easily disappear there.

Late one November afternoon, two weeks past his fortieth birthday, he closed his rented apartment on Hollywood Boulevard; taking leave of no one, he drove unhurriedly toward the freeway entrance. There he surrendered control to the electronic highway net, which seized his car and pulled it into the traffic flow. The net governed him as far as Covina; when he saw Forest Lawn's statuary-speckled hilltop coming up on his right, he readied himself to resume driving. A mile beyond the vast cemetery a blinking sign told him he was on his own, and he took the wheel. The car continued to slice inland at the same velocity, as mechanical as iron, of 140 kilometers per hour. With each moment the recent past dropped from him, bit by bit.

Can you drown in the desert? Let's give it a try, God. I'll make a bargain with you. You let me drown out there. All right? And I'll give myself to you. Let me sink into the sand; let me bathe in it; let it wash Mars out of my soul; let it drown me, God; let it drown me. Free me from Mars and I'm m all yours, God. Is it a deal? Drown me in the desert and I'll surrender at last. I'll surrender.

❋

At twilight he was in Banning. Some gesture of farewell to civilization seemed suddenly appropriate, and he risked stopping to have dinner at a small Mexican restaurant. It was crowded with families enjoying a night out, which made Oxenshuer fear he would be recognized. Look, someone would cry, there's the Mars astronaut, there's the one who came back! But of course no one spotted him. He had grown a bushy, sandy moustache that nearly obliterated his thin, tense lips. His body, lean and wide-shouldered, no longer had an astronaut's springy erectness; in the nineteen months since his return from the red planet he had begun to stoop a little, to cultivate a roundedness of the upper back, as if some leaden weight beneath his breastbone were tugging him forward and downward. Besides, spacemen are quickly forgotten. How long had anyone remembered the names of the heroic lunar teams of his youth? Borman, Lovell, and Anders. Armstrong, Aldrin, and Collins. Scott, Irwin, and Worden. Each of them had had a few gaudy weeks of fame, and then they had disappeared into the blurred pages of the almanac, all, perhaps, except Armstrong: children learned about him at school. His one small step: he would become a figure of myth, up there with Columbus and Magellan. But the others? Forgotten. Yes. Yesterday's heroes. Oxenshuer, Richardson, and Vogel. Who? Oxenshuer, Richardson, and Vogel. That's Oxenshuer right over there, eating tamales and enchiladas, drinking a bottle of Double-X. He's the one who came back. Had some sort of breakdown and left his wife. Yes. That's a funny name, Oxenshuer. Yes. He's the one who came back. What about the other two? They died. Where did they die, daddy? They died on Mars, but Oxenshuer came back. What were their names again? Richardson and Vogel. They died. Oh. On Mars. Oh. And Oxenshuer didn't. What were their names again?

Unrecognized, safely forgotten, Oxenshuer finished his meal and returned to the freeway. Night had come by this time. The moon was nearly full; the mountains, clearly outlined against the darkness, glistened with a coppery sheen. There is no moonlight on Mars except the feeble, hasty glow of Phobos, dancing in and out of eclipse on its nervous journey from west to east. He had found Phobos disturbing; nor had he cared for fluttery Deimos, starlike, a tiny rocketing point of light. Oxenshuer drove onward, leaving the zone of urban sprawl behind, entering the true desert, pockmarked here and there by resort towns: Palm Springs, Twenty-nine Palms, Desert Hot Springs. Beckoning billboards summoned him to the torpid pleasures of whirlpool baths and saunas. These temptations he ignored without difficulty. Dryness was what he sought.

Once he was east of Indio he began looking for a place to abandon the car; but he was still too close to the southern boundaries of Joshua Tree National Monument, and he did not want to make camp this near to any area that might be patrolled by park rangers. So he kept driving until the moon was high and he was deep into the Chuckwalla country, with nothing much except sand dunes and mountains and dry lake beds between him and the Arizona border. In a stretch where the land seemed relatively flat he slowed the car almost to an idle, killed his lights, and swerved gently off the road, following a vague northeasterly course; he gripped the wheel tightly as he jounced over the rough, crunchy terrain. Half a kilometer from the highway Oxenshuer came to a shallow sloping basin, the dry bed of some ancient lake. He eased down into it until he could no longer see the long yellow tracks of headlights on the road, and knew he must be below the line of sight of any passing vehicle. Turning the engine off, he locked the car—a strange prissiness here, in the midst of nowhere!—took his backpack from the trunk, slipped his arms through the shoulder straps, and, without looking back, began to walk into the emptiness that lay to the north.

As he walks he composes a letter that he will never send.

Dear Claire, I wish I had been able to say goodbye to you before I left Los Angeles. I regretted only that: leaving town without telling you. But I was afraid to call. I draw back from you. You say you hold no grudge against me over Dave's death; you say it couldn't possibly have been my fault, and of course you're right. And yet I don't dare face you, Claire. Why is that? Because I left your husband's body on Mars and the guilt of that is choking me? But a body is only a shell, Claire. Dave's body isn't Dave, and there wasn't anything I could do for Dave. What is it, then, that comes between us? Is it my love, Claire, my guilty love for my friend's widow? Eh? That love is salt in my wounds, that love is sand in my throat, Claire. Claire. Claire. I can never tell you any of this, Claire. I never will. Goodbye. Pray for me. Will you pray?

His years of grueling NASA training for Mars served him well now. Powered by ancient disciplines, he moved swiftly, feeling no strain even with forty-five pounds on his back. He had no trouble with the uneven footing. The sharp chill in the air did not bother him, though he wore only light clothing, slacks and shirt and a flimsy cotton vest. The solitude, far from oppressing him, was actually a source of energy: a couple of hundred kilometers away in Los Angeles it might be the ninth decade of the twentieth century, but this was a prehistoric realm, timeless, unscarred by man, and his spirit expanded in his self-imposed isolation. Conceivably every footprint he made was the first human touch this land had felt. That grey, pervasive sense of guilt, heavy on him since his return from Mars, held less weight here beyond civilization's edge.

This wasteland was the closest he could come to attaining Mars on Earth. Not really close enough, for too many things broke the illusion: the great gleaming scarred moon, and the succulent terrestrial vegetation, and the tug of Earth's gravity, and the faint white glow on the leftward horizon that he imagined emanated from the cities of the coastal strip. But it was as close to Mars in flavor as he could manage. The Peruvian desert would have been better, only he had no way of getting to Peru.

An approximation. It would suffice.

A trek of at least a dozen kilometers left him still unfatigued, but he decided, shortly after midnight, to settle down for the night. The site he chose was a small level quadrangle bounded on the north and south by spiky, ominous cacti—chollas and prickly pears—and on the east by a maze of scrubby mesquite; to the west, a broad alluvial fan of tumbled pebbles descended from the nearby hills. Moonlight, raking the area sharply, highlighted every contrast of contour: the shadows of cacti were unfathomable inky pits and the tracks of small animals—lizards and kangaroo rats—were steep-walled canyons in the sand. As he slung his pack to the ground two startled rats, browsing in the mesquite, noticed him belatedly and leaped for cover in wild, desperate bounds, frantic but delicate. Oxenshuer smiled at them.

On the twentieth day of the mission Richardson and Vogel went out, as planned, for the longest extravehicular on the schedule, the ninety-kilometer crawler-jaunt to the Gulliver site. Goddamned well about time, Dave Vogel had muttered, when the EVA okay had at last come floating up, time-lagged and crackly, out of far-off Mission Control. All during the eight-month journey from Earth, while the brick-red face of Mars was swelling patiently in their portholes, they had argued about the timing of the big Marswalk, an argument that had begun six months before launch date. Vogel, insisting that the expedition was the mission's most important scientific project, had wanted to do it first, to get it done and out of the way before mishaps might befall them and force them to scrub it. No matter that the timetable decreed it for Day Twenty. The timetable was too conservative. We can overrule Mission Control, Vogel said. If they don't like it, let them reprimand us when we get home. But Richardson, though, he wouldn't go along. Houston knows best, he kept saying. He always took the side of authority. First we have to get used to working on Mars, Dave. First we ought to do the routine stuff close by the landing site, while we're getting acclimated. What's our hurry? We've got to stay here a month until the return window opens, anyway. Why breach the schedule? The scientists know what they're doing, and they want us to do everything in its proper order, Richardson said. Vogel, stubborn, eager, seething, thought he would find an ally in Oxenshuer. You vote with me, John. Don't tell me you give a crap about Mission Control! Two against one and Bud will have to give in. But Oxenshuer, oddly, took Richardson's side. He hesitated to deviate from the schedule. He wouldn't be making the long extravehicular himself in any case; he had drawn the short straw; he was the man who'd d be keeping close to the ship all the time. How then could he vote to alter the carefully designed schedule and send Richardson off, against his will, on a risky and perhaps ill-timed adventure? No, Oxenshuer said. Sorry, Dave, it isn't my place to decide such things. Vogel appealed anyway to Mission Control, and Mission Control said wait till Day Twenty, fellows. On Day Twenty Richardson and Vogel suited up and went out. It was the ninth EVA of the mission, but the first that would take anyone more than a couple of kilometers from the ship.

Oxenshuer monitored his departing companions from his safe niche in the control cabin. The small video screen showed him the path of their crawler as it diminished into the somber red plain. You're well named, rusty old Mars. The blood of fallen soldiers stains your soil.

Your hills are the color of the flames that lick conquered cities. Jouncing westward across Solis Lacus, Vogel kept up a running commentary. Lots of dead nothing out here, Johnny. It's as bad as the Moon. A prettier color, though. Are you reading me? I'm reading you, Oxenshuer said. The crawler was like a submarine mounted on giant preposterous wheels. Joggle, joggle, joggle, skirting craters and ravines, ridges and scarps. Pausing now and then so Richardson could pop a geological specimen or two into the gunnysack. Then onward, westward, westward. Heading bumpily toward the site where the unmanned Ares IV Mars Lander, almost a decade earlier, had scraped some Martian microorganisms out of the ground with the Gulliver sampling device.

> "Gulliver" is a culture chamber that inoculates itself with a sample of soil. The sample is obtained by two 7½-meter lengths of kite line wound on small projectiles. When the projectiles are fired, the lines unwind and fall to the ground. A small motor inside the chamber then reels them in, together with adhering soil particles. The chamber contains a growth medium whose organic nutrients are labeled with radioactive carbon. When the medium is inoculated with soil, the accompanying microorganisms metabolize the organic compounds and release radioactive carbon dioxide. This diffuses to the window of a Geiger counter, where the radioactivity is measured. Growth of the microbes causes the rate of carbon dioxide production to increase exponentially with time—an indication that the gas is being formed biologically. Provision is also made for the injection, during the run, of a solution containing a metabolic poison which can be used to confirm the biological origin of the carbon dioxide and to analyze the nature of the metabolic reactions.

All afternoon the crawler traversed the plain, and the sky deepened from dark purple to utter black, and the untwinkling stars, which on Mars are visible even by day, became more brilliant with the passing hours, and Phobos came streaking by, and then came little hovering Deimos; and Oxenshuer, wandering around the ship, took readings on this and that and watched his screen and listened to Dave Vogel's chatter; and Mission Control offered a comment every little while. And during these hours the Martian temperature began its nightly slide down the centigrade ladder. A thousand kilometers away, an inversion of thermal gradients unexpectedly developed, creating fierce currents in the tenuous Martian atmosphere, ripping gouts of red sand loose from the hills, driving wild scarlet clouds eastward toward the Gulliver site. As the sandstorm increased in intensity, the scanner satellites in orbit around Mars detected it and relayed pictures of it to Earth, and after the normal transmission lag it was duly noted at Mission Control as a potential hazard to the men in the crawler, but somehow—the NASA hearings did not succeed in fixing blame for this inexplicable communications failure—no one passed the necessary warning along to the three astronauts on Mars. Two hours after he had finished his solitary dinner aboard the ship, Oxenshuer heard Vogel say, "Okay, Johnny, we've finally reached the Gulliver site, and as soon as we have our lighting system set up we'll get out and see what the hell we have here." Then the sandstorm struck in full fury. Oxenshuer heard nothing more from either of his companions.

Making camp for the night, he took first from his pack his operations beacon, one of his NASA souvenirs. By the sleek instrument's cool, inexhaustible green light he laid out his bedroll in the flattest, least pebbly place he could find; then, discovering himself far from sleepy, Oxenshuer set about assembling his solar still. Although he had no idea how long he would stay in the desert—a week, a month, a year, forever—he had brought perhaps a month's supply of food concentrates with him, but no water other than a single canteen's worth, to tide him through thirst on this first night. He could not count on finding wells or streams here, any more than he had on Mars, and, unlike the kangaroo rats, capable of living indefinitely on nothing but dried seeds, producing water metabolically by the oxidation of carbohydrates, he would not be able to dispense entirely with fresh water. But the solar still would see him through.

He began to dig.

Methodically he shaped a conical hole a meter in diameter, half a meter deep, and put a wide-mouthed two-liter jug at its deepest point. He collected pieces of cactus, breaking off slabs of prickly pear but ignoring the stiletto-spined chollas, and placed these along the slopes of the hole. Then he lined the hole with a sheet of clear plastic film, weighted by rocks in such a way that the plastic came in contact with the soil only at the hole's rim and hung suspended a few centi-meters above the cactus pieces and the jug. The job took him twenty minutes. Solar energy would do the rest: as sunlight passed through the plastic into the soil and the plant material, water would evaporate, condense in droplets on the underside of the plastic, and trickle into the jug. With cactus as juicy as this, he might be able to count on a liter a day of sweet water out of each hole he dug. The still was emergency gear developed for use on Mars; it hadn't done anyone any good there, but Oxenshuer had no fears of running dry in this far more hospitable desert.

Enough. He shucked his pants and crawled into his sleeping bag. At last he was where he wanted to be: enclosed, protected, yet at the same time alone, unsurrounded, cut off from his past in a world of dryness.

He could not yet sleep; his mind ticked too actively. Images out of the last few years floated insistently through it and had to be purged, one by one. To begin with, his wife's face. (Wife? I have no wife. Not now.) He was having difficulty remembering Lenore's features, the shape of her nose, the turn of her lips, but a general sense of her existence still burdened him. How long had they been married? Eleven years, was it? Twelve? The anniversary? March 30, 31? He was sure he had loved her once. What had happened? Why had he recoiled from her touch?

—No, please, don't do that. I don't want to yet.

—You've been home three months, John.

Her sad green eyes. Her tender smile. A stranger, now. His ex-wife's face turned to mist and the mist congealed into the face of Claire Vogel. A sharper image: dark glittering eyes, the narrow mouth, thin cheeks framed by loose streamers of unbound black hair. The widow Vogel, dignified in her grief, trying to console him.

—I'm sorry, Claire. They just disappeared, is all. There wasn't anything I could do.

—John, John, it wasn't your fault. Don't let it get you like this.

—I couldn't even find the bodies. I wanted to look for them, but it was all sand everywhere, sand, dust, the craters, confusion, no signal, no landmarks, no way, Claire, no way.

—It's all right, John. What do the bodies matter? You did your best. I know you did.

Her words offered comfort but no absolution from guilt. Her embrace—light, chaste—merely troubled him. The pressure of her heavy breasts against him made him tremble. He remembered Dave Vogel, halfway to Mars, speaking lovingly of Claire's breasts. Her jugs, he called them. Boy, I'd like to have my hands on my lady's jugs right this minute! And Bud Richardson, more annoyed than amused, telling him to cut it out, to stop stirring up fantasies that couldn't be satisfied for another year or more.

Claire vanished from his mind, driven out by a blaze of flashbulbs. The hovercameras, hanging in midair, scanning him from every angle. The taut, earnest faces of the newsmen, digging deep for human interest. See the lone survivor of the Mars expedition! See his tortured eyes! See his gaunt cheeks! There's the President himself, folks, giving John Oxenshuer a great big welcome back to Earth! What thoughts must be going through this man's mind, the only human being to walk the sands of an alien world and return to our old down-to-Earth planet! How keenly he must feel the tragedy of the two lost astronauts he left behind up there! There he goes now, there goes John Oxenshuer, disappearing into the debriefing chamber—

Yes, the debriefings. Colonel Schmidt, Dr. Harkness, Commander Thompson, Dr. Burdette, Dr. Horowitz, milking him for data. Their voices carefully gentle, their manner informal, their eyes all the same betraying their single-mindedness.

—Once again, please, Captain Oxenshuer. You lost the signal, right, and then the backup line refused to check out, you couldn't get any telemetry at all. And then?

—And then I took a directional fix, I did a thermal scan and tripled the infrared, I rigged an extension lifeline to the sample-collector and went outside looking for them. But the collector's range was only ten kilometers. And the dust storm was too much. The dust storm. Too damned much. I went five hundred meters and you ordered me back into the ship. Didn't want to go back, but you ordered me.

—We didn't want to lose you too, John.

—But maybe it wasn't too late, even then. Maybe.

—There was no way you could have reached them in a short-range vehicle.

—I would have figured some way of recharging it. If only you had let me. If only the sand hadn't been flying around like that. If. Only.

—I think we've covered the point fully.

—Yes. May we go over some of the topographical data now, Captain Oxenshuer?

—Please. Please. Some other time.

It was three days before they realized what sort of shape he was in. They still thought he was the old John Oxenshuer, the one who had amused himself during the training period by reversing the inputs on his landing simulator, just for the hell of it, the one who had surreptitiously turned on the unsuspecting Secretary of Defense just before a Houston press conference, the one who had sung bawdy carols at a pious Christmas party for the families of the astronauts in '86. Now, seeing him darkened and turned in on himself, they concluded eventually that he had been transformed by Mars, and they sent him, finally, to the chief psychiatric team, Mendelson and McChesney.

—How long have you felt this way, Captain?

—I don't know. Since they died. Since I took off for Earth. Since I entered Earth's atmosphere. I don't know. Maybe it started earlier. Maybe it was always like this.

—What are the usual symptoms of the disturbance?

—Not wanting to see anybody. Not wanting to talk to anybody. Not wanting to be with anybody. Especially myself. I'm so goddamned sick of my own company.

—And what are your plans now?

—Just to live quietly and grope my way back to normal.

—Would you say it was the length of the voyage that upset you most, or the amount of time you had to spend in solitude on the homeward leg, or your distress over the deaths of—

—Look, how would I know?

—Who'd know better?

—Hey, I don't believe in either of you, you know? You're figments. Go away. Vanish.

—We understand you're putting in for retirement and a maximum disability pension, Captain.

—Where'd you hear that? It's a stinking lie. I'm going to be okay before long. I'll be back on active duty before Christmas, you got that?

—Of course, Captain.

—Go. Disappear. Who needs you?

—John, John, it wasn't your fault. Don't let it get you like this.

—I couldn't even find the bodies. I wanted to look for them, but it was all sand everywhere, sand, dust, the craters, confusion, no signal, no landmarks, no way, Claire, no way.

The images were breaking up, dwindling, going. He saw scattered glints of light slowly whirling overhead, the kaleidoscope of the heavens, the whole astronomical psychedelia swaying and cavorting, and then the sky calmed, and then only Claire's face remained, Claire and the minute red disc of Mars. The events of the nineteen months contracted to a single star-bright point of time, and became as nothing, and were gone. Silence and darkness enveloped him. Lying tense and rigid on the desert floor, he stared up defiantly at Mars, and closed his eyes, and wiped the red disc from the screen of his mind, and slowly, gradually, reluctantly, he surrendered himself to sleep.

Voices woke him. Male voices, quiet and deep, discussing him in an indistinct buzz. He hovered a moment on the border between dream and reality, uncertain of his perceptions and unsure of his proper response; then his military reflexes took over and he snapped into instant wakefulness, blinking his eyes open, sitting up in one quick move, rising to a standing position in the next, poising his body to defend itself.

He took stock. Sunrise was maybe half an hour away; the tips of the mountains to the west were stained with early pinkness. Thin mist shrouded the low-lying land. Three men stood just beyond the place where he had mounted his beacon. The shortest one was as tall as he, and they were desert-tanned, heavy-set, strong and capable-looking. They wore their hair long and their beards full; they were oddly dressed, shepherd-style, in loose belted robes of light green muslin or linen. Although their expressions were open and friendly and they did not seem to be armed, Oxenshuer was troubled by awareness of his vulnerability in this emptiness, and he found menace in their presence. Their intrusion on his isolation angered him. He stared at them warily, rocking on the balls of his feet.

One, bigger than the others, a massive thick-cheeked blue-eyed man, said, "Easy. Easy, now. You look all ready to fight."

"Who are you? What do you want?"

"Just came to find out if you were okay. You lost?"

Oxenshuer indicated his neat camp, his backpack, his bedroll. "Do I seem lost?"

"You're a long way from anywhere," said the man closest to Oxenshuer, one with shaggy yellow hair and a cast in one eye.

"Am I? I thought it was just a short hike from the road."

The three men began to laugh. "You don't know where the hell you are, do you?" said the squint-eyed one. And the third one, dark-bearded, hawk-featured, said, "Look over thataway." He pointed behind Oxenshuer, to the north. Slowly, half anticipating trickery, Oxenshuer turned. Last night, in the moonlit darkness, the land had seemed level and empty in that direction, but now he beheld two steeply rising mesas a few hundred meters apart, and in the opening between them he saw a low wooden palisade, and behind the palisade the flat-roofed tops of buildings were visible, tinted orange-pink by the spreading touch of dawn. A settlement out here? But the map showed nothing, and, from the looks of it, that was a town of some two or three thousand people. He wondered if he had somehow been transported by magic during the night to some deeper part of the desert. But no: there was his solar still, there was the mesquite patch; there were last night's prickly pears. Frowning, Oxenshuer said, "What is that place in there?"

"The City of the Word of God," said the hawk-faced one calmly.

"You're lucky," said the squint-eyed one. "You've been brought to us almost in time for the Feast of St. Dionysus. When all men are made one. When every ill is healed."

Oxenshuer understood. Religious fanatics. A secret retreat in the desert. The state was full of apocalyptic cults, more and more of them now that the end of the century was only about ten years away and millennial fears were mounting. He scowled. He had a native Easterner's innate distaste for Californian irrationality. Reaching into the reservoir of his own decaying Catholicism, he said thinly, "Don't you mean St. Dionysius? With an *I*? Dionysus was the Greek god of wine."

"Dionysus," said the big blue-eyed man. "Dionysius is somebody else, some Frenchman. We've heard of him. Dionysus is who we mean." He put forth his hand. "My name's Matt, Mr. Oxenshuer. If you stay for the Feast, I'll stand brother to you. How's that?"

The sound of his name jolted him. "You've heard of me?"

"Heard of you? Well, not exactly. We looked in your wallet."

"We ought to go now," said the squint-eyed one. "Don't want to miss breakfast."

"Thanks," Oxenshuer said, "but I think I'll pass up the invitation. I came out here to get away from people for a little while."

"So did we," Matt said.

"You've been called," said Squint-eye hoarsely. "Don't you realize that, man? You've been called to our city. It wasn't any accident you came here."

"No?"

"There aren't any accidents," said Hawk-face. "Not ever. Not in the breast of Jesus, not ever a one. What's written is written. You were called, Mr. Oxenshuer. Can you say no?" He put his hand lightly on Oxenshuer's arm. "Come to our city. Come to the Feast. Look, why do you want to be afraid?"

"I'm not afraid. I'm just looking to be alone."

"We'll let you be alone, if that's what you want," Hawk-face told him. "Won't we, Matt? Won't we, Will? But you can't say no to our city. To our saint. To Jesus. Come along, now. Will, you carry his pack. Let him walk into the city without a burden." Hawk-face's sharp, forbidding features were softened by the glow of his fervor. His dark eyes gleamed. A strange, persuasive warmth leaped from him to Oxenshuer. "You won't say no. You won't. Come sing with us. Come to the Feast. Well?"

"Well?" Matt asked also.

"To lay down your burden," said squint-eyed Will. "To join the singing. Well? Well?"

"I'll go with you," Oxenshuer said at length. "But I'll carry my own pack."

They moved to one side and waited in silence while he assembled his belongings. In ten minutes everything was in order. Kneeling, adjusting the straps of his pack, he nodded and looked up. The early sun was full on the city now, and its rooftops were bright with a golden radiance. Light seemed to stream upward from them; the entire desert appeared to blaze in that luminous flow.

"All right," Oxenshuer said, rising and shouldering his pack. "Let's go." But he remained where he stood, staring ahead. He felt the city's golden luminosity as a fiery tangible force on his cheeks, like the outpouring of heat from a crucible of molten metal. With Matt leading the way, the three men walked ahead, single file, moving fast. Will, the squint-eyed one, bringing up the rear, paused to look back questioningly at Oxenshuer, who was still standing entranced by the sight of that supernal brilliance. "Coming," Oxenshuer murmured. Matching the pace of the others, he followed them briskly over the parched, sandy wastes toward the City of the Word of God.

There are places in the coastal desert of Peru where no rainfall has ever been recorded. On the Paracas Peninsula, about eleven miles south of the port of Pisco, the red sand is absolutely bare of all vegetation, not a leaf, not a living thing; no stream enters the ocean nearby. The nearest human habitation is several miles away, where wells tap underground water and a few sedges line the beach. There is no more arid area in the western hemisphere; it is the epitome of loneliness and desolation. The psychological landscape of Paracas is much the same as that of Mars. John Oxenshuer, Dave Vogel, and Bud Richardson spent three weeks camping there in the winter of 1987, testing their emergency gear and familiarizing themselves with the emotional texture of the Martian environment. Beneath the sands of the peninsula are found the desiccated bodies of an ancient people unknown to history, together with some of the most magnificent textiles that the world has ever seen. Natives seeking salable artifacts have rifled the necropolis of Paracas, and now the bones of its occupants lie scattered on the surface, and the winds alternately cover and uncover fragments of the coarser fabrics, discarded by the diggers, still soft and strong after nearly two millennia.

Vultures circle high over the Mojave. They would pick the bones of anyone who died here. There are no vultures on Mars. Dead men become mummies, not skeletons, for nothing decays on Mars. What has died on Mars remains buried in the sand, invulnerable to time, imperishable, eternal. Perhaps archaeologists, bound on a futile but inevitable search for the remains of the lost races of old Mars, will find the withered bodies of Dave Vogel and Bud Richardson in a mound of red soil, ten thousand years from now.

At close range the city seemed less magical. It was laid out in the form of a bull's-eye, its curving streets set in concentric rings behind the blunt-topped little palisade, evidently purely symbolic in purpose, that rimmed its circumference between the mesas. The buildings were squat stucco affairs of five or six rooms, unpretentious and undistinguished, all of them similar if not identical in style: pastel-hued structures of the sort found everywhere in southern California. They seemed to be twenty or thirty years old and in generally shabby condition; they were set close together and close to the street, with no gardens and no garages. Wide avenues leading inward pierced the rings of buildings every few hundred meters. This seemed to be entirely a residential district, but no people were in sight, either at windows or on the streets, nor were there any parked cars; it was like a movie set, clean and empty and artificial. Oxenshuer's footfalls echoed loudly. The silence and surreal emptiness troubled him. Only an occasional child's tricycle, casually abandoned outside a house, gave evidence of recent human presence.

As they approached the core of the city, Oxenshuer saw that the avenues were narrowing and then giving way to a labyrinthine tangle of smaller streets, as intricate a maze as could be found in any of the old towns of Europe; the bewildering pattern seemed deliberate and carefully designed, perhaps for the sake of shielding the central section and making it a place apart from the antiseptic, prosaic zone of houses in the outer rings. The buildings lining the streets of the maze had an institutional character: they were three and four stories high, built of red brick, with few windows and pinched, unwelcoming entrances. They had the look of nineteenth-century hotels; possibly they were warehouses and meeting halls and places of some municipal nature. All were deserted. No commercial establishments were visible, no shops, no restaurants, no banks, no loan companies, no theaters, no newsstands. Such things were forbidden, maybe, in a theocracy such as Oxenshuer suspected this place to be. The city plainly had not evolved in any helter-skelter free-enterprise fashion, but had been planned down to its last alleyway for the exclusive use of a communal order whose members were beyond the bourgeois needs of an ordinary town.

Matt led them sure-footedly into the maze, infallibly choosing connecting points that carried them steadily deeper toward the center. He twisted and turned abruptly through juncture after juncture, never once doubling back on his track. At last they stepped through one passageway barely wide enough for Oxenshuer's pack, and he found himself in a plaza of unexpected size and grandeur. It was a vast open space, roomy enough for several thousand people, paved with cobbles that glittered in the harsh desert sunlight. On the right was a colossal building two stories high that ran the entire length of the plaza, at least three hundred meters; it looked as bleak as a barracks, a dreary utilitarian thing of clapboard and aluminum siding painted a dingy drab green, but all down its plaza side were tall, radiant stained-glass windows, as incongruous as pink gardenias blooming on a scrub oak. A towering metal cross rising high over the middle of the pointed roof settled all doubts; this was the city's church. Facing it across the plaza was an equally immense building, no less unsightly, built to the same plan but evidently secular, for its windows were plain and it bore no cross. At the far side of the plaza, opposite the place where they had entered it, stood a much smaller structure of dark stone in an implausible Gothic style, all vaults and turrets and arches. Pointing to each building in turn, Matt said, "Over there's the house of the god. On this side's the dining hall. Straight ahead, the little one, that's the house of the Speaker. You'll meet him at breakfast. Let's go eat."

> ...Captain Oxenshuer and Major Vogel, who will spend the next year and a half together in the sardine-can environment of their spaceship as they make their round trip journey to Mars and back, are no strangers to one another. Born on the same day—November 4, 1949—in Reading, Pennsylvania, they grew up together, attending the same elementary and high schools as classmates and sharing a dormitory room as undergraduates at Princeton. They dated many of the same girls; it was Captain Oxenshuer who introduced Major Vogel to his future wife, the former Claire Barnes, in 1973. "You might say he stole her from me," the tall, slender astronaut likes to tell interviewers, grinning to show he holds no malice over the incident. In a sense Major Vogel returned the compliment, for Captain Oxenshuer has been married since March 30, 1978, to the major's first cousin, the former Lenore Reiser, whom he met at his friend's wedding reception. After receiving advanced scientific degrees—Captain Oxenshuer in meteorology and celestial mechanics, Major Vogel in geology and space navigation—they enrolled together in the space program in the spring of 1979 and shortly afterward were chosen as members of the original thirty-six-man group of trainees for the first manned flight to the red

planet. According to their fellow astronauts, they quickly distinguished themselves for their quick and imaginative responses to stress situations, for their extraordinarily deft teamwork, and also for their shared love of high-spirited pranks and gags, which got them in trouble more than once with sober-sided NASA officials. Despite occasional reprimands, they were regarded as obvious choices for the initial Mars voyage, to which their selection was announced on March 19, 1985. Colonel Walter ("Bud") Richardson, named that day as command pilot for the Mars mission, cannot claim to share the lifelong bonds of companionship that link Captain Oxenshuer and Major Vogel, but he has been closely associated with them in the astronaut program for the past ten years and long ago established himself as their most intimate friend. Colonel Richardson, the third of this country's three musketeers of interplanetary exploration, was born in Omaha, Nebraska, on the 5th of June, 1948. He hoped to become an astronaut from earliest childhood onward, and...

They crossed the plaza to the dining hall. Just within the entrance was a dark-walled low-ceilinged vestibule; a pair of swinging doors gave access to the dining rooms beyond. Through windows set in the doors Oxenshuer could glimpse dimly-lit vastnesses to the left and the right, in which great numbers of solemn people, all clad in the same sort of flowing robes as his three companions, sat at long bare wooden tables and passed serving bowls around. Nick told Oxenshuer to drop his pack and leave it in the vestibule; no one would bother it, he said. As they started to go in, a boy of ten erupted explosively out of the left-hand doorway, nearly colliding with Oxenshuer. The boy halted just barely in time, backed up a couple of paces, stared with shameless curiosity into Oxenshuer's face, and, grinning broadly, pointed to Oxenshuer's bare chin and stroked his own as if to indicate that it was odd to see a man without a beard. Matt caught the boy by the shoulders and pulled him against his chest; Oxenshuer thought he was going to shake him, to chastise him for such irreverence, but no, Matt gave the boy an affectionate hug, swung him far overhead, and tenderly set him down. The boy clasped Matt's powerful forearms briefly and went sprinting through the righthand door.

"Your son?" Oxenshuer asked.

"Nephew. I've got two hundred nephews. Every man in this town's my brother, right? So every boy's my nephew."

—If I could have just a few moments for one or two questions, Captain Oxenshuer.

—Provided it's really just a few moments. I'm due at Mission Control at 0830, and—

—I'll confine myself, then, to the one topic of greatest relevance to our readers. What are your feelings about the Deity, Captain? Do you, as an astronaut soon to depart for Mars, believe in the existence of God?

—My biographical poop-sheet will tell you that I've been known to go to Mass now and then.

—Yes, of course, we realize you're a practicing member of the Catholic faith, but, well, Captain, it's widely understood that for some astronauts religious observance is more of a public-relations matter than a matter of genuine spiritual urgings. Meaning no offense, Captain, we're trying to ascertain the actual nature of your relationship, if any, to the Divine Presence, rather than—

—All right. You're asking a complicated question and I don't see how I can give an easy answer. If you're asking whether I literally believe in the Father, Son, and Holy Ghost, whether I think Jesus came down from heaven for our salvation and was crucified for us and was buried and on the third day rose again and ascended into heaven, I'd have to say no. Not except in the loosest metaphorical sense. But I do believe—ah—suppose we say I believe in the existence of an organizing force in the universe, a power of sublime reason that makes everything hang together, an underlying principle of rightness. Which we can call God for lack of a better name. And which I reach toward, when I feel I need to, by way of the Roman Church, because that's how I was raised.

—That's an extremely abstract philosophy, Captain.

—Abstract. Yes.

—That's an extremely rationalistic approach. Would you say that your brand of cool rationalism is characteristic of the entire astronaut group?

—I can't speak for the whole group. We didn't come out of a single mold. We've got some all-American boys who go to church every Sunday and think that God Himself is listening in person to every word they say, and we've got a couple of atheists, though I won't tell you who, and we've got guys who just don't care one way or the other. And I can tell you we've got a few real mystics, too, some out-and-out guru types. Don't let the uniforms and hair-cuts fool you. Why, there are times when I feel the pull of mysticism myself.

—In what way?

—I'm not sure. I get a sense of being on the edge of some sort of cosmic breakthrough. An awareness that there may be real forces just beyond my reach, not abstractions but actual functioning dynamic entities, which I could attune myself to if I only knew how to find the key. You feel stuff like that when you go into space, no matter how much of a rationalist you think you are. I've felt it four to five times, on training flights, on orbital missions. I want to feel it again. I want to break through. I want to reach God, am I making myself clear? I want to reach God.

—But you say you don't literally believe in Him, Captain. That sounds contradictory to me.

—Does it really?

—It does, sir.

—Well, if it does, I don't apologize. I don't have to think straight all the time. I'm entitled to a few contradictions. I'm capable of holding a couple of diametrically opposed beliefs. Look, if I want to flirt with madness a little, what's it to you?

—Madness, Captain?

—Madness. Yes. That's exactly what it is, friend. There are times when Johnny Oxenshuer is tired of being so goddamned sane. You can quote me on that. Did you get it straight? There are times when Johnny Oxenshuer is tired of being so goddamned sane. But don't print it until I've blasted off for Mars, you hear me? I don't want to get bumped from this mission for incipient schizophrenia. I want to go. Maybe I'll find God out there this time, you know? And maybe I won't. But I want to go.

—I think I understand what you're saying, sir. God bless you, Captain Oxenshuer. A safe voyage to you.

—Sure. Thanks. Was I of any help?

Hardly anyone glanced up at him, only a few of the children, as Matt led him down the long aisle toward the table on the platform at the back of the hall. The people here appeared to be extraordinarily self-contained, as if they were in possession of some wondrous secret from which he would be forever excluded, and the passing of the serving bowls seemed far more interesting to them than the stranger in their midst. The smell of scrambled eggs dominated the great room. That heavy, greasy odor seemed to expand and rise until it squeezed out all the air. Oxenshuer found himself choking and gagging. Panic seized him. He had never imagined he could be thrown into terror by the smell of scrambled eggs. "This way," Matt called. "Steady on, man. You all right?" Finally they reached the raised table. Here sat only men, dignified and serene of mien, probably the elders of the community. At the head of the table was one who had the unmistakable look of a high priest. He was well past seventy—or eighty or ninety—and his strong-featured leathery face was seamed and gullied; his eyes were keen and intense, managing to convey both a fierce tenacity and an all-encompassing warm humanity. Small-bodied, lithe, weighing at most a hundred pounds, he sat ferociously erect, a formidably commanding little man. A metallic embellishment of the collar of his robe was, perhaps, the badge of his status. Leaning over him, Matt said in exaggeratedly clear, loud tones, "This here's John. I'd like to stand brother to him when the Feast comes, if I can. John, this here's our Speaker."

Oxenshuer had met popes and presidents and secretaries-general, and, armored by his own standing as a celebrity, had never fallen into foolish awe-kindled embarrassment. But here he was no celebrity; he was no one at all, a stranger, an outsider, and he found himself lost before the Speaker. Mute, he waited for help. The old man said, his voice as melodious and as resonant as a cello, "Will you join our meal, John? Be welcome in our city."

Two of the elders made room on the bench. Oxenshuer sat at the Speaker's left hand; Matt sat beside him. Two girls of about fourteen brought settings: a plastic dish, a knife, a fork, a spoon, a cup. Matt served him: scrambled eggs, toast, sausages. All about him the clamor of eating went on. The Speaker's plate was empty. Oxenshuer fought back nausea and forced himself to attack the eggs. "We take all our meals together," said the Speaker. "This is a closely knit community, unlike any community I know on Earth." One of the serving girls said pleasantly, "Excuse me, brother," and, reaching over Oxenshuer's shoulder, filled his cup with red wine. Wine for breakfast? They worship Dionysus here, Oxenshuer remembered.

—The Speaker said, "We'll house you. We'll feed you. We'll love you. We'll lead you to God. That's why you're here, isn't it? To get closer to Him, eh? To enter into the ocean of Christ."

✹

—What do you want to be when you grow up, Johnny?

—An astronaut, ma'am. I want to be the first man to fly to Mars.

No. He never said any such thing.

✹

Later in the morning he moved into Matt's house, on the perimeter of the city, overlooking one of the mesas. The house was merely a small green box, clapboard outside, flimsy beaverboard partitions inside: a sitting room, three bedrooms, a bathroom. No kitchen or dining room. ("We take all our meals together.") The walls were bare: no icons, no crucifixes, no religious paraphernalia of any kind. No television, no radio, hardly any personal possessions at all in evidence: a shotgun, a dozen worn books and magazines, some spare robes and extra boots in a closet, little more than that. Matt's wife was a small quiet woman in her late thirties, soft-eyed, submissive, dwarfed by her burly husband. Her name was Jean. There were three children, a boy of about twelve and two girls, maybe nine and seven. The boy had had a room of his own; he moved uncomplainingly in with his sisters, who doubled up in one bed to provide one for him, and Oxenshuer took the boy's room. Matt told the children their guest's name, but it drew no response from them. Obviously they had never heard of him. Were they even aware that a spaceship from Earth had lately journeyed to Mars? Probably not. He found that refreshing: for years Oxenshuer had had to cope with children paralyzed with astonishment at finding themselves in the presence of a genuine astronaut. Here he could shed the burdens of fame.

He realized he had not been told his host's last name. Somehow it seemed too late to ask Matt directly, now. When one of the little girls came wandering into his room he said, "What's your name?"

"Toby," she said, showing a gap-toothed mouth.

"Toby what?"

"Toby. Just Toby."

No surnames in this community? All right. Why bother with surnames in a place where everyone knows everyone else? Travel light, brethren, travel light, strip away the excess baggage.

Matt walked in and said, "At council tonight I'll officially apply to stand brother to you. It's just a formality. They've never turned an application down."

"What's involved, actually?"

"It's hard to explain until you know our ways better. It means I'm, well, your spokesman, your guide through our rituals."

"A kind of sponsor?"

"Well, sponsor's the wrong word. Will and Nick will be your sponsors. That's a different level of brotherhood, lower, not as close. I'll be something like your godfather, I guess; that's as near as I can come to the idea. Unless you don't want me to be. I never consulted you. Do you want me to stand brother to you, John?"

It was an impossible question. Oxenshuer had no way to evaluate any of this. Feeling dishonest, he said, "It would be a great honor, Matt."

Matt said, "You got any real brothers? Flesh kin?"

"No. A sister in Ohio." Oxenshuer thought a moment. "There once was a man who was like a brother to me. Knew him since childhood. As close as makes no difference. A brother, yes."

"What happened to him?"

"He died. In an accident. A long way from here."

"Terrible sorry," Matt said. "I've got five brothers. Three of them outside; I haven't heard from them in years. And two right here in the city. You'll meet them. They'll accept you as kin. Everyone will.

"What did you think of the Speaker?" Matt said.

"A marvelous old man. I'd like to talk with him again."

"You'll talk plenty with him. He's my father, you know."

Oxenshuer tried to imagine this huge man springing from the seed of the spare-bodied, compactly built Speaker and could not make the connection. He decided Matt must be speaking metaphorically again. "You mean, the way that boy was your nephew?"

"He's my true father," Matt said. "I'm flesh of his flesh." He went to the window. It was open about eight centimeters at the bottom. "Too cold for you in here, John?"

"It's fine."

"Gets cold, sometimes, these winter nights."

Matt stood silent, seemingly sizing Oxenshuer up. Then he said, "Say, you ever do any wrestling?"

"A little. In college."

"That's good."

"Why do you ask?"

"One of the things brothers do here, part of the ritual. We wrestle some. Especially the day of the Feast. It's important in the worship. I wouldn't want to hurt you any when we do. You and me, John. We'll do some wrestling before long, just to practice up for the Feast, okay? Okay?"

They let him go anywhere he pleased. Alone, he wandered through the city's labyrinth, that incredible tangle of downtown streets, in early afternoon. The maze was cunningly constructed, one street winding into another so marvelously that the buildings were drawn tightly together and the bright desert sun could barely penetrate; Oxenshuer walked in shadow much of the way. The twisting mazy passages baffled him. The purpose of this part of the city seemed clearly symbolic: everyone who dwelled here was compelled to pass through these coiling interlacing streets in order to get from the commonplace residential quarter, where people lived in isolated family groupings, to the dining hall, where the entire community together took the sacrament of food, and to the church, where redemption and salvation were to be had. Only when purged of error and doubt, only when familiar with the one true way (or was there more than one way through the maze? Oxenshuer wondered.) could one attain the harmony of communality. He was still uninitiated, an outlander; wander as he would, dance tirelessly from street to cloistered street, he would never get there unaided.

He thought it would be less difficult than it had first seemed to find his way from Matt's house to the inner plaza, but he was wrong: the narrow, meandering streets misled him, so that he sometimes moved away from the plaza when he thought he was going toward it, and, after pursuing one series of corridors and intersections for fifteen minutes, he realized that he had merely returned himself to one of the residential streets on the edge of the maze. Intently, he tried again. An astronaut trained to maneuver safely through the trackless wastes of Mars ought to be able to get about in one small city. Watch for landmarks, Johnny. Follow the pattern of the shadows. He clamped his lips, concentrated, plotted a course. As he prowled he occasionally saw faces peering briefly at him out of the upper windows of the austere warehouselike buildings that flanked the street. Were they smiling? He came to one group of streets that seemed familiar to him, and went in and in, until he entered an alleyway closed at both ends, from which the only exit was a slit barely wide enough for a man if he held his breath and slipped through sideways. Just beyond, the metal cross of the church stood outlined against the sky, encouraging him: he was nearly to the end of the maze. He went through the slit and found himself in a cul-de-sac; five minutes of close inspection revealed no way to go on. He retraced his steps and sought another route.

One of the bigger buildings in the labyrinth was evidently a school. He could hear the high, clear voices of children chanting mysterious hymns. The melodies were conventional seesaws of piety, but the words were strange:

> Bring us together. Lead us to the ocean.
> Help us to swim. Give us to drink.
> Wine in my heart today,
> Blood in my throat today,
> Fire in my soul today,
> All praise, O God, to thee.

Sweet treble voices, making the bizarre words sound all the more grotesque. Blood in my throat today. Unreal city. How can it exist? Where does the food come from? Where does the wine come from? What do they use for money? What do the people do with themselves all day? They have electricity: what fuel keeps the generator running? They have running water. Are they hooked into a public utility district's pipelines, and if so why isn't this place on my map? Fire in my soul today. Wine in my heart today. What are these feasts, who are these saints? This is the god who burns like fire. This is the god whose name is music. This is the god whose soul is wine. You were called, Mr. Oxenshuer. Can you say no? You can't say no to our city. To our saint. To Jesus. Come along, now?

Where's the way out of here?

Three times a day, the whole population of the city went on foot from their houses through the labyrinth to the dining hall. There appeared to be at least half a dozen ways of reaching the central plaza, but, though he studied the route carefully each time, Oxenshuer was unable to keep it straight in his mind. The food was simple and nourishing, and there was plenty of it. Wine flowed freely at every meal. Young boys and girls did the serving, jubilantly hauling huge platters of food from the kitchen; Oxenshuer had no idea who did the cooking, but he supposed the task would rotate among the women of the community. (The men had other chores. The city, Oxenshuer learned, had been built entirely by the freely contributed labor of its own inhabitants. Several new houses were under construction now. And there were irrigated fields beyond the mesas.) Seating in the dining hall was random at the long tables, but people generally seemed to come together in nuclear-family groupings. Oxenshuer met Matt's two brothers, Jim and Ernie, both smaller men than Matt but powerfully built. Ernie gave Oxenshuer a hug, a quick, warm, impulsive gesture. "Brother," he said. "Brother! Brother!"

The Speaker received Oxenshuer in the study of his residence on the plaza, a dark ground-floor room, the walls of which were covered to ceiling height with shelves of books. Most people here affected a casual hayseed manner, an easy drawling rural simplicity of speech that implied little interest in intellectual things, but the Speaker's books ran heavily to abstruse philosophical and theological themes, and they looked as though they had all been read many times. Those books confirmed Oxenshuer's first fragmentary impression of the Speaker: that this was a man of supple, well-stocked mind, sophisticated, complex. The Speaker offered Oxenshuer a cup of cool tart wine. They drank in silence. When he had nearly drained his cup, the old man calmly hurled the dregs to the glossy slate floor. "An offering to Dionysus," he explained.

"But you're Christians here," said Oxenshuer.

"Yes, of course we're Christians! But we have our own calendar of saints. We worship Jesus in the guise of Dionysus and Dionysus in the guise of Jesus. Others might call us pagans, I suppose. But where there's

Christ, is there not Christianity?" The Speaker laughed. "Are you a Christian, John?"

"I suppose. I was baptized. I was confirmed. I've taken communion. I've been to confession now and then."

"You're of the Roman faith?"

"More that faith than any other," Oxenshuer said.

"You believe in God?"

"In an abstract way."

"And in Jesus Christ?"

"I don't know," said Oxenshuer uncomfortably. "In a literal sense, no. I mean, I suppose there was a prophet in Palestine named Jesus, and the Romans nailed him up, but I've never taken the rest of the story too seriously. I can accept Jesus as a symbol, though. As a metaphor of love. God's love."

"A metaphor for all love," the Speaker said. "The love of God for mankind. The love of mankind for God. The love of man and woman, the love of parent and child, the love of brother and brother, every kind of love there is. Jesus is love's spirit. God is love. That's what we believe here. Through communal ecstasies we are reminded of the new commandment He gave unto us, That ye love one another. And as it says in Romans, Love is the fulfilling of the law. We follow His teachings; therefore we are Christians."

"Even though you worship Dionysus as a saint?"

"Especially so. We believe that in the divine madnesses of Dionysus we come closer to Him than other Christians are capable of coming. Through revelry, through singing, through the pleasures of the flesh, through ecstasy, through union with one another in body and in soul—through these we break out of our isolation and become one with Him. In the life to come we will all be one. But first we must live this life and share in the creation of love, which is Jesus, which is God. Our goal is to make all beings one with Jesus, so that we become droplets in the ocean of love which is God, giving up our individual selves."

"This sounds Hindu to me, almost. Or Buddhist."

"Jesus is Buddha. Buddha is Jesus."

"Neither of them taught a religion of revelry."

"Dionysus did. We make our own synthesis of spiritual commandments. And so we see no virtue in self-denial, since that is the contradiction of love. What is held to be virtue by others is sin to us. And vice versa, I would suppose."

"What about the doctrine of the virgin birth? What about the virginity of Jesus himself? The whole notion of purity through restraint and asceticism?"

"Those concepts are not part of our belief, friend John."

"But you do recognize the concept of sin?"

"The sins we deplore," said the Speaker, "are such things as coldness, selfishness, aloofness, envy, maliciousness, all those things that hold one man apart from another. We punish the sinful by engulfing them in love. But we recognize no sins that arise out of love itself or out of excess of love. Since the world, especially the Christian world, finds our principles hateful and dangerous, we have chosen to withdraw from that world."

"How long have you been out here?" Oxenshuer asked.

"Many years. No one bothers us. Few strangers come to us. You are the first in a very long time."

"Why did you have me brought to your city?"

"We knew you were sent to us," the Speaker said.

At night there were wild frenzied gatherings in certain tall windowless buildings in the depths of the labyrinth. He was never allowed to take part. The dancing, the singing, the drinking, whatever else went on, these things were not yet for him. Wait till the Feast, they told him, wait till the Feast, then you'll be invited to join us. So he spent his evenings alone. Some nights he would stay home with the children. No babysitters were needed in this city, but he became one anyway, playing simple dice games with the girls, tossing a ball back and forth with the boy, telling them stories as they fell asleep. He told them of his flight to Mars, spoke of watching the red world grow larger every day, described the landing, the alien feel of the place, the iron-red sands, the tiny glinting moons. They listened silently, perhaps fascinated, perhaps not at all interested: he suspected they thought he was making it all up. He never said anything about the fate of his companions.

Some nights he would stroll through town, street after quiet street, drifting in what he pretended was a random way toward the downtown maze. Standing near the perimeter of the labyrinth—even now he could not find his way around in it after dark, and feared getting lost if he went in too deep—he would listen to the distant sounds of the celebration, the drumming, the chanting, the simple, repetitive hymns:

This is the god who burns like fire
This is the god whose name is music
This is the god whose soul is wine

And he would also hear them sing:

Tell the saint to heat my heart
Tell the saint to give me breath
Tell the saint to quench my thirst

And this:

Leaping shouting singing stamping
Rising climbing flying soaring
Melting joining loving blazing
Singing soaring joining loving

Some nights he would walk to the edge of the desert, hiking out a few hundred meters into it, drawing a bleak pleasure from the solitude, the crunch of sand beneath his boots, the knifeblade coldness of the air, the forlorn gnarled cacti, the timorous kangaroo rats, even the occasional scorpion. Crouching on some gritty hummock, looking up through the cold brilliant stars to the red dot of Mars, he would think of Dave Vogel, would think of Bud Richardson, would think of Claire, and of himself, who he had been, what he had lost. Once, he remembered, he had been a high-spirited man who laughed easily, expressed affection readily and openly, enjoyed joking, drinking, running, swimming, all the active outgoing things. Leaping shouting singing stamping. Rising climbing flying soaring. And then this deadness had come over him, this zombie absence of response, this icy shell. Mars had stolen him from himself. Why? The guilt? The guilt, the guilt, the guilt—he had lost himself in guilt. And now he was lost in the desert. This implausible town. These rites, this cult. Wine and shouting. He had no idea how long he had been here. Was Christmas approaching? Possibly it was only a few days away. Blue plastic Yule trees were sprouting in front of the department stores on Wilshire Boulevard. Jolly red Santas pacing the sidewalk. Tinsel and glitter. Christmas might be an appropriate time for the Feast of St. Dionysus. The Saturnalia revived. Would the Feast come soon? He anticipated it with fear and eagerness.

Late in the evening, when the last of the wine was gone and the singing was over, Matt and Jean would return, flushed, wine-drenched, happy, and through the thin partition separating Oxenshuer's room from theirs would come the sounds of love, the titanic poundings of their embraces, far into the night.

—Astronauts are supposed to be sane, Dave.

—Are they? Are they really, Johnny?

—Of course they are.

—Are you sane?

—I'm sane as hell, Dave.

—Yes. Yes. I'll bet you think you are.

—Don't you think I'm sane?

—Oh, sure, you're sane, Johnny. Saner than you need to be. If anybody asked me to name him one sane man, I'd say John Oxenshuer. But you're not all that sane. And you've got the potential to become very crazy.

—Thanks.

—I mean it as a compliment.

—What about you? You aren't sane?

—I'm a madman, Johnny. And getting madder all the time.

—Suppose NASA finds out that Dave Vogel's a madman?

—They won't, my friend. They know I'm one hell of an astronaut, and so by definition I'm sane. They don't know what's inside me. They can't. By definition, they wouldn't be NASA bureaucrats if they could tell what's inside a man.

—They know you're sane because you're an astronaut?

—Of course, Johnny. What does an astronaut know about the irrational? What sort of capacity for ecstasy does he have, anyway? He trains for ten years; he jogs in a centrifuge; he drills with computers, he runs a thousand simulations before he dares to sneeze; he thinks in spaceman jargon; he goes to church on Sundays and doesn't pray; he turns himself into a machine so he can run the damnedest machines anybody ever thought up. And to outsiders he looks deader than a banker, deader than a stockbroker, deader than a sales manager. Look at him, with his 1975 haircut and his 1965 uniform. Can a man like that even know what a mystic experience is? Well, some of us are really like that. They fit the official astronaut image. Sometimes I think you do, Johnny, or at least that you want to. But not me. Look, I'm a yogi. Yogis train for decades so they can have a glimpse of the All. They subject their bodies to crazy disciplines. They learn highly specialized techniques. A yogi and an astronaut aren't all that far apart, man. What I do, it's not so different from what a yogi does, and it's for the same reason. It's so we can catch sight of the White Light. Look at you, laughing! But I mean it, Johnny. When that big fist knocks me into orbit, when I see the whole world hanging out there, it's a wild moment for me, it's ecstasy, it's nirvana. I live for those moments. They make all the NASA crap worthwhile. Those are breakthrough moments, when I get into an entirely new realm. That's the only reason I'm in this. And you know something? I think it's the same with you, whether you know it or not. A mystic thing, Johnny, a crazy thing, that powers us, that drives us on. The yoga of space. One day you'll find out. One day you'll see yourself for the madman you really are. You'll open up to all the wild forces inside you, the lunatic drives that sent you to NASA. You'll find out you weren't just a machine after all; you weren't just a stockbroker in a fancy costume; you'll find out you're a yogi, a holy man, an ecstatic. And you'll see what a trip you're on, you'll see that controlled madness is the only true secret and that you've always known the Way. And you'll set aside everything that's left of your old straight self. You'll give yourself up completely to forces you can't understand and don't want to understand. And you'll love it, Johnny. You'll love it.

When he had stayed in the city about three weeks—it seemed to him that it had been about three weeks, though perhaps it had been two or four—he decided to leave. The decision was nothing that came upon him suddenly; it had always been in the back of his mind that he did not want to be here, and gradually that feeling came to dominate him. Nick had promised him solitude while he was in the city, if he wanted it, and indeed he had had solitude enough, no one bothering him, no one making demands on him, the city functioning perfectly well without any contribution from him. But it was the wrong kind of solitude. To be alone in the middle of several thousand people was worse than camping by himself in the desert. True, Matt had promised him that after the Feast he would no longer be alone. Yet Oxenshuer wondered if he really wanted to stay here long enough to experience the mysteries of the

Feast and the oneness that presumably would follow it. The Speaker spoke of giving up all pain as one enters the all-encompassing body of Jesus. What would he actually give up, though—his pain or his identity? Could he lose one without losing the other? Perhaps it was best to avoid all that and return to his original plan of going off by himself in the wilderness.

One evening after Matt and Jean had set out for the downtown revels, Oxenshuer quietly took his pack from the closet. He checked all his gear, filled his canteen, and said goodnight to the children. They looked at him strangely, as if wondering why he was putting on his pack just to go for a walk, but they asked no questions. He went up the broad avenue toward the palisade, passed through the unlocked gate, and in ten minutes was in the desert, moving steadily away from the City of the Word of God.

It was a cold, clear night, very dark, the stars almost painfully bright, Mars very much in evidence. He walked roughly eastward, through choppy countryside badly cut by ravines, and soon the mesas that flanked the city were out of sight. He had hoped to cover eight or ten kilometers before making camp, but the ravines made the hike hard going; when he had been out no more than an hour one of his boots began to chafe him and a muscle in his left leg sprang a cramp. He decided he would do well to halt. He picked a campsite near a stray patch of Joshua trees that stood like grotesque sentinels, stiff-armed and bristly, along the rim of a deep gully. The wind rose suddenly and swept across the desert flats, agitating their angular branches violently. It seemed to Oxenshuer that those booming gusts were blowing him the sounds of singing from the nearby city:

> I go to the god's house and his fire consumes me
> I cry the god's name and his thunder deafens me
> I take the god's cup and his wine dissolves me

He thought of Matt and Jean, and Ernie who had called him brother, and the Speaker who had offered him love and shelter, and Nick and Will his sponsors. He retraced in his mind the windings of the labyrinth until he grew dizzy. It was impossible, he told himself, to hear the singing from this place. He was at least three or four kilometers away. He prepared his campsite and unrolled his sleeping bag. But it was too early for sleep; he lay wide awake, listening to the wind, counting the stars, playing back the chants of the city in his head. Occasionally he dozed, but only for fitful intervals, easily broken. Tomorrow, he thought, he would cover twenty-five or thirty kilometers, going almost to the foothills of the mountains to the east, and he would set up half a dozen solar stills and settle down for a leisurely reexamination of all that had befallen him.

The hours slipped by slowly. About three in the morning he decided he was not going to be able to sleep, and he got up, dressed, paced along the gully's edge. A sound came to him: soft, almost a throbbing purr. He saw a light in the distance. A second light. The sound redoubled, one purr overlaid by another. Then a third light, farther away. All three lights in motion. He recognized the purring sounds now: the engines of dune-cycles. Travellers crossing the desert in the middle of the night? The headlights of the cycles swung in wide circular orbits around him. A search party from the city? Why else would they be driving like that, cutting off acres of desert in so systematic a way?

Yes. Voices. "John? Jo—ohn! Yo, John!"

Looking for him. But the desert was immense; the searchers were still far off. He need only take his gear and hunker down in the gully, and they would pass him by.

"Yo, John! Jo—ohn!"

Matt's voice.

Oxenshuer walked down the slope of the gully, paused a moment in its depths, and, surprising himself, started to scramble up the gully's far side. There he stood in silence a few minutes, watching the circling dune-cycles, listening to the calls of the searchers. It still seemed to him that the wind was bringing him the songs of the city people. This is the god who burns like fire. This is the god whose name is music. Jesus waits. The saint will lead you to bliss, dear tired John. Yes. Yes. At last he cupped his hands to his mouth and shouted, "Yo! Here I am! Yo!"

Two of the cycles halted immediately; the third, swinging out far to the left, stopped a little afterward. Oxenshuer waited for a reply, but none came.

"Yo!" he called again. "Over here, Matt! Here!"

He heard the purring start up. Headlights were in motion once more, the beams traversing the desert and coming to rest. On him. The cycles approached. Oxenshuer re-crossed the gully, collected his gear, and was waiting again on the cityward side when the searchers reached him. Matt, Nick, Will.

"Spending a night out?" Matt asked. The odor of wine was strong on his breath.

"Guess so."

"We got a little worried when you didn't come back by midnight. Thought you might have stumbled into a dry wash and hurt yourself some. Wasn't any cause for alarm, though, looks like." He glanced at Oxenshuer's pack, but made no comment. "Long as you're all right, I guess we can leave you to finish what you were doing. See you in the morning, okay?"

He turned away. Oxenshuer watched the men mount their cycles.

"Wait," he said.

Matt looked around.

"I'm all finished out here," Oxenshuer said. "I'd appreciate a lift back to the city."

"It's a matter of wholeness," the Speaker said. "In the beginning, mankind was all one. We were in contact. The communion of soul to soul. But then it all fell apart. *'In Adam's Fall we sinned all,'* remember? And that Fall, that original sin, John, it was a falling apart, a falling away from one another, a falling into the evil of strife. When we were in Eden we were more than simply one family, we were one being, one universal entity; and we came forth from Eden as individuals, Adam and Eve, Cain and Abel. The original universal being broken into pieces. Here, John, we seek to put the pieces back together. Do you follow me?"

"But how is it done?" Oxenshuer asked.

"By allowing Dionysus to lead us to Jesus," the old man said. "And in the saint's holy frenzy to create unity out of opposites. We bring the hostile tribes together. We bring the contending brothers together. We bring man and woman together."

Oxenshuer shrugged. "You talk only in metaphors and parables."

"There's no other way."

"What's your method? What's your underlying principle?"

"Our underlying principle is mystic ecstasy. Our method is to partake of the flesh of the god, and of his blood."

"It sounds very familiar. Take; eat. This is my body. This is my blood. Is your Feast a High Mass?"

The Speaker chuckled. "In a sense. We've made our synthesis between paganism and orthodox Christianity, and we've tried to move backward from the symbolic ritual to the literal act. Do you know where Christianity went astray? The same place all other religions have become derailed. The point at which spiritual experience was replaced by rote worship. Look at your Jews, muttering about Pharaoh in a language they've forgotten. Look at your Christians, lining up at the communion rail for a wafer and a gulp of wine, and never once feeling the terror and splendor of knowing that they're eating their god! Religion becomes doctrine too soon. It becomes professions of faith, formulas, talismans, emptiness. 'I believe in God the Father Almighty, creator of heaven and earth, and in Jesus Christ his only son, our Lord, who was conceived by the Holy Spirit, born from the Virgin Mary—" Words. Only words. We don't believe, John, that religious worship consists in reciting narrative accounts of ancient history. We want it to be immediate. We want it to be real. We want to *see* our god. We want to *taste* our god. We want to *become* our god."

"How?"

"Do you know anything about the ancient cults of Dionysus?"

"Only that they were wild and bloody, with plenty of drinking and revelry and maybe human sacrifices."

"Yes. Human sacrifices," the Speaker said. "But before the human sacrifices came the divine sacrifices, the god who dies, the god who gives up his life for his people. In the prehistoric Dionysiac cults the god himself was torn apart and eaten, he was the central figure in a mystic rite of destruction in which his ecstatic worshippers feasted on his raw flesh, a sacramental meal enabling them to be made full of the god and take on blessedness, while the dead god became the scapegoat for man's sins. And then the god was reborn and all things were made one by his rebirth. So in Greece, so in Asia Minor, priests of Dionysus were ripped to pieces as surrogates for the god, and the worshippers partook of blood and meat in cannibalistic feasts of love, and in more civilized times animals were sacrificed in place of men, and still later, when the religion of Jesus replaced the various Dionysiac religions, bread and wine came to serve as the instruments of communion, metaphors for the flesh and blood of the god. On the symbolic level it was all the same. To devour the god. To achieve contact with the god in the most direct way. To experience the rapture of the ecstatic state, when one is possessed by the god. To unite that which society has forced asunder. To break down all boundaries. To rip off all shackles. To yield to our saint, our mad saint, the drunken god who is our saint, the mad saintly god who abolishes walls and makes all things one. Yes, John? We integrate through disintegration. We dissolve in the great ocean. We burn in the great fire. Yes, John? Give your soul gladly to Dionysus the Saint, John. Make yourself whole in his blessed fire. You've been divided too long." The Speaker's eyes had taken on a terrifying gleam. "Yes, John? Yes? Yes?"

In the dining hall one night Oxenshuer drinks much too much wine. The thirst comes upon him gradually and unexpectedly; at the beginning of the meal he simply sips as he eats, in his usual way, but the more he drinks, the more dry his throat becomes, until by the time the meat course is on the table he is reaching compulsively for the carafe every few minutes, filling his cup, draining it, filling, draining. He becomes giddy and boisterous; someone at the table begins a hymn, and Oxenshuer joins in, though he is unsure of the words and keeps losing the melody. Those about him laugh, clap him on the back, sing even louder, beckoning to him, encouraging him to sing with them. Ernie and Matt match him drink for drink, and now whenever his cup is empty they fill it before he has a chance. A serving girl brings a full carafe. He feels a prickling in his earlobes and at the tip of his nose, feels a band of warmth across his chest and shoulders, and realizes he is getting drunk, but he allows it to happen. Dionysus reigns here. He has been sober long enough. And it has occurred to him that his drunkenness perhaps will inspire them to admit him to the night's revels. But that does not happen. Dinner ends. The Speaker and the other old men who sit at his table file from the hall; it is the signal for the rest to leave. Oxenshuer stands. Falters. Reels. Recovers. Laughs. Links arms with Matt and Ernie. "Brothers," he says. "Brothers!" They go from the hall together, but outside, in the great cobbled plaza, Matt says to him, "You better not go wandering in the desert tonight, man, or you'll break your neck for sure." So he is still excluded. He goes back through the labyrinth with Matt and Jean to their house, and they help him into his room and give him a jug of wine in case he still feels the thirst, and then they leave him. Oxenshuer sprawls on his bed. His head is spinning. Matt's boy looks in and asks if everything's all right. "Yes," Oxenshuer tells him. "I just need to lie down some." He feels embarrassed over being so helplessly intoxicated, but he reminds himself that in this city of Dionysus no one need apologize for taking too much wine. He closes his eyes and waits for a little stability to return. In the darkness a vision comes to him: the death of Dave Vogel. With strange brilliant clarity Oxenshuer sees the landscape of Mars spread out on the screen of his mind, low snubby hills sloping down to broad crater-pocked plains, gnarled desolate boulders, purple sky, red gritty particles blowing about. The extravehicular crawler well along on its journey westward toward the Gulliver site, Richardson driving, Vogel busy taking pictures, operating the myriad sensors, leaning into the microphone to describe everything he sees. They are at the Gulliver site now, preparing to leave the crawler, when they are surprised by the sudden onset of the sandstorm. Without warning the sky is red with billowing capes of sand, driving down on them like snowflakes in a blizzard. In the first furious moment of the storm the vehicle is engulfed; within minutes sand is piled a meter high on the crawler's domed transparent roof; they can see nothing, and the sandfall steadily deepens as the storm gains in intensity. Richardson grabs the controls, but the wheels of the crawler will not grip. "I've never seen anything like this," Vogel mutters. The vehicle has extendible perceptors on stalks, but when Vogel pushes them out to their full reach he finds that they are even then hidden by the sand. The crawler's eyes are blinded; its antennae are buried. They are drowning in sand. Whole dunes are descending on them. "I've never seen anything like this," Vogel says again. "You can't imagine it, Johnny. It hasn't been going on five minutes and we must be under three or four meters of sand already." The crawler's engine strains to free them. "Johnny? I can't hear you, Johnny. Come in, Johnny." All is silent on the ship-to-crawler transmission belt. "Hey, Houston," Vogel says, "we've got this goddamned sandstorm going, and I seem to have lost contact with the ship. Can you raise him for us?" Houston does not reply. "Mission Control, are you reading me?" Vogel asks. He still has some idea of setting up a crawler-to-Earth-to-ship relay, but slowly it occurs to him that he has lost contact with Earth as well. All transmissions have ceased. Sweating suddenly in his spacesuit, Vogel shouts into the microphone, jiggles controls, plugs in the fail-safe communications banks only to find that everything has failed; sand has invaded the crawler and holds them in a deadly blanket. "Impossible," Richardson says. "Since when is sand an insulator for radio waves?" Vogel shrugs.

"It isn't a matter of insulation, dummy. It's a matter of total systems breakdown. I don't know why." They must be ten meters underneath the sand now. Entombed. Vogel pounds the hatch, thinking that if they can get out of the crawler somehow they can dig their way to the surface through the loose sand, and then—and then what? Walk back ninety kilometers to the ship? Their suits carry thirty-six-hour breathing supplies. They would have to average two and a half kilometers an hour, over ragged cratered country, in order to get there in time; and with this storm raging their chances of surviving long enough to hike a single kilometer are dismal. Nor does Oxenshuer have a backup crawler in which he could come out to rescue them, even if he knew their plight; there is only the flimsy little one-man vehicle that they use for short-range geological field trips in the vicinity of the ship. "You know what?" Vogel says. "We're dead men, Bud." Richardson shakes his head vehemently. "Don't talk garbage. We'll wait out the storm, and then we'll get the hell out of here. Meanwhile we better just pray." There is no conviction in his voice, however. How will they know when the storm is over? Already they lie deep below the new surface of the Martian plain, and everything is snug and tranquil where they are. Tons of sand hold the crawler's hatch shut. There is no escape. Vogel is right: they are dead men. The only remaining question is one of time. Shall they wait for the crawler's air supply to exhaust itself, or shall they take some more immediate step to hasten the inevitable end, going out honorably and quickly and without pain? Here Oxenshuer's vision falters. He does not know how the trapped men chose to handle the choreography of their deaths. He knows only that whatever their decision was, it must have been reached without bitterness or panic, and that the manner of their departure was calm. The vision fades. He lies alone in the dark. The last of the drunkenness has burned itself from his mind.

"Come on," Matt said. "Let's do some wrestling."

It was a crisp winter morning, not cold, a day of clear, hard light. Matt took him downtown, and for the first time Oxenshuer entered one of the tall brick-faced buildings of the labyrinth streets. Inside was a large, bare gymnasium, unheated, with bleak yellow walls and threadbare purple mats on the floor. Will and Nick were already there. Their voices echoed in the cavernous room. Quickly Matt stripped down to his undershorts. He looked even bigger naked than clothed; his muscles were thick and rounded, his chest was formidably deep, his thighs were pillars. A dense covering of fair curly hair sprouted everywhere on him, even his back and shoulders. He stood at least two meters tall and must have weighed close to 110 kilos. Oxenshuer, tall but not nearly so tall as Matt, well built but at least twenty kilos lighter, felt himself badly outmatched. He was quick and agile, at any rate: perhaps those qualities would serve him. He tossed his clothing aside.

Matt looked him over closely. "Not bad," he said. "Could use a little more meat on the bones."

"Got to fatten him up some for the Feast, I guess," Will said. He grinned amiably. The three men laughed; the remark seemed less funny to Oxenshuer.

Matt signaled to Nick, who took a flask of wine from a locker and handed it to him. Uncorking it, Matt drank deeply and passed the flask to Oxenshuer. It was different from the usual table stuff: thicker, sweeter, almost a sacramental wine. Oxenshuer gulped it down. Then they went to the center mat.

They hunkered into crouches and circled one another tentatively, outstretched arms probing for an opening. Oxenshuer made the first move. He slipped in quickly, finding Matt surprisingly slow on his guard and unsophisticated in defensive technique. Nevertheless, the big man was able to break Oxenshuer's hold with one fierce toss of his body, shaking him off easily and sending him sprawling violently backward. Again they circled. Matt seemed willing to allow Oxenshuer every initiative. Warily Oxenshuer advanced, feinted toward Matt's shoulders, seized an arm instead; but Matt placidly ignored the gambit and somehow pivoted so that Oxenshuer was caught in the momentum of his own onslaught, thrown off balance, vulnerable to a bearhug. Matt forced him to the floor. For thirty seconds or so Oxenshuer stubbornly resisted him, arching his body; then Matt pinned him. They rolled apart and Nick proffered the wine again. Oxenshuer drank, gasping between pulls. "You've got good moves," Matt told him. But he took the second fall even more quickly, and the third with not very much greater effort. "Don't worry," Will murmured to Oxenshuer as they left the gym. "The day of the Feast, the saint will guide you against him."

✺

Every night, now, he drinks heavily, until his face is flushed and his mind is dizzied. Matt, Will, and Nick are always close beside him, seeing to it that his cup never stays dry for long. The wine makes him hazy and groggy, and frequently he has visions as he lies in a stupor on his bed, recovering. He sees Claire Vogel's face glowing in the dark, and the sight of her wrings his heart with love. He engages in long dreamlike imaginary dialogues with the Speaker on the nature of ecstatic communion. He sees himself dancing in the god-house with the other city folk, dancing himself to exhaustion and ecstasy. He is even visited by St. Dionysus. That saint has a youthful and oddly innocent appearance, with a heavy belly, plump thighs, curling golden hair, a flowing golden beard; he looks like a rejuvenated Santa Claus. "Come," he says softly. "Let's go to the ocean." He takes Oxenshuer's hand and they drift through the silent dark streets, toward the desert, across the swirling dunes, floating in the night, until they reach a broad-bosomed sea, moonlight blazing on its surface like cold white fire. What sea is this? The saint says, "This is the sea that brought you to the world, the undying sea that carries every mortal into life. Why do you ever leave the sea? Here. Step into it with me." Oxenshuer enters. The water is warm, comforting, oddly viscous. He gives himself to it, ankle-deep, shin-deep, thigh-deep; he hears a low murmuring song rising from the gentle waves, and he feels all sorrow going from him, all pain, all sense of himself as a being apart from others. Bathers bob on the breast of the sea. Look: Dave Vogel is here, and Claire, and his parents, and his grandparents, and thousands more whom he does not know, millions, even, a horde stretching far out from shore, all the progeny of Adam, even Adam himself, yes, and Mother Eve, her soft pink body aglow in the water. "Rest," the saint whispers. "Drift. Float. Surrender. Sleep. Give yourself to the ocean, dear John." Oxenshuer asks if he will find God in this ocean. The saint replies, "God is the ocean. And God. is within you. He always has been. The ocean is God. You are God. I am God. God is everywhere, John, and we are His indivisible atoms. God is everywhere. But before all else, God is within you."

What does the Speaker say? The Speaker speaks Freudian wisdom. Within us all, he says, there dwells a force, an entity—call it the unconscious; it's as good a name as any—that from its hiding place dominates and controls our lives, though its workings are mysterious and opaque to us. A god within our skulls. We have lost contact with that god, the Speaker says; we are unable to reach it or to comprehend its powers, and so we are divided against ourselves, cut off from the chief source of our strength and cut off, too, from one another: the god that is within me no longer has a way to reach the god that is within you, though you and I both came out of the same primordial ocean, out of that sea of divine unconsciousness in which all being is one. If we could tap that force, the Speaker says, if we could make contact with that hidden god, if we could make it rise into consciousness or allow ourselves to submerge into the realm of unconsciousness, the split in our souls would be healed and we would at last have full access to our godhood. Who knows what kind of creatures we would become then? We would speak, mind to mind. We would travel through space or time, merely by willing it. We would work miracles. The errors of the past could be undone; the patterns of old griefs could be rewoven. We might be able to do anything, the Speaker says, once we have reached that hidden god and transformed ourselves into the gods we were meant to be. Anything. Anything. Anything.

This is the dawn of the day of the Feast. All night long the drums and incantations have resounded through the city; he has been alone in the house, for not even the children were there; everyone was dancing in the plaza, and only he, the uninitiated, remained excluded from the revels. Much of the night he could not sleep. He thought of using wine to lull himself, but he feared the visions the wine might bring, and let the flask be. Now it is early morning, and he must have slept, for he finds himself fluttering up from slumber, but he does not remember having slipped down into it. He sits up. He hears footsteps, someone moving through the house. "John? You awake, John?" Matt's voice. "In here," Oxenshuer calls.

They enter his room: Matt, Will, Nick. Their robes are spotted with splashes of red wine, and their faces are gaunt, eyes red-rimmed and unnaturally bright; plainly they have been up all night. Behind their fatigue, though, Oxenshuer perceives exhilaration. They are high, very high, almost in an ecstatic state already, and it is only the dawn of the day of the Feast. He sees that their fingers are trembling. Their bodies are tense with expectation.

"We've come for you," Matt says. "Here. Put this on."

He tosses Oxenshuer a robe similar to theirs. All this time Oxenshuer has continued to wear his mundane clothes in the city, making him a marked man, a conspicuous outsider. Naked, he gets out of bed and picks up his undershorts, but Matt shakes his head. Today, he says, only robes are worn. Oxenshuer nods and pulls the robe over his bare body. When he is robed he steps forward; Matt solemnly embraces him, a strong warm hug, and then Will and Nick do the same. The four men leave the house. The long shadows of dawn stretch across the avenue that leads to the labyrinth; the mountains beyond the city are tipped with red. Far ahead, where the avenue gives way to the narrower streets, a tongue of black smoke can be seen licking the sky. The reverberations of the music batter the sides of the buildings. Oxenshuer feels a strange onrush of confidence and is certain he could negotiate the labyrinth unaided this morning; as they reach its outer border he is actually walking ahead of the others, but sudden confusion confounds him, an inability to distinguish one winding street from another comes over him, and he drops back in silence, allowing Matt to take the lead.

Ten minutes later they reach the plaza.

It presents a crowded, chaotic scene. All the city folk are there, some dancing, some singing, some beating on drums or blowing into trumpets, some lying sprawled in exhaustion. Despite the chill in the air, many robes hang open, and more than a few of the citizens have discarded their clothing entirely. Children run about, squealing and playing tag. Along the front of the dining hall a series of wine barrels has been installed, and the wine. gushes freely from the spigots, drenching those who thrust cups forward or simply push their lips to the flow. To the rear, before the house of the Speaker, a wooden platform has sprouted, and the Speaker and the city elders sit enthroned upon it. A gigantic bonfire has been kindled in the center of the plaza, fed by logs from an immense woodpile—hauled no doubt from some storehouse in the labyrinth—that occupies some twenty square meters. The heat of this blaze is enormous, and it is the smoke from the bonfire that Oxenshuer was able to see from the city's edge.

His arrival in the plaza serves as a signal. Within moments, all is still. The music dies away; the dancing stops; the singers grow quiet; no one moves. Oxenshuer, flanked by his sponsors Nick and Will and preceded by his brother Matt, advances uneasily toward the throne of the Speaker. The old man rises and makes a gesture, evidently a blessing.

"Dionysus receives you into his bosom," the Speaker says, his resonant voice traveling far across the plaza. "Drink, and let the saint heal your soul. Drink, and let the holy ocean engulf you. Drink. Drink."

"Drink," Matt says, and guides him toward the barrels. A girl of about fourteen, naked, sweat-shiny, wine-soaked, hands him a cup. Oxenshuer fills it and puts it to his lips. It is the thick, sweet wine, the sacramental wine that he had had on the morning he had practiced wrestling with Matt. It slides easily down his throat; he reaches for more, and then for more when that is gone.

At a signal from the Speaker, the music begins again. The frenzied dancing resumes. Three naked men hurl more logs on the fire and it blazes up ferociously, sending sparks nearly as high as the tip of the cross above the church. Nick and Will and Matt lead Oxenshuer into a circle of dancers who are moving in a whirling, dizzying step around the fire, shouting, chanting, stamping against the cobbles, flinging their arms aloft. At first Oxenshuer is put off by the uninhibited corybantic motions and finds himself self-conscious about imitating them, but as the wine reaches his brain he sheds all embarrassment, and prances with as much gusto as the others: he ceases to be a spectator of himself and becomes fully a participant. Whirl. Stamp. Fling. Shout. Whirl. Stamp. Fling. Shout. The dance centrifuges his mind; pools of blood collect at the walls of his skull and flush the convolutions of his cerebellum as he spins. The heat of the fire makes his skin glow. He sings:

Tell the saint to heat my heart
Tell the saint to give me breath
Tell the saint to quench my thirst

Thirst. When he has been dancing so long that his breath is fire in his throat, he staggers out of the circle and helps himself freely at a spigot. His greed for the thick wine astonishes him. It is as if he has been parched for centuries, every cell of his body shrunken and withered, and only the wine can restore him.

Back to the circle again. His head throbs; his bare feet slap the cobbles; his arms claw the sky. This is the god whose name is music. This is the god whose soul is wine. There are ninety or a hundred people in the central circle of dancers now, and other circles have formed in the corners of the plaza, so that the entire square is a nest of dazzling interlocking vortices of motion. He is being drawn into these vortices, sucked out of himself; he is losing all sense of himself as a discrete individual entity.

Leaping shouting singing stamping
Rising climbing flying soaring
Melting joining loving blazing
Singing soaring joining loving

"Come," Matt murmurs. "It's time for us to do some wrestling." He discovers that they have constructed a wrestling pit in the far corner of the plaza, over in front of the church. It is square, four low wooden borders about ten meters long on each side, filled with the coarse sand of the desert. The Speaker has shifted his lofty seat so that he now faces the pit; everyone else is crowded around the place of the wrestling, and all dancing has once again stopped. The crowd opens to admit Matt and Oxenshuer. Not far from the pit Matt shucks his robe; his powerful naked body glistens with sweat. Oxenshuer, after only a moment's hesitation, strips also. They advance toward the entrance of the pit. Before they enter, a boy brings them each a flask of wine. Oxenshuer, already feeling wobbly and hazy from drink, wonders what more wine will do to his physical coordination, but he takes the flask and drinks from it in great gulping swigs. In moments it is empty. A young girl offers him another. "Just take a few sips," Matt advises. "In honor of the god." Oxenshuer does as he is told. Matt is sipping from a second flask too; without warning, Matt grins and flings the contents of his flask over Oxenshuer. Instantly Oxenshuer retaliates. A great cheer goes up; both men are soaked with the sticky red wine. Matt laughs heartily and claps Oxenshuer on the back. They enter the wrestling pit.

Wine in my heart today,
Blood in my throat today,
Fire in my soul today,
All praise, O God, to thee.

They circle one another warily. Brother against brother. Romulus and Remus, Cain and Abel, Osiris and Set: the ancient ritual, the timeless conflict. Neither man offers. Oxenshuer feels heavy with wine, his brain clotted, and yet a strange lightness also possesses him; each time he puts his foot down against the sand the contact gives him a little jolt of ecstasy. He is excitingly aware of being alive, mobile, vigorous. The sensation grows and possesses him, and he rushes forward suddenly, seizes Matt, tries to force him down. They struggle in almost motionless rigidity. Matt will not fall, but his counterthrust is unavailing against Oxenshuer. They stand locked, body against sweat-slick, wine-drenched body, and after perhaps two minutes of intense tension they give up their holds by unvoiced agreement, backing away trembling from one another. They circle again. Brother. Brother. Abel. Cain. Oxenshuer crouches. Extends his hands, groping for a hold. Again they leap toward one another. Again they grapple and freeze. This time Matt's arms pass like bands around Oxenshuer, and he tries to lift Oxenshuer from the ground and hurl him down. Oxenshuer does not budge. Veins swell in Matt's forehead, and, Oxenshuer suspects, in his own. Faces grow crimson. Muscles throb with sustained effort. Matt gasps, loosens his grip, tries to step back; instantly Oxenshuer steps to one side of the bigger man, catches his arm, pulls him close. Once more they hug. Each in turn, they sway but do not topple. Wine and exertion blur Oxenshuer's vision; he is intoxicated with strain. Heaving, grabbing, twisting, shoving, he goes around and around the pit with Matt, until abruptly he experiences a dimming of perception, a sharp moment of blackout, and when his senses return to him he is stunned to find himself wrestling not with Matt but with Dave Vogel. Childhood friend, rival in love, comrade in space. Vogel, closer to him than any brother of the flesh, now here in the pit with him: thin, sandy hair, snub nose, heavy brows, thick-muscled shoulders. "Dave!" Oxenshuer cries. "Oh, Christ, Dave! Dave!" He throws his arms around the other man. Vogel gives him a mild smile and tumbles to the floor of the pit. "Dave!" Oxenshuer shouts, falling on him. "How did you get here, Dave?" He covers Vogel's body with his own. He embraces him with a terrible grip. He murmurs Vogel's name, whispering in wonder, and lets a thousand questions tumble out. Does Vogel reply? Oxenshuer is not certain. He thinks he hears answers, but they do not match the questions. Then Oxenshuer feels fingers tapping his back. "Okay, John," Will is saying. "You've pinned him fair and square. It's all over. Get up, man."

"Here, I'll give you a hand," says Nick.

In confusion Oxenshuer rises. Matt lies sprawled in the sand, gasping for breath, rubbing the side of his neck, nevertheless still grinning. "That was one hell of a press," Matt says. "That something you learned in college?"

"Do we wrestle another fall now?" Oxenshuer asks.

"No need. We go to the god-house now," Will tells him. They help Matt up. Flasks of wine are brought to them; Oxenshuer gulps greedily. The four of them leave the pit, pass through the opening crowd, and walk toward the church.

Oxenshuer has never been in here before. Except for a sort of altar at the far end, the huge building is wholly empty: no pews, no chairs, no chapels, no pulpit, no choir. A mysterious light filters through the stained-glass windows and suffuses the vast open interior space. The Speaker has already arrived; he stands before the altar. Oxenshuer, at a whispered command from Matt, kneels in front of him. Matt kneels to Oxenshuer's left; Nick and Will drop down behind them. Organ music, ghostly, ethereal, begins to filter from concealed grillwork. The congregation is assembling; Oxenshuer hears the rustle of people behind him, coughs, some murmuring. The familiar hymns soon echo through the church.

I go to the god's house and his fire consumes me
I cry the god's name and his thunder deafens me
I take the god's cup and his wine dissolves me

Wine. The Speaker offers Oxenshuer a golden chalice. Oxenshuer sips. A different wine: cold, thin. Behind him a new hymn commences, one that he has never heard before, in a language he does not understand. Greek? The rhythms are angular and fierce; this is the music of the Bacchantes, this is an Orphic song, alien and frightening at first, then oddly comforting. Oxenshuer is barely conscious. He comprehends nothing. They are offering him communion. A wafer on a silver dish: dark bread, crisp, incised with an unfamiliar symbol. Take; eat. This is my body. This is my blood. More wine. Figures moving around him, other communicants coming forward. He is losing all sense of time and place. He is departing from the physical dimension and drifting across the breast of an ocean, a great warm sea, a gentle undulating sea that bears him easily and gladly. He is aware of light, warmth, hugeness, weightlessness; but he is aware of nothing tangible. The wine. The wafer. A drug in the wine, perhaps? He slides from the world and into the universe. This is my body. This is my blood. This is the experience of wholeness and unity. I take the god's cup and his wine dissolves me. How calm it is here. How empty. There's no one here, not even me. And everything radiates a pure warm light. I float. I go forth. I. I. I. John Oxenshuer. John Oxenshuer does not exist. John Oxenshuer is the universe. The universe is John Oxenshuer. This is the god whose soul is wine. This is the god whose name is music. This is the god who burns like fire. Sweet flame of oblivion. The cosmos is expanding like a balloon. Growing. Growing. Go, child, swim out to God. Jesus waits. The saint, the mad saint, the boozy old god who is a saint, will lead you to bliss, dear John. Make yourself whole. Make yourself into nothingness. I go to the god's house and his fire consumes me. Go. Go. Go. I cry the god's name and his thunder deafens me. *Dionysus! Dionysus!*

All things dissolve. All things become one.

This is Mars. Oxenshuer, running his ship on manual, lets it dance lightly down the final 500 meters to the touchdown site, touching up the yaw and pitch, moving serenely through the swirling red clouds that his rockets are kicking free. Contact light. Engine stop. Engine arm, off.

—All right, Houston, I've landed at Gulliver Base.

His signal streaks across space. Patiently he waits out the lag and gets his reply from Mission Control at last:

—Roger. Are you ready for systems checkout prior to EVA?

—Getting started on it right now, Houston.

He runs through his routines quickly, with the assurance born of total familiarity. All is well aboard the ship; its elegant mechanical brain ticks beautifully and flawlessly. Now Oxenshuer wriggles into his backpack, struggling a little with the cumbersome life-support system; putting it on without any fellow astronauts to help him is more of a chore than he expected, even under the light Martian gravity. He checks out his primary oxygen supply, his ventilating system, his water-support loop, his communications system. Helmeted and gloved and fully sealed, he exists now within a totally self-sufficient pocket universe. Unshipping his power shovel, he tests its compressed-air supply. All systems go.

—Do I have a go for cabin depressurization, Houston?

—You are go for cabin depress, John. It's all yours. Go for cabin depress.

He gives the signal and waits for the pressure to bleed down. Dials flutter. At last he can open the hatch. We have a go for EVA, John. He hoists his power shovel to his shoulder and makes his way carefully down the ladder. Boots bite into red sand. It is midday on Mars in this longitude, and the purple sky has a warm auburn glow. Oxenshuer approaches the burial mound. He is pleased to discover that he has relatively little excavating to do; the force of his rockets during the descent has stripped much of the overburden from his friends' tomb. Swiftly he sets the shovel in place and begins to cut away the remaining sand. Within minutes the glistening dome of the crawler is visible in several places. Now Oxenshuer works more delicately, scraping with care until he has revealed the entire dome. He flashes his light through it and sees the bodies of Vogel and Richardson. They are unhelmeted, and their suits are open: casual dress, the best outfit for dying. Vogel sits at the crawler's controls, Richardson lies just behind him on the floor of the vehicle. Their faces are dry, almost fleshless, but their features are still expressive, and Oxenshuer realizes that they must have died peaceful deaths, accepting the end in tranquility. Patiently he works to lift the crawler's dome. At length the catch yields and the dome swings upward. Climbing in, he slips his arms around Dave Vogel's body and draws it out of the spacesuit. So light: a mummy, an effigy. Vogel seems to have no weight at all. Easily Oxenshuer carries the parched corpse over to the ship. With Vogel in his arms he ascends the ladder. Within, he breaks out the flag-sheathed plastic container NASA has provided and tenderly wraps it around the body. He stows Vogel safely in the ship's hold. Then he returns to the crawler to get Bud Richardson. Within an hour the entire job is done.

—Mission accomplished, Houston.

The landing capsule plummets perfectly into the Pacific: .. The recovery ship, only three kilometers away, makes for the scene while the helicopters move into position over the bobbing spaceship. Frogmen come forth to secure the flotation collar: the old, old routine. In no time at all the hatch is open. Oxenshuer emerges. The helicopter closest to the capsule lowers its recovery basket, Oxenshuer disappears into the capsule, returning a moment later with Vogel's shrouded body, which he passes across to the swimmers. They load it into the basket and it goes up to the helicopter. Richardson's body follows, and then Oxenshuer himself.

The President is waiting on the deck of the recovery ship. With him are the two widows, black-garbed, dry-eyed, standing straight and firm. The President offers Oxenshuer a warm grin and grips his hand.

—A beautiful job, Captain Oxenshuer. The whole world is grateful to you.

—Thank you, sir.

Oxenshuer embraces the widows. Richardson's wife first: a hug and some soft murmurs of consolation. Then he draws Claire close, conscious of the television cameras. Chastely he squeezes her. Chastely he presses his cheek briefly to hers.

—I had to bring him back, Claire. I couldn't rest until I recovered those bodies.

—You didn't need to, John.

—I did it for you.

He smiles at her. Her eyes are bright and loving.

There is a ceremony on deck. The President bestows posthumous medals on Richardson and Vogel. Oxenshuer wonders whether the medals will be attached to the bodies, like morgue tags, but no, he gives them to the widows. Then Oxenshuer receives a medal for his dramatic return to Mars. The President makes a little speech. Oxenshuer pretends to listen, but his eyes are on Claire more often than not.

With Claire sitting beside him, he sets forth once more out of Los Angeles via the San Bernardino Freeway, eastward through the plastic suburbs, through Alhambra and Azusa, past the Covina Hills Forest Lawn, through San Bernardino and Banning and Indio, out into the desert. It is a bright late-winter day, and recent rains have greened the hills and coaxed the cacti into bloom. He keeps a sharp watch for landmarks: flatlands, dry lakes.

—I think this is the place. In fact, I'm sure of it.

He leaves the freeway and guides the car northeastward. Yes, no doubt of it: there's the ancient lake bed, and there's his abandoned automobile, looking ancient also, rusted and corroded, its hood up, its wheels and engine stripped by scavengers long ago. He parks this car beside it, gets out, dons his backpack. He beckons to Claire.

—Let's go. We've got some hiking ahead of us.

She smiles timidly at him. She leaves the car and presses herself lightly against him, touching her lips to his. He begins to tremble.

—Claire. Oh, God, Claire.

—How far do we have to walk?

—Hours.

He gears his pace to hers. If necessary, they will camp overnight and go on into the city tomorrow, but he hopes they can get there before sundown. Claire is a strong hiker, and he is confident she can cover the distance in five or six hours, but there is always the possibility that he will fail to find the twin mesas. He has no compass points, no maps, nothing but his own intuitive sense of the city's location to guide him. They walk steadily northward. Neither of them says very much. Every half hour they pause to rest; he puts down his pack and she hands him the canteen. The air is mild and fragrant. Jackrabbits boldly accompany them. Blossoms are everywhere. Oxenshuer, transfigured by love, wants to leap and soar.

—We ought to be seeing those mesas soon.

—I hope so. I'm starting to get tired, John.

—We can stop and make camp if you like.

—No. No. Let's keep going. It can't be much farther, can it? They keep going. Oxenshuer calculates they have covered twelve or thirteen kilometers already. Even allowing for some straying from course, they should be getting at least a glimpse of the mesas by this time, and it troubles him that they are not in view. If he fails to find them in the next half hour, he will make camp, for he wants to avoid hiking after sundown.

Suddenly they breast a rise in the desert and the mesas come into view, two steep wedges of rock, dark grey against the sand. The shadows of late afternoon partially cloak them, but there is no mistaking them.

—There they are, Claire. Out there.

—Can you see the city?

—Not from this distance. We've come around from the side, somehow. But we'll be there before very long.

At a faster pace, now, they head down the gentle slope and into the flats. The mesas dominate the scene. Oxenshuer's heart pounds, not entirely from the strain of carrying his pack. Ahead wait Matt and Jean, Will and Nick, the Speaker, the god-house, the labyrinth. They will welcome Claire as his woman; they will give them a small house on the edge of the city; they will initiate her into their rites. Soon. Soon. The mesas draw near.

—Where's the city, John?

—Between the mesas.

—I don't see it.

—You can't really see it from the front. All that's visible is the palisade, and when you get very close you can see some rooftops above it.

—But I don't even see the palisade, John. There's just an open space between the mesas.

—A shadow effect. The eye is easily tricked.

But it does seem odd to him. At twilight, yes, many deceptions are possible; nevertheless he has the clear impression from here that there is nothing but open space between the mesas. Can these be the wrong mesas? Hardly. Their shape is distinctive and unique; he could never confuse those two jutting slabs with other formations. The city, then? Where has the city gone? With each step he takes he grows more perturbed. He tries to hide his uneasiness from Claire, but she is tense, edgy, almost panicky now, repeatedly asking him what has happened, whether they are lost. He reassures her as best he can. This is the right place, he tells her. Perhaps it's an optical illusion that the city is invisible, or perhaps some other kind of illusion, the work of the city folk.

—Does that mean they might not want us, John? And they're hiding their city from us?

—I don't know, Claire.

—I'm frightened.

—Don't be. We'll have all the answers in just a few minutes.

When they are about 500 meters from the face of the mesas Claire's control breaks. She whimpers and darts forward, sprinting through the cacti toward the opening between the mesas. He calls out to her, tells her to wait for him, but she runs on, vanishing into the deepening shadows. Hampered by his unwieldy pack, he stumbles after her, gasping for breath. He sees her disappear between the mesas. Weak and dizzy, he follows her path, and in a short while comes to the mouth of the canyon.

There is no city.

He does not see Claire.

He calls her name. Only mocking echoes respond. In wonder he penetrates the canyon, looking up at the steep sides of the mesas, remembering streets, avenues, houses.

—Claire?

No one. Nothing. And now night is coming. He picks his way over the rocky, uneven ground until he reaches the far end of the canyon, and looks back at the mesas, and outward at the desert, and he sees no one. The city has swallowed her and the city is gone.

—Claire! Claire!

Silence.

He drops his pack wearily, sits for a long while, finally lays out his bedroll. He slips into it but does not sleep; he waits out the night, and when dawn comes he searches again for Claire, but there is no trace of her. All right. All right. He yields. He will ask no questions. He shoulders his pack and begins the long trek back to the highway.

By mid-morning he reaches his car. He looks back at the desert, ablaze with noon light. Then he gets in and drives away.

He enters his apartment on Hollywood Boulevard. From here, so many months ago, he first set out for the desert; now all has come around to the beginning again. A thick layer of dust covers the cheap utilitarian furniture. The air is musty. All the blinds are drawn closed. He wanders aimlessly from hallway to living room, from living room to bedroom, from bedroom to kitchen, from kitchen to hallway. He kicks off his boots and sprawls out on the threadbare living-room carpet, face down, eyes closed. So tired. So drained. I'll rest a bit.

"John?"

It is the Speaker's voice.

"Let me alone," Oxenshuer says. "I've lost her. I've lost you. I think I've lost myself."

"You're wrong. Come to us, John."

"I did. You weren't there."

"Come now. Can't you feel the city calling you? The Feast is over. It's time to settle down among us."

"I couldn't find you."

"You were still lost in dreams, then. Come now. Come. The saint calls you. Jesus calls you. Claire calls you."

"Claire?"

"Claire," he says.

Slowly Oxenshuer gets to his feet. He crosses the room and pulls the blinds open. This window faces Hollywood Boulevard; but, looking out, he sees only the red plains of Mars, eroded and cratered, glowing in purple noon light. Vogel and Richardson are out there, waving to him. Smiling. Beckoning. The faceplates of their helmets glitter by the cold gleam of the stars. Come on, they call to him. We're waiting for you. Oxenshuer returns their greeting and walks to another window. He sees a lifeless wasteland here too. Mars again, or is it only the Mojave Desert? He is unable to tell. All is dry, all is desolate, all is beautiful with the serene transcendent beauty of desolation. He sees Claire in the middle distance. Her back is to him; she is moving at a steady, confident pace toward the twin mesas. Between the mesas lies the City of the Word of God, golden and radiant in the warm sunlight. Oxenshuer nods. This is the right moment. He will go to her. He will go to the city. The Feast of St. Dionysus is over and the city calls to him.

Bring us together. Lead us to the ocean.
Help us to swim. Give us to drink.
Wine in my heart today,
Blood in my throat today,
Fire in my soul today,

All praise, O God, to thee.

Oxenshuer runs in long loping strides. He sees the mesas; he sees the city's palisade. The sound of far-off chanting throbs in his ears. "This way, brother!" Matt shouts. "Hurry, John!" Claire cries. He runs. He stumbles, and recovers, and runs again. Wine in my heart today. Fire in my soul today. "God is everywhere," the saint tells him. "But before all else, God is within you." The desert is a sea, the great warm cradling ocean, the undying mother sea of all things, and Oxenshuer enters it gladly, and drifts, and floats, and lets it take hold of him and carry him wherever it will.

WHAT WE LEARNED FROM THIS MORNING'S NEWSPAPER

And here we have a story built around one of the most familiar of all science-fictional concepts, the supposed advantages to be had by getting an advance peek at tomorrow's news. In the olden days every pulpster in the business had a crack at writing the story that was usually called something like "The Man Who Saw Tomorrow," with results that usually were as predictable to the reader as they would have been to the protagonist, although in the hands of real masters the theme carried plenty of impact. (I think particularly of C.M. Kornbluth's acidulous little story, "Dominoes," and Philip K. Dick's novel The World Jones Made.*)*

Playing games with time has long been one of my own obsessions as a storyteller, and so it's not surprising that I, too, have written "The Man Who Saw Tomorrow," not once but a number of times. Here's one example. I feel no guilt whatever over having offered the world yet another the-next-day's-newspaper story. My version of the theme has its own original touches, its own individual stylistic flourishes, its own properly Silverbergian ending, and so be it: here it is, without apologies. I wrote it in January, 1972, and Bob Hoskins published it in the fourth volume of his anthology Infinity.

1.

I got home from the office as usual at 6:47 this evening and discovered that our peaceful street has been in some sort of crazy uproar all day. The newsboy it seems came by today and delivered the New York Times for Wednesday December 1 to every house on Redbud Crescent. Since today is Monday November 22 it follows therefore that Wednesday December 1 is the middle of next week. I said to my wife are you sure that this really happened? Because I looked at the newspaper myself before I went off to work this morning and it seemed quite all right to me.

At breakfast time the newspaper could be printed in Albanian and it would seem quite all right to you my wife replied. Here look at this. And she took the newspaper from the hall closet and handed it all folded up to me. It looked just like any other edition of the *New York Times* but I saw what I had failed to notice at breakfast time, that it said Wednesday December 1.

Is today the 22nd of November I asked? Monday?

It certainly is my wife told me. Yesterday was Sunday and tomorrow is going to be Tuesday and we haven't even come to Thanksgiving yet. Bill what are we going to do about this?

I glanced through the newspaper. The front page headlines were nothing remarkable I must admit, just the same old *New York Times* stuff that you get any day when there hasn't been some event of cosmic importance. NIXON, WITH WIFE, TO VISIT 3 CHINESE CITIES IN 7 DAYS. Yes. 10 HURT AS GUNMEN SHOOT WAY INTO AND OUT OF BANK. All right. GROUP OF 10, IN ROME, BEGINS NEGOTIATING REALIGNMENT OF CURRENCIES. Okay. The same old *New York Times* stuff and no surprises. But the paper was dated Wednesday December 1 and that was a surprise of sorts I guess.

This is only a joke I told my wife.

Who would do such a thing for a joke? To print up a whole newspaper? It's impossible Bill.

It's also impossible to get next week's newspaper delivered this week you know or hadn't you considered what I said?

She shrugged and I picked up the second section. I opened to page fifty which contained the obituary section and I admit I felt quite queasy for a moment since after all this might not be any joke and what would it be like to find my own name there? To my relief the people whose obituaries I saw were Harry Rogoff Terry Turner Dr. M. A. Feinstein and John Millis. I will not say that the deaths of these people gave me any pleasure but better them than me of course. I even looked at the death notices in small type but there was no listing for me. Next I turned to the sports section and saw KNICKS' STREAK ENDED, 110-109. We had been talking about going to get tickets for that game at the office and my first thought now was that it isn't worth bothering to see it. Then I remembered you can bet on basketball games and I knew who was going to win and that made me feel very strange. So also I felt odd to look at the bottom of page sixty-four where they had the results of the racing at Yonkers Raceway and then quickly flip flip flip I was on page sixty-nine and the financial section lay before my eyes. DOW INDEX RISES BY 1.61 TO 831.34 the headline said. National Cash Register was the most active stock closing at 27 off $\frac{1}{4}$. Then Eastman Kodak 88 down $1\frac{1}{8}$. By this time I was starting to sweat very hard and I gave my wife the paper and took off my jacket and tie.

I said how many people have their newspaper?

Everybody on Redbud Crescent she said that's eleven houses altogether.

And nowhere beyond our street?

No the others got the ordinary paper today we've been checking on that.

Who's we I asked?

Marie and Cindy and I she said. Cindy was the one who noticed about the paper first and called me and then we all got together and talked about it. Bill what are we going to do? We have the stock market prices and everything Bill.

If it isn't a joke I told her.

It looks like the real paper doesn't it Bill?

I think I want a drink I said. My hands were shaking all of a sudden and the sweat was still coming. I had to laugh because it was just the other Saturday night some of us were talking about the utter predictable regularity of life out here in the suburbs the dull smooth sameness of it all. And now this. The newspaper from the middle of next week. It's like God was listening to us and laughed up His sleeve and said to Gabriel or whoever it's time to send those stuffed shirts on Redbud Crescent a little excitement.

2.

After dinner Jerry Wesley called and said we're having a meeting at our place tonight Bill can you and your lady come?

I asked him what the meeting was about and he said it's about the newspaper.

Oh yes I said. The newspaper. What about the newspaper?

Come to the meeting he said I really don't want to talk about this on the phone.

Of course we'll have to arrange a sitter Jerry.

No you won't we've already arranged it he told me. The three Fischer girls are going to look after all the kids on the block. So just come over around quarter to nine.

Jerry is an insurance broker very successful at that he has the best house on the Crescent, two-story Tudor style with almost an acre of land and a big paneled rumpus room in the basement. That's where the meeting took place. We were the seventh couple to arrive and soon after us the Maxwells the Bruces and the Thomasons came in. Folding chairs were set out and Cindy Wesley had done her usual great trays of canapés and such and there was a lot of liquor, self-service at the bar. Jerry stood up in front of everybody and grinned and said I guess you've all been wondering why I called you together this evening. He held up his copy of the newspaper. From where I was sitting I could make out only one headline clearly it was 10 HURT AS GUNMEN SHOOT WAY INTO AND OUT OF BANK but that was enough to enable me to recognize it as the newspaper.

Jerry said did all of you get a copy of this paper today?

Everybody nodded.

You know Jerry said that this paper gives us some extraordinary opportunities to improve our situation in life. I mean if we can accept it as the real December 1 edition and not some kind of fantastic hoax then I don't need to tell you what sort of benefits we can get from it, right?

Sure Bob Thomason said but what makes anybody think it isn't a hoax? I mean next week's newspaper who could believe that?

Jerry looked at Mike Nesbit. Mike teaches at Columbia Law and is more of an intellectual than most of us.

Mike said well of course the obvious conclusion is that somebody's playing a joke on us. But have you looked at the newspaper closely?

Every one of those stories has been written in a perfectly legitimate way. There aren't any details that ring false. It isn't like one of those papers where the headlines have been cooked up but the body of the text is an old edition. So we have to consider the probabilities. Which sounds more fantastic? That someone would take the trouble of composing an entire fictional edition of the *Times* setting it in type printing it and having it delivered or that through some sort of fluke of the fourth dimension we've been allowed a peek at next week's newspaper? Personally I don't find either notion easy to believe but I can accept fourth-dimensional hocus-pocus more readily than I can the idea of a hoax. For one thing unless you've had a team the size of the *Times'* own staff working on this newspaper it would take months and months to prepare it and there's no way that anybody could have begun work on the paper more than a few days in advance because there are things in it that nobody could have possibly known as recently as a week ago. Like the Phase Two stuff and the fighting between India and Pakistan.

But how could we get next week's newspaper Bob Thomason still wanted to know?

I can't answer that said Mike Nesbit. I can only reply that I am willing to accept it as genuine. A miracle if you like.

So am I said Tim McDermott and a few others said the same.

We can make a pile of money out of this thing said Dave Bruce.

Everybody began to smile in a strange strained way. Obviously everybody had looked at the stock market stuff and the racetrack stuff and had come to the same conclusions.

Jerry said there's one important thing we ought to find out first. Has anybody here spoken about this newspaper to anybody who isn't currently in this room?

People said nope and uh-uh and not me.

Good said Jerry. I propose we keep it that way. We don't notify the *Times* and we don't tell Walter Cronkite and we don't even let our brother-in-law on Dogwood Lane know, right? We just put our newspapers away in a safe place and quietly do whatever we want to do about the information we've got. Okay? Let's put that to a vote. All in favor of stamping this newspaper top secret raise your right hand.

Twenty-two hands went up.

Good said Jerry. That includes the kids you realize. If you let the kids know anything they'll want to bring the paper to school for show and tell for Christ's sake. So cool it you hear?

Sid Fischer said are we going to work together on exploiting this thing or do we each act independently?

Independently said Dave Bruce.

Right independently said Bud Maxwell.

It went all around the room that way. The only one who wanted some sort of committee system was Charlie Harris. Charlie has bad luck in the stock market and I guess he was afraid to take any risks even with a sure thing like next week's paper. Jerry called for a vote and it came out ten to one in favor of individual enterprise. Of course if anybody wants to team up with anybody else I said there's nothing stopping anybody.

As we started to adjourn for refreshments Jerry said remember you only have a week to make use of what you've been handed. By the first of December this is going to be just another newspaper and a million other people will have copies of it. So move fast while you've got an advantage.

3.

The trouble is when they give you only next week's paper you don't ordinarily have a chance to make a big killing in the market. I mean stocks don't generally go up fifty per cent or eighty per cent in just a few trading sessions. The really broad swings take weeks or months to develop. Still and all I figured I could make out all right with the data I had. For one thing there evidently was going to be a pretty healthy rally over the next few days. According to the afternoon edition of the *Post* that I brought home with me the market had been off seven on the 22nd, closing with the Dow at 803.15, the lowest all year. But the December 1 *Times* mentioned "`a stunning two-day advance" and the average finished at 831.34 on the 30th. Not bad. Then too I could work on margin and other kinds of leverage to boost my return. We're going to make a pile out of this I told my wife.

If you can trust that newspaper she said.

I told her not to worry. When we got home from Jerry's I spread out the *Post* and the *Times* in the den and started hunting for stocks that moved up at least ten percent between November 22 and November 30. This is the chart I made up:

Stock	Nov 22 close	Nov 30 high
Levitz Furniture	89½	103¾
Bausch & Lomb	133	149
Natomas	45¼	57
Disney	99	116¾
EG&G	19¼	23¾

Spread your risk Bill I told myself. Don't put all your eggs in one basket. Even if the newspaper was phony I couldn't get hurt too badly if I bought all five. So at half past nine the next morning I phoned my broker and told him I wanted to do some buying in the margin account at the opening. He said don't be in a hurry Bill the market's in lousy shape. Look at yesterday there were 201 new lows this market's going to be under 750 by Christmas. You can see from this that he's an unusual kind of broker since most of them will never try to discourage you from placing an order that'll bring them a commission. But I said no I'm playing a hunch I want to go all out on this and I put in buys on Levitz Bausch Natomas Disney and EG&G. I used the margin right up to the hilt and then some. Okay I told myself if this works out the way you hope it will you've just bought yourself a vacation in Europe and a new Chrysler and a mink for the wife and a lot of other goodies. And if not? If not you just lost yourself a hell of a lot of money Billy boy.

4.

Also I made some use out of the sports pages.

At the office I looked around for bets on the Knicks vs. the SuperSonics next Tuesday at the Garden. A couple of guys wondered why I was interested in action so far ahead but I didn't bother to answer and finally I got Eddie Martin to take the Knicks by eleven points. Also I got Marty Felks to take Milwaukee by eight over the Warriors that same night. Felks thinks Abdul-Jabbar is the best center the game ever had and he'll always bet the Bucks but my paper had it that the Warriors would cop it, 106-103. At lunch with the boys from Leclair & Anderson I put down $250 with Butch Hunter on St Louis over the Giants on

Sunday. Next I stopped off at the friendly neighborhood Off-track Betting Office and entered a few wagers on the races at Aqueduct. My handy guide to the future told me that the Double paid $52.40 and the third Exacta paid $62.20, so I spread a little cash on each. Too bad there were no $2,500 payoffs that day but you can't be picky about your miracles can you?

5.

Tuesday night when I got home I had a drink and asked my wife what's new and she said everybody on the block had been talking about the newspaper all day and some of the girls had been placing bets and phoning their brokers. A lot of the women here play the market and even the horses though my wife is not like that, she leaves the male stuff strictly to me.

What stocks were they buying I asked?

Well she didn't know the names. But a little while later Joni Bruce called up for a recipe and my wife asked her about the market and Joni said she had bought Winnebago Xerox and Transamerica. I was relieved at that because I figured it might look really suspicious if everybody on Redbud Crescent suddenly phoned in orders the same day for Levitz Bausch Disney Natomas and EG&G. On the other hand what was I worrying about nobody would draw any conclusions and if anybody did we could always say we had organized a neighborhood investment club. In any case I don't think there's any law against people making stock market decisions on the basis of a peek at next week's newspaper. Still and all who needs publicity and I was glad we were all buying different stocks.

I got the paper out after dinner to check out Joni's stocks. Sure enough Winnebago moved up from 33¼ to 38 , Xerox from 105¾ to 111 , and Transamerica from 14 to 17. I thought it was dumb of Joni to bother with Xerox getting only a six percent rise since it's the percentages where you pay off but Winnebago was up better than ten percent and Transamerica close to twenty percent. I wished I had noticed Transamerica at least although no sense being greedy, my own choices would make out all right.

Something about the paper puzzled me. The print looked a little blurry in places and on some pages I could hardly read the words. I didn't remember any blurry pages. Also the paper it's printed on seemed a different color, darker grey, older-looking. I compared it with the newspaper that came this morning and the December I issue was definitely darker. A paper shouldn't get old-looking that fast, not in two days.

I wonder if something's happening to the paper I said to my wife.

What do you mean?

Like it's deteriorating or anyway starting to change.

Anything can happen said my wife. It's like a dream you know and in dreams things change all the time without warning.

6.

Wednesday November 24. I guess we just have to sweat this thing out so far the market in general isn't doing much one way or the other. This afternoon's *Post* gives the closing prices there was a rally in the morning but it all faded by the close and the Dow is down to 798.63. However my own five stocks all have had decent upward moves Tues and Wed so maybe I shouldn't worry. I have four points profit in Bausch already two in Natomas five in Levitz two in Disney three-quarters in EG&G and even though that's a long way from the quotations in the Dec 1 newspaper it's better than having losses, also there's still that "stunning two-day advance" due at the end of the month. Maybe I'm going to make out all right. Winnebago Transamerica and Xerox are also up a little bit. Market's closed tomorrow on account of Thanksgiving.

7.

Thanksgiving Day. We went to the Nesbits in the afternoon. It used to be that people spent Thanksgiving with their own kin their aunts uncles grandparents cousins et cetera but you can't do that out here in a new suburb where everybody comes from someplace far away so we eat the turkey with neighbors instead. The Nesbits invited the Fischers the Harrises the Thomasons and us with all the kids of course too. A big noisy gathering. The Fischers came very late so late that we were worried and thinking of sending someone over to find out what was the matter. It was practically time for the turkey when they showed up and Edith Fischer's eyes were red and puffy from crying.

My God my God she said I just found out my older sister is dead.

We started to ask the usual meaningless consoling questions like was she a sick woman and where did she live and what did she die of? And Edith sobbed and said I don't mean she's dead yet I mean she's going to die next Tuesday.

Next Tuesday Tammy Nesbit asked? What do you mean I don't understand how you can know that now. And then she thought a moment and she did understand and so did all the rest of us. Oh Tammy said the newspaper.

The newspaper yes Edith said. Sobbing harder.

Edith was reading the death notices Sid Fischer explained God knows why she was bothering to look at them just curiosity I guess and all of a sudden she lets out this terrible cry and says she sees her sister's name. Sudden passing, a heart attack.

Her heart is weak Edith told us. She's had two or three bad attacks this year.

Lois Thomason went to Edith and put her arms around her the way Lois does so well and said there there Edith it's a terrible shock to you naturally but you know it must have been inevitable sooner or later and at least the poor woman isn't suffering any more.

But don't you see Edith cried. She's still alive right now maybe if I phone and say go to the hospital right away they can save her? They might put her under intensive care and get ready for the attack before it even comes. Only I can't say that can I? Because what can I tell her? That I read about her death in next week's newspaper? She'll think I'm crazy and she'll laugh and she won't pay any attention to me. Or maybe she'll get very upset and drop dead right on the spot all on account of me. What can I do oh God what can I do?

You could say it was a premonition my wife suggested. A very vivid dream that had the ring of truth to you. If your sister puts any faith at all in things like that maybe she'll decide it can't hurt to see her doctor and then—

No Mike Nesbit broke in you mustn't do any such thing Edith. Because they can't save her. No way. They didn't save her when the time came.

The time hasn't come yet said Edith.

So far as we're concerned said Mike the time has already come because we have the newspapers that describe the events of November 30 in the past tense. So we know your sister is going to die and to all intents and purposes is already dead. It's absolutely certain because it's in the newspaper and if we accept the newspaper as authentic then it's a record of actual events beyond any hope of changing.

But my sister Edith said.

Your sister's name is already on the roll of the dead. If you interfere now it'll only bring unnecessary aggravation to her family and it won't change a thing.

How do you know it won't Mike?

The future mustn't be changed Mike said. For us the events of that one day in the future are as permanent as any event in the past. We don't dare play around with changing the future not when it's already signed sealed and delivered in that newspaper. For all we know the future's like a house of cards. If we pull one card out say your sister's life we might bring the whole house tumbling down. You've got to accept the decree of fate Edith. You've got to. Otherwise there's no telling what might happen.

My sister Edith said. My sister's going to die and you won't let me do anything to save her.

8.

Edith carrying on like that put a damper on the whole Thanksgiving celebration. After a while she pulled herself together more or less but she couldn't help behaving like a woman in mourning and it was hard for us to be very jolly and thankful with her there choking back the sobs. The Fischers left right after dinner and we all hugged Edith and told her how sorry we were. Soon afterward the Thomasons and the Harrises left too.

Mike looked at my wife and me and said I hope you aren't going to run off also.

No I said not yet there's no hurry is there?

We sat around some while longer. Mike talked about Edith and her sister. The sister can't be saved he kept saying. And it might be very dangerous for everybody if Edith tries to interfere with fate.

To get the subject away from Edith we started talking about the stock market. Mike said he had bought Natomas Transamerica and Electronic Data Systems which he said was due to rise from 36¾ on November 22 to 47 by the 30th. I told him I had bought Natomas too and I told him my other stocks and pretty soon he had his copy of the December 1 paper out so we could check some of the quotations.

Looking over his shoulder I observed that the print was even blurrier than it had seemed to me Tuesday night which was the last occasion I had examined my paper and also the pages seemed very grey and rough.

What do you think is going on I said? The paper definitely seems to be deteriorating.

It's entropic creep he said.

Entropic creep?

Entropy you know is the natural tendency of everything in nature to come apart at the seams as time goes along. These newspapers must be subject to unusually strong entropic strains because of their anomalous position out of their proper place in time. I've been noticing how the print is getting harder to read and I wouldn't be surprised if it became completely illegible in another couple of days.

We hunted up the prices of my stocks in his paper and the first one we saw was Bausch & Lomb hitting a high of 149¾ on November 30.

Wait a second I said I'm sure the high is supposed to be 149 even.

Mike thought it might be an effect of the general blurriness but no it was still quite clear on that page of stock market quotations and it said 149¾. I looked up Natomas and the high that was listed was 56 . I said I'm positive it's 57. And so on with several other stocks. The figures didn't jibe with what I remembered. We had a friendly little discussion about that and then it became not so friendly as Mike implied my memory was faulty and in the end I jogged down the street to my place and got my own copy of the paper. We spread them both out side by side and compared the quotes. Sure enough the two were different. Hardly any quote in his paper matched those in mine, all of them off an eighth here, a quarter there. What was even worse the figures didn't quite match the ones I had noted down on the first day. My paper now gave the Bausch high for November 30 as 149½ and Natomas as 56½ and Disney as 117. Levitz 104, EG&G 23 . Everything seemed to be sliding around.

It's a bad case of entropic creep Mike said.

I wonder if the newspapers were ever identical to each other I said. We should have compared them on the first day. Now we'll never know whether we all had the same starting point.

Let's check out the other pages Bill.

We compared things. The front page headlines were all the same but there were little differences in the writing. The classified ads had a lot of rearrangements. Some of the death notices were different. All in all the papers were similar but not anything like identical.

How can this be happening I asked? How can words on a printed page be different one day from another?

How can a newspaper from the future get delivered in the first place Mike asked?

9.

We phoned some of the others and asked about stock prices. Just trying to check something out we explained. Charlie Harris said Natomas was quoted at 56 and Jerry Wesley said it was 57¼ and Bob Thomason found that the whole stock market page was too blurry to read although he thought the Natomas quote was 57½. And so on. Everybody's paper slightly different.

Entropic creep. It's hitting hard.

What can we trust? What's real?

10.

Saturday afternoon Bob Thomason came over very agitated. He had his newspaper under his arm. He showed it to me and said look at this Bill how can it be? The pages were practically falling apart and they were completely blank. You could make out little dirty traces where there once had been words but that was all. The paper looked about a million years old.

I got mine out of the closet. It was in bad shape but not that bad. The print was faint and murky yet I could still make some things out clearly. Natomas 56¼. Levitz Furniture 103½ . Disney 117¼. New numbers all the time.

Meanwhile out in the real world the market has been rallying for a couple of days right on schedule and all my stocks are going up. I may go crazy but it looks at least like I'm not going to take a financial beating.

11.

Monday night November 29. One week since this whole thing started. Everybody's newspaper is falling apart. I can read patches of print on two or three pages of mine and the rest is pretty well shot. Dave Bruce says his paper is completely blank the way Bob's was on Saturday. Mike's is in better condition but it won't last long. They're all getting eaten up by entropy. The market rallied strongly again this afternoon. Yesterday the Giants got beaten by St. Louis and at lunch today I collected my winnings from Butch Hunter. Yesterday also Sid and Edith Fischer left suddenly for a vacation in Florida. That's where Edith's sister lives, the one who's supposed to die tomorrow.

12.

I can't help wondering whether Edith did something about her sister after all despite the things Mike said to her Thanksgiving.

13.

So now it's Tuesday night November 30 and I'm home with the *Post* and the closing stock prices. Unfortunately I can't compare them with the figures in my copy of tomorrow's *Times* because I don't have the paper any more it turned completely to dust and so did everybody else's but I still have the notes I took the first night when I was planning my market action. And I'm happy to say everything worked out perfectly despite the effects of entropic creep. The Dow Industrials closed at 831.34 today which is just what my record says. And look at this list of highs for the day where my broker sold me out on the nose:

Levitz Furniture	103¾
Bausch & Lomb	149
Natomas	57
Disney	116¾
EG&G	23¾

So whatever this week has cost me in nervous aggravation it's more than made up in profits.

Tomorrow is December 1 finally and it's going to be funny to see that newspaper again. With the headlines about Nixon going off to China and the people wounded in the bank robbery and the currency negotiations in Rome. Like an old friend coming home.

14.

I suppose everything has to balance out. This morning before breakfast I went outside as usual to get the paper and it was sitting there in the bushes but it wasn't the paper for Wednesday December 1 although this is in fact Wednesday December 1. What the newsboy gave me this morning was the paper for Monday November 22 which I never actually received the day of the first mixup.

That in itself wouldn't be so bad. But this paper is full of stuff I don't remember from last Monday. As though somebody had reached into last week and switched everything around, making up a bunch of weird events. Even though I didn't get to see the *Times* that day I'm sure I would have heard about the assassination of the Governor of Missouri. And the earthquake in Peru that killed ten thousand people. And Mayor Lindsay resigning to become Nixon's new Secretary of State. Especially about Mayor Lindsay resigning to become Nixon's new Secretary of State. This paper *has* to be a joke.

But what about the one we got last week? How about those stock prices and the sports results?

When I get into the city this morning I'm going to stop off first thing at the New York Public Library and check the file copy of the November 22 *Times*. I want to see if the library's copy is anything like the one I just got.

What kind of newspaper am I going to get tomorrow?

15.

Don't think I'm going to get to work at all today. Went out after breakfast to get the car and drive to the station and the car wasn't there nothing was there just grey everything grey no lawn no shrubs no trees none of the other houses in sight just grey like a thick fog swallowing everything up at ground level. Stood there on the front step afraid to go into that grey. Went back into the house woke up my wife told her. What does it mean Bill she asked what does it mean why is it all grey? I don't know I said. Let's turn on the radio. But there was no sound out of the radio nothing on the TV not even a test pattern the phone line dead too everything dead and I don't know what's happening or where we are I don't understand any of this except that this must be a very bad case of entropic creep. All of time must have looped back on itself in some crazy way and I don't know anything I don't understand a thing.

Edith what have you done to us?

I don't want to live here any more I want to cancel my newspaper subscription I want to see my house I want to get away from here back into the real world but how how I don't know it's all grey grey grey everything grey nothing out there just a lot of grey.

THE MUTANT SEASON

This little story has an odd history appended to it. Roger Elwood, he who edited innumerable anthologies of new stories in the 1970s, phoned me one day in January, 1972 and asked if I could—as a favor—hurriedly write something for a book for young readers he was doing called Androids, Time Machines, and Blue Giraffes. *The stories were supposed to follow themes—robots, mutants, time travel, space travel, etc.—and for some reason he had come up short in the mutant category.*

I was in a short-story-writing phase then, and even though I had no particular mutant-theme idea sitting around waiting to be written, I sat right down and improvised a six-page story about a tribe of mutants who regularly gather at a holiday resort, but who, being mutants, visit the resort off season so that they will remain inconspicuous. It was the sort of decent, professional job that I had learned to turn out on demand many years earlier, when I was just beginning my career and had discovered that if I made myself useful to editors who were having inventory problems I'd find it very much easier to pay my rent each month.

Elwood was happy with the story, and so, I suppose, were the readers of his book. I had earned $75 in not very many hours—$75 was still a visible amount of money in 1972—and had earned a little karmic credit by doing an editor a favor, besides. I put "The Mutant Season" out of my mind and went on to other things.

It remained out of my mind for fifteen years—until the ingenious Byron Preiss, a man who until his untimely death in 2005 earned a nice living by coming up with unusual ideas for books and finding people to write them, suggested to me that "The Mutant Season" might very successfully be turned into a series of novels by some younger writer, with a fee going to me for supplying the underlying concept. I responded with polite incredulity. My hastily written 1200-word story to be spun out not simply into a novel but a series of novels? Was he serious? Yes, indeed, he was. My story had merely provided a flicker of insight into the subterranean and surreptitious world of mutants living among us; the idea deserved exploration at much greater length, he said. I shrugged. All right, I told him. Go ahead. You have my blessing.

Byron promptly got the mighty Doubleday-Bantam publishing combine interested in the project: a quartet of books. Now came the job of finding writers to write them. I mildly suggested that my wife, who had begun writing science fiction under her maiden name of Karen Haber and had had every story she had written so far accepted for publication—an impressive total of three short stories, I think, or maybe four—might be a good candidate to do one of the books. This was in the summer of 1987, at the World Science Fiction Convention in Brighton, England. Byron, a man who did nothing by halves, instantly decided that Karen would be the ideal choice to write all four novels. Lou Aronica of Bantam, also a man given to taking bold visionary leaps, enthusiastically seconded the proposal, even though it involved hiring a writer who had no more than a few short stories to her credit to produce four books. I was startled, but maintained an amiable silence as this discussion unfolded. Karen was silent too, but hers was the silence of shock, not of diplomacy. Then and there the deal was put together: Karen would expand my tiny story of 1972 into a vast saga spanning hundreds of thousands of words.

The weird thing is that it all worked out. Karen laboriously constructed the first volume over a period of seven or eight months, and—behold—it was okay. "So that's how you write a novel," she said, and set about doing the second one. It was a lot easier for her than the first, and a better book besides. Then came the third...and the fourth. The publisher was pleased, the sales figures were satisfying, and she moved on to other book-length projects.

I've been entangled in the publishing world more than half a century now. You would think that I've seen just about everything, and you would be right. But new surprises always seem to come along. "The Mutant Season"—mine of 1972—did indeed give rise to four substantial novels, written by my very own Significant Other. Wonders never do cease, do they? At any rate, here's the story that started it all.

THE MUTANT SEASON

It snowed yesterday, three inches. Today a cruel wind comes ripping off the ocean, kicking up the snowdrifts. This is the dead of winter, the low point of the year. This is the season when the mutants arrive. They showed up ten years ago, the same six families as always, renting all the beach houses on the north side of Dune Crest Road. They like to come here in winter when the vacationers are gone and the beaches are empty. I guess they don't enjoy having a lot of normals around. In winter here there's just the little hard core of year-round residents like us. And we don't mind the mutants so long as they don't bother us.

I can see them now, frolicking along the shore, kids and grownups. The cold doesn't seem to affect them at all. It would affect me plenty, being outside in this weather, but they don't even trouble themselves with wearing overcoats. Just light windbreakers and pullovers. They have thicker skins than we do, I guess—leathery-looking, shiny, apple-green—and maybe a different metabolism. They could almost be people from some other planet, but no, they're all natives of the USA, just like you and me. Mutants, that's all. Freaks is what we used to call them. But of course you mustn't call them that now.

Doing their mutant tricks. They can fly, you know. Oh, it isn't really flying, it's more a kind of jumping and soaring, but they can go twenty, thirty feet in the air and float up there about three or four minutes. Levitation, they call it. A bunch of them are levitating right out over the ocean, hanging high above the breakers. It would serve them right to drop and get a soaking. But they don't ever lose control. And look, two of them are having a snowball fight without using their hands, just picking up the snow with their minds and wadding it into balls and tossing it around. Telekinesis, that's called.

I learn these terms from my older daughter Ellen. She's seventeen. She spends a lot of time hanging around with one of the mutant kids. I wish she'd stay away from him.

Levitation. Telekinesis. Mutants renting beach houses. It's a crazy world these days.

Look at them jumping around. They look happy, don't they?

It's three weeks since they came. Cindy, my younger girl—she's nine—asked me today about mutants. What they are. Why they exist.

I said, There are all different kinds of human beings. Some have brown skins and woolly hair, some have yellow skins and slanted eyes, some have—

Those are the races, she said. I know about races. The races look different outside but inside they're pretty much all the same. But the mutants are really different. They have special powers and some of them have strange bodies. They're more different from us than other races are, and that's what I don't understand.

They're a special kind of people, I told her. They were born different from everybody else.

Why?

You know what genes are, Cindy?

Sort of, she said. We're just starting to study about them.

Genes are what determine how our children will look. Your eyes are brown because I have the gene for brown eyes, see? But sometimes there are sudden changes in a family's genes. Something strange gets in. Yellow eyes, maybe. That would be a mutation. The mutants are people who had something strange happen to their genes some time back, fifty, a hundred, three hundred years ago, and the change in the genes became permanent and was handed down from parents to children. Like the gene for the floating they do. Or the gene for their shiny skin. There are all sorts of different mutant genes.

Where did the mutants come from?

They've always been here, I said.

But why didn't anybody ever talk about them? Why isn't there anything about the mutants in my schoolbooks?

It takes time for things to get into schoolbooks, Cindy. Your books were written ten or fifteen years ago. People didn't know much about mutants then and not much was said about them, especially to children your age. The mutants were still in hiding. They lived in out-of-the-way places and disguised themselves and concealed their powers.

Why don't they hide any more?

Because they don't need to, I said. Things have changed. The normal people accept them. We've been getting rid of a lot of prejudices in the last hundred years. Once upon a time anybody who was even a little strange made other people uncomfortable. Any sort of difference—skin color, religion, language—caused trouble, Cindy. Well, we learned to accept people who aren't like ourselves. We even accept people who aren't quite human, now. Like the mutants.

If you accept them, she said, why do you get angry when Ellen goes walking on the beach with what's-his-name?

Ellen's friend went back to college right after the Christmas holidays. Tim, his name is. He's a junior at Cornell. I think she's spending too much time writing long letters to him, but what can I do?

My wife thinks we ought to be more sociable toward them. They've been here a month and a half and we've just exchanged the usual token greetings—friendly nods, smiles, nothing more. We don't even know their names. I could get along without knowing them, I said. But all right. Let's go over and invite them to have drinks with us tonight.

We went across to the place Tim's family is renting. A man who might have been anywhere from thirty-five to fifty-five answered the door. It was the first time I ever saw any of them up close. His features were flat and his eyes were set oddly far apart, and his skin was so glossy it looked like it had been waxed. He didn't ask us in. I was able to see odd things going on behind him in the house—people floating near the ceiling, stuff like that. Standing there at the door, feeling very uneasy and awkward, we hemmed and hawed and finally said what we had come to say. He wasn't interested. You can tell when people aren't interested in being mixed with. Very coolly he said they were busy now, expecting guests, and couldn't drop by. But they'd be in touch.

I bet that's the last we hear of them. A standoffish bunch, keeping to themselves, setting up their own ghetto.

Well, never mind. I don't need to socialize with them. They'll be leaving in another couple of weeks anyway.

How fast the cycle of the months goes around. First snowstorm of the season today, a light one, but it's not really winter yet. I guess our weird friends will be coming back to the seashore soon.

Three of the families moved in on Friday and the other three came today. Cindy's already been over visiting. She says this year Tim's family has a pet, a mutant dog, no less, a kind of poodle only with scaly skin and bright red eyes, like marbles. Gives me the shivers. I didn't know there were mutant dogs.

I was hoping Tim had gone into the army or something. No such luck. He'll be here for two weeks at Christmastime. Ellen's already counting the days.

I saw the mutant dog out on the beach. If you ask me, that's no dog, that's some kind of giant lizard. But it barks. It does bark. And wags its tail. I saw Cindy hugging it. She plays with the younger mutant kids just as though they're normals. She accepts them and they accept her. I suppose it's healthy. I suppose their attitudes are right and mine are wrong. But I can't help my conditioning, can I? I don't want to be prejudiced. But some things are ingrained when we're very young.

Ellen stayed out way past midnight tonight with Tim.

Tim at our house for dinner this evening. He's a nice kid, have to admit. But so strange-looking. And Ellen made him show off levitation for us. He frowns a little and floats right up off the ground. A freak, a circus freak. And my daughter's in love with him.

His winter vacation will be over tomorrow. Not a moment too soon, either.

Another winter nearing its end. The mutants clear out this week. On Saturday they had a bunch of guests—mutants of some other type, no less! A different tribe. The visitors were tall and thin, like walking skeletons, very pale, very solemn. They don't speak out loud: Cindy says they talk with their minds. Telepaths. They seem harmless enough, but I find this whole thing very scary. I imagine dozens of bizarre strains existing within mankind, alongside mankind, all kinds of grotesque mutant types breeding true and multiplying. Now that they've finally surfaced, now that we've discovered how many of them there really are, I started to wonder what new surprises lie ahead for us so-called normals. Will we find ourselves in a minority in another couple of generations? Will those of us who lack superpowers become third-class citizens?

I'm worried.

Summer. Fall. Winter. And here they come again. Maybe we can be friendlier with them this year.

Last year, seven houses. This year they've rented nine. It's good to have so many people around, I guess. Before they started coming it was pretty lonesome here in the winters.

Looks like snow. Soon they'll be here. Letter from Ellen, saying to get her old room ready. Time passes. It always does. Things change. They always do. Winter comes round in its season, and with it come our strange friends. Their ninth straight year here. Can't wait to see Ellen.

Ellen and Tim arrived yesterday. You see them down on the beach? Yes, they're a good-looking young couple. That's my grandson with them. The one in the blue snowsuit. Look at him floating—bet he's nine feet off the ground! Precocious, that's him. Not old enough to walk yet. But he can levitate pretty well, let me tell you.

CAUGHT IN THE ORGAN DRAFT

One big issue during the turbulent period of American life that we remember as the Vietnam era—from 1965 to 1972, roughly—was the question of the citizen's responsibilities to his government at a time when the government is engaged in activities of which the citizen strongly disapproves. The war that the United States then was waging in Southeast Asia, to the bewilderment and fury of many of its people, was the specific stimulus for the reexamination of civic duties that was going on. Our entanglement in Vietnam and neighboring countries had pretty much wound down by the time I wrote this story, in February of 1972, but the sociopolitical effects of the conflict still were very much in evidence, as indeed they continue to be even now, a generation later.

"Caught in the Organ Draft" is not explicitly a Vietnam story—I don't think I ever actually wrote one—but it does explore, along with various other things, the idea of conscription for an unpopular cause, and tries to avoid the obvious conclusions while nevertheless addressing the inescapable realities. I wrote it for a book called And Walk Now Gently Through the Fire, *edited by the then-ubiquitous Roger Elwood. Some of Elwood's dozens of collections of science-fiction stories were superb, some were mediocre, some were execrable. This was one of the better ones, calling forth fine work by Philip Jose Farmer, Barry Malzberg, R.A. Lafferty, and half a dozen others. The ostensible theme of the book was biochemistry and its impact on the human condition, but Vietnam, unsurprisingly, provided a secret subtext for most of the stories.*

Look there, Kate, down by the promenade. Two splendid seniors, walking side by side near the water's edge. They radiate power, authority, wealth, assurance. He's a judge, a senator, a corporation president, no doubt, and she's—what?—a professor emeritus of international law, let's say. There they go toward the plaza, moving serenely, smiling, nodding graciously to passersby. How the sunlight gleams in their white hair! I can barely stand the brilliance of that reflected aura: it blinds me, it stings my eyes. What are they, eighty, ninety, a hundred years old? At this distance they seem much younger—they hold themselves upright, their backs are straight, they might pass for being only fifty or sixty. But I can tell. Their confidence, their poise, mark them for what they are. And when they were nearer I could see their withered cheeks, their sunken eyes. No cosmetics can hide that. These two are old enough to be our great-grandparents. They were well past sixty before we were even born, Kate. How superbly their bodies function! But why not? We can guess at their medical histories. She's had at least three hearts, he's working on his fourth set of lungs, they apply for new kidneys every five years, their brittle bones are reinforced with hundreds of skeletal snips from the arms and legs of hapless younger folk, their dimming sensory apparatus is aided by countless nerve-grafts obtained the same way, their ancient arteries are freshly sheathed with sleek teflon. Ambulatory assemblages of second-hand human parts, spliced here and there with synthetic or mechanical organ substitutes, that's all they are. And what am I, then, or you? Nineteen years old and vulnerable. In their eyes I'm nothing but a ready stockpile of healthy organs, waiting to serve their needs. Come here, son. What a fine strapping young man you are! Can you spare a kidney for me? A lung? A choice little segment of intestine? Ten centimeters of your ulnar nerve? I need a few pieces of you, lad. You won't deny a distinguished elder like me what I ask, will you? Will you?

Today my draft notice, a small crisp document, very official-looking, came shooting out of the data slot when I punched for my morning mail. I've been expecting it all spring; no surprise, no shock, actually rather an anticlimax now that it's finally here. In six weeks I am to report to Transplant House for my final physical exam—only a formality, they wouldn't have drafted me if I didn't already rate top marks as organ-reservoir potential—and then I go on call. The average call time is about two months. By autumn they'll be carving me up. Eat, drink, and be merry, for soon comes the surgeon to my door.

A straggly band of senior citizens is picketing the central headquarters of the League for Bodily Sanctity. It's a counter-demonstration, an anti-anti-transplant protest, the worst kind of political statement, feeding on the ugliest of negative emotions. The demonstrators carry glowing signs that say:

BODILY SANCTITY—OR BODILY SELFISHNESS?

And:

YOU OWE YOUR LEADERS YOUR VERY LIVES

And:

LISTEN TO THE VOICE OF EXPERIENCE

The picketers are low-echelon seniors, barely across the qualifying line, the ones who can't really be sure of getting transplants. No wonder they're edgy about the League. Some of them are in wheelchairs and some are encased right up to the eyebrows in portable life-support systems. They croak and shout bitter invective and shake their fists. Watching the show from an upper window of the League building, I shiver with fear and dismay. These people don't just want my kidneys or my lungs. They'd take my eyes, my liver, my pancreas, my heart, anything they might happen to need.

I talked it over with my father. He's forty-five years old—too old to have been personally affected by the organ draft, too young to have needed any transplants yet. That puts him in a neutral position, so to speak, except for one minor factor: his transplant status is 5-G. That's quite high on the eligibility list, not the top-priority class but close enough. If he fell ill tomorrow and the Transplant Board ruled that his life would be endangered if he didn't get a new heart or lung or kidney, he'd be given one practically immediately. Status like that simply has to influence his objectivity on the whole organ issue. Anyway, I told him I was planning to appeal and maybe even to resist. "Be reasonable," he said, "be rational, don't let your emotions run away with you. Is it worth jeopardizing your whole future over a thing like this? After all, not everybody who's drafted loses vital organs."

"Show me the statistics," I said. "Show me."

He didn't know the statistics. It was his impression that only about a quarter or a fifth of the draftees actually got an organ call. That tells you how closely the older generation keeps in touch with the situation—and my father's an educated man, articulate, well-informed. Nobody over the age of thirty-five that I talked to could show me any statistics. So I showed them. Out of a League brochure, it's true, but based on certified National Institute of Health reports. Nobody escapes. They always clip you, once you qualify. The need for young organs inexorably expands to match the pool of available organpower. In the long run they'll get us all and chop us to bits. That's probably what they want, anyway. To rid themselves of the younger members of the species, always so troublesome, by cannibalizing us for spare parts, and recycling us, lung by lung, pancreas by pancreas, through their own deteriorating bodies.

Fig. 4. On March 23, 1964, this dog's own liver was removed and replaced with the liver of a nonrelated mongrel donor. The animal was treated with azathioprine for four months and all therapy then stopped. He remains in perfect health 6 years after transplantation.

The war goes on. This is, I think, its fourteenth year. Of course they're beyond the business of killing now. They haven't had any field engagements since '93 or so, certainly none since the organ draft legislation went into effect. The old ones can't afford to waste precious young bodies on the battlefield. So robots wage our territorial struggles for us, butting heads with a great metallic clank, laying land mines and twitching their sensors at the enemy's mines, digging tunnels beneath his screens, et cetera, et cetera. Plus, of course, the quasi-military activity—economic sanctions, third-power blockades, propaganda telecasts beamed as overrides from merciless orbital satellites, and stuff like that. It's a subtler war than the kind they used to wage: nobody dies. Still, it drains national resources. Taxes are going up again this year, the fifth or sixth year in a row, and they've just slapped a special Peace Surcharge on all metal-containing goods, on account of the copper shortage. There once was a time when we could hope that our crazy old leaders would die off or at least retire for reasons of health, stumbling away to their country villas with ulcers or shingles or scabies or scruples and allowing new young peacemakers to take office. But now they just go on and on, immortal and insane, our senators, our cabinet members, our generals, our planners. And their war goes on and on too, their absurd, incomprehensible, diabolical, self-gratifying war.

I know people my age or a little older who have taken asylum in Belgium or Sweden or Paraguay or one of the other countries where Bodily Sanctity laws have been passed. There are about twenty such countries, half of them the most progressive nations in the world and half of them the most reactionary. But what's the sense of running away? I don't want to live in exile. I'll stay here and fight.

Naturally they don't ask a draftee to give up his heart or his liver or some other organ essential to life, say his medulla oblongata. We haven't yet reached that stage of political enlightenment at which the government feels capable of legislating fatal conscription. Kidneys and lungs, the paired organs, the dispensable organs, are the chief targets so far. But if you study the history of conscription over the ages you see that it can always be projected on a curve rising from rational necessity to absolute lunacy. Give them a fingertip, they'll take an arm. Give them an inch of bowel, they'll take your guts. In another fifty years they'll be drafting hearts and stomachs and maybe even brains, mark my words; let them get the technology of brain transplants together and nobody's skull will be safe. It'll be human sacrifice all over again. The only difference between us and the Aztecs is one of method: we have anaesthesia, we have antisepsis and asepsis, we use scalpels instead of obsidian blades to cut out the hearts of our victims.

MEANS OF OVERCOMING THE HOMOGRAFT REACTION

The pathway that has led from the demonstration of the immunological nature of the homograft reaction and its universality to the development of relatively effective but by no means completely satisfactory means of overcoming it for therapeutic purposes is an interesting one that can only be touched upon very briefly. The year 1950 ushered in a new era in transplantation immunobiology in which the discovery of various means of weakening or abrogating a host's response to a homograft—such as sublethal whole body X-irradiation, or treatment with certain adrenal corticosteroid hormones, notably cortisone—began to influence the direction of the mainstream of research and engender confidence that a workable clinical solution might not be too far off. By the end of the decade, powerful immuno-suppressive drugs, such as 6-mercaptopurine, had been shown to be capable of holding in abeyance the reactivity of dogs to renal homografts, and soon afterward this principle was successfully extended to man.

Is my resistance to the draft based on an ingrained abstract distaste for tyranny in all forms or rather on the mere desire to keep my body intact? Could it be both, maybe? Do I need an idealistic rationalization at all? Don't I have an inalienable right to go through my life wearing my own native-born kidneys?

The law was put through by an administration of old men. You can be sure that all laws affecting the welfare of the young are the work of doddering moribund ancients afflicted with angina pectoris, atherosclerosis, prolapses of the infundibulum, fulminating ventricles, and dilated viaducts. The problem was this: not enough healthy young people were dying of highway accidents, successful suicide attempts, diving-board miscalculations, electrocutions, and football injuries; therefore there was a shortage of transplantable organs. An effort to restore the death penalty for the sake of creating a steady supply of state-controlled cadavers lost out in the courts. Volunteer programs of organ donation weren't working out too well, since most of the volunteers were criminals who signed up in order to gain early release from prison: a lung reduced your sentence by five years, a kidney got you three years off, and so on. The exodus of convicts from the jails under this clause wasn't so popular among suburban voters. Meanwhile there was an urgent and mounting need for organs; a lot of important seniors might in fact die if something didn't get done fast. So a coalition of senators from all four parties rammed the organ-draft measure through the upper chamber in the face of a filibuster threat from a few youth-oriented members. It had a much easier time in the House of Representatives, since nobody in the House ever pays much attention to the text of a bill up for a vote, and word had been circulated on this one that if it passed, everybody over sixty-five who had any political pull at all could count on living twenty or thirty extra years, which to a Representative means a crack at ten to fifteen extra terms of office. Naturally there have been court challenges, but what's the use? The average age of the eleven Justices of the Supreme Court is seventy-eight. They're human and mortal. They need our flesh. If they throw out the organ draft now, they're signing their own death warrants.

For a year and a half I was the chairman of the anti-draft campaign on our campus. We were the sixth or seventh local chapter of the League for Bodily Sanctity to be organized in this country, and we were real activists. Mainly we would march up and down in front of the draft board offices carrying signs proclaiming things like:

KIDNEY POWER

And:

A MAN'S BODY IS HIS CASTLE

And:

THE POWER TO CONSCRIPT ORGANS
IS THE POWER TO DESTROY LIVES

We never went in for the rough stuff, though, like bombing organ-transplant centers or hijacking refrigeration trucks. Peaceful agitation, that was our motto. When a couple of our members tried to swing us to a more violent policy, I delivered an extemporaneous two-hour speech arguing for moderation. Naturally I was drafted the moment I became eligible.

⁂

"I can understand your hostility to the draft," my college advisor said. "It's certainly normal to feel queasy about surrendering important organs of your body. But you ought to consider the countervailing advantages. Once you've given an organ you get a 6-A classification, Preferred Recipient, and you remain forever on the 6-A roster. Surely you realize that this means that if you ever need a transplant yourself, you'll automatically be eligible for one, even if your other personal and professional qualifications don't lift you to the optimum level. Suppose your career plans don't work out and you become a manual laborer, for instance. Ordinarily you wouldn't rate even a first look if you developed heart disease, but your Preferred Recipient status would save you. You'd get a new lease on life, my boy."

I pointed out the fallacy inherent in this. Which is that as the number of draftees increases, it will come to encompass a majority or even a totality of the population, and eventually everybody will have 6-A Preferred Recipient status by virtue of having donated, and the term Preferred Recipient will cease to have any meaning. A shortage of transplantable organs would eventually develop as each past donor stakes his claim to a transplant when his health fails, and in time they'd have to arrange the Preferred Recipients by order of personal and professional achievement anyway, for the sake of arriving at some kind of priorities within the 6-A class, and we'd be right back where we are now.

Fig. 7. The course of a patient who received antilymphocyte globulin (ALG) before and for the first four months after renal homotransplantation. The donor was an older brother. There was no early rejection. Prednisone therapy was started forty days postoperatively. Note the insidious onset of late rejection after cessation of globulin therapy. This was treated by a moderate increase in the maintenance doses of steroids. This delayed complication occurred in only two of the first twenty recipients of intrafamilial homografts who were treated with ALG. It has been seen with about the same low frequency in subsequent cases. (By permission of Surg. Gynec. Obstet. *126 (1968): p. 1023.)*

So I went down to Transplant House today, right on schedule, to take my physical. A couple of my friends thought I was making a tactical mistake by reporting at all; if you're going to resist, they said, resist at every point along the line. Make them drag you in for the physical. In purely idealistic (and ideological) terms I suppose they're right. But there's no need yet for me to start kicking up a fuss. Wait till they actually say, We need your kidney, young man. Then I can resist, if resistance is the course I ultimately choose. (Why am I wavering? Am I afraid of the damage to my career plans that resisting might do? Am I not entirely convinced of the injustice of the entire organ-draft system? I don't know. I'm not even sure that I am wavering. Reporting for your physical isn't really a sellout to the system.) I went, anyway. They tapped this and X-rayed that and peered into the other thing. Yawn, please. Bend over, please. Cough, please. Hold out your left arm, please. They marched me in front of a battery of diagnostat machines and I stood there hoping for the red light to flash—tilt, get out of here!—but I was, as expected, in perfect physical shape, and I qualified for call. Afterward I met Kate and we walked in the park and held hands and watched the glories of the sunset and discussed what I'll do, when and if the call comes. *If?* Wishful thinking, boy!

If your number is called you become exempt from military service, and they credit you with a special $750 tax deduction every year. Big deal.

Another thing they're very proud of is the program of voluntary donation of unpaired organs. This has nothing to do with the draft, which—thus far, at least—requisitions only paired organs, organs that can be spared without loss of life. For the last twelve years it's been possible to walk into any hospital in the United States and sign a simple release form allowing the surgeons to slice you up. Eyes, lungs, heart, intestines, pancreas, liver, anything, you give it all to them. This process used to be known as suicide in a simpler era and it was socially disapproved of, especially in times of labor shortages. Now we have a labor surplus, because even though our population growth has been fairly slow since the middle of the century, the growth of labor-eliminating mechanical devices and processes has been quite rapid, even exponential.

Therefore, to volunteer for this kind of total donation is considered a deed of the highest social utility, removing as it does a healthy young body from the overcrowded labor force and at the same time providing some elder statesman with the assurance that the supply of vital organs will not unduly diminish. Of course you have to be crazy to volunteer, but there's never been any shortage of lunatics in our society.

If you're not drafted by the age of twenty-one, through some lucky fluke, you're safe. And a few of us do slip through the net, I'm told. So far there are more of us in the total draft pool than there are patients in need of transplants. But the ratios are changing rapidly. The draft legislation is still relatively new. Before long they'll have drained the pool of eligible draftees, and then what? Birth rates nowadays are low; the supply of potential draftees is finite. But death rates are even lower; the demand for organs is essentially infinite. I can give you only one of my kidneys, if I am to survive; but you, as you live on and on, may require more than one kidney transplant. Some recipients may need five or six sets of kidneys or lungs before they finally get beyond hope of repair at age 170 or so. As those who've given organs come to requisition organs later on in life, the pressure on the under-21 group will get even greater. Those in need of transplants will come to outnumber those who can donate organs, and everybody in the pool will get clipped. And then? Well, they could lower the draft age to 17 or 16 or even 14. But even that's only a short-term solution. Sooner or later, there won't be enough spare organs to go around.

Will I stay? Will I flee? Will I go to court? Time's running out. My call is sure to come up in another few weeks. I feel a tickling sensation in my back, now and then, as though somebody's quietly sawing at my kidneys.

Cannibalism. At Chou-kou-tien, Dragon Bone Hill, twenty-five miles south-west of Peking, paleontologists excavating a cave early in the twentieth century discovered the fossil skulls of Peking Man, *Pithecanthropus pekinensis.* The skulls had been broken away at the base, which led Franz Weidenreich, the director of the Dragon Bone Hill digs, to speculate that Peking Man was a cannibal who had killed his own kind, extracted the brains of his victims through openings in the base of their skulls, cooked and feasted on the cerebral meat—there were hearths and fragments of charcoal at the site—and left the skulls behind in the cave as trophies. To eat your enemy's flesh: to absorb his skills, his strengths, his knowledge, his achievements, his virtues. It took mankind five hundred thousand years to struggle upward from cannibalism. But we never lost the old craving, did we? There's still easy comfort to gain by devouring those who are younger, stronger, more agile than you. We've improved the techniques, is all. And so now they eat us raw, the old ones, they gobble us up, organ by throbbing organ. Is that really an improvement? At least Peking Man cooked his meat.

Our brave new society, where all share equally in the triumphs of medicine, and the deserving senior citizens need not feel that their merits and prestige will be rewarded only by a cold grave—we sing its praises all the time. How pleased everyone is about the organ draft! Except, of course, a few disgruntled draftees.

The ticklish question of priorities. Who gets the stockpiled organs? They have an elaborate system by which hierarchies are defined. Supposedly a big computer drew it up, thus assuring absolute godlike impartiality. You earn salvation through good works: accomplishments in career and benevolence in daily life win you points that nudge you up the ladder until you reach one of the high-priority classifications, 4-G or better. No doubt the classification system is impartial and is administered justly. But is it rational? Whose needs does it serve? In 1943, during World War II, there was a shortage of the newly discovered drug penicillin among the American military forces in North Africa. Two groups of soldiers were most in need of its bene-fits: those who were suffering from infected battle wounds and those who had contracted venereal disease. A junior medical officer, working from self-evident moral principles, ruled that the wounded heroes were more deserving of treatment than the self-indulgent syphilitics. He was overruled by the medical officer in charge, who observed that the VD cases could be restored to active duty more quickly, if treated; besides, if they remained untreated they served as vectors of further infection. Therefore he gave them the penicillin and left the wounded groaning on their beds of pain. The logic of the battlefield, incontrovertible, unassailable.

The great chain of life. Little creatures in the plankton are eaten by larger ones, and the greater plankton falls prey to little fishes, and little fishes to bigger fishes, and so on up to the tuna and the dolphin and the shark. I eat the flesh of the tuna and I thrive and flourish and grow fat, and store up energy in my vital organs. And am eaten in turn by the shriveled wizened seniors. All life is linked. I see my destiny.

In the early days, rejection of the transplanted organ was the big problem. Such a waste! The body failed to distinguish between a beneficial though alien organ and an intrusive, hostile microorganism. The mechanism known as the immune response was mobilized to drive out the invader. At the point of invasion enzymes came into play, a brush-fire war designed to rip down and dissolve the foreign substances. White corpuscles poured in via the circulatory system, vigilant phagocytes on the march. Through the lymphatic network carne antibodies, high-powered protein missiles. Before any technology of organ grafts could be developed, methods had to be devised to suppress the immune response. Drugs, radiation treatment, metabolic shock—one way or another, the organ-rejection problem was long ago conquered. I can't conquer my draft-rejection problem. Aged and rapacious legislators, I reject you and your legislation.

My call notice came today. They'll need one of my kidneys. The usual request. "You're lucky," somebody said at lunchtime. "They might have wanted a lung."

Kate and I walk into the green glistening hills and stand among the blossoming oleanders and corianders and frangipani and whatever. How good it is to be alive, to breathe this fragrance, to show our bodies to the bright sun! Her skin is tawny and glowing. Her beauty makes me weep. She will not be spared. None of us will be spared. I go first, then she, or is it she ahead of me? Where will they make the incision? Here, on her smooth rounded back? Here, on the flat taut belly? I can see the high priest standing over the altar. At the first blaze of dawn his shadow falls across her. The obsidian knife that is clutched in his upraised hand has a terrible fiery sparkle. The choir offers up a discordant hymn to the god of blood. The knife descends.

My last chance to escape across the border. I've been up all night, weighing the options. There's no hope of appeal. Running away leaves a bad taste in my mouth. Father, friends, even Kate, all say stay, stay, stay, face the music. The hour of decision. Do I really have a choice? I have no choice. When the time comes, I'll surrender peacefully.

I report to Transplant House for conscriptive donative surgery in three hours.

After all, he said coolly, what's a kidney? I'll still have another one, you know. And if that one malfunctions, I can always get a replacement. I'll have Preferred Recipient status, 6-A, for what that's worth. But I won't settle for my automatic 6-A. I know what's going to happen to the priority system; I'd better protect myself. I'll go into politics. I'll climb. I'll attain upward mobility out of enlightened self-interest, right? Right. I'll become so important that society will owe me a thousand transplants. And one of these years I'll get that kidney back. Three or four kidneys, fifty kidneys, as many as I need. A heart or two. A few lungs. A pancreas, a spleen, a liver. They won't be able to refuse me anything.

I'll show them. I'll show them. I'll out-senior the seniors. There's your Bodily Sanctity activist for you, eh? I suppose I'll have to resign from the League. Goodbye, idealism. Goodbye, moral superiority. Goodbye, kidney. Goodbye, goodbye, goodbye.

It's done. I've paid my debt to society. I've given up unto the powers that be my humble pound of flesh. When I leave the hospital in a couple of days, I'll carry a card testifying to my new 6-A status.

Top priority for the rest of my life.

Why, I might live for a thousand years.

MANY MANSIONS

Here's an example of mainstream contemporary-literature modes carried over into science fiction, something I've done now and again throughout my entire career. (A very early story called "The Songs of Summer" owed a great deal to Faulkner's As I Lay Dying. *I've channeled Joseph Conrad on a number of occasions. One passage in my novel* Son of Man *employs William Burroughs' cut-up technique. And so forth.) This is another, and I think it was a successful transplantation.*

Somewhere in the mid-1960s Robert Coover wrote a funny, frantic story called "The Babysitter," in which a narrative situation is dissected and refracted in an almost Cubist fashion into dozens of short scenes, some of which are deliberately contradictory of others. I read it and admired it and saw what Coover had done as a perfect way to approach the paradoxes of the time-travel story, in which a single act of transit through time can generate a host of parallel time-tracks. I had written plenty of time-travel stories before—the theme is a particular favorite of mine—but Coover had shown me a completely new way to do it.

So off I went, killing off grandfathers and having characters meeting themselves both coming and going, in what is probably the most complex short story of temporal confusion since Robert A. Heinlein's "By His Bootstraps." (Or Heinlein's much later "All You Zombies—"). I had a wonderful time doing it, which was important, because in that complicated segment of my life—this was February, 1972, when I was midway through the chaotic transition from a lifetime in New York to a wholly new incarnation as a Californian—writing usually was neither easy nor particularly pleasant for me. Terry Carr published the story in the third of his Universe *anthologies, and it has been reprinted several times since. I can't read it even now without chuckling over its dizzy pace and lunatic inventiveness.*

The debt to Coover's original story, I thought, was obvious. But over the past thirty-plus years a grand total of one reader has asked me whether I had had "The Babysitter" in mind when I wrote "Many Mansions." (I never do learn. Many years later, when I wrote a story called "The Secret Sharer" that translated the plot of Conrad's classic novella into science-fictional terms, and hung Conrad's original title on my story just so everyone would understand what I was doing, a reader wrote an angry letter to the editor of the magazine where my story appeared, complaining that I had stolen the title of a famous story by Joseph Conrad. Maybe I should attach explanatory footnotes to these things.)

It's been a rough day. Everything gone wrong. A tremendous tie-up on the freeway going to work, two accounts cancelled before lunch, now some inconceivable botch by the weather programmers. It's snowing outside. Actually snowing. He'll have to go out and clear the driveway in the morning. He can't remember when it last snowed. And of course a fight with Alice again. She never lets him alone. She's at her most deadly when she sees him come home exhausted from the office. Ted why don't you this, Ted get me that. Now, waiting for dinner, working on his third drink in forty minutes, he feels one of his headaches coming on. Those miserable killer headaches that can destroy a whole evening. What a life! He toys with murderous fantasies. Take her out by the reservoir for a friendly little stroll, give her a quick hard shove with his shoulder. She can't swim. Down, down, down. Glub. Goodbye, Alice. Free at last.

In the kitchen she furiously taps the keys of the console, programming dinner just the way he likes it. Cold vichyssoise, baked potato with sour cream and chives, sirloin steak blood-rare inside and charcoal-charred outside. Don't think it isn't work to get the meal just right, even with the autochef. All for him. The bastard. Tell me, why do I sweat so hard to please him? Has he made me happy? What's he ever done for me except waste the best years of my life? And he thinks I don't know about his other women. Those lunchtime quickies. Oh, I wouldn't mind at all if he dropped dead tomorrow. I'd be a great widow—so dignified at the funeral, so strong, hardly crying at all. And everybody thinks we're such a close couple. Married eleven years and they're still in love. I heard someone say that only last week. If they only knew the truth about us. If they only knew.

Martin peers out the window of his third-floor apartment in Sunset Village. Snow. I'll be damned. He can't remember the last time he saw snow. Thirty, forty years back, maybe, when Ted was a baby. He absolutely can't remember. White stuff on the ground when? The mind gets wobbly when you're past eighty. He still can't believe he's an old man. It rocks him to realize that his grandson Ted, Martha's boy, is almost forty. I bounced that kid on my knee and he threw up all over my suit. Four years old then. Nixon was President. Nobody talks much about Tricky Dick these days. Ancient history. McKinley, Coolidge, Nixon. Time flies. Martin thinks of Ted's wife, Alice. What a nice tight little ass she has. What a cute pair of jugs. I'd like to get my hands on them. I really would. You know something, Martin? You're not such an old ruin yet. Not if you can get it up for your grandson's wife.

His dreams of drowning her fade as quickly as they came. He is not a violent man by nature. He knows he could never do it. He can't even bring himself to step on a spider; how then could he kill his wife? If she'd die some other way, of course, without the need of his taking direct action, that would solve everything. She's driving to the hairdresser on one of those manual-access roads she likes to use, and her car swerves on an icy spot, and she goes into a tree at eighty kilometers an hour. Good. She's shopping on Union Boulevard, and the bank is blown up by an activist; she's nailed by flying debris. Good. The dentist gives her a new anaesthetic and it turns out she's fatally allergic to it. Puffs up like a blowfish and dies in five minutes. Good. The police come, long faces, snuffly noses. Terribly sorry, Mr. Porter. There's been an awful accident. Don't tell me it's my wife, he cries. They nod lugubriously. He bears up bravely under the loss, though.

"You can come in for dinner now," she says. He's sitting slouched on the sofa with another drink in his hand. He drinks more than any man she knows, not that she knows all that many. Maybe he'll get cirrhosis and die. Do people still die of cirrhosis, she wonders, or do they give them liver transplants now? The funny thing is that he still turns her on, after eleven years. His eyes, his face, his hands. She despises him but he still turns her on.

The snow reminds him of his young manhood, of his days long ago in the East. He was quite the ladies' man then. And it wasn't so easy to get some action back in those days, either. The girls were always worried about what people would say if anyone found out. What people would say! As if doing it with a boy you liked was something shameful. Or they'd worry about getting knocked up. They made you wear a rubber. How awful that was: like wearing a sock. The pill was just starting to come in, the original pill, the old one-a-day kind. Imagine a world without the pill! ("Did they have dinosaurs when you were a boy, grandpa?") Still, Martin had made out all right. Big muscular frame, strong earnest features, warm inquisitive eyes. You'd never know it to look at me now. I wonder if Alice realizes what kind of stud I used to be. If I had the money I'd rent one of those time machines they've got now and send her back to visit myself around 1950 or so. A little gift to my younger self. He'd really rip into her. It gives Martin a quick riffle of excitement to think of his younger self ripping into Alice. But of course he can't afford any such thing.

As he forks down his steak he imagines being single again. Would I get married again? Not on your life. Not until I'm good and ready, anyway, maybe when I'm fifty-five or sixty. Me for bachelorhood for the time being, just screwing around like a kid. To hell with responsibilities. I'll wait two, three weeks after the funeral, a decent interval, and then I'll go off for some fun. Hawaii, Tahiti, Fiji, someplace out there. With Nolie. Or Maria. Or Ellie. Yes, with Ellie. He thinks of Ellie's pink thighs, her soft heavy breasts, her long radiant auburn hair. Two weeks in Fiji with Ellie. Two weeks in Ellie with Fiji. Yes. Yes. Yes. 'Is the steak rare enough for you, Ted?' Alice asks. 'It's fine,' he says.

She goes upstairs to check the children's bedroom. They're both asleep, finally. Or else faking it so well that it makes no difference. She stands by their beds a moment, thinking, I love you, Bobby, I love you, Tink. Tink and Bobby, Bobby and Tink. I love you even though you drive me crazy sometimes. She tiptoes out. Now for a quiet evening of television. And then to bed. The same old routine. Christ. I don't know why I go on like this. There are times when I'm ready to explode. I stay with him for the children's sake, I guess. Is that enough of a reason?

He envisions himself running hand in hand along the beach with Ellie. Both of them naked, their skins bronzed and gleaming in the tropical sunlight. Palm trees everywhere. Grains of pink sand under foot. Soft transparent wavelets lapping the shore. A quiet cove. "No one can see us here," Ellie murmurs. He sinks down on her firm sleek body and enters her.

A blazing band of pain tightens like a strip of hot metal across Martin's chest. He staggers away from the window, dropping into a low crouch as he stumbles toward a chair. The heart. Oh, the heart! That's what you get for drooling over Alice. Dirty old man. "Help," he calls feebly. "Come on, you filthy machine, help me!" The medic, activated by the key phrase, rolls silently toward him. Its sensors are already at work scanning him, searching for the cause of the discomfort. A telescoping steel-jacketed arm slides out of the medic's chest and, hovering above Martin, extrudes an ultrasonic injection snout. "Yes," Martin murmurs, "that's right, damn you, hurry up and give me the drug!" Calm. I must try to remain calm. The snout makes a gentle whirring noise as it forces the relaxant into Martin's vein. He slumps in relief. The pain slowly ebbs. Oh, that's much better. Saved again. Oh. Oh. Oh. Dirty old man. Ought to be ashamed of yourself.

Ted knows he won't get to Fiji with Ellie or anybody else. Any realistic assessment of the situation brings him inevitably to the same conclusion. Alice isn't going to die in an accident, any more than he's likely to murder her. She'll live forever. Unwanted wives always do. He could ask for a divorce, of course. He'd probably lose everything he owned, but he'd win his freedom. Or he could simply do away with himself. That was always a temptation for him. The easy way out, no lawyers, no hassles. So it's that time of the evening again. It's the same every night. Pretending to watch television, he secretly indulges in suicidal fantasies.

Bare-bodied dancers in gaudy luminous paint gyrate lasciviously on the screen, nearly large as life. Alice scowls. The things they show on TV nowadays! It used to be that you got this stuff only on the X-rated channels, but now it's everywhere. And look at him, just lapping it up! Actually she knows she wouldn't be so stuffy about the sex shows except that Ted's fascination with them is a measure of his lack of interest in her. Let them show screwing and all the rest on TV, if that's what people want. I just wish Ted had as much enthusiasm for me as he does for the television stuff. So far as sexual permissiveness in general goes, she's no prude. She used to wear nothing but trunks at the beach, until Tink was born and she started to feel a little less proud of her figure. But she still dresses as revealingly as anyone in their crowd. And gets stared at by everyone but her own husband. He watches the TV cuties. His other women must use him up. Maybe I ought to step out a bit myself, Alice thinks. She's had her little affairs along the way. Not many, nothing very serious, but she's had some. Three lovers in eleven years, that's not a great many, but it's a sign that she's no puritan. She wonders if she ought to get involved with somebody now. It might move her life off dead center while she still has the chance, before boredom destroys her entirely. "I'm going up to wash my hair," she announces. "Will you be staying down here till bedtime?"

There are so many ways he could do it. Slit his wrists. Drive his car off the bridge. Swallow Alice's whole box of sleeping tabs. Of course those are all old-fashioned ways of killing yourself. Something more modern would be appropriate. Go into one of the black taverns and start making loud racial insults? No, nothing modern about that. It's very 1975. But something genuinely contemporary does occur to him. Those time machines they've got now: suppose he rented one and went back, say, sixty years, to a time when one of his parents hadn't yet been born. And killed his grandfather. Find old Martin as a young man and slip a knife into him. If I do that, Ted figures, I should instantly and painlessly cease to exist. I would never have existed, because my mother wouldn't ever have existed. Poof. Out like a light. Then he realizes he's fantasizing a murder again. Stupid: if he could ever murder anyone, he'd murder Alice and be done with it. So the whole fantasy is foolish. Back to the starting point is where he is.

She is sitting under the hair-dryer when he comes upstairs. He has a peculiarly smug expression on his face, and as soon as she turns the dryer off she asks him what he's thinking about. 'I may have just invented a perfect murder method,' he tells her. "Oh?" she says. He says, "You rent a time machine. Then you go back a couple of generations and murder one of the ancestors of your intended victim. That way you're murdering the victim too, because he won't ever have been born if you kill off one of his immediate progenitors. Then you return to your own time. Nobody can trace you because you don't have any fingerprints on file in an era before your own birth. What do you think of it?" Alice shrugs. "It's an old one," she says. "It's been done on television a dozen times. Anyway, I don't like it. Why should an innocent person have to die just because he's the grandparent of somebody you want to kill?"

They're probably in bed together right now, Martin thinks gloomily. Stark naked side by side. The lights are out. The house is quiet. Maybe they're smoking a little grass. Do they still call it grass, he wonders, or is there some new nickname now? Anyway the two of them turn on. Yes. And then he reaches for her. His hands slide over her cool, smooth skin.

He cups her breasts. Plays with the hard little nipples. Sucks on them. The other hand wandering down to her parted thighs. And then she. And then he. And then they. And then they. Oh, Alice, he murmurs. Oh, Ted, Ted, she cries. And then they. Go to it. Up and down, in and out. Oh. Oh. Oh. She claws his back. She pumps her hips. Ted! Ted! Ted! The big moment is arriving now. For her, for him. Jackpot! Afterward they lie close for a few minutes, basking in the afterglow. And then they roll apart. Goodnight, Ted. Goodnight, Alice. Oh, Jesus. They do it every night, I bet. They're so young and full of juice. And I'm all dried up. Christ, I hate being old. When I think of the man I once was. When I think of the women I once had. Jesus. Jesus. God, let me have the strength to do it just once more before I die. And leave me alone for two hours with Alice.

She has trouble falling asleep. A strange scene keeps playing itself out obsessively in her mind. She sees herself stepping out of an upright coffin-size box of dark grey metal, festooned with dials and levers. The time machine. It delivers her into a dark, dirty alleyway, and when she walks forward to the street she sees scores of little antique automobiles buzzing around. Only they aren't antiques, they're the current models. This is the year 1947. New York City. Will she be conspicuous in her futuristic clothes? She has her breasts covered, at any rate. That's essential back here. She hurries to the proper address, resisting the temptation to browse in shop windows along the way. How quaint and ancient everything looks. And how dirty the streets are. She comes to a tall building of red brick. This is the place. No scanners study her as she enters. They don't have annunciators yet or any other automatic home-protection equipment. She goes upstairs in an elevator so creaky and unstable that she fears for her life. Fifth floor. Apartment 5-J. She rings the doorbell. *He* answers. He's terribly young, only twenty-four, but she can pick out signs of the Martin of the future in his face, the strong cheekbones, the searching blue eyes. "Are you Martin Jamieson?" she asks. "That's right," he says. She smiles. "May I come in?" "Of course," he says. He bows her into the apartment. As he momentarily turns his back on her to open the coat closet she takes the heavy steel pipe from her purse and lifts it high and brings it down on the back of his head. *Thwock*. She takes the heavy steel pipe from her purse and lifts it high and brings it down on the back of his head. *Thwock*. She takes the heavy steel pipe from her purse and lifts it high and brings it down on the back of his head. *Thwock.*

Ted and Alice visit him at Sunset Village two or three times a month. He can't complain about that; it's as much as he can expect. He's an old, old man and no doubt a boring one, but they come dutifully, sometimes with the kids, sometimes without. He's never gotten used to the idea that he's a great-grandfather. Alice always gives him a kiss when she arrives and another when she leaves. He plays a private little game with her, copping a feel at each kiss. His hand quickly stroking her butt. Or sometimes when he's really rambunctious it travels lightly over her breast. Does she notice? Probably. She never lets on, though. Pretends it's an accidental touch. Most likely she thinks it's charming that a man of his age would still have at least a vestige of sexual desire left. Unless she thinks it's disgusting, that is.

The time-machine gimmick, Ted tells himself, can be used in ways that don't quite amount to murder. For instance. "What's that box?" Alice asks. He smiles cunningly. "It's called a panchronicon," he says. "It gives you a kind of televised reconstruction of ancient times. The salesman loaned me a demonstration sample." She says, "How does it work?" "Just step inside," he tells her. "It's all ready for you." She starts to enter the machine, but then, suddenly suspicious, she hesitates on the threshold. He pushes her in and slams the door shut behind her. *Wham!* The controls are set. Off goes Alice on a one-way journey to the Pleistocene. The machine is primed to return as soon as it drops her off. That isn't murder, is it? She's still alive, wherever she may be, unless the sabre-tooth tigers have caught up with her. So long, Alice.

In the morning she drives Bobby and Tink to school. Then she stops at the bank and post office. From ten to eleven she has her regular session at the identity-reinforcement parlor. Ordinarily she would go right home after that, but this morning she strolls across the shopping center plaza to the office that the time-machine people have just opened. TEMPONAUTICS, LTD, the sign over the door says. The place is empty except for two machines, no doubt demonstration models, and a bland-faced, smiling salesman. "Hello," Alice says nervously. "I just wanted to pick up some information about the rental costs of one of your machines."

Martin likes to imagine Alice coming to visit him by herself some rainy Saturday afternoon. "Ted isn't able to make it today," she explains. "Something came up at the office. But I knew you were expecting us, and I didn't want you to be disappointed. Poor Martin, you must lead such a lonely life." She comes close to him. She is trembling. So is he. Her face is flushed and her eyes are bright with the unmistakable glossiness of desire. He feels a sense of sexual excitement too, for the first time in ten or twenty years, that tension in the loins, that throbbing of the pulse. Electricity. Chemistry. His eyes lock on hers. Her nostrils flare, her mouth goes taut. "Martin," she whispers huskily. "Do you feel what I feel?" "You know I do," he tells her. She says, "If only I could have known you when you were in your prime!" He chuckles. "I'm not altogether senile yet," he cries exultantly. Then she is in his arms and his lips are seeking her fragrant breasts.

"Yes, it came as a terrible shock to me," Ted tells Ellie. "Having her disappear like that. She simply vanished from the face of the earth, as far as anyone can determine. They've tried every possible way of tracing her and there hasn't been a clue." Ellie's flawless forehead furrows in a fitful frown. "Was she unhappy?" she asks, "Do you think she may have done away with herself?" Ted shakes his head. "I don't know. You live with a person for eleven years and you think you know her pretty well, and then one day something absolutely incomprehensible occurs and you realize how impossible it is ever to know another human being at all. Don't you agree?" Ellie nods gravely. "Yes, oh, yes, certainly!" she says. He smiles down at her and takes her hands in his. Softly he says, "Let's not talk about Alice any more, shall we? She's gone and that's all I'll ever know." He hears a pulsing symphonic crescendo of shimmering angelic choirs as he embraces her and murmurs, "I love you, Ellie. I love you."

She takes the heavy steel pipe from her purse and lifts it high and brings it down on the back of his head. *Thwock*. Young Martin drops instantly, twitches once, lies still. Dark blood begins to seep through the dense blond curls of his hair. How strange to see Martin with golden hair, she thinks, as she kneels beside his body. She puts her hand to the bloody place, probes timidly, feels the deep indentation. Is he dead? She isn't sure how to tell. He isn't moving. He doesn't seem to be breathing. She wonders if she ought to hit him again, just to make certain. Then she remembers something she's seen on television, and takes her mirror from her purse. Holds it in front of his face. No cloud forms. That's pretty conclusive: you're dead, Martin. R.I.P. Martin Jamieson, 1923-1947. Which means that Martha Jamieson Porter (1948-) will never now be conceived, and that automatically obliterates the existence of her son Theodore Porter (1968-). Not bad going, Alice, getting rid of unloved husband and miserable shrewish mother-in-law all in one shot. Sorry, Martin. Bye-bye, Ted. (R.I.P. Theodore Porter, 1968-1947. Eh?) She rises, goes into the bathroom with the steel pipe and carefully rinses it off. Then she puts it back into her purse. Now to go back to the machine and return to 2006, she thinks. To start my new life. But as she leaves the apartment, a tall, lean man steps out of the hallway shadows and clamps his hand powerfully around her wrist. "Time Patrol," he says crisply, flashing an identification badge. "You're under arrest for temponautic murder, Mrs. Porter."

Today has been a better day than yesterday, low on crises and depressions, but he still feels a headache coming on as he lets himself into the house. He is braced for whatever bitchiness Alice may have in store for him this evening. But, oddly, she seems relaxed and amiable. "Can I get you a drink, Ted?" she asks. "How did your day go?" He smiles and says, "Well, I think we may have salvaged the Hammond account after all. Otherwise nothing special happened. And you? What did you do today, love?" She shrugs. "Oh, the usual stuff," she says. "The bank, the post office, my identity-reinforcement session."

If you had the money, Martin asks himself, how far back would you send her? 1947, that would be the year, I guess. My last year as a single man. No sense complicating things. Off you go, Alice baby, to 1947. Let's make it March. By June I was engaged and by September Martha was on the way, though I didn't find that out until later. Yes: March, 1947. So Young Martin answers the doorbell and sees an attractive girl in the hall, a woman, really, older than he is, maybe thirty or thirty-two. Slender, dark-haired, nicely constructed. Odd clothing: a clinging grey tunic, very short, made of some strange fabric that flows over her body like a stream. How it achieves that liquid effect around the pleats is beyond him. "Are you Martin Jamieson?" she asks. And quickly answers herself. "Yes, of course, you must be. I recognize you. How handsome you were!" He is baffled. He knows nothing, naturally, about this gift from his aged future self. "Who are you?" he asks. "May I come in first?" she says. He is embarrassed by his lack of courtesy and waves her inside. Her eyes glitter with mischief. "You aren't going to believe this," she tells him," but I'm your grandson's wife."

"Would you like to try out one of our demonstration models?" the salesman asks pleasantly. "There's absolutely no cost or obligation." Ted looks at Alice. Alice looks at Ted. Her frown mirrors his inner uncertainty. She also must be wishing that they had never come to the Temponautics showroom. The salesman, pattering smoothly onward, says, "In these demonstrations we usually send our potential customers fifteen or twenty minutes into the past. I'm sure you'll find it fascinating. While remaining in the machine, you'll be able to look through a viewer and observe your own selves actually entering this very showroom a short while ago. Well? Will you give it a try? You go first, Mrs. Porter. I assure you it's going to be the most unique experience you've ever had." Alice, uneasy, tries to back off, but the salesman prods her in a way that is at once gentle and unyielding, and she steps reluctantly into the time machine. He closes the door. A great business of adjusting fine controls ensues. Then the salesman throws a master switch. A green glow envelopes the machine and it disappears, although something transparent and vague—retinal after-image? the ghost of the machine?—remains dimly visible. The salesman says, "She's now gone a short distance into her own past. I've programmed the machine to take her back eighteen minutes and keep her there for a total elapsed interval of six minutes, so she can see the entire opening moments of your visit here. But when I return her to Now Level, there's no need to match the amount of elapsed time in the past, so that from our point of view she'll have been absent only some thirty seconds. Isn't that remarkable, Mr. Porter? It's one of the many extraordinary paradoxes we encounter in the strange new realm of time travel." He throws another switch. The time machine once more assumes solid form. "Voila!" cries the salesman. "Here is Mrs. Porter, returned safe and sound from her voyage into the past." He flings open the door of the time machine. The passenger compartment is empty. The salesman's face crumbles. "Mrs. Porter?" he shrieks in consternation. "Mrs. Porter? I don't understand! How could there have been a malfunction? This is impossible! Mrs. Porter? *Mrs. Porter?*"

She hurries down the dirty street toward the tall brick building. This is the place. Upstairs. Fifth floor, apartment 5-J. As she starts to ring the doorbell, a tall, lean man steps out of the shadows and clamps his hand powerfully around her wrist. "Time Patrol," he says crisply, flashing an identification badge. "You're under arrest for contemplated temponautic murder, Mrs. Porter."

"But I haven't any grandson," he sputters. "I'm not even mar—" She laughs. "Don't worry about it!" she tells him. "You're going to have a daughter named Martha and she'll have a son named Ted and I'm going to marry Ted and we'll have two children named Bobby, and Tink. And you're going to live to be an old, old man. And that's all you need to know. Now let's have a little fun." She touches a catch at the side of her tunic and the garment falls away in a single fluid cascade. Beneath it she is naked. Her nipples stare up at him like blind pink eyes. She beckons to him. "Come on!" she says hoarsely. "Get undressed, Martin! You're wasting time!"

Alice giggles nervously. "Well, as a matter of fact," she says to the salesman, "I think I'm willing to let my husband be the guinea pig. How about it, Ted?" She turns toward him. So does the salesman. "Certainly, Mr. Porter. I know you're eager to give our machine a test run, yes?" No, Ted thinks, but he feels the pressure of events propelling him willy-nilly. He gets into the machine. As the door closes on him he fears that claustrophobic panic will overwhelm him; he is reassured by the sight of a handle on the door's inner face. He pushes on it and the door opens, and he steps out of the machine just in time to see his earlier self coming into the Temponautics showroom with Alice. The salesman is going forward to greet them. Ted is now eighteen minutes into his own past. Alice and the other Ted stare at him, aghast. The salesman whirls and exclaims, "Wait a second, you aren't supposed to get out of—" How stupid they all look! How bewildered! Ted laughs in their faces. Then he rushes past them, nearly knocking his other self down, and erupts into the shopping-center plaza. He sprints in a wild frenzy of exhilaration toward the parking area. Free, he thinks. I'm free at last. And I didn't have to kill anybody.

Suppose I rent a machine, Alice thinks, and go back to 1947 and kill Martin? Suppose I really do it? What if there's some way of tracing the crime to me? After all, a crime committed by a person from 2006 who goes back to 1947 will have consequences in our present day. It might change all sorts of things. So they'd want to catch the criminal and punish him, or better yet prevent the crime from being committed in the first place. And the time machine company is bound to know what year I asked them to send me to. So maybe it isn't such an easy way of committing a perfect crime. I don't know. God, I can't understand any of this. But perhaps I can get away with it. Anyway, I'm going to give it a try. I'll show Ted he can't go on treating me like dirt.

They lie peacefully side by side, sweaty, drowsy, exhausted in the good exhaustion that comes after a first-rate screw. Martin tenderly strokes her belly and thighs. How smooth her skin is, how pale, how transparent! The little blue veins so clearly visible. "Hey," he says suddenly. "I just thought of something. I wasn't wearing a rubber or anything. What if I made you pregnant? And if you're really who you say you are. Then you'll go back to the year 2006 and you'll have a kid and he'll be his own grandfather, won't he?" She laughs. "Don't worry much about it," she says.

A wave of timidity comes over her as she enters the Temponautics office. This is crazy, she tells herself. I'm getting out of here. But before she can turn around, the salesman she spoke to the day before materializes from a side room and gives her a big hello. Mr. Friesling. He's practically rubbing his hands together in anticipation of landing a contract. "So nice to see you again, Mrs. Porter." She nods and glances worriedly at the demonstration models. "How much would it cost," she asks, "to spend a few hours in the spring of 1947?"

Sunday is the big family day. Four generations sitting down to dinner together: Martin, Martha, Ted and Alice, Bobby and Tink. Ted rather enjoys these reunions, but he knows Alice loathes them, mainly because of Martha. Alice hates her mother-in-law. Martha has never cared much for Alice, either. He watches them glaring at each other across the table. Meanwhile old Martin stares lecherously at the gulf between Alice's breasts. You have to hand it to the old man, Ted thinks. He's never lost the old urge. Even though there's not a hell of a lot he can do about gratifying it, not at his age. Martha says sweetly, "You'd look ever so much better, Alice dear, if you'd let your hair grow out to its natural color." A sugary smile from Martha. A sour scowl from Alice. She glowers at the older woman. "This *is* its natural color," she snaps.

Mr. Friesling hands her the standard contract form. Eight pages of densely packed type. "Don't be frightened by it, Mrs. Porter. It looks formidable but actually it's just a lot of empty legal rhetoric. You can show it to your lawyer, if you like. I can tell you, though, that most of our customers find no need for that." She leafs through it. So far as she can tell, the contract is mainly a disclaimer of responsibility. Temponautics, Ltd, agrees to bear the brunt of any malfunction caused by its own demonstrable negligence, but wants no truck with acts of God or with accidents brought about by clients who won't obey the safety regulations. On the fourth page Alice finds a clause warning the prospective renter that the company cannot be held liable for any consequences of actions by the renter which wantonly or wilfully interfere with the already determined course of history. She translates that for herself: *If you kill your husband's grandfather, don't blame us if you get in trouble.* She skims the remaining pages. "It looks harmless enough," she says. "Where do I sign?"

As Martin comes out of the bathroom he finds Martha blocking his way. "Excuse me," he says mildly, but she remains in his path. She is a big fleshy woman. At fifty-eight she affects the fashions of the very young, with grotesque results; he hates that aspect of her. He can see why Alice dislikes her so much. "Just a moment," Martha says. "I want to talk to you, Father." "About what?" he asks. "About those looks you give Alice. Don't you think that's a little too much? How tasteless can you get?" "Tasteless? Are you anybody to talk about taste, with your face painted green like a fifteen-year old?" She looks angry: he's scored a direct hit. She replies, "I just think that at the age of eighty-two you ought to have a greater regard for decency than to go staring down your own grandson's wife's front." Martin sighs. "Let me have the staring, Martha. It's all I've got left."

He is at the office, deep in complicated negotiations, when his autosecretary bleeps him and announces that a call has come in from a Mr. Friesling, of the Union Boulevard Plaza office of Temponautics, Ltd. Ted is puzzled by that: what do the time machine people want with him? Trying to line him up as a customer? "Tell him I'm not interested in time trips," Ted says. But the autosecretary bleeps again a few moments later. Mr. Friesling, it declares, is calling in reference to Mr. Porter's credit standing. More baffled than before, Ted orders the call switched over to him. Mr. Friesling appears on the desk screen. He is small-featured and bright-eyed, rather like a chipmunk. "I apologize for troubling you, Mr. Porter," he begins. "This is strictly a routine credit check, but it's altogether necessary. As you surely know, your wife has requested rental of our equipment for a fifty-nine-year time jaunt, and inasmuch as the service fee for such a trip exceeds the level at which we extend automatic credit, our policy requires us to ask you if you'll confirm the payment schedule that she has requested us to—" Ted coughs violently. "Hold on," he says. "My wife's going on a time jaunt? What the hell, this is the first time I've heard of that!"

She is surprised by the extensiveness of the preparations. No wonder they charge so much. Getting her ready for the jaunt takes hours. They inoculate her to protect her against certain extinct diseases. They provide her with clothing in the style of the mid-twentieth century, ill-fitting and uncomfortable. They give her contemporary currency, but warn her that she would do well not to spend any except in an emergency, since she will be billed for it at its present-day numismatic value, which is high. They make her study a pamphlet describing the customs and historical background of the era and quiz her in detail. She learns that she is not under any circumstances to expose her breasts or genitals in public while she is in 1947. She must not attempt to obtain any mind-stimulating drugs other than alcohol. She should not say anything that might be construed as praise of the Soviet Union or of Marxist philosophy. She must bear in mind that she is entering the past solely as an observer, and should engage in minimal social interaction with the citizens of the era she is visiting. And so forth. At last they decide it's safe to let her go. "Please come this way, Mrs. Porter," Friesling says.

After staring at the telephone a long while, Martin punches out Alice's number. Before the second ring he loses his nerve and disconnects. Immediately he calls her again. His heart pounds so furiously that the medic, registering alarm on its delicate sensing apparatus, starts toward him. He waves the robot away and clings to the phone. Two rings. Three. Ah. "Hello?" Alice says. Her voice is warm and rich and feminine. He has his screen switched off. "Hello? Who's there?"

Martin breathes heavily into the mouthpiece. Ah. Ah. Ah. Ah. "Hello? Hello? Hello? Listen, you pervert, if you phone me once more—" *Ah. Ah. Ah.* A smile of bliss appears on Martin's withered features. Alice hangs up. Trembling, Martin sags in his chair. Oh, that was good! He signals fiercely to the medic. "Let's have the injection now, you metal monster!" He laughs. Dirty old man.

❋

Ted realizes that it isn't necessary to kill a person's grandfather in order to get rid of that person. Just interfere with some crucial event in that person's past, is all. Go back and break up the marriage of Alice's grandparents, for example. (How? Seduce the grandmother when she's eighteen? "I'm terribly sorry to inform you that your intended bride is no virgin, and here's the documentary evidence." They were very grim about virginity back then, weren't they?) Nobody would have to die. But Alice wouldn't ever be born.

❋

Martin still can't believe any of this, even after she's slept with him. It's some crazy practical joke, most likely. Although he wishes all practical jokes were as sexy as this one. "Are you really from the year 2006?" he asks her. She laughs prettily. "How can I prove it to you?" Then she leaps from the bed. He tracks her with his eyes as she crosses the room, breasts jiggling gaily. What a sweet little body. How thoughtful of my older self to ship her back here to me. If that's what really happened. She fumbles in her purse and extracts a handful of coins. "Look here," she says. "Money from the future. Here's a dime from 1993. And this is a two-dollar piece from 2001. And here's an old one, a 1979 Kennedy half-dollar." He studies the unfamiliar coins. They have a greasy look, not silvery at all. Counterfeits? They won't necessarily be striking coins out of silver forever. And the engraving job is very professional. A two-dollar piece, eh? Well, you never can tell. And this. The half-dollar. A handsome young man in profile. "Kennedy?" he says. "Who's Kennedy?"

❋

So this is it at last. Two technicians in grey smocks watch her, sober-faced, as she clambers into the machine. It's very much like a coffin, just as she imagined it would be. She can't sit down in it; it's too narrow. Gives her the creeps, shut up in here. Of course, they've told her the trip won't take any apparent subjective time, only a couple of seconds. *Woosh!* and she'll be there. All right. They close the door. She hears the lock clicking shut. Mr. Friesling's voice comes to her over a loudspeaker. "We wish you a happy voyage, Mrs. Porter. Keep calm and you won't get into any difficulties." Suddenly the red light over the door is glowing. That means the jaunt has begun: she's traveling backward in time. No sense of acceleration, no sense of motion. One, two, three. The light goes off. That's it. I'm in 1947, she tells herself. Before she opens the door, she closes her eyes and runs through her history lessons. World War II has just ended. Europe is in ruins. There are forty-eight states. Nobody has been to the moon yet or even thinks much about going there. Harry Truman is President. Stalin runs Russia, and Churchill—is Churchill still Prime Minister of England? She isn't sure. Well, no matter. I didn't come here to talk about prime ministers. She touches the latch and the door of the time machine swings outward.

He steps from the machine into the year 2006. Nothing has changed in the showroom. Friesling, the two poker-faced technicians, the sleek desks, the thick carpeting, all the same as before. He moves bouncily. His mind is still back there with Alice's grandmother. The taste of her lips, the soft urgent cries of her fulfillment. Who ever said all women were frigid in the old days? They ought to go back and find out. Friesling smiles at him. "I hope you had a very enjoyable journey, Mr.—ah—" Ted nods. "Enjoyable and useful," he says. He goes out. Never to see Alice again—how beautiful! The car isn't where he remembers leaving it in the parking area. You have to expect certain small peripheral changes, I guess. He hails a cab, gives the driver his address. His key does not fit the front door. Troubled, he thumbs the annunciator. A woman's voice, not Alice's, asks him what he wants. "Is this the Ted Porter residence?" he asks. "No, it isn't," the woman says, suspicious and irritated. The name on the doorplate, he notices now, is McKenzie. So the changes are not all so small. Where do I go now? If I don't live here, then where? "Wait!" he yells to the taxi, just pulling away. It takes him to a downtown cafe, where he phones Ellie. Her face, peering out of the tiny screen, wears an odd frowning expression. "Listen, something very strange has happened," he begins, "and I need to see you as soon as—" "I don't think I know you," she says. "I'm Ted," he tells her. "Ted who?" she asks.

How peculiar this is, Alice thinks. Like walking into a museum diorama and having it come to life. The noisy little automobiles. The ugly clothing. The squat, dilapidated twentieth-century buildings. The chaos. The oily, smoky smell of the polluted air. Wisps of dirty snow in the streets. Cans of garbage just sitting around as if nobody's ever heard of the plague. Well, I won't stay here long. In her purse she carries her kitchen carver, a tiny nickel-jacketed laser-powered implement. Steel pipes are all right for dream fantasies, but this is the real thing, and she wants the killing to be quick and efficient. Criss, cross, with the laser beam, and Martin goes. At the street corner she pauses to check the address. There's no central info number to ring for all sorts of useful data, not in these primitive times; she must use a printed telephone directory, a thick tattered book with small smeary type. Here he is: Martin Jamieson, 504 West Forty-fifth. That's not far. In ten minutes she's there. A dark brick structure, five or six stories high, with spidery metal fire escapes running down its face. Even for its day it appears unusually run-down. She goes inside. A list of tenants is posted just within the front door. Jamieson, 3-A. There's no elevator and of course no liftshaft. Up the stairs. A musty hallway lit by a single dim incandescent bulb. This is Apartment 3-A. Jamieson. She rings the bell.

Ten minutes later Friesling calls back, sounding abashed and looking dismayed: "I'm sorry to have to tell you that there's been some sort of error, Mr. Porter. The technicians were apparently unaware that a credit check was in process, and they sent Mrs. Porter off on her trip while we were still talking." Ted is shaken. He clutches the edge of the desk. Controlling himself with an effort, he says, "How far back was it that she wanted to go?" Friesling says, "It was fifty-nine years. To 1947." Ted nods grimly. A horrible idea has occurred to him. 1947 was the year that his mother's parents met and got married. What is Alice up to?

The doorbell rings. Martin, freshly showered, is sprawled out naked on his bed, leafing through the new issue of Esquire and thinking vaguely of going out for dinner. He isn't expecting any company. Slipping into his bathrobe, he goes toward the door. "Who's there?" he calls. A youthful, pleasant female voice replies, "I'm looking for Martin Jamieson." Well, okay. He opens the door. She's perhaps twenty-seven, twenty-eight years old, very sexy, on the slender side but well built. Dark hair, worn in a strangely boyish short cut. He's never seen her before. "Hi," he says tentatively. She grins warmly at him. "You don't know me," she tells him, "but I'm a friend of an old friend of yours. Mary Chambers? Mary and I grew up together in—ah—Ohio. I'm visiting New York for the first time, and Mary once told me that if I ever come to New York I should be sure to look up Martin Jamieson, and so—may I come in?" "You bet," he says. He doesn't remember any Mary Chambers from Ohio. But what the hell, sometimes you forget a few. What the hell.

He's much more attractive than she expected him to be. She has always known Martin only as an old man, made unattractive as much by his coarse lechery as by what age has done to him. Hollow-chested, stoop-shouldered, pleated jowly face, sparse strands of white hair, beady eyes of faded blue—a wreck of a man. But this Martin in the doorway is sturdy, handsome, untouched by time, brimming with life and vigor and virility. She thinks of the carver in her purse and feels a genuine pang of regret at having to cut this robust boy off in his prime. But there isn't such a great hurry, is there? First we can enjoy each other, Martin. And then the laser.

"When is she due back?" Ted demands. Friesling explains that all concepts of time are relative and flexible; so far as elapsed time at Now Level goes, she's already returned. "What?" Ted yells. "Where is she?"

Friesling does not know. She stepped out of the machine, bade the Temponautics staff a pleasant goodbye, and left the showroom. Ted puts his hand to his throat. What if she's already killed Martin? Will I just wink out of existence? Or is there some sort of lag, so that I'll fade gradually into unreality over the next few days? "Listen," he says raggedly, "I'm leaving my office right now and I'll be down at your place in less than an hour. I want you to have your machinery set up so that you can transport me to the exact point in space and time where you just sent my wife." "But that won't be possible," Friesling protests. "It takes hours to prepare a client properly for—" Ted cuts him off. "Get everything set up, and to hell with preparing me properly," he snaps. "Unless you feel like getting slammed with the biggest negligence suit since this time-machine thing got started, you better have everything ready when I get there."

He opens the door. The girl in the hallway is young and good-looking, with close-cropped dark hair and full lips. Thank you, Mary Chambers, whoever you may be. "Pardon the bathrobe," he says, "but I wasn't expecting company." She steps into his apartment. Suddenly he notices how strained and tense her face is. Country girl from Ohio, suddenly having second thoughts about visiting a strange man in a strange city? He tries to put her at her ease. "Can I get you a drink?" he asks. "Not much of a selection, I'm afraid, but I have scotch, gin, some blackberry cordial—" She reaches into her purse and takes something out. He frowns. Not a gun, exactly, but it does seem like a weapon of some sort, a little glittering metal device that fits neatly in her hand. "Hey," he says, "what's—" "I'm so awfully sorry, Martin," she whispers, and a bolt of terrible fire slams into his chest.

She sips the drink. It relaxes her. The glass isn't very clean, but she isn't worried about picking up a disease, not after all the injections Friesling gave her. Martin looks as if he can stand some relaxing too. "Aren't you drinking?" she asks. "I suppose I will," he says. He pours himself some gin. She comes up behind him and slips her hand into the front of his bathrobe. His body is cool, smooth, hard. "Oh, Martin," she murmurs. "Oh! Martin!"

Ted takes a room in one of the commercial hotels downtown. The first thing he does is try to put a call through to Alice's mother in Chillicothe. He still isn't really convinced that his little time-jaunt flirtation has retroactively eliminated Alice from existence. But the call convinces him, all right. The middle-aged woman who answers is definitely not Alice's mother. Right phone number, right address—he badgers her for the information—but wrong woman. "You don't have a daughter named Alice Porter?" he asks three or four times. "You don't know anyone in the neighborhood who does? It's important." All right. Cancel the old lady, ergo cancel Alice. But now he has a different problem. How much of the universe has he altered by removing Alice and her mother? Does he live in some other city, now, and hold some other job? What has happened to Bobby and Tink? Frantically he begins phoning people. Friends, fellow workers, the man at the bank. The same response from all of them: blank stares, shakings of the head. We don't know you, fellow. He looks at himself in the mirror. Okay, he asks himself. Who am I?

Martin moves swiftly and purposefully, the way they taught him to do in the army when it's necessary to disarm a dangerous opponent. He lunges forward and catches the girl's arm, pushing it upward before she can fire the shiny whatzis she's aiming at him. She turns out to be stronger than he anticipated, and they struggle fiercely for the weapon. Suddenly it fires. Something like a lightning bolt explodes between them and knocks him to the floor, stunned. When he picks himself up he sees her lying near the door with a charred hole in her throat.

The telephone's jangling clatter brings Martin up out of a dream in which he is ravishing Alice's luscious young body. Dry-throated, gummy-eyed, he reaches a palsied hand toward the receiver. "Yes?" he says. Ted's face blossoms on the screen. "Grandfather!" he blurts. "Are you all right?" "Of course I'm all right," Martin says testily. "Can't you tell? What's the matter with you, boy?" Ted shakes his head. "I don't know," he mutters. "Maybe it was only a bad dream. I imagined that Alice rented one of those time machines and went back to 1947. And tried to kill you so that I wouldn't ever have existed." Martin snorts. "What idiotic nonsense! How can she have killed me in 1947 when I'm here alive in 2006?"

Naked, Alice sinks into Martin's arms. His strong hands sweep eagerly over her breasts and shoulders and his mouth descends to hers. She shivers with desire. "Yes," she murmurs tenderly, pressing herself against him. "Oh, yes, yes, yes!" They'll do it and it'll be fantastic. And afterward she'll kill him with the kitchen carver while he's lying there savoring the event. But a troublesome thought occurs. If Martin dies in 1947, Ted doesn't get to be born in 1968. Okay. But what about Tink and Bobby? They won't get born either, not if I don't marry Ted. I'll be married to someone else when I get back to 2006, and I suppose I'll have different children. Bobby? Tink? What am I doing to you? Sudden fear congeals her, and she pulls back from the vigorous young man nuzzling her throat. "Wait," she says. "Listen, I'm sorry. It's all a big mistake. I'm sorry, but I've got to get out of here right away!"

So this is the year 1947. Well, well, well. Everything looks so cluttered and grimy and ancient. He hurries through the chilly streets toward his grandfather's place. If his luck is good and if Friesling's technicians have calculated things accurately, he'll be able to head Alice off. That might even be her now, that slender woman walking briskly half a block ahead of him. He steps up his pace. Yes, it's Alice, on her way to Martin's. Well done, Friesling! Ted approaches her warily, suspecting that she's armed. If she's capable of coming back to 1947 to kill Martin, she'd kill him just as readily. Especially back here where neither one of them has any legal existence. When he's close to her he says in a low, hard, intense voice, "Don't turn around, Alice. Just keep walking as if everything's perfectly normal." She stiffens. "Ted?" she cries, astonished. "Is that you, Ted?" "Damned right it is." He laughs harshly. "Come on. Walk to the corner and turn to your left around the block. You're going back to your machine and you're going to get the hell out of the twentieth century without harming anybody. I know what you were trying to do, Alice. But I caught you in time, didn't I?"

Martin is just getting down to real business when the door of his apartment bursts open and a man rushes in. He's middle-aged, stocky, with weird clothes—the ultimate in zoot suits, a maze of vividly contrasting colors and conflicting patterns, shoulders padded to resemble shelves—and a wild look in his eyes. Alice leaps up from the bed. "Ted!" she screams. "My God, what are you doing here?" "You murderous bitch," the intruder yells. Martin, naked and feeling vulnerable, his nervous system stunned by the interruption, looks on in amazement as the stranger grabs her and begins throttling her. "Bitch! Bitch! Bitch!" he roars, shaking her in a mad frenzy. The girl's face is turning black. Her eyes are bugging. After a long moment Martin breaks finally from his freeze. He stumbles forward, seizes the man's fingers, peels them away from the girl's throat. Too late. She falls limply and lies motionless. "Alice!" the intruder moans. "Alice, Alice, what have I done?" He drops to his knees beside her body, sobbing. Martin blinks. "You killed her," he says, not believing that any of this can really be happening. "You actually killed her?"

Alice's face appears on the telephone screen. Christ, how beautiful she is, Martin thinks, and his decrepit body quivers with lust. "There you are," he says. "I've been trying to reach you for hours. I had such a strange dream that something awful had happened to Ted—and then your phone didn't answer, and I began to think maybe the dream was a premonition of some kind, an omen, you know—" Alice looks puzzled. "I'm afraid you have the wrong number, sir," she says sweetly, and hangs up.

She draws the laser and the naked man cowers back against the wall in bewilderment. "What the hell is this?" he asks, trembling. "Put that thing down, lady. You've got the wrong guy." "No," she says. "You're the one I'm after. I hate to do this to you, Martin, but I've got no choice. You have to die." "Why?" he demands. "*Why?*" "You wouldn't understand it even if I told you," she says. She moves her finger toward the discharge stud. Abruptly there is a frightening sound of cracking wood and collapsing plaster behind her, as though an earthquake has struck. She whirls and is appalled to see her husband breaking down the door of Martin's apartment. "I'm just in time!" Ted exclaims. "Don't move, Alice!" He reaches for her. In panic she fires without thinking. The dazzling beam catches Ted in the pit of the stomach and he goes down, gurgling in agony, clutching at his belly as he dies.

The door falls with a crash and this character in peculiar clothing materializes in a cloud of debris, looking crazier than Napoleon. It's incredible, Martin thinks. First an unknown broad rings his bell and invites herself in and takes her clothes off, and then, just as he's about to screw her, this happens. It's pure Marx Brothers, only dirty. But Martin's not going to take any crap. He pulls himself away from the panting, gasping girl on the bed, crosses the room in three quick strides, and seizes the newcomer. "Who the hell are you?" Martin demands, slamming him hard against the wall. The girl is dancing around behind him. "Don't hurt him!" she wails. "Oh, please, don't hurt him!"

Ted certainly hadn't expected to find them in bed together. He understood why she might have wanted to go back in time to murder Martin, but simply to have an affair with him, no, it didn't make sense. Of course, it was altogether likely that she had come here to kill and had paused for a little dalliance first. You never could tell about women, even your own wife. Alley cats, all of them. Well, a lucky thing for him that she had given him these few extra minutes to get here. "Okay," he says. "Get your clothes on, Alice. You're coming with me." "Just a second, mister," Martin growls. "You've got your goddamned nerve, busting in like this." Ted tries to explain, but the words won't come. It's all too complicated. He gestures mutely at Alice, at himself, at Martin. The next moment Martin jumps him and they go tumbling together to the floor.

"Who are you?" Martin yells, banging the intruder repeatedly against the wall. "You some kind of detective? You trying to work a badger game on me?" Slam. Slam. Slam. He feels the girl's small fists pounding on his own back. "Stop it!" she screams. "Let him alone, will you? He's my husband!" *"Husband!"* Martin cries. Astounded, he lets go of the stranger and swings around to face the girl. A moment later he realizes his mistake. Out of the corner of his eye he sees that the intruder has raised his fists high above his head like clubs. Martin tries to get out of the way, but no time, no time, and the fists descend with awful force against his skull.

Alice doesn't know what to do. They're rolling around on the floor, fighting like wildcats, now Martin on top, now Ted. Martin is younger and bigger and stronger, but Ted seems possessed by the strength of the insane; he's gone berserk. Both men are bloody-faced, and furniture is crashing over everywhere. Her first impulse is to get between them and stop this crazy fight somehow. But then she remembers that she has come here as a killer, not as a peacemaker. She gets the laser from her purse and aims it at Martin, but then the combatants do a flip-flop and it is Ted who is in the line of fire. She hesitates. It doesn't matter which one she shoots, she realizes after a moment. They both have to die, one way or another. She takes aim. Maybe she can get them both with one bolt. But as her finger starts to tighten on the discharge stud, Martin suddenly gets Ted in a bearhug and, half lifting him, throws him five feet across the room. The back of Ted's neck hits the wall and there is a loud *crack*. Ted slumps and is still. Martin gets shakily to his feet. "I think I killed him," he says. "Christ, who the hell was he?" "He was your grandson," Alice says and begins to shriek hysterically.

Ted stares in horror at the crumpled body at his feet. His hands still tingle from the impact. The left side of Martin's head looks as though a pile-driver has crushed it. "Good God in heaven," Ted says thickly, "what have I done? I came here to protect him and I've killed him! I've killed my own grandfather!" Alice, wide-eyed, futilely trying to cover her nakedness by folding one arm across her breasts and spreading her other hand over her loins, says, "If he's dead, why are you still here? Shouldn't you have disappeared?" Ted shrugs. "Maybe I'm safe as long as I remain here in the past. But the moment I try to go back to 2006, I'll vanish as though I've never been. I don't know. I don't understand any of this. What do you think?"

Alice steps uncertainly from the machine into the Temponautics showroom. There's Friesling. There are the technicians. Friesling says, smiling, "I hope you had a very enjoyable journey, Mrs.—ah—uh' He falters. "I'm sorry," he says, reddening, "but your name seems to have escaped me." Alice says, "It's, ah, Alice—uh—do you know, the second name escapes me too?"

The whole clan has gathered to celebrate Martin's eighty-third birthday. He cuts the cake, and then one by one they go to him to kiss him. When it's Alice's turn, he deftly spins her around so that he screens her from the others and gives her rump a good hearty pinch. "Oh, if I were only fifty years younger!" he sighs.

It's a warm springlike day. Everything has been lovely at the office—three new accounts all at once—and the trip home on the freeway was a breeze. Alice is waiting for him, dressed in her finest and most sexy outfit, all ready to go out. It's a special day. Their eleventh anniversary. How beautiful she looks! He kisses her, she kisses him, he takes the tickets from his pocket with a grand flourish. "Surprise," he says. "Two weeks in Hawaii, starting next Tuesday! Happy anniversary!" "Oh, Ted!" she cries. "How marvelous! I love you, Ted darling!" He pulls her close to him again. "I love you, Alice dear."